DAVID ROSE AND THE FORBIDDEN TOURNAMENT

A
"David Rose" Novel
by
Daryl Rothman

DAVID ROSE AND THE FORBIDDEN TOURNAMENT
David Rose – Book 2
Copyright © 2022 by Daryl Rothman

SECOND EDITION SOFTCOVER
ISBN: 1622535669
ISBN-13: 978-1-62253-566-8

Editor: Lane Diamond
Cover Artist: D. Robert Pease
Interior Designer: Lane Diamond

EVOLVED PUBLISHING™
www.EvolvedPub.com
Butler, Wisconsin, USA

Printed in Book Antiqua font.

BOOKS BY DARYL ROTHMAN

"DAVID ROSE" SERIES
Book 1: *The Awakening of David Rose*
Book 2: *David Rose and the Forbidden Tournament*
Book 3: *David Rose and the Days of Awe*

STAND-ALONE NOVELS
Gospel

DEDICATION

For Dad,
Gone, but never forgotten. This tale speaks a bit of the nature
of Man, and so too a bit of angels. The better angels of my
nature, I owe so very much to you.

CHAPTER 1
Between Worlds

THE CEMETERY GATES LOOMED LIKE
sentinels as they approached, but David Rose retained
scant faith in the barriers between worlds. He strode
through the entrance with Rachel struggling to keep
pace, her little hand gripping his. Their father believed
them to be at Robert's, which, in fact, they had been. He
would not approve of their current destination, particularly
Rachel's inclusion in the matter. Behind them, a low whirring
played over the pavement. David didn't look back,
knowing it was Chester in his wheelchair, accompanied
by Robert and Amanda. They were the only ones David
had told, the only ones he planned to tell.

That meant their worlds had changed forever,
too.

It grew darker as they went, the pale illumination
of the occasional lamppost fading like a flare at sea.
Roughly a quarter mile in, the road terminated in a
circle. David waited for his friends to catch up.

He eyed Amanda. "Here?"

She nodded and looked around. "She'll be here."

"She" was Audrey DaMone, Amanda's friend and their
grade's resident Goth chick—familiar, Amanda maintained,
with the ways of the occult. David didn't know Audrey
well, but she seemed cool enough—different, but cool.
And who was he to talk about different? High school
had no shortage of cliques, and being different was often

- 1 -

your ticket to being ostracized. The "cool" kids were typically the ones doing the ostracizing, but Amanda was unlike most of the cool kids. She was kind to everyone, regardless of their classification along the continuum of high school stereotypes.

Amanda's left hand flashed blue. She looked at her phone, pressed some buttons, then slid it into her back pocket. "She's in the mausoleum."

Chester shut off his wheelchair. "On foot from here, then," he said, and then, with a hint of admonition, "cenotaph."

"What's that?" Robert asked, helping Chester up. "A creature from Greek mythology?"

"In fact, no," Chester replied. "She said mausoleum, referring, naturally, to the Langston monument. But despite conventional wisdom, its being an empty grave makes it, by definition, a cenotaph."

Amanda smiled, clearly unaffronted. Even on a late-night graveyard excursion, Chester was still, inimitably, Chester.

Robert withdrew the cane from the customized sheath at the rear of the wheelchair and handed it to their friend.

"Thanks," Chester said, before turning to David. "For the record, I oppose this course of action. There are serious matters to which we must attend."

David peered into the blackness. "Duly noted."

"I think it's up ahead." Amanda beckoned.

David remembered spotting the large tomb months ago when he'd been there with Marcel. The three Langston brothers had perished on an aircraft carrier in World War II, the type of tragedy which ultimately fueled changes to the rules of engagement concerning deployment of family members. Their bodies were never recovered and so the mausoleum — cenotaph — sat empty, a tribute to a family's sacrifice. David wasn't certain why Audrey had chosen this spot, but other matters pressed in on him. He needed to know the significance of the mirror, and Amanda believed her friend might be able to help.

"Come on," he said.

Robert gestured at the wheelchair. "Okay to leave it?"

"It would," Chester replied, "be an audacious getaway."

It was dark, the terrain uneven in spots, and Robert walked alongside Chester.

Amanda caught up to David and Rachel, who grabbed her hand with her free one.

David turned the mirror over in his hand as they went. Marcel had pressed it into his palm that last time he'd seen him, on the moors at Kane Manor — small, compact, circular, about the size of a drink coaster. It closed like a locket, and David had not even thought to open it until the flight home, and when he did, there had been a note inside.

Many, yet one.

Naturally, he had questions, but Marcel was not there to ask, nor did David know how to reach him. Marcel had assured him he would be in touch, but that it was better for now — safer — for them to let the path between them grow cold. An unsettling notion, but David trusted him implicitly.

The mirror appeared pedestrian at first, but upon closer inspection, its faded exterior suggested something else entirely. It didn't just look old; it looked ancient, the kind of ancient that froze you in your tracks because history seemed to be whispering to you. He remembered when he was young—maybe Rachel's age—his parents taking him to see an exhibit of the Dead Sea Scrolls. They tried to explain what it was, and he'd understood—not their words, really, but the gravity of the thing. Felt it. It was the same with the mirror. If only Marcel had taken one moment more to tell him what he was supposed to do with it.

There was something else, something so fleeting that he wouldn't have thought twice of it, had life been anything other than it had been in the last year. He'd snapped the mirror shut on the flight, but just as he did, he'd detected something in the small, round glass.

Someone.

Not him.

He'd flipped it back open, but it was only him looking back, and it hadn't happened since.

"I see a light." Rachel squeezed his hand again and pointed.

"That's it," David said. He waited for the others, then proceeded toward the faint glow. He brushed against tombstones twice as he walked, feeling on each occasion as though he should apologize. As they neared the tomb, the hazy illumination grew brighter, conforming to the shape of the structure. When they reached it, David paused, his hand on the cold, stone door.

Rachel tugged at his hand and whispered, "Are the ghosts awake?"

"No ghosts," he said, and immediately something knotted inside him, the way it always did when he knew he may have made a promise he could not keep. He pushed open the heavy, creaking door.

One unfamiliar with Audrey DaMone might have at first believed they'd indeed seen a ghost. She was pale, strikingly so, and her long, black hair accentuated the effect. Her olive eyes gleamed in the glow from the ring of candles she'd assembled.

"Come in," she said, and they did. "Please shut the door."

Robert was last to step inside, following Chester. He shut the door behind him.

Rachel was the only one who didn't need to crouch. Audrey sat at the far end of the structure, cross-legged, and gestured for them to sit. Rachel scrambled onto her brother's lap; Amanda sat to their right. Opposite them, Robert helped Chester lower to the ground, then sat beside him. The candles encircled an inscribed monument to the Langston brothers. The small flames danced, throwing new shadows upon the walls.

Audrey turned to David. "Did you bring it?"

He handed her the mirror.

She didn't open it, but stared at its exterior, rolling it from one side to the other. The candlelight shifted again, glinting off a small ring that intersected Audrey's lower lip.

Rachel pointed. "Does that hurt?"

"Rachel," David said.

"Oh, she's fine," Audrey assured him. She smiled at Rachel. "Not a bit." She returned her attention to the mirror, and finally opened it. She gasped as the candles shuddered and swooned. "Where did you get this?"

"A friend," David replied. "It's all I can tell you."

"If I am to divine the secrets of such a thing, I need to know more."

Before David could reply, Chester spoke up. "No offense meant, but what are your credentials for divining such things?"

"I have studied them," Audrey said. "The occult. Dark magic. Ancient cultures."

"Fair enough," said Chester. "But what makes you so sure this object has anything to do with any of that?"

Audrey straightened. "I didn't say I was sure. Maybe you will just have to go on faith." She addressed David. "It would help matters if you could tell me a bit more."

"I'm sorry," David said. "I can't. Maybe you'll just have to go on faith, too."

Audrey regarded him a moment, then the mirror. "It holds secrets, and quite possibly more than that. I feel it. I am not just saying that—it's not like I have anything at stake. I'm just telling you what I believe. I feel something, but when I look into this glass, I see only myself. This object was not intended for me." She looked at David as intently as she had the item he'd handed her. "But you saw something else, didn't you? You must have."

David inhaled. "Yes."

Audrey nodded. "Jing."

"Excuse me?"

"Magic mirror," Chester interjected. "According to the Chinese Daoists."

"Yes," Audrey said. "Magic mirrors, also called divination mirrors. The Daoists believed them to be a gateway to the spiritual worlds. The circular shape represents the infinite and connecting nature of the universe. They were used for many things — understanding the past, predicting the future, even exorcisms." A worried look crept over her face. "It's not for that, is it?"

David shrugged. "I really hope not."

Rachel nestled her head against his chest, and Amanda softly stroked her hair.

Audrey closed the mirror, clasped it between her hands and spoke in a low voice. "If that is what this is, then it's something very powerful, not only in what it reveals, but in how it may be used by one who possesses it."

Robert raised an eyebrow. "Used?"

"Some believe he who is pure in spirit may call upon the forces of nature, of Heaven and Earth, in moments of need."

"Your knowledge is impressive," Chester said. "But as you alluded to earlier, much of this is constructed on faith. You are, as far as I am aware, correct in that which you presented, but it still comes down to notions of magic, and supernatural things — unprovable things."

"Not necessarily." Audrey touched David's arm. "Do you want to try?"

David looked down at Rachel. The advancing hour and Amanda's touch had lulled her. He extended his hand to Audrey, and she gave him the locket. For a moment, she closed her hand around his.

"Remember," she said. "It took considerable time and practice to achieve mastery of the mirror. Its power derives from all forms of energy — living and passed on, earthy and spiritual. Opening the gates between worlds is no easy matter, and closing them may be harder yet. I have no way of knowing what or whom you're summoning, or if they'll come, or if something else might."

"Something else?"

Audrey cast a quick glance at Rachel.

David still wasn't sure how much of any of this he believed, but Audrey clearly felt they stood a greater chance of discovering the mirror's secrets here, in the graveyard. Now, she was warning him that this place just might conjure more than they bargained for.

"Spirits?" he mouthed.

Audrey nodded. "Maybe. A place of purgatory, perhaps."

Purgatory. All David remembered was it was related to notions of the afterlife, and something told him not in a good way. If spirits roamed these hallowed grounds — here, now — that meant they weren't, of course, in Heaven. And if they weren't in Heaven, then.... He looked at Audrey, unsure because of Rachel how to best phrase his question, but Audrey read his eyes.

"Purgatory is not what most people think," she said. "Most people, for whatever reason, think it is a version of — well, you know. It's not. It's a place for souls destined for Heaven, but which haven't made it yet. Their lives on Earth were not quite good enough for eternal grace so they wait — a terrible limbo, waiting for their time, waiting for the light."

David drew a deep breath and then exhaled. The candlelight danced. "And what do you think?" he asked her.

Audrey managed a faint smile. "I really don't know. I just want you to be sure, before you try."

"Thank you, but I know what I saw before, and I think I know *who*. I think he'll come again." He drew another breath, slowly exhaled, and opened the locket.

Only him, and nothing else, but it was the worst sort of nothing, the sort you knew wouldn't last long.

Rachel shifted in her brother's lap, her eyes fluttering open and growing rapt.

It was still just David in the mirror, and the gray nothingness around him, but now the nothingness was deepening, turning upon itself, like an ancient voice seeking articulation. The candles swayed again, the flames cowering, and the tomb grew cold on this warm summer night. Rachel's fingertips dug into her brother's arms as a loud *whoosh* sounded, and the candles went out. For a moment, sheer blackness.... Things were always darkest where the light had just been.

"David...." Rachel buried her head in his chest, and he held her tightly.

"Robert, if you please," Chester said. Some shuffling and grunting ensued as Robert helped Chester to his feet. A moment later, a slender prism of light pierced the gloom. Chester had switched on his phone's flashlight, and he directed it toward the ground, away from direct contact with anyone's eyes.

Robert shoved the door open, and helped Chester extricate himself from the structure. Amanda stepped out next, followed by David and Rachel, and finally Audrey, who had hurriedly scooped up her candlesticks and placed them in the small crate in which she'd brought them.

"Carry me," Rachel told David.

They proceeded slowly, Chester lighting the way with his phone. Audrey and Amanda walked alongside each other, the candlesticks clanking in dull rhythm with every step.

Rachel's face sat inches from David's, and when he glanced in her eyes, they were wide and bearing an expression he wasn't certain he'd ever seen.

He stopped in his tracks, his own eyes widening. Something had buzzed him, *touched* him, or at least come close enough to create a sharp, chilled gust. He could see in the eyes of his sister she'd felt it too.

Amanda nudged Audrey, and said, "Wait." She then turned back to David. "Are you okay?"

Robert and Chester stopped and looked back too.

At that moment, the strangest of impulses rushed over him: he must put his sister away from him. From the moment things had started falling apart, slipping away, his instinct had been to pull her closer, to protect her at all costs, but whatever was setting upon them now was — surely — after *him*. This was his burden to bear, not Rachel's or anyone else's, and while he might not prevail in whatever this fight really was, damn if he would let Rachel be harmed in the crossfire. He set her down and backed away, then held up his hands to deter her as she cried out and began to scamper back to him.

"Rachel!"

She stopped at the sharpness in her brother's voice.

"Rachel." Softer now. "Stand back, okay. It'll be safer." He backed farther away, each step clawing at his conscience, searing into him.

The others had stopped as well, watching with incredulity the events unfolding before them.

"No one move!" David called. "They're after me." He braced for the next assault from... whatever they were. He tensed, but the next rush never came, and in that awful sliver of time when one realizes he's made the gravest of errors, David understood why.

He prepared to spring forward but paused. He'd learned things were all too often not what they seemed, but as his mind attempted to register what was transpiring before them, like one of those rapid-turning flipbooks, he'd no idea how things seemed, no frame of reference against which to even hazard a comparison. This was something else entirely, something that defied somethingness, and so he stopped, hoping down to his bones that in so doing, he would not be failing Rachel yet again. Still, he had to be sure.

Those diving, darting bits of luminescence that had pursued them now encircled his sister, having slowed ever slightly, and they coalesced like a halo above her. David shielded his face as he attempted to make eye contact with Rachel—it was not that the hovering ring was emanating light, but rather *was* light, of a sort David had never seen. Whatever it was, it had issued forth from the darkened depths of the cemetery, a macabre yet entrancing reanimation. His eyes adjusted and locked with his sister's, and he was surprised to see the calm—and something more than that—pooling within.

The ring began to descend over her, and David shot forward but was instantly repelled, as though by an electrified fence. He stumbled to the ground, his skin pricking with an unearthly voltage, more incapacitating than painful.

"David!" Amanda rushed to his side and helped him up.

As he straightened, he realized the shimmering sphere was regarding him. Even in a world where the impossible had become probable, this seemed unfathomable, but as he stared, the ring was shifting, transforming, devolving away from what moments before had been the incandescent sum of its parts.

The *it* became *they*—faces, spirits, ghosts—and they beheld him with eyes that could not be eyes, but which pierced him, nevertheless. They didn't want him, and they didn't want him near. Within the sunken orbs welled a profound sorrow. Their "bodies" trailed out behind them like tails of a comet—wispy, glowing tendrils now slowly contracting back as the ring reconstituted itself and slowly turned back toward Rachel. These things—whatever they were—broke over her like a cloud, touching her, nuzzling her, it seemed.

A strange serenity welled up in David, as it had in those fleeting moments with Malea in the water. Was this yet another wrinkle in the world he thought he knew, another new reality? He inched forward. New reality or not, there was one gospel that compelled him always.

"Rachel," he said, and slowly extended his arms.

The apparitions scattered in apparent agitation, some breaking ranks and darting at David once again, but now Rachel held out her arms, as she had with the great stag at Kane Manor.

"It's okay," she said.

David was not entirely sure to whom she was speaking, but there was no mistaking the effect her words had, as the apparitions turned back to her, slowing, fluttering, calming. David glanced at his friends; each stared in various states of wonder, except Chester, who looked with an expression of severe assessment, as if in so doing he might somehow extricate that which he beheld from the muddled depths of incomprehension.

"Amazing," said Audrey, her voice trailing off, eyes locked onto the otherworldly nimbus. "They're drawn to her."

"Rachel," David said again. "We have to go."

"They're scared," Rachel said. "They're lost."

David inched closer, remaining focused on his sister, doing his best to ignore the angry buzzing. He held out a hand. Another jolt besieged him, and he flinched but didn't fall back.

"No!" Rachel exclaimed.

David braced and extended his hand again, and this time Rachel stepped forward and grasped it. They began to walk, their friends quickly following.

The ring disintegrated once more and roiled in distress; the apparitions darted and dived around them, coalescing back into the vaporous halo before splintering off again. Their agitation grew louder and more persistent, like a cloud of hungry mosquitoes.

"Keep my hand," David called over the hum. "Keep walking."

They did, David guiding his sister past and around headstones that rose as jutting silhouettes, gleaming into focus under the seething, spectral glow. A profound incongruity gnawed at him. For whatever reason, he'd been chosen as a principal in this ancient game, had already been thrust into the chaos and mystery of converging worlds. But that was no reason to drag anyone else into it, especially the people he cared about most. Even if he could no longer accomplish it for himself, he wished more than anything that he could somehow return things to the way they had once been for everyone else — slam the door to other worlds and lock it shut, no matter what might rise up pounding from the other side. Yet, as they walked past graves and approached the road from which they'd veered, the drone deafening and the glow blinding, he knew in his heart that it was well too late.

When they at last reached the interior road, Robert helped Chester into his wheelchair.

Their last few steps would not be easy: their thrumming escort roared into a disorienting cacophony and swirled violently about them. David wondered if they would be pursued all the way home; indeed, he wondered if they would *get* home.

He needn't wait long for an answer, for as soon as he and Rachel crossed over to the road, the spirits flattened and were jolted back.

"They cannot cross," Audrey said.

The spirits circled and fomented, some breaking ranks and trying the barrier once again, rebuffed each time like moths at a bug lantern. Gradually, it began to fade, like retreating fog, but a few wisps lingered behind, near Rachel. They were distinct figures now — faces, young and old and varied, imploring Rachel with mournful eyes.

She held out a hand, but David gently pulled her back.

"I'm sorry," she said, eyes glistening in the lingering glow.

The drone faded out as they headed toward the entrance, gradually replaced by the low whirring of Chester's wheelchair and clanking of Audrey's candles. Bits of reality beckoned: streetlights, the sound of passing vehicles, the yammering of a dog... trademarks of familiarity bestowing small measures of comfort. Clinging to pillars which had forever supported all one understood of the world, did not always bespeak denial. Sometimes it was a way to cope, a way to steady oneself, before opening doors you never knew were there.

***

HE EXPECTED HIS FATHER'S EYES TO

be tinged with admonition, but when he opened the front door to their house and saw him standing there in the foyer, he registered something more.

"I'm sorry," David said, pinning his hopes on a preemptive apology. "I should have called. We just ran a little late."

"More than a little," his father said, his tone severe. "We'll talk about it later." He glanced toward the living room before turning back to his son. "You have a visitor."

CHAPTER 2
But a Messenger

"MARCEL!" DAVID BURST PAST HIS father into the living room, but the individual who rose from the couch to meet him was not Marcel. He was a short man who strode forward, extended his hand, and addressed David in a somewhat high-pitched voice.

"I am sorry to disappoint. I am but a messenger on your friend's behalf."

David's father appeared at the edge of the living room, holding a very tired-looking Rachel. "I'm going to put her to bed," he said. He regarded their guest. "You're certain you wouldn't like anything?"

The man smiled. "Thank you, no. I do not wish to impose upon you any more than I have."

David's father nodded and headed to the stairwell with Rachel.

Their guest turned back to David and said, "Master Rose."

"David," he said.

"David. And I am Herm—you may call me Herman. Shall we sit?"

They did. Herman regarded him with an almost reverent expression that David found unsettling. He knew it was well-intended, that Herman, like Marcel and Kane and apparently countless others, regarded him as some vital piece of their great puzzle, a key player in their grand game, but he wanted nothing to do with it. He didn't want to be exalted — or hunted — for something he could scarcely remember and, at any rate, had not chosen for himself.

Nonetheless, he trusted Marcel, and if he'd dispatched this man to see him, then David needed to trust *him* too. They were, after all, his best chance at achieving that which he wanted most.

"Marcel sent you?"

Herman smiled. "Indeed yes, but I do not begrudge the duty. I have traveled far greater distances, to be sure." A light flickered behind his eyes.

The footfalls upon the second-floor hallway diminished, a door squeaked open, and it was apparent her father was putting Rachel to bed.

Herman glanced toward the stairwell, then back at David. "He doesn't know, then? I rather suspected otherwise."

"He doesn't believe."

Herman raised an eyebrow. "But he was there, yes? When you awakened?"

David eyed the stairwell. "He was, but he couldn't see what I saw, couldn't feel what I felt. And Kane was just too good."

Herman nodded. "I can only imagine how hard it is, wishing you could see Marcel, wanting to tell your father, wanting to find your mother — new worlds, new yous, boundless possibility. But I imagine, in so many ways, you feel ever more alone."

David looked down, but after a moment lifted his head and met Herman's gaze. He blinked fiercely and nodded.

"Allow yourself these sentiments," Herman said, "but do not despair. Alone as you might in your darkest moments believe yourself to be, take heart that this is not true. Many walk beside you, even when you cannot see."

David took a deep breath, exhaled. "What now?"

"You have been awakened," Herman said. "You now walk in concurrent worlds. It will be all too easy to become consumed with those newer ones, because they are newer, because they simmer with magic — some parts wondrous, some parts dark — but stay mindful, Master Rose... David... of that world you've always known. The others will beckon soon enough, but for now, I suggest you try to live as normally as possible — no easy thing, I grant you."

"What about school?" David asked. "Friends?" Memories of his duel with Donovan swept over him. "These... abilities I have.... Should I hide them?"

Herman smiled, as though impressed with the question. "You must exercise your best judgment."

David wanted to roll his eyes. Why did it always seem there were half-answers, elusive clues, deepening mysteries? He vaguely got the concept that it might somehow be better to discover these things on his own, but he hadn't asked for any of this, and it would have suited him just as well to be handed the entire playbook at once.

"The woman," he suddenly said.

Herman raised an eyebrow.

"Malea... she said something to me, something about a gathering, I think. What is that?"

Herman's expression suggested that were the individual in question present, he would most assuredly admonish her, but his features quickly softened. "Yes, the Great Assembling, and it is why caution is paramount, for the lines between worlds have already begun to blur. Doorways have been opened."

"Donovan," said David. "Our past lives."

"Not only that. You can imagine the difficulty attempting to render comprehensible a story whose plot has thickened for millennia."

"Yes," said David, recalling the infusion of memories that had flooded him at Tintagel.

Herman glanced upstairs. "Our time grows short. The mirror... have you discovered its purpose?"

"Maybe," David said. "I saw someone... me—the other me."

"*Another* you."

David inhaled deeply. "But just that once."

Herman nodded. "I see."

"Will you teach me?"

Herman regarded him wistfully. "It is not my place to do so, though I can only imagine your anxiousness." He smiled. "Great wonders await, but your ability to navigate them will benefit the more from waiting for Marcel. I caution you that meddling with these powers before that time might prove unwise."

David sighed. Always, there seemed to be such equivocations, irksome shades of gray. *New worlds beckon, but wait for Marcel to show you. We don't know when that might be. Great power sits at your fingertips, but grasping it could have dire consequences.* It was like he'd finally arrived at a great door behind which awaited the answers he'd for so very long sought, only to be told to come back later. He longed for swift and decisive movement, such as he'd felt when Arondight had come alive in his hands, but he would try to wait... for now... again.

"How unwise?" he asked.

The floorboards creaked above them and they glanced upwards.

Herman spoke quietly. "The immortals walk in worlds known to no others, see things no one else sees. Good or evil, they stand out like beacons to one another." Herman leaned closer. "You are awakened," he said. "From this day forward, as you discover your powers, as you step further into this new world, it gives off signals."

"Others will see it?" David asked. "Others like me?"

"Others will see it, and others will come."

The floorboards creaked again, louder this time; his father was returning.

Herman arose, and David did likewise. By the time David's father had rejoined them, Herman had moved to the front door.

"You're leaving?"

"I'm afraid I must," Herman said. He gestured upstairs with a tilt of his head. "Your precious angel, she is all right?"

"I think so, David father said. "She's asleep. Of course, it's hard to really know what all right is, given all that has happened, especially for one so young."

Herman nodded. "Indeed, it is, sir. Indeed, it is. She has endured much. You all have. She is lucky to have you."

"We are lucky to have her."

Herman appeared solemn but once more his eyes glinted as he nodded. "We all are."

Herman shook their hands a final time before pulling the door open and stepping out into the night.

David's father peered out at their driveway, and up and down the street. A curious look lit over his features. "Can I give you a ride? Call you a cab?"

"Thank you, no," Herman said. "My conveyance awaits just around the corner."

David observed him, that glint more pronounced in the darkness.

"Farewell for now, friends." Herman turned and headed off on foot.

David remembered something, something so obvious he shook his head that he hadn't thought to broach it until now. He watched their visitor diminishing into the spectral glare of the streetlights—quaint and quiet houses, the occasional returning vehicle, the shrill song of cicadas. Tomorrow, adults would go to work, and kids of all ages would set about their summer plans—normal stuff. Trouble was, that term had flipped within the reservoir of David's understanding, in this new world where up was down, day was night, and time a thing more uncertain still.

"Wait!"

Herman stopped and turned, his shadow flaring like wings upon the pavement.

David broke into a trot. "There was one other," he said upon reaching him.

Herman regarded him.

"One other time it happened, with the mirror. Tonight, in fact—at the cemetery."

"Whom did you see?"

David hesitated. "Not in there," he said. "Not exactly. We tried to see if it would work... see who might come, and they did, only... not from the mirror."

Herman's brow furrowed.

David could feel his heart begin to accelerate, as had become customary during times like this, when unnerving notions began churn within him.

"What did you see?" asked Herman.

David cast a glance back to his house, to where his dad stood peering out at them from the doorway. "Ghosts," he said. "Ghosts, or spirits or something. They were after Rachel, but not to hurt her, more like wanting her to stay, or to go with her. It was the strangest thing." He searched Herman's eyes. "Is that part of all this? Part of who I am?"

Herman placed a hand on David's shoulder, his eyes kind but hard-set. "I'm afraid that is something quite more."

CHAPTER 3
Tributaries

A STORM WAS GATHERING ON THE
far horizon. David couldn't be certain when it would
arrive, only that it would. An expanding plume of
rain clouds loomed in an otherwise gleaming quadrant
of midday sky, pierced here and there by shafts of
sunlight, as though bored by travelers from worlds
beyond. But such doors, David knew, had already been
flung open, and he needed to be ready for whoever — or
whatever — might next come barreling through.

"David," his father said.

He'd retrieved his bike and now turned to find his father
leaning in the doorway, still in his pajamas. He looked
haggard, beat. It was the weekend, so he hadn't shaved, but
it was more than that. He looked to David not unlike Mr.
Cheswick that day he and Amanda had come calling.

"Hey," David responded.

"Where you off to?"

"Library."

His father frowned. "Library? It's summer. That's
great, but I don't recall that being one of your hangouts."

David shrugged.

"Wait." His father's eyes narrowed. "You're not
still chasing down conspiracy theories, are you?"

David tensed, but remained silent.

"David, you have to let it go. Crazy things
happened, yes, but they were accidents. Donovan was a

very troubled kid. I am sorry all of it happened, especially after what happened to your mother, but...."

"Dad...."

His father walked over to him and placed his hands on his shoulders. "But if you're still trying to find some connection between the two, you're setting yourself up for terrible disappointment." He glanced up at Rachel's window. "And you won't be the only one."

David bit his lip, fighting to restrain his anger. He felt his father's concern, but still simmered over his lack of faith in his son. He turned away, severing his father's grip.

"I gotta go." He took one last glance back.

His father frowned, then nodded and shuffled back inside, disappearing into the shadows.

David turned to go but there came a rapping from above, and he looked up and saw Rachel in the window. She waved, and he waved back, but he winced on account of the melancholy in her eyes. He conjured a smile and waved again, and when her face brightened just a bit, he turned and pedaled into the street. He had work to do.

***

HIS FATHER HAD BEEN RIGHT — IT was not his normal hangout — but the library was Chester's suggestion, and their friend grinned from behind the pile of books he'd already assembled, upon seeing them approach.

"Until today," said Robert, "I would have told you it would be impossible to get me to the library in the summer, much less a Saturday."

"When you have eliminated the impossible," said Chester, "whatever remains, however improbable, must be the truth."

David grinned. "You've said that before."

Chester nodded. "Holmes," he said. "The Sign of the Four."

And it was this group of four in which David would again place his trust. They joined Chester at his table, near the reference section at the far end of the building. Robert sat adjacent Chester, Amanda alongside David.

"We're having a secret meeting to explore a mystery," Robert said, "and this is our gathering place?"

"If we wish to find clues about the future," Chester rejoined, "it is often helpful to look to the past. Books have an uncanny way of being helpful toward that end."

Robert rolled his eyes.

"Honored to be part of the team," Amanda said, "and I want to help, but which mystery are we trying to solve? What happened with Kane, with Donovan... with your mom?"

"I don't know," David replied. "All of it, I guess."

Amanda nodded. "So where to start?"

"How about the beginning?" Robert smirked.

Chester leaned forward and clasped his hands. "His sarcasm notwithstanding, I dare say our friend is right."

"But I don't know what that means anymore," David said. He regarded each of them. "Beginning of the strange things at school? Beginning of life without Mom? Beginning of being Lancelot?"

"One life at a time, I think," said Chester. "Let's start with this one. No one besides you has any experience with the rest of it, and so our ability to help you is far greater if we start with the world we know."

"Okay," said Amanda, "then what do we know? When did the strange things begin to happen?"

"When we lost Mom," David said. His friends regarded him solemnly. "Probably before that, but that's what I remember."

Amanda touched his shoulder. "Okay, then let's start there."

David leaned back, folded his arms behind his head, and inhaled deeply. "Stuff really started after that night—nightmares, fights, the feeling there was always something, or someone, after me." He eyed his friends. "I guess it turns out there was. And then last fall, almost a year after Mom had disappeared, when I saw Malea...." He glanced at Robert. "When you pulled me from the creek."

For a few moments, only the faint tick of the wall clock sounded, like slow-dripping water.

"And then," David resumed, "all the stuff with Donovan and Kathy, all the stuff at school, Marcel, Cheswick. The obsession with conflicts and feuds, trying to awaken me, Rendicott, Cerratus...."

"Kane," added Chester. "Don't forget Kane. He orchestrated—from all you've said—the entire thing, including everything and everyone at school—even, as far as he knew, anyway, Marcel."

David nodded, and in his mind's eye he saw him now—Kane, standing before him as he had when they'd left the castle, his eyes burning once more into David's, as if to say, *'I told you we'd meet again.'* David felt his fists balling. Yes, Kane had orchestrated the confrontation with Donovan—and nearly cost him and David their lives—but David's thoughts had roamed back to another day, the one in the woods at the Moreland place, when he'd discovered the torn piece of cloth. His friends were right—it could have been anyone's—but in his heart, he knew; Kane had been there that terrible night, responsible for either the disappearance or death of his mother. How he now wished he would have run him through, in the shadow of the great eclipse, instead of handing Arondight over like a dutiful subject. It was his, after all — Lancelot's, not Kane's, whoever, and whatever, Kane was.

But, no. His fists slowly unclenched, and he exhaled. Their time would come — his and Kane's. This he knew in his bones, but not quite yet, not while Kane remained his best chance at finding his mother. It was tough, though, really tough — at times excruciating. Theirs was a plot centuries in the making, and yet at times he felt it was all he could do to wait just one moment more.

"Damn," David said. A water bottle he'd brought had tipped over and the lid hadn't been well-fastened, and a small stream coursed forth onto the table.

"Here," said Amanda, pulling a few tissues from her bag and handing them to David.

He began blotting the spill, dabbing at the little tributaries which had started to run across the table, but suddenly stopped, staring.

"What's wrong?" asked Amanda.

"Malea," David replied. "The naiad." He straightened up, the sopping tissues clutched in his hand. "She saved my life, in the cave with Merlin." He shook his head, then saw his friends exchange glances, and drew back at their dubious expressions.

"Sorry," Amanda said. She touched his shoulder. "We believe you, but you must understand some of this is still hard to process. We've been taught our whole lives stories like that can't be real."

David nodded and sank slowly into his chair. "I know. There are still times I think that too, except that I'm living them."

Chester leaned forward. "I must echo what Amanda said. We are still trying to process all this. Immortality is one thing: I'm a skeptic, even though I've seen things now, such as at the cemetery, which I would have previously thought impossible. I recognize there are logical aspects, though, ties to beliefs in religion and afterlife and such. Even with the Arthurian stuff, while most scholars ascribe it to legend, the argument may be tendered that there is a historical basis. Yet even if they existed — Arthur, Lancelot, Gawain — they were people. Merlin too. Perhaps a sorcerer, or practitioner of the occult, but human. But this creature you speak of...."

"Malea."

"Malea. What you have described requires an acceptance of a race belonging, until now, purely to mythology."

Amanda reached for one of the books on the table — *Legends & Lore of Greek Mythology* — and began leafing through. "What did you call her?"

"Not me," said David. "Marcel. He called her a naiad."

Amanda nodded and continued leafing.

"I suggest we follow her lead," Chester said. "I've taken the liberty of securing some possible sources." He handed a book to each of them.

Robert groaned. "No one said there'd be homework."

"There will be more than a bit," Chester said.

"Naiads?" David asked, fetching up his book.

Chester shook his head. "Divide and conquer," he said. "Malea was just one of the unusual things that has happened to you. We must try to understand all of it — the powers, the conflict, the idea of immortality... everything. Just start looking. When uncertain what we are looking for, the best course is to keep our eyes open and let it find us."

David raised an eyebrow. "Holmes again?"

Chester grinned widely. "McVee," he said. "I think if there are clues in here, we'll know them when we see them. Amanda, any luck?"

"Maybe." She cast a glance at each of them, before returning her gaze to a passage in her book. "According to Greek Mythology, the Naiads were female spirits, nymphs. There were different types, having dominion over different bodies of water, from fountains and ponds up to rivers, streams, even the sea." She glanced up at David. "That's where you saw her, right? Malea? In water?"

David nodded. "First in the creek when it was flooding over, then again in the cave, by the sea."

"Most naiads were associated with fresh water, others with salt water, but sometimes the distinction blurred within the belief of the ancient Greeks that the world's waters interlocked as one overall system, emanating from caverns deep in the sea." Amanda paused again and looked up.

"It follows," David said. "I saw her in fresh water and sea water. I saw her two different places across the globe. Pretty sure she didn't board a plane."

Robert leaned forward. "But what's her role in all this? I mean, she gives some vague warning in the creek, then throws down with Merlin—I can't believe I'm saying any of this—with Merlin, in a sea cave in England."

David shrugged. "Not sure her role, only that she seems to be on our side, which, had you been in that cave, you'd agree is a very good thing."

"A good thing indeed," Amanda said. "While often revered or worshipped, naiads could also be fearsome and dangerous, possessing of impassioned tempers and capable of great jealousy." She glanced back up. "You better stay on her good side."

CHAPTER 4
Darkness and Light

RACHEL'S DADDY HAD GIVEN HER breakfast, and they'd talked for quite a while. She could tell he was worried about her, but she was worried about him. She'd seen him talking to her brother outside before David pedaled off, and when he'd shuffled back into their house, he'd looked so pale to her, so tired. In England, he had seemed more like his old self, when he was protecting his children, but now it was clear he and David had problems again, and that everything was taking a toll on him. She understood—he'd been through a lot. Her too. Some of it had been fun, actually—flying in an airplane, getting to stay in a castle, making friends with the beautiful stag. There was plenty she hadn't liked, too—Kathy, Kane, those awful brothers, Donovan trying to hurt David.

And the ghosts: the one that Donovan had turned into that night she ran away in the thunderstorm, and the ones last night at the graveyard, even though those ones hadn't been so scary. They seemed to like her, but... this was all just a lot to think about. She wanted to do things she liked to do, was used to doing, like playing with friends, reading with David, laughing with her dad. She and David had a job to do too, a promise to keep. Mama was out there... somewhere... waiting for them to find her. Daddy was having too hard a time, so it was up to her and David, and so, even ghosts were just going to have to understand.

She wished David had taken her with him today. She knew he was probably meeting his friends and they would be talking about things — about the graveyard, about England... about Mama. She might not have understood everything they'd be saying but she still felt she should be there. It was her mama — hers and David's — after all, and David was her brother. He had been through so much too.

A chill ran through her as she recalled how Donovan had nearly killed him with the sword. Something had lit up inside her, even from as far away as she'd been, something that told her David was in danger. It had been, and was now, the strangest of feelings — so many things at once. Deep in her heart, she trusted and knew that they would always take care of her — David, their father, Mama too, wherever she was and whenever they found her. But right alongside that feeling, which made her feel every bit as safe and warm as when she snuggled with her stuffed animals beneath her comforter, lived another feeling, every bit as real, even if she couldn't quite find the words to figure out what it was. That something inside her had known, even before seeing, that David was in danger that day. That special something told her that, just as there were those she could depend upon, there were also those who depended upon her.

She wished David would be home soon. Their father was downstairs, probably in his study, maybe sitting in the dark like he used to right after Mama had disappeared. She grabbed up her bear for company, slipped from her room, and treaded down the hallway to David's room. He wasn't there, but she nudged the door cautiously nonetheless. The sky was darkening through his window, but something caught her eye in the ribbon of light that segmented the otherwise dim room — something shiny.

She squinted and shuffled over to the bed where the mirror lay, the one David had returned from England with, and which had seemed to start all the trouble last night at the cemetery. She scampered onto the bed and knelt over the unusual object, seeing already, in this new light, things she'd not noticed before. It still was old-looking — *real* old — but at the same time not old at all. It didn't look new, either, not exactly, but rather... well... different. It was about as pretty as anything she'd ever seen, not unlike the fancy stained-glass windows at church when they used to go, but not quite that either.

Some different world rose from the surface of the glass itself in the thin shaft of sunlight, a faraway-looking mountain range unlike any she'd ever seen, like something from one of her storybooks. Her eyes widened but then started to grow heavy, and she lay back and held the mirror over her, and stared in through rapidly drowsing vision. It was calling to her, this risen place, of this she was quite sure. It had come to fetch her with golden chariots pulled by the most beautiful horses she'd ever seen. She smiled at the sound of their approach, at their rhythmic hoofbeats, so soft and insistent.

***

THE MORNING PASSED, AND WITH NO answers and fleeting clues that seemed to evaporate as quickly as they'd suggested themselves, it became apparent they were there for the long haul. They gave Robert some money, and he walked across the street to the burger place and brought back lunch. They ate and read and conferred, and ate and read and conferred some more, each using the restroom once or twice, getting up and pacing about and stretching a bit. David was amazed when, what seemed not that much later, he glanced up and saw it was almost closing time.

"Time is short," Chester said. He scanned their group. "Robert, anything?"

"Just some of the same stuff from class," Robert replied. "Hatfields-McCoys, the War of the Roses... no pun intended."

Chester turned his attention to David. "Anything catch your eye?"

"Not really. Lots of what we've studied, like conflict and death as universal themes, all that stuff. A danse macabre. Remember all those paintings and stuff?"

"Indeed," Chester replied. "Anything else?"

"Not really, other than the Biblical stuff, I guess."

Chester arched an eyebrow. "Such as?"

David glanced between his notes and his assigned book.

"This says there are ancient Biblical origins to conflict." He flipped to a page he had marked. "The Old Testament refers to a Book of Life, where God records the deeds of the righteous and unrighteous, and who in the next year is marked for life and marked for death. It talks about one of six Heavenly envoys who mark the righteous for life. The Book of Jubilees refers to two separate books — those who walk in darkness are marked as enemies of God and written into the Book of Death, but for those who walk in light and protect others from evil, they shall awaken to everlasting life." He looked up. "All conflict, according to this, roots back to these origins — good and bad, light and dark, life and death."

No one spoke, and the silence seemed to press in

upon them.

"Light and dark," Amanda said suddenly, softly, as though to herself. "There's something here too." Her voice had subsided to a whisper — fitting, perhaps, given the venue — but her eyes glazed with a faraway look, and she read as though she'd forgotten anyone else were present. "Legend holds that in the timeless battle between good and evil and light and dark, allegiances formed and fractured throughout the centuries, lines became blurred, unclear, gray."

She glanced up at David — causing his heart to dance, as always — before returning to her page.

"But good and evil and light and dark still existed, ever and always, and there came into being immortal soldiers of each, those who would forever embody and fight for the kind of world they wished to see, and which, through their perseverance, they might one day bring about. They carry the torch of righteousness and are watched over in turn by guardians of their own, benevolent souls who, if necessary, have and will make the ultimate sacrifice to protect them and keep the torch ablaze. But always have these soldiers of light been burdened by a blighted shadow, mercenaries of darkness who believe that only when the fires of light and goodness are extinguished may they prevail and cast the world into an eternity of despair."

They regarded one another, no sound now, save for their own breathing and the quiet rhythm of the clock. It was only when the overheads flickered off, leaving just the pale glow of the auxiliary lighting, that David looked and saw it was closing time.

Ms. Duffy, the longtime librarian with spectacles perched far down on her nose, shuffled over. "Time to go," she said in a kindly voice.

"I wonder," said Chester, "if we might just have a

few minutes more?"

Ms. Duffy consulted her watch. "All right, Chester. For you... ten minutes."

"And I wonder if we might go downstairs?"

A conflicted look swam over the librarian's face. "All right," she finally said. "Ten minutes."

"Obliged."

Ms. Duffy turned and disappeared into the now shadowed recesses from which she'd approached.

"I'm not sure whether to be impressed or mortified," said Robert. "You have special library privileges?"

"Try to contain your envy," Chester said.

Chester and Robert took the elevator down, and when they emerged, David and Amanda were awaiting them. Together they proceeded into the dim rectangular space laid out before them. The auxiliary lighting provided scant illumination, and though a cobbling of brick-sized windows lined the periphery of this cellar-like space, the waning daylight hung thinly about, frittering away beneath the descending cloak of night.

David could see through one of these small openings that the moon had risen in the deeply purpling sky, crescent and alabaster, its glow waxing their faces in chalky incandescence, like disembodied heads bobbing along the aisles.

"I didn't even know there was a lower level," Robert said. "What are we looking for?"

Chester tendered a sheepish nod toward a section of books to their left.

David peered through the gloom. "Occult?"

Chester shrugged. "I'm not saying I believe, but we are attempting to get inside the heads of those who do."

Amanda's eyes narrowed and she stepped toward

the shelf and retrieved a book from just over Robert's shoulder. "Daoist Mythology and Traditions." She furrowed her brow and glanced at David. "Daoist. Didn't Audrey say something about that?"

David nodded and stepped closer to her, peering through the pallor at that book she held. "Something to do with the mirror," he said.

Amanda raised her wrist to her eyes and squinted at her watch. "Not much time." She flipped to the index of her selection. A moment later she nodded, whispered a page number to herself, and flipped back the other direction until she had it. She read silently a while, her lips moving, and finally paused and glanced up. "Listen to this. Ancient Buddhist priests used Magic Mirrors to reveal to disciples that form in which they might be reborn. According to the more ancient texts, on the back of the mirror, or sometimes on the glass itself, are found strange and divine landscapes. Sometimes, depending on the exact mirror, various images would appear in different light."

Robert nudged David. "Have you seen any of that?"

David thought. "Maybe," he said. "It definitely had an ancient and unusual look, but what had most surprised me was when I thought I saw... well, you know."

Robert looked from him to Amanda. "What does it all mean?"

She returned her gaze to the book. In the heavy silence, the muted creaking of the old building and the whisper of the wind in the trees seemed frightfully loud.

Chester consulted his watch.

Amanda read. "The various metals with which the mirrors were constructed were believed possessing of magical properties. The Daoists believed spirits were made visible by Magic Mirrors. The reflection in the mirror is thought to be the image of one's soul."

They each regarded David.

"As the possessor gazes into the mirror, the changing images reflect the various images of the individual's past lives. If a person looks into the mirror and does not...." Amanda swallowed hard, and a nervous look spread over her moonlit face.

"What is it?' David said.

Amanda regarded him uneasily, then returned to the page. "If a person looks in the mirror and does not recognize his own countenance, it is believed a sign his own death is near."

David shifted as three sets of eyes fell upon him. "I mean, what does that even mean? If I have past lives, is it a sign if I don't recognize my present one? Or any of them?" He laughed, an unconvincing sound. "Plus, it said mythology, right? Daoist mythology? Mythology may not be real. And it's not even Arthur stuff, you know? Might not even be connected, right?"

"Right," Chester said. "It is indeed mythology, and we've no way of knowing of any connection to these other experiences you've endured."

David smiled weakly.

"Do you have the mirror with you?' Chester asked. "Perhaps we may have another look."

David reached into his backpack and fumbled around. "Damn. I thought I did. Must have fallen out on my bed."

Amanda held up a hand, eyes on the page. "It may not be all doom and gloom," she said. "The Daoist priests used the mirrors to ward evil, to observe the true shape or nature of a spirit, human or animal, as one might indeed, in truth, be the other. When used properly, the mirrors were thought to possess the ability to render the invisible visible, and so therefore the true form of an evil spirit would be in the mirror, revealed."

"Well," said Robert, "that's cool."

"Mythology," Chester said. "Remember."

Robert nodded toward David. "Tell him."

"Be cautioned," Amanda resumed, "that these properties do not position the mirror itself as a weapon, but merely a tool. It may reveal the enemy, but in that telling moment, the individual must be prepared of his own devices to wage battle."

"Yeah," said David. "I kinda figured. Is that all?"

A door creaked at the top of the stairwell. "Chester? Time is up, I'm afraid!"

"We'll be right up!" Chester called. "Thank you!"

David turned to Amanda.

"One thing more," she said. "The Tunnel of Light." Her eyes narrowed in the darkness. "To increase his or her power over the one being observed, a possessor of the Magic Mirror, if so trained, can evoke a Tunnel of Light, a phenomenon of unbridled power achievable only through intense concentration and focus. The practitioner can, in so doing, observe everyone and everything within the continuum of their focus, even sensing, feeling, and seeing those things manifesting great distances — or even lifetimes — away."

"Well," said Robert. "That's kinda freaky, but still cool."

David touched Amanda's shoulder, and she looked up.

"What does it mean," he asked. "Feel? Like, inside, emotionally? Or, really *feel*? Touch?"

She peered back down at the page. "The tunnel permits a kinetic connection between practitioner and subject, spiritually binding them and permitting, in some instances, a linkage of vast, even psychic influence." She narrowed her eyes further and flipped to the next page. "On rare occasions, a practitioner became so accomplished in the practice and powers of the mirror that he might, through intense meditation, imagine and project a whirling, smoke-like vortex, boring through time and space. Known by some as a Tube of Light, this vortex comprises a far more potent conductor, capable of transforming particle response, exerting a strong, even dangerous influence on the subject positioned at the opposite end of the tunnel. Once the light overtakes and consumes the person on the far end, he or she may be compelled into actions against their will, held spellbound and, in the rarest of instances, according to legend, even physically contacted."

Amanda stopped, exhaled, and looked up. In the shadowed silence, the clock on the wall ticked conspicuously.

"Chester, I'm afraid I must insist

"Coming, Ms. Duffy." Chester signaled his friends. "We have to go."

Amanda closed the book and returned it to its place on the shelf. As they shuffled back toward the elevator, Amanda leaned in toward David and whispered, "Where did you say you left that mirror?"

CHAPTER 5
Gathering Night

HE PEDALED HOME BY MOONLIGHT, wracked with the sort of worry with which he'd by now grown so familiar. When he cornered onto their street and neared their house, the strange disunion of shadow and light that marked it did nothing to allay these fears. Only the lamplight in the study illuminated the lower level, but it was what he observed on the second floor that set his heart to hammering. He'd not left the light in his room on, of this he was certain, but now emanated from it a most peculiar glow. His eyes cast quickly over to Rachel's room: dark as the gathering night.

When he came in, he glanced edgewise over to the study, but didn't break stride as he headed for the stairwell. A tallow light lined the bottom of the door, behind which, he knew, sat their father, either sleeping or lost in what had become one of his many stupors.

He took the stairs two at a time. Upon reaching the corridor, he glimpsed another band of illumination emitting from beneath his own door, brighter though— much brighter. He darted to his door and burst in and, despite the seemingly endless parade of strange things to which he'd become accustomed, was frozen by what he beheld.

Rachel lay splayed on his bed, the mirror clutched in one of her tiny hands, arm bent at her side as though she'd been knocked back. Her eyes would flutter, freeze wide and rapt, then flutter and close again. The mirror seemed ablaze in her hand, gold and gleaming and engulfing the entire room in its luster. What apprehended David's attention most was the small but expanding vortex rising from it, like some miniature waterspout emanating from the ring of fire encircling the glass, mushrooming within that funnel of light which had birthed it, toward what end he could not know, and could not chance.

"Rachel!" He darted to the bed.

The sound of his voice seemed to break the trance, and Rachel's eyes widened. She turned toward him, but then noticed the strange spiral rising toward her within the glowing column of light. She seemed uncertain what to do, and started to raise the mirror for closer inspection.

"No!" David tumbled onto the bed and snatched up the mirror, after which the vortex paused, suspended, before shimmering like a mirage and evaporating, as if never there. The glass itself, however, continued roiling, undulant, smoking with movement and hypnotic imagery.

Rachel scampered to her knees and scooted behind her brother as the unworldly spectacle played out before them.

It was scattering — the picture and its inhabitants — but the trace remnants that lingered on the edges of David's perception chilled him — a picture — or, more aptly, a *sense* — of some other world of which he could offer no account, even with his realization of and budding connection to other, past worlds of his own. He wondered if Rachel had seen it too, just now, over his shoulder, before it bled away into nothingness. Maybe it was what she'd been looking at all that time, before he'd burst in; maybe it was what had rendered her in such a state as he'd discovered her. And no wonder: of all that had happened to him, something about this unnerved him more than any of it. It wasn't that what he'd glimpsed was all terrible — it seemed to him some bits of it had been, but there had also been beauty and light. It was in the totality of the thing, in what he'd seen or thought he'd seen — on a gut level, or whatever was deeper than that in a person, whatever existed in your blood and bones. It brought a great foreboding for which he had neither the time — the march of urgent footsteps reverberated from the stairwell outside his door — nor the capacity to process.

He snapped the mirror shut and slid it under his pillow. The footsteps sounded from the hallway, louder. David turned to Rachel and put a finger to his lips.

She nodded and put a finger to her own.

A hand settled on the doorknob, and now his door swung open. Their father stood in the doorway peering in at his children, gaunt and bloodshot in the pale hallway light.

"I heard something," he said, his sunken eyes casting about the room. "Saw something too, a light, but...." He scratched his head.

"You saw something up here, down there?" David asked.

His father stared. "Well, I heard something," he said. "I can't even describe it. What's going on? Is everything okay?"

"Yeah," David said. "Nothing going on."

Much as he was frustrated with him, their father was clearly lost and struggling, and David took no joy in distressing him further. Nonetheless, if he would not, or could not, be an ally, then there was little choice but to leave him somewhat in the dark.

Rachel sidled out from behind her brother, hopped down from the bed, and went to their father. "Everything's fine, Daddy," she said, hugging his waist.

A helpless smile flickered across his ragged features. He hugged his daughter and kissed her atop the head. "If you say so, angel." He glanced once more at David. "I'll make dinner."

***

JUST BEYOND MORELAND FARMS, THE

Evergreen River wound its way through the valley, its brick-colored waters snaking past hillsides and browning fields, and if the sun were right, tinting emerald beneath the namesake timber that lined its banks. When they got to the berm overlooking the river, they stopped pedaling, and sat beside one another on their bikes, watching the shimmering waters.

"We'll be able to drive here in a few months," Amanda said.

David nodded. "So many things changing."

Amanda smiled and inched her bike closer. "So many things changing." Her sunlit eyes traced thoughtfully over the river. "But not everything." She twisted on her bike until their eyes met. "When was the time of Arthur? Fifth century? Sixth?"

"That's what they say."

"Well, what's that, fifteen-hundred years? Even if you were part of that world — part of that time — I bet this river looked pretty much the same, had you stood here. Maybe different on land, but I mean the river itself. It was there, just as it's here now, just as it'll be here in another fifteen-hundred years, and probably much longer than that."

David stared out at the coursing waters.

"It's just like other things," she continued. "Things that flow inside us, always there, like your devotion to Rachel, and to your mom."

David held her gaze. "More than that."

Amanda smiled.

David turned back toward the river, fighting to suppress the grin that threatened at any moment to crest boyish and huge across his features. He peeked at Amanda, who seemed to be moderating a smile of her own. They hadn't even kissed yet—not that he dared presume they would—but there in the dying light of this summer day, despite all that was happening, it occurred to him that this feeling here and now—this feeling of her—was as that river they beheld, fixing within him a course which he would, one way or another, forever abide.

"What's next?" Amanda asked, her voice lifting like small wings onto the breeze. A few sun-kissed wisps of hair danced across her forehead.

David could not imagine anyone, or anything, more beautiful. "I don't know." Truly, he did not.

She nodded, accepting.

They stared out at the river, which ran segmented in slats of shadow and glimmering gold, as though two rivers ran there. A colony of gulls fluttered suddenly and noisily into view, their frantic wing beats rippling like sheaves of paper lost to the wind. They rose darkly against the bruising sky, seemed to suspend in formation for a moment, before wheeling from sight.

"I can only imagine," said Amanda, "how much you have on your mind—the immortality, the magic, Kane, Marcel, Malea." She shook her head. "Amazing. How do you keep perspective? Keep your focus?"

He turned to her. "I don't know that I do."

She smiled. "Well, maybe not always. I mean, who could? But when all's said and done, you do, and that's what I think I admire most." She turned more fully toward him, penetrating his eyes with her own, reflecting the fire of sunset, awash as ever in kindness.

She was, he knew, right—there was so very much on his mind, except it all seemed far away just then. He felt himself falling in, like he had with Malea, but that had been the lure of something ancient and supernatural. He would take this moment over any other, for it was real in the here and now, breathing and alive.

Amanda leaned toward him and nuzzled her cheek to his.

Yes, this moment triumphed over any other, for its power lived not in any magic, but in the heavenly press of cheek upon cheek, in the scant millimeters separating lips from lips. He closed his eyes as he felt the sweep of her mouth across his cheek, and the petal kiss upon the corner of his trembling mouth.

"In the end," she said, "you'll know."

CHAPTER 6
Open Locks

"Double, double toil and trouble;
Fire burn and caldron bubble.
Fillet of a fenny snake,
In the caldron boil and bake;
Eye of newt and toe of frog,
Wool of bat and tongue of dog,
Adder's fork and blind-worm's sting,
Lizard's leg and howlet's wing,
For a charm of powerful trouble,
Like a hell-broth boil and bubble."

SHE WAS THE MOST ENDEARING
witch on the planet, by his way of thinking. Amanda did summer drama, and David had been thrilled to attend the performance that evening at the community theater just a mile or so from his home. When it was over, Amanda came out and hugged him and thanked him for coming, before returning backstage for the after-party with her cast mates.

He'd walked to the play, and though his father texted and offered to pick him up, he politely declined, preferring to savor the exhilaration of Amanda's affection on the stroll home.

He set out beneath a night sky deep-set and starless. But for the palest slip of moonlight, he walked in darkness past Deer Creek and quiet subdivisions, and along the sidewalk that snaked past the cemetery. A car went past, maybe two; his mind was elsewhere. Somewhere a dog barked. The graveyard did not unnerve him, despite recent events. He felt, if anything, a certain solidarity with the dead, maybe because of what he was, or maybe because, like the dead, he longed to be left in peace. As he paced along to the rhythm of his own footsteps, the crimping gates and towering oaks looming over him, that strange intuition with which he'd grown so familiar told him this was not to be.

He was being followed—never a comforting realization, especially for one at whose heels entire lifetimes had come nipping. It was all still so very new and uncertain, even the moment-to-moment navigation of daily life here in this world he'd always known—just the feel of things, the sense of things. Was day really day and night really night? And how long before either transformed like the wind?

Fair is foul and foul is fair.

And so it was, with all that awaited and all that must be done, he wasn't the least bit confident in his ability to perceive things accurately, including his current apprehension.

But there it was. *There.* That feeling... not so dissimilar from that moment at Tintagel when Donovan—Gawain— had wielded Galatine against him. The moon had succumbed behind an inky veil, but something snared his attention, and as he squinted through the gates at the strange shadow shaping up within the cemetery, he shivered despite the warm evening.

Where are those ancient powers when I need them?

He turned and resumed walking, more briskly now. His heart jumped as a loud clang rang out, followed by an equally jarring rasp of metal upon metal.

"I admire one who partakes in theatre!" cried a voice from somewhere behind him. "By the pricking of my thumbs, something wicked this way comes...."

Who the hell could it be? Donovan? One of Kane's men? Marcel had insisted neither was likely, but then, who? His mind scrambled frantically back to Herman's visit, something he'd warned David of....

He flinched again as another clang reverberated, closer this time—then another. He cornered onto the next street, which abutted the cemetery for one more block but would lead to subdivisions where he could cut through to his own. He pressed on, taking long strides, keeping watch out of the corner of his eyes. When at last he reached the edge of the cemetery grounds, he cornered one more time, near the entrance, to sojourn the final leg home.

"Open locks, whoever knocks."

They'd come face to face.

The man took a step backward, sword in hand, and executed a bow. "Master Rose."

David reached for his own sword, for Arondight, but quickly remembered he did not possess the hallowed weapon—Kane did. The moon slipped its cover, revealing in its illumination a well-proportioned and distinguished-looking man in a long coat. He looked thirty-something, maybe forty, but if he was what David thought he was, what was age... for either of them? He glanced about, hoping for a car or other passers-by.

"Alexander LaGrange," the man said, and sheathed his sword. He eyed David up and down, his face crinkling in curiosity. "Setting out unarmed, at this time of Assembly?"

David took a slight step backwards. "Isn't it forbidden here?" He gestured beyond the man. "Holy ground?"

LaGrange chuckled heartily. "Me thinks you've watched too many movies, lad — 'there can be only one' and all that nonsense." He fixed his eyes upon David's. "There is only who lives and one who dies."

"How did you —"

"Find you?" LaGrange raised an eyebrow. "You are young indeed in your education. Signals, lad. Signals. Not intended for me, no doubt, but here I be." His eyes burned through the darkness. "And I've lived too many lifetimes to fail now."

David wanted to break his gaze, wanted to run, but he regarded this new adversary straight on and held his ground.

Where are the others? The other hims?

"But I'm not without honor," LaGrange said. "I'll not dispatch an unarmed man."

David exhaled.

LaGrange turned and stared back into the shadows of the cemetery. "We shall find you a weapon here."

David felt his eyes widen. "What? No!" He took another step back. "I need a sword — my sword. But —"

"We duel now!" LaGrange seethed. "I have not traveled this far and long for nothing. We fight now, 'less you prefer I pursue you home, and involve what others we might find there?"

"No!"

"Very well, then." LaGrange outstretched his arm congenially and gestured to the dark recesses beyond, as though welcoming David to a new home. "Follow me." He whirled about with a rapid sweep of his coat. "I'm sure we can find something suitable."

David watched LaGrange stride off into the darkness, and considered for a moment seizing the opportunity to flee, but what LaGrange had threatened lingered upon his heart. He took an uneasy step forward, as though any next such step might prove the one past the point of no return.

"Come on, then!" LaGrange's voice trumpeted from the shadows. "Let us tarry no further."

David inhaled deeply, his heart revving. He gritted his teeth and increased his gait.

Has it all come to this? Been for this?

Had he survived at Tintagel, awakened into this new world, and traveled in spirit through centuries all to have it end here, like this, at the hands of this stranger of whom he recalled not a thing? It seemed unbecoming, not just for him, but for it all — the game, this dark and ancient world that seemed to all its other participants so damn important. It couldn't be.

He walked over and down hills that rolled black as ink. Rows of headstones ghosted into view as he passed, and sprawling oaks materialized vast and bone-colored. When a few minutes later LaGrange shaped back into sight, poised alongside a row of graves, something knotted in David's stomach as he realized where he'd been lured.

No coincidences in this new world.

"A proper spot for you to fall," said LaGrange. "Beside your dearest mother."

David met his gaze in the moonlight. "Don't speak of her. Not ever."

LaGrange dismissed him with an impatient wave. "Ours is a world that does not suffer such sensitivities." He cast his eyes about. "Now, to find you a proper implement...." Something caught LaGrange's attention at the end of the row of stones, on the ground near the fence line.

David knew which stone was his mother's, even in the darkness, but he dare not become transfixed — LaGrange had bestowed him a momentary reprieve. He reached again but not for his missing sword, not even for his phone. He withdrew from his back pocket the mirror, turned slightly to shield it with his body, and thumbed open the cover.

LaGrange bent over whatever he'd spotted by the fence line, and David could hear metal clanking about.

He glanced quickly into the mirror, toward what end, he couldn't be sure — toward any end but this.

Nothing... at first. Just the cold, dull glass, dark save for the trace of moonlight it reflected.

"These should do!" called LaGrange, his tone almost cheerful, accompanied by more clanging.

David did not look up.

"I say," called LaGrange. "What have you got there?"

"Nothing." David fumbled to snap the mirror shut but it was too late. He had seen nothing in the mirror — no past lives, no other worlds, not even his own reflection, owing to both the darkness and his haste. But now, a thin but vivid glow radiated from the glass. He got the lid shut and closed his fist tight around it, but no matter: the light bore through him like an x-ray, through his hand and into the heavy darkness, displacing it utterly with its mushrooming incandescence.

David turned back to LaGrange, the cat — and God knew what else — well out of the bag.

LaGrange grasped in either hand a discarded, spear-like slat from the iron fencing. As the two immortals regarded one another in the unearthly glow, LaGrange's eyes grew wide.

"Oh, now you'd be a special one, wouldn't you?" His tongue flicked quickly over his lips. "Better yet." He tossed one of the spears.

David snatched it from the air, already in battle position. The blinding light had at last subsided, and David shoved the mirror back into his pocket.

LaGrange settled into an attack posture, poised the spear above him as one might a javelin, and regarded David with glinting eyes. "You understand this, don't you lad? About immortality, about our world? It's no get out of jail free card. You can die, once you've awakened — *really* die."

David narrowed his eyes, angled his body to oppose LaGrange, and raised the tapered iron instrument above his shoulder. "I understand, and you should too."

He'd no idea whether such bravado emanated from somewhere else inside him, from other hims or other times. It mattered not. All he knew was his body was roiling, his blood searing, much as when Donovan had attacked, when he'd been jolted in a life-saving instant into some gladiatorial imperative he even now scarcely understood. And even if there was none of this, no mythical, muscle memory to call upon, he was not about to succumb easily, not to this time-jumping assassin, not to anyone. He'd made a promise, more than one, and though he'd just as soon this stranger evaporate back to wherever he'd come from, he'd kill him if he had to, or die trying.

"That's the spirit, lad," said LaGrange, advancing forward. "Go down swinging." And swing LaGrange did, bringing the spear forward and down with a great flourish.

David met the assault full on, striding into a guard position, his own weapon transferred into a two-handed grip. The collision reverberated like a bell tower, a seismic percussion. David's head throbbed, but this was good—it had to have been heard for miles, and now, perhaps, someone would come.

LaGrange appeared unconcerned. He swung his spear back up in a great arc, its trajectory carving the air in a violent whistle, and once more leapt forward in attack.

David parried the blow again, eliciting another ear-splitting detonation, but this time there was more, as a searing light erupted at the confluence of their weapons.

The mirror again? David briefly wondered. *No, that's impossible. It's in my back pocket.*

Whatever the cause, it expanded with such force as to send both combatants flying backwards. The slat flew from David's hands, and he rolled aside a moment before its pointed end impaled the earth where his head had just been. The illumination faded as quickly as it had come, and David's eyes widened as another figure resolved slowly into view.

"Fontaine," LaGrange spat. "What the devil are you doing here?"

"Keeping an eye on devils like you," replied the voice that David had so longed to hear. "You know such rogue behavior is not looked upon kindly. A time and place for everything."

David gathered himself and scrambled to his feet. *Where did Marcel come from?*

He stepped forward, but Marcel motioned him away with a quick but certain wave of his hand.

"You shouldn't meddle," said LaGrange, who had likewise returned to his feet and faced Marcel with weapon in hand, but there was something in his voice now, the first trace of uncertainty, and as David regarded the surreal turn of events, he detected a flicker of fear in the dark eyes of this wayward immortal. "It's a good way to get yourself killed."

David's heart hammered. Maybe LaGrange was nervous, maybe not, but he'd just threatened Marcel, who stood mere feet away... unarmed, from what David could see. He bent to retrieve the spear, to offer it up to his friend and mentor, but once more Marcel seemed to divine his intentions.

"David," he said. "Stand back."

David hesitated, then did as instructed.

"I'm afraid I don't have the time to argue," Marcel told LaGrange. "Are you certain you wish to pursue this matter?"

David watched as the color slowly drained from LaGrange immortal, and his heart pounded. Something about Marcel... not just what he was saying but how he was saying it. Also odd was the unmistakable trepidation welling up in this strange adversary, who clearly was lethal in his own right, having survived this supernatural contest throughout the centuries, vanquishing who knew how many others in his wake.

LaGrange eyed Marcel, who stood calmly, before lowering his spear and taking a small step backwards. He cast a final glance at David, then returned his attention to the one who'd spoiled his intentions on this evening.

"We'll meet again," he said, tossing the spear and retreating into the shadows.

"You should very much hope," Marcel said, "that we do not."

And with that, LaGrange was gone.

David rushed to Marcel, who turned just in time to receive his embrace.

"It's good to see you," David said. "How did you know where to find me?"

"It's good to see you too, Master Rose," Marcel said. "And I knew because you called me."

David released his grip and stepped back. "I did?"

Marcel smiled. "Indeed. You are at this moment in possession of that item I bestowed upon you on the moors, am I correct?"

David grinned. "You are correct, but I don't think I called you.... I don't know, it all happened so fast."

Marcel put an arm on his shoulder. "As things tend to in this world, especially for one so new to it. It'll get better. As for the mirror, I urge caution. Much as it aided you here tonight, its powers are, as you've seen, unpredictable, and profound."

David started to reply, but just then neighboring church bells sounded, harkening the top of the hour. One chime, two, tolling in the stillness of this summer night... three, four... nine in total, and as the last echoes faded, it occurred to him, there again in a graveyard, that so much of late seemed marked by death and time — never enough of one, far too much of the other.

He looked at Marcel. "Will you come over?"

"Regrettably, I cannot." He nodded in the direction ahead. "Let us walk."

"Where have you been?" David asked as they went.

"I'm afraid I'm only disappointing you tonight," Marcel said. "But I cannot tell you — not yet, anyway. It would endanger you even more so, and that is not something I am willing to do."

"You're not disappointing me," David said. "You saved my life."

Marcel smiled. "Well, I'm not so sure you couldn't have taken him."

David couldn't suppress a grin. "Really?"

"Really." Marcel paused and turned to him. "Not merely because of skill, though you possess far more of it than you know, because there is always someone more skilled, more powerful." He gripped David's shoulders much like his father used to, eyes glinting in the wash of moonlight that ebbed between the overhanging oak limbs and hung about like smoke. "It is not these things which shall, at the end of all things, see you through."

He held David's gaze, conveying more in the small and silent space between them than words ever could. Only when David nodded did Marcel relinquish his grip, and together they resumed walking, each step bringing them closer to the iron archway that marked the entrance of these sacred grounds.

"Will you come back?" David's voice sounded small to himself, childlike.

"Always," Marcel said. "You must train. I will return as soon as possible. I just don't know when that will be. I am...." He trailed off, as if to that place in question. "...looking for something."

"Like Kane?"

"Like Kane."

"What if I need you?"

Marcel stopped, and David did too. Marcel regarded him with the same gentility that more than anything—more than *everything*—defined him. "Then call."

David smiled. "The mirror."

"The mirror, if you must, but again, I urge caution. Even the most expert practitioners have failed to fully harness its powers." He regarded David solemnly. "For now, call upon it only in the direst of circumstances, and in that moment, should it come, concentrate with all your mind and all your heart. Envision what you want, and why you want it." He looked David squarely in the eyes. "Okay?"

"Okay, but then how *do* I reach you? Unless you've got a phone now?"

It was Marcel's turn to grin. "Don't worry yourself about it, Master Rose. If you need me, truly need me, I'll know."

They reached the lamppost that loomed over the archway, and by its pale light walked out of the shadows. Marcel accompanied him until David's house shaped up within the moonlit distance, and there they paused and embraced once more.

Then, almost as quickly as he'd appeared, Marcel turned and walked briskly away into the darkness, and was gone.

CHAPTER 7
Breadcrumbs

WHEN DAVID LOOKED OUT HIS window and saw their father's car still in the driveway, he knew his dad must have called in sick to work again. He used the bathroom, dressed, and went downstairs.

Rachel was curled up on the couch, shrouded in the morning light, watching cartoons and hugging a pillow to her chest.

"Hey," David said. "Did you have breakfast yet?"

She glanced over. "Daddy says he'll make me something."

"I'll do it. What do you want?"

She crinkled her nose in contemplation. "Peanut butter and jelly," she finally proclaimed.

David nodded, and headed to the kitchen.

Only a few slices of bread remained, and he shook the bag out to get to them. When he'd finished making the sandwich, he brushed his hands together and summoned Rachel to the kitchen. He poured himself some cereal, and some juice for both of them, and joined his sister at the table.

They ate silently a while, Rachel chewing her sandwich with a faraway look, but at length she looked up at him and said, "What was it?"

David swallowed his swig of juice and clanked down his glass. "What was what?"

"That *thing*," she said, her voice a touch impatient. "That spinning thing."

David regarded her, then fixed upon his half-full glass, canting it slightly, watching the swirling liquid within. "I don't know. That mirror has lots of powers, but it could be dangerous. Don't touch it again, okay? Don't get near it."

Rachel picked up her sandwich. "You didn't cut the crust off."

"Sorry."

"It's okay, I can do it."

They finished eating, and when David took up her plate, Rachel said, "Lots of stuff happening."

He brushed the crumbs from her plate into the trash, and rattled the plate and his bowl into the sink. "Yeah... lots... but it'll be okay."

"I know," she said, and scooted from her chair and stood before him. "But we have to keep our promise." She looked up at him, index finger raised. "We have to find her."

David stopped as Rachel, as always, had distilled things down to their essence. After all that had transpired, not the least of which was Marcel's revelation that he believed their mother still alive, finding her needed to remain at the forefront of all things. He looked down at his sister. "I know."

Rachel lowered her finger, appearing for the moment satisfied, spun, and headed from the kitchen.

David turned on the faucet and began to rinse the dishes.

"Hey!"

He looked up to see Rachel paused in the entranceway, pointing at the kitchen floor. "What?"

"You spilled." She giggled.

He followed her gaze to the floor, where a trail of breadcrumbs laced in a thin arc across the tiles. "Very funny." He smirked and grabbed a broom.

Rachel giggled again before disappearing into the living room.

David detached the dustpan from the broom handle, bent at the end of the trail, then paused, stared, and straightened back up. A smattering of crumbs must have escaped the bag when he'd shaken it out. They'd scattered in a rather evenly spread arrangement, perhaps six inches separating each one in their trajectory across the floor. David retreated slowly until his back pressed against the counter, and propped the broom against the wall. The muted sounds of Rachel's cartoons came from the living room, and their father, he knew, was sequestered in his darkened study. He wasn't certain why, but he flicked off the light switch and stood peering at the crumbs in the haze of morning light.

Rachel, of course, was right. *Lots happening.* Castles, swords, wizards, magic mirrors — entire worlds sprung up, old and new, but in the end, only one thing mattered. If he believed their mother to still be alive — and he would allow himself to believe no less — then it only followed that clues had been left behind, perhaps even by her own hand, if only he knew where — and how — to look. A raft of clouds eased into view, and the kitchen fell momentarily into shadow. David squinted through the darkness at the trail of crumbs, which snaked across the floor in their strange ellipse, suggesting a pathway he knew not, but suggesting it, nevertheless. He stared a moment longer, absorbing that which, for the moment, defied resolution, then grabbed the broom and flicked the lights back on.

***

HE MARVELED AT THE WONDER OF

it all, the notion that he had all these past lives — *was* all these past lives — but now that he was awakened, he had to confront the reality of the thing, and reality was not always wondrous. Reality could kill. He knew that his first life, of course, his incipient soul, was in so many ways key to the whole thing, but while Lancelot might be the beginning, he was far from the end. He needed to know more of them, those lives — more of *him*. He needed to get at least a glimpse at them, that he might understand them, and come to know and even channel their greatest virtues. But how?

He wished Marcel could have stayed. Marcel would know, could teach David how to journey back those lifetimes to find himself, and to return stronger. Marcel could show him how to step back and properly look at things, like one of those 3D pictures you stared at, trying desperately to make sense of it before realizing you indeed were looking too closely, and had to step back in order to make things out.

He was a composite, after all, the sum of his parts. He just needed to discover what those parts were — those other bits of the picture, those pieces of the puzzle. It was every bit the mystery as the clues he was seeking about this world, about his mom — every bit as elusive as the breadcrumbs, if you looked at them too closely, if you only examined them one at a time. You had to step back, had to know where to look, and for now, with no Marcel there to guide him and his father slipping deeper by the day, he was on his own. Again.

He had the mirror, and that was something, as good a place to start as any. Clearly it had powers, held secrets, and while the prudent thing might be to wait for Marcel, David's blood roiled with incontestable urgency. He didn't think he could look his sister in the eyes next time and tell her he'd done nothing. No. He might have to step back to find the right path, but once he did, he must go forward. If other hims wished to follow, so be it, but either way, he was going.

Right now, he was going to where it all began — the woods and creek, where he'd been chased by the Gentry brothers and first encountered Malea. Maybe it was conducive to magic there, maybe not, but he couldn't very well do all this out in the open. He could go to the graveyard, but after what had happened that night a few weeks ago, it was probably wise to steer clear. The dead had a way of finding him, anyway.

On this pleasant Saturday morning, only a handful of people milled about. A woman walked her dog, and a man walked alongside his young son, who pedaled his bicycle excitedly, if unsteadily, upon the sidewalk that ran parallel to the woods.

When all had shrunk from view, David cut across the field to the creek. He walked briskly alongside it, until a few minutes later he'd arrived at the drainage tunnel. There hadn't been much rain of late, and he skipped across the creek without incident. It grew immediately darker under the canopy of foliage at the tree line. He thought briefly about wading to the tunnel, but knew in his heart she wouldn't be in there. *Malea*. She didn't sit waiting in a drainage tunnel. With the waterways of the world her chariots, she'd been here that day for a specific reason. Besides, he didn't feel her, as odd a consideration as that might be. He'd come to feel things, to sense them — people, danger — the increasing signs of this dark world. He'd felt it with LaGrange.

After a glance across the creek and field to ensure no one else might see him, he turned and angled slowly into the woods, the afternoon shading darker with each step. When he'd entered far enough, he sat down beneath a massive oak and withdrew the mirror from his pocket. It was quiet, save for the occasional twittering of birds and rustling of small life amongst the leaf litter. He'd no idea how this was supposed to work, and it occurred to him the safer course of action would be to wait for Marcel, but the pang of hemorrhaging time gnawed relentlessly at him. He thought about Chester, the most logical and level-headed of their bunch. How would he approach this? David chuckled. There was little chance their friend would, under any circumstance, attempt to summon past lives through a mirror. But, he mused, what if he did? What was the wisest way to go about it? He breathed in, the earthy scent soothing, and exhaled deeply. He should begin with what he knew of the mysterious object, however little that might be.

Marcel had given it to him, and that seemed as important a detail as any. David recalled the face when he'd peeked at the mirror for the first time, and all that had happened that night in the graveyard with Rachel and his friends, and later with LaGrange. And of course, he remembered the close call with Rachel that night in his room. Clearly, the mirror possessed powers, none of which he was yet convinced were anything but dark and dangerous. His thoughts drifted to Amanda, as they increasingly did of late. He couldn't help it. He wished she were here beside him, but hadn't wanted to endanger her. Now, in the still of the hushed woods, her voice echoed in his memory.

'Ancient Buddhist priests,' she'd shared that day at the library, 'used magic mirrors to reveal to disciples that *form in which they might be reborn. The Daoists believed spirits were made visible by Magic Mirrors. The reflection in the mirror is thought to be the image of one's soul.'*

A small rustling sounded nearby, and he glanced to observe a shying squirrel at the tree opposite him. They regarded one another momentarily before the rodent darted off.

Amanda's words slowly returned. *'As the possessor gazes into the mirror, the changing images reflect the various images of the individual's past lives.'*

Past lives. The notion still bewildered him. Was there ever getting used to such a thing? *Past lives... and not just one.* He knew the one, and that was enough for a lifetime, but there were more.

He'd begun to run the math in his mind: Lancelot had lived around fifteen centuries ago, and if he'd been reborn even just once a century since, that meant.... He'd always stop himself, so unnerving was the entire consideration. He twirled the mirror slowly in his hand and squinted against the spliced sunlight filtering through the gaps in the forest canopy. He wondered how old these trees were. Centuries? Had he seen them before? He glanced back down at the mirror. It wasn't how often he'd *lived* that unnerved him, but how often he'd *died*. Immortality glittered through endless volumes of literature, and the imagination of a world, but this was the underbelly of the thing, the part that didn't shine. How many times had he lived and died, and most important of all, could any of it keep him alive long enough this go-around, to fulfill the task to which he was forsworn?

He fell.

He found it unsettling on any number of levels, not the least of which was the fact he was already seated, propped there against the sturdy trunk of the towering oak. Yet fall he did, through time and space and the fortress of all he'd ever known—the world that was. That world faded fast, the forest growing pitch, falling away before his rapt and staring eyes.

This, he knew, was impossible. *'When you have eliminated the impossible,'* said Holmes, *'whatever remains, however improbable, must be the truth...'* from *The Sign of the Four*, his favorite Holmes novel. Now, as earth and sky and even the oaks crumbled away before him, another four flashed across the failing landscape of his consciousness. Horses. He was sure they were horses, there a moment, then gone, but burned indelibly into his mind. He'd seen a red horse, and a white one, another one black, and one pale. Dark figures sat atop each— there and then gone.

Something haunted him about the image, pulled at him like the incontestable draw of this strange gravity. The unnerving sense that rather than falling away, they had risen up, though how and from where he could not know. Still, as all went black and he plummeted through this cold and starless sky, something dreadful knotted in the pit of soul, assuring him that, in time, he would.

Time... the more he realized he'd had, the less he seemed to have left.

He breathed in deeply, and the world seemed to pause with him, and he opened the mirror.

CHAPTER 8
No Time for Memories

HIS FIRST THOUGHT WAS, *RACHEL will be worried*, and on the heels of this: *who is Rachel?*

He'd sauntered to the western edge of his property, and propped a boot upon the fence, squinting against the sunset, when this strangest of considerations drifted in. He shook his head, his dark mane sweeping across his face. It was summer, hot, the grasses and fields wilting, but all around him the violet clusters sprung up, as always — ever since he could remember.

But this was no time for memories.

Watkins was coming for him, and he'd best be ready. It was going to be dicey, either way. Dispatching a mortal, unless absolutely necessary, was frowned upon; being killed by one was hardly a more appealing option. Incapacitating him seemed the best of precious few alternatives, but even this was fraught with difficulty: theirs was to be a dual to the death, and where death had been promised, anything less would not be tolerated by the people. How little they knew — the townsfolk — about death, life, and so much else, but he couldn't begrudge them this. This was their only go-around.

The day's last light flattened out beneath a watercolor sky, a line of fire burning the horizon into wedges of purple and pink. He squinted more intently, detecting movement against the glare, and watched as small, marionette figures shaped darkly from the twilight, distant silhouettes moving slowly, almost imperceptibly, but coming.

His hand moved instinctively to his side, despite the space between them, and his heart kicked into a gallop that seemed to outpace the cadence of his adversary. It belied the confidence of one who'd lived as long as he, but he hoped he'd never lose it entirely, that abiding bite of agitation, for then complacency would follow, and in their world, where complacency traveled, death inevitably rode side-saddle.

Rachel.

There it was again.

Must get back.

He shook his head again and blinked furiously. Next time he saw Marcel, perhaps he could glean some answers about these voices in his head. *Yes, Marcel... he can help. Maybe he can get me out of here.*

Another shake of his head and beads of sweat flew from his furrowed brow. The approaching figures resolved into clarity, as if emboldened into greater stature, both man and beast, with each step forward. *Let them come.* He'd faced it all, and learned through lifetimes that it was not the size or weaponry of the combatant, but the depth of his enmity, and of the latter, there was never the slightest shortage, the world over.

Today it was Watkins, and whatever slight was perceived between them — a woman, an insult, a dispute, honor. Yet where was the honor in killing? Was the scourge of this antipathy sated by further hostilities, or fed by them? Did not the answer lie in something different?

His fingers twitched at his side. The world continued to get it wrong, and he no better. He could make out Watkins' face now, and that of his accomplices, Rennard and Filmore. Watkins' eyes narrowed and glinted above the methodical clopping of hooves, the small plumes rising in their wake.

He pushed back from the fence, walked to the gate of his property, unlatched and swung it open, welcoming those who would see him dead.

His visitors nodded at this gesture as they guided their horses forward. Filmore even touched the brim of his hat.

"You sure yous don't want Ellington here to witness?" Watkins called over his shoulder.

He responded, "We answer to a greater judge," and swung the gate back closed.

Watkins steered his steed about. "And you're about to meet him."

The visitors dismounted and hitched their horses to the trough. Rennard and Filmore ambled a short distance off in opposite directions, leaving a lane between them. Watkins paced off toward the north, some five meters, before pirouetting back around, his fingers dancing on his right holster.

Wait. This is crazy. I've never shot a gun.

He clenched his eyes, trying to will away this most untimely of intrusions. Of course, he'd shot a gun—too many times—but these foreign thoughts invaded. They came as his own thoughts, yet felt as if words from another.

He inhaled deeply, then opened his eyes and fixed them upon Watkins, who stood glaring in the day's failing light.

"Your time is up, Duncan!" Watkins spat.

It all happened in a blink—yet he saw it all in excruciating detail: Watkins pulling on him and his pistol glinting, his own weapon sliding free of its holster and slicing upward through the dusk. All fell quiet, no dark and no light, only the enveloping gray of gun smoke. He closed his eyes, savoring this briefest of reprieves. The moment was coming. One way or the other, it always came.

Duncan.

The gunfighter had called him Duncan. Now he watched as Watkins' comrades rushed to the side of their stricken friend, who lie writhing in the dust against the blue-tinged slate of falling night.

He'd wounded his adversary, but not fatally.

Once satisfied the men didn't aim to pull on him, he holstered his weapon, turned about, and headed home.

Home.

Duncan's, maybe, but not *his.* His waited somewhere back through the hazy labyrinth of time, a half mile or so beyond the woods where he'd left himself, and where he could only hope and presume he still remained, propped against the thick trunk of the oak.

How the hell am I supposed to get back?

The mirror had conducted him here, that much was certain. His hands grasped at his sides, but instead of pockets, they found, of course, holsters. He was brand new at this straddling of lives and lifetimes, and so couldn't be entirely certain, but he doubted very much that he or any gunslinger of the time had earned a fearsome reputation based upon their skills with a pocket mirror.

Nonetheless, he couldn't very well shoot his way back home, and so he needed to find it.

He pushed open the door of Duncan's cabin, and cast his gaze about the darkened quarters. When he stepped forward, the floor creaked, and a hearty bark issued forth from the obscurity, followed by the rapid patter of a quadruped approach. The hound shaped up out of the darkness and nuzzled his outstretched hand.

"Hey, Charlie," he said.

He crossed the room in Duncan's body toward an aft window, where framed in a pale slip of moonlight stood a wood table, bare save for a kerosene lamp and a scattering of matchsticks. Charlie's ears twitched at the pop of the match, and he circled anxiously. David watched himself head to a cupboard, open it, and retrieve a few biscuits from a jar. He turned, and Charlie sat, tail whooshing across the floor, as his master scattered the biscuits before him.

He found a canteen full of water, took a few deep gulps, then wiped his mouth, unhitched his gun belt and placed it on the table. He set about looking for the mirror, but there weren't many places to look in this threadbare dwelling, and his search went unrequited. He went to the door and opened it and looked out into the night. Charlie sidled past him and sauntered into the yard, sniffing and snorting at the ground until he settled upon a copse of bushes upon which to conduct his business.

Perhaps he didn't need the mirror. Perhaps if he slept, he would awaken back under the oak. Maybe it was as simple as that. He exhaled deeply, and shook his head at his own folly. Nothing was that simple in this world.

The dog had disappeared somewhere into the evening, not far though — David could hear him sniffing and snuffling somewhere among the bushes.

"Charlie!" He whistled sharply, and a moment later, the hound came bounding out of the shadows and skittered into the cabin.

Any uncertainty regarding the era into which he'd been catapulted had evaporated in his futile search for the mirror—there was no indoor plumbing. His subsequent use of the outhouse behind the cabin struck him as possibly the most unnerving development of this whole ordeal, but as he settled into Duncan's bed in the lone adjoining room, he grudgingly ceded there had been worse things—darkness and death and centuries-old sinister schemes.

Yeah, all that.

Charlie approached the bed, regarded the figure atop it, and sniffed the air. He nuzzled David's hand—Duncan's hand—and only when that hand patted him several times upon the head did he slink over to a far corner of the room, circle twice, and ease to the ground with a sigh.

David closed his eyes, those eyes which were not his own, yet were, in this bed and home and place and time at once alien and familiar. A current of unconsciousness rolled in, despite his racing thoughts, and he felt himself quickly succumbing, fading beneath the rising tide. It occurred to him that he ought to resist, to swim for it, but he was so very tired, and as the surface grew more and more distant, a peaceful resignation overcame him.

Just before his eyes sealed shut, he had the strangest vision—a hand outstretched, from that fading world, reaching.

CHAPTER 9
A Journey across Lifetimes

"WE'VE GOT TO STOP MEETING THIS way."

David couldn't see himself, but he was pretty sure he smiled. *Robert. Again.* He opened his eyes, no easy task, and squinted up at his best friend.

"What day is it?" he asked.

Robert frowned. "Um, Thursday. What day did you think it was?"

David groaned and eased to his feet. "I really don't know. Seems like I was gone for days."

"Gone? You mean, here?" Robert nodded at the mirror in David's hand. "Or does it have something to do with that?"

David followed Robert's gaze down to the object in question, surprised at first to spot it there, and nodded.

"I didn't think you were supposed to mess with that thing," Robert said. "All sorts of crazy stuff I saw in there."

David lifted the mirror to his eyes, apprehensively, but saw only himself and the oak at his back. He exhaled and eased the mirror shut. "What did you see?"

"You," Robert said. "You, but not you. Here, but not here. You wouldn't wake up at first — either of you — and, well, so I reached in to get you."

David nodded slowly. "Thanks."

They stood silently a while, both recalling, David suspected, that fateful day not far from this very spot, when Robert had pulled him from the roaring creek. So much had happened since then, but how much further had he gotten in his quest for the truth? Each day in this strange, new world seemed to bring far more questions than answers.

He was unsure how much time had passed when his best friend at last nudged him from his ruminations.

"Let's go home," Robert said.

***

"THANKS FOR REMEMBERING."

David shrugged. "Of course, man."

Chester forced a smile. "You were the only one."

"Come on," David said. "The day is young."

Indeed, it was. David had texted Chester early that morning to wish him a happy birthday and see if he wanted to hang out a bit. Chester had gratefully accepted, and now they sat at Evergreen Tea House, Chester's favorite hangout—except for the library—sipping their beverages as the sun breached the horizon in brushstrokes of pink and blue. Chester blew across the rim of his tea, the steam undulating back like ripples in a lake.

"One more year," David said, cautiously bringing his latte to his lips.

Chester raised an eyebrow.

"Until you'll be driving. You'll be the first."

Chester inhaled deeply and sipped his tea. "Will I?"

David frowned. "Come on, man, I've seen plenty of people who.... Plenty of people. They use hand controls and stuff. Right?"

Chester shrugged. "Sure, some do."

They sat quietly a while. Four youth about their age—two guys and two girls—sat down at an adjacent table. David couldn't help but notice a slight smirk on the face of one of the guys.

"Too early for cake?" David asked. "Come on, they have all sorts of stuff here. Let me get you something."

Chester smiled, but dismissed the notion with a wave of his hand. "No thank you." He took a sip, gazed out a moment at the awakening day, and turned back to meet the gaze of his friend. "But I might have something for you."

"What do you mean?"

Chester leaned forward.

David noticed the same guy at the adjacent table looking at Chester, then snickering to his friends. Something in him began to roil, but he set it aside and focused on the topic at hand.

"You remember our conversation a few months back, at my house, about the handwriting?"

David paused mid-sip. "Um, yeah, it kinda blew the whole case open, you know?"

Chester permitted himself a grin. "Well, having said that, I fear that in so doing, I created for you more questions than answers."

David eyed his friend and said, "Before that day, I *had no* answers. If it created more questions, so be it, but I would have been lost without you."

Chester smiled and nodded. "I appreciate that, but I think it's time to consider some of the possible answers, no?"

David leaned forward, grasping his mug with both hands. He felt his heart rev up, as it did whenever he stood at the precipice of a possible breakthrough. So often, it was Chester who had shown him the way.

"What did we learn?" Chester inquired.

David took a sip, stretched his arms out over his head, and sat back. "Let me think: that I'm immortal; that immortality exists, that centuries-old assholes kidnapped my mom and orchestrated an impossibly complex cover-up, all part of some cosmic destiny, and that someone I thought was a friend tried to kill me because he was pissed off at me from like a thousand years ago?" David put an index finger to his chin. "And... oh yeah, that some water nymph from another world would fight Merlin — *Merlin* — in a cave, as part of all that." He smiled at Chester. "What did I miss?"

Chester sipped, smiled, and set down his mug. "Well, that's the thing, isn't it? What *did* you miss? What did *we* miss?"

David felt stares upon them from the next table, but leaned forward and addressed his friend. "I don't know, probably a lot. Sometimes I don't even know even know where to begin. Sometimes I feel that I'm so very close — *presque vu*, as Marcel told me — at the brink of an epiphany."

Chester grinned. "I seemed to be upon the verge of comprehension — "

David knew from the inflection of Chester's voice that he was quoting something.

" — without the power to comprehend as men, at times, find themselves upon the brink of remembrance, without being able, in the end, to remember."

Chester sipped his tea. If he was aware of the carrying-on at the next table, he didn't show it.

"Holmes?" David guessed. "Dupin?"

Chester's eyes glinted. "The latter. *Murders in the Rue Morgue.*"

"I should have guessed."

Chester waved this off, but now his eyes narrowed. "What's important is that Marcel may well have been right." Chester's gaze traveled momentarily outside, then returned. "He was right about a lot—right about things none of us would have conceived possible."

David nodded. "And now what? He's gone, for now, and I feel lost."

Chester tapped his index finger upon his mug. "An understandable sentiment, to say the least—new worlds, new realities, like a thousand towering trees sprung up before you without warning, and no matter how much you crane your neck, it is, from that vantage, impossible to see everything."

David brought his beverage to his lips, but it had gone cold. He set it back down and said, "Yeah, so now what?" His coffee lolled placidly in the mug.

Chester sat back in his chair, glanced again outside. "Now you step back. Now *we* step back, that we might see the forest for the trees."

David looked up from his mug... waited.

"Marcel left," Chester continued, "but he did not leave you empty-handed."

"The mirror," David said quietly.

"The mirror, yes, but the mirror is a tool, however mysterious and compelling, and a tool is only as important as its purpose."

"My past lives," David said, quieter still. "So I can see who I was, who I am, and learn how to use those powers." He stared into his mug.

"A conduit," Chester said. "A link between lives, between worlds."

David raised his gaze back to his friend and nodded.

"One possessing of great power," continued Chester, "and great peril, as you have learned."

"That is true."

Chester's drink had gone cold too, and he set it aside. "So that's a good start," he said. "We're beginning to see more of the forest, and farther up along the trees. Let's press on, then."

More snickering came from the near table, and David shot them a glance.

"Pay them no mind," said Chester. "So then... we have determined the tool's purpose, to a degree."

David sighed. He thought of Rachel, and of promises made. "To a degree? This just can't be easy, can it?"

Chester sighed. "I fear not, but that doesn't mean it's impossible. You've illuminated some of the purposes of the mirror."

David raised an eyebrow. "Some? Transporting me to and from past lives? Channeling ghosts? It's like something out of a sci-fi movie. That's only *part* of it?"

"Indeed, it is."

"Can you just cut to the QED," David implored his friend. "Please?"

"Ah, where's the fun in that?" Chester quipped, but now his voice lowered. "But truly, I wish I could make that so. Alas, a journey across lifetimes does not appear poised to be a short one. All the more critical we do not misstep along the way."

"I know."

"You have captured quite aptly what the mirror *does*," Chester noted. "What it enables you to do."

"And?"

"And so, it is incumbent upon us to understand why you are to do it."

David frowned. "Well, like I said, I think it's to connect with my past lives, learn about them and channel the powers."

Chester continued like an encouraging teacher. "Yes, but even still, why do those things? Toward what end?"

David looked at his friend, and remembered a promise. "To find my mom."

"Yes, absolutely, and Marcel wants to help you do that, no doubt. But why the mirror, specifically?"

David regarded his friend. He began to reply, but stopped.

"Take your time," said Chester. "It's a lot."

David managed a grin. No one pulled off an understatement like Chester McVee.

"To be ready," David said. "For what, I really don't know. Malea spoke of a Great Assembling, whatever that is."

"Right, and while so much remains to be learned, might we reasonably conclude what happened with Donovan had a lot to do with it? So too with this LaGrange fellow?"

"I guess so." David rubbed his neck. "They both seemed to want me dead."

"Right," Chester replied evenly. "I can only imagine how unnerving a notion that is, and I do not wish to distress you further, but it is my hope that understanding these matters as fully and quickly as possible can only serve to thwart any further such efforts, and enemies."

"I know," David said. "Thank you." He looked down a moment, then back up. "I still can't help but feel badly for Donovan, even though he tried to kill me."

"*Facilis descensus* Averno," Chester said.

"More Dupin?"

"Indeed, though he slightly misspoke it in the narrative, from *The Purloined Letter*. The descent to Avernus, or the Underworld, is easy. Not meaning to forecast Donavan's eternal destination, but merely offering a modicum of empathy. Life is full of temptations, and it is all too easy, for any of us, to fall."

David glanced out the window. "Yeah."

"And that brings to bear another consideration," Chester said. "For all these powers, these talents and abilities and perhaps knowledge and experience of lifetimes past that you apparently now possess, have you considered the possibility of their equally potent counterparts?"

David couldn't suppress another grin. "I know that wasn't Latin, but it may as well have been."

Chester chuckled. "I mean to say, as with anyone, whether the most remarkable or commonplace person in history, no matter how extraordinary one's attributes, he or she, like anyone, possesses no shortage of flaws and vulnerabilities. If you have now, somehow, become linked to any number of past personas, you bear simultaneously the privilege of their best features and abilities, as well as the burden of their worst."

David nodded slowly.

"So then, Marcel, while exhorting caution, nevertheless bestowed the mirror, that you might practice and prepare, not only in the manner of mastering powers and skills, but perhaps, too, becoming aware of and learning to ward off those less estimable traits."

They fell silent a spell, before David replied. "Hey, did you think you'd ever be saying these things?"

Chester regarded him silently.

"Advising me about past lives... magic mirrors... all that."

Chester grinned sheepishly. "Not in the slightest. I would have, in fact, likely been the first to denounce such folly."

"And now?"

"Now... everything has changed."

When a short while later they exited the establishment, the sun near full apex, David spotted them immediately, the kids from the adjacent table... waiting.

"Come on," Chester said. "Ignore them. I'm used to it."

David bit his lip, then nodded and turned to head the other direction with his friend.

"That's right, gimp. Better head the other way!"

Chester continued as if he hadn't heard.

David paused a moment, then turned around.

"Yeah, come on, man, what you gonna do about it?" teased the one who'd been glaring and snickering inside.

David headed toward him.

"David!"

"Don't worry," David called back to Chester. "I've got this."

The kid straightened up from the car against which he'd been leaning, and motioned David onward. "We'll see about that," he said.

David strode forward, unsure still how to summon the requisite powers, much less which ones, yet confident they would come—as they had way back when with Gillespie, in the hypnosis session with Cerratus, and under the eclipse with Donovan, AKA Gawain. He retained eye contact, reasonably sure the rest of the entourage would stand aside. If they didn't... well, they'd get what was coming too. A few feet away now, he balled his fists and waited for the surge of power and adrenaline.

And waited.

When it didn't come, he swung anyway, and missed. His adversary connected, hard enough and square enough that David felt his lip split as he flew backwards and fell to the pavement. He managed to brace himself and keep his head from impacting the concrete, and then the kid was upon him, snarling down like Donovan had at Tintagel. He parried the kid's ensuing blows, deflecting them just enough to prevent additional direct hits, but he was tiring quickly. He could hear people shouting, including Chester and the kid's friends, and before long, a handful of adults came running and separated the two combatants.

It all became a blur: a sea of faces, a medley of discordant voices, a dread of the disappointment this latest trouble would provoke in his dad. One consideration, however, gnawed at him above all else.

They didn't come.

CHAPTER 10
Worlds Away

THE FIRST FEW MONTHS AFTER THEIR
mother's disappearance, their father had set the table
each night at her spot for dinner. This at first seemed a
contradiction, given how he'd said they must move on,
but David knew deep inside he missed her terribly. And
so, when Rachel asked that evening if they should put a
plate out for her Mama, David very much hoped she
would not be disappointed.

They sat in the unlit dining room, the last light of
day bisecting the room and providing ample
illumination. Their father sat silently at the far end of the
table, the shadowed end, his children flanking him to
either side.

"Daddy, can I?"

"I don't know, baby," their father replied quietly.
His gaze traveled between his children. "I don't want
you to—"

"—get my hopes up," his daughter finished. "I
know."

David suppressed a grin.

"Well, then," said their father, "you understand my
concern."

David recognized the flickering in his sister's eyes,
and spoke up before she could retort. "She does. We
both do, but it's just a way to remember her, pay
respect." He lowered his voice. "It helps her cope."

"It's not that!" Rachel poked a fork in his direction, and he held his up hand. She eyed him uncertainly, then their father, before easing back in her chair.

"See," said their father. "It only gets her worked up. And you—" He motioned at David's still swollen lip. "—getting in fights again."

"It had nothing to do with that," David said.

They ate silently. Though mere feet apart, their father appeared to David worlds away. Their mother had always sat opposite him, at the other end of the oval table, their children between them. David's eyes traced from his father to his sister, to their mother's empty place—so little space between them, yet so much. His hope had stirred back at Tintagel, when his father had charged in when Donovan—Gawain—attacked him, when he'd stood up to Kane, but he hadn't been able to bring himself to let him fully in, to open the door to the entirety of this new world. David could only imagine how impossible it would seem to an already jaded adult, and so, he hadn't told his father about Merlin, or Malea, or the full truth of any of this. Not surprisingly, as the days and weeks passed, and with all that had transpired, their father retreated further still.

"Okay."

David looked up.

"Okay," their father said again. "You can set out her spot."

A smile flashed across Rachel's face, and she scrambled down from her chair.

"But don't go getting ideas," their father said, raising a finger. "You know I worry."

"I know," said David, pushing back from his chair to go help Rachel. "We won't."

Ideas had a way of forcing their way in, though, and even some things Rachel was coming to understand, their father could not — *would* not.

"We can't tell him yet," David told her quietly, handing her a plate from the cupboard. "He's not ready." He crouched before her. "Okay?"

"Okay," she said.

They stepped quietly back into the dining room, pausing momentarily in the shrinking splice of daylight. Their father looked up from the end of the table, shrouded in the advancing gloom. Though David knew it was impossible, his father appeared even farther away than before.

Rachel stepped around the unoccupied chair, set down a plate, and said, "For you, Mama."

***

A STORM CAME, POWERFUL ENOUGH

to knock out the power, and this, along with the darkened skies, rendered the house near pitch black, even though it was morning. David looked toward his door and listened for the pattering. It didn't take long, and he sat up in his bed as Rachel's wide-eyed countenance materialized in the hazy opening in the doorway.

"Come on," he said.

"My light is broke," she said, pushing his door open and padding over to his bed.

He smiled. "Power's out from the storm. They're all out. It's okay. It'll come back on eventually."

Rachel scrambled up onto his bed, and he slid over so she could nestle beside him. "When?"

"I don't know," he said. "Usually doesn't take too long, but it always come back on. We just have to wait."

Her face crinkled in contemplation. "Is Daddy at work?"

"Yep."

She suddenly grabbed his arm. "What if the lights are broke where he is too? What if he can't see?"

David laughed. "He's fine. It may not even be out there, and if it is, they'll do the same thing as here—they'll just wait. Some buildings have backup systems anyway, so it never gets completely dark."

Rachel eased back down onto the pillow and said, "We need that."

The wind picked up, whistling through the trees and over houses, and David thought about the tree house he and Donovan had built, and wondered if it would have withstood such gales. The sky rumbled with increasing volume and frequency, making Rachel start, so David decided to make a game of it. They each took to guessing the number of seconds between flashes of lightning and the ensuing repercussion. The lightning danced upon the wall like a campfire bowing in the wind.

The lull between flash and bang gradually increased, and when lightning became sporadic and the thunder a distant murmur, David rose and pulled back the curtains. A dull, gray light permeated the room. Rachel's face dropped when he unsuccessfully tried the light, but he smiled and summoned her from the bed.

"It'll be on soon," he assured her. "And see... daylight now. Go get dressed. I'll make some breakfast." He stepped over to his window as Rachel grudgingly eased from the bed. "Let's be quick. Soon as the lighting is over, we'll go outside. There's something I want you to see."

CHAPTER 11
The Rainbow Prophecy

WHEN THEY STEPPED FROM THEIR house and Rachel spied the rainbow glittering against the backdrop of berry sky, she beamed and asked if he would take her to it. They walked past Deer Creek Elementary, her hand in his, and past the cemetery, where not long ago at all, the dead had awakened beneath them.

"Hey!"

David hadn't realized he'd sped up, tugging his sister along. "Sorry," he said, glancing briefly toward the tombstones.

They cut through a few subdivisions, doing their best to keep their gleaming destination in view. Rachel maintained an impressive monologue of typical seven-year-old things, naming everything they passed or saw, and David was glad for this, glad that she could still, at least in moments, be allowed to just be a kid. When they cornered into the next subdivision, David stopped. He'd pondered what he might tell Rachel once she noticed they weren't getting closer to the rainbow, or maybe that it had disappeared.

Except it hadn't... and, they were.

It was hardly lost upon him that what they now beheld was a practical impossibility. *'You can't reach the end of a rainbow,'* he could hear Chester admonishing, *'because it isn't there. It will always remain the same distance away. Raindrops act as prisms, splitting light into bands of color — an optical illusion.'*

"Cool!" Rachel gawked at the monolith of color before them.

David might have elected a different word. It was spellbinding, doubtless — a glimmering crescent of impossibly vivid hues — but this quality — *any* quality — was unsettling in something which *should not be.* Yet there it was — physical, tangible, solid, wholly incongruous, yet not. This was the most unsettling thing of all: that his world had in the last year become so blurred with paradox, it rendered yet one more bombshell merely part of his new normal. His world — the one here and now — was no longer his *only* world.

"Come *on.*" Rachel tugged hard, transfixed by what to her must have seemed a fairytale come true.

Less certain, David gently pulled her back.

"David! Hey, David!" He turned and spotted a girl in jeans and a black tank top emerging from the stoop of a nearby home. "Hey, Rachel!"

Audrey DaMone. David hadn't known where she lived, but was rather glad for the interruption. He smiled as she hustled over.

"What are you guys doing out here?" Audrey bent over to hug Rachel, who pointed skyward.

"Ah," Audrey acknowledged. "The rainbow."

David turned to her. "So, you see it?"

Audrey shrugged. "Well, barely. It's far away, and kinda fading, but yeah, I see it."

David furrowed his brow.

"It's right *there,*" Rachel said.

Audrey eyed her, and then David. "Okay," she said, patting Rachel's back. She turned to David, and he nodded slowly.

"Sometimes," Audrey said after a moment, "we see what we want to."

David regarded the towering phenomenon. "Not so sure I want to be seeing this," he said.

"Sometimes," Audrey amended, "we see what we need to see."

"Not so sure of that either."

They stared ahead, spellbound — two by what they saw, one by what she didn't.

"So, what now?" Audrey finally asked.

David inhaled deeply, let it out. "Walk with us?"

Audrey nodded slowly and turned to him. "You'll have to tell me what you see."

David nodded and squeezed Rachel's hand. "Don't let go," he told her.

They set off slowly, like Dorothy's first uneasy steps upon the yellow brick road. Audrey made sure not to pace ahead of them. She walked haltingly, one hand slightly extended, as though blindfolded. A man and his little dog passed them the opposite way, and an occasional vehicle trundled by. David glanced at each passerby as if to gauge the reaction to the otherworldly sight they surely couldn't have missed, but which, he knew, they had. A few minutes later, he lightly pressed Rachel's hand, and they slowed. He glanced at Audrey, who had stopped just behind them.

"We're close."

Audrey managed a faint smile and said, "Okay, careful now."

"Hey," David said, after a quick glance at his sister. "It's a rainbow. They're good things, right?"

Audrey remained silent.

"You all right?" David asked her.

She nodded, but wore a faraway look. "Are you assuming I'll know about rainbow mythology?"

David craned his neck at the incandescent spectacle. "I don't assume anything anymore."

"Good," said Audrey, "because a lot of people do. I'm *that* girl. The goth girl. The pierced girl. The tatted girl. The girl in black. The girl who knows about myths and legends and magic."

"You do know about that," David said softly. "Just like Chester knows about so much. It's not a bad thing. It's cool, but it doesn't define you."

Audrey's eyes glistened. "It does for some." She brushed her forearm across her face, and kicked softly at a few pebbles. "Do you ever wonder why Chester knows so much? Why he reads so much, studies, immerses himself in things?"

"I think I know."

Audrey nodded sadly. "Maybe we're drawn to some things because of being rejected by others."

David regarded her, and started to say something, then stopped, empty. What powers, what wisdom, what words, could he offer for a hurting heart? He looked down and saw that Rachel had withdrawn her hand and taken Audrey's.

Audrey smiled as Rachel led her forward, David pacing alongside. A minute on, Audrey nudged his shoulder. "Warriors," she said.

"What?"

"Warriors of the Rainbow Prophecy... the Cree Indian nation.... There are other versions, other tribes."

David held them up. "So... you *do* know about this."

She grinned sheepishly. "I *happen* to know a little about it."

David smiled. "Well?"

Audrey glanced down at Rachel, then turned back to David. "The Cree believed the time would come, if the polluting and deforestation and exploitation of the earth continued, that fish would die in the streams, birds fall from the sky, trees crumble, and mankind would cease to exist."

David eyed her. "What's that got to do with rainbows?"

"That was like a century ago," Audrey said. "Things have gotten far worse since then, worse than anyone could have imagined — the pollution, climate change, the utter ravaging of the natural world."

David frowned. "Yeah... but rainbows?"

Rachel looked up at Audrey.

"The Rainbow Prophecy," Audrey said, "refers to the keepers of these legends, of the rituals. They believe these things will be needed when time comes to bring the world back to health." She stared ahead at that pageant she could not behold. "They believe these legendary beings will return on a dawn of awakening, and all people will unite in justice, peace, and harmony — people of all nations, all colors, all creeds. The Rainbow Prophecy."

David let it sink in as his gaze traveled up the towering display. "But this is an actual rainbow." He glanced back at her. "You know... happy things, color and light, a pot of gold."

Audrey breathed deeply. "It's why I said be careful." She softened her voice. "I just know the legends. I don't know what is really true. Is it what we'll find at the end of the rainbow, or what will, perhaps, find us?"

"I've been asking myself that for a while now."

They stood, staring and silent.

"So," Audrey finally said, "what do you want to do?"

David shrugged. "Want has nothing to do with it. Anything that could be a clue, anything that could move us closer to...." He glanced down at his sister, then back up.

"I understand," Audrey replied. "Just be careful."

They moved slowly onward. The subdivision terminated in a vast, plowed field, which David recognized as the far end of Moreland Farms. The near end of the rainbow arched from the soil, glimmering like a hologram at the point of intersection and radiating a spectrum of color beyond anything his mind could register. He glanced down at Rachel, who'd maintained her grip with Audrey, but now sought out her brother's hand with her free one.

"It's so pretty," Rachel said.

They stood, transfixed, as an eerie still fell over the expanse. A flock of crows rose suddenly from nearby grasses and soared, in full throat, toward the cover of the nearby woods.

Audrey touched David's shoulder. "How close?"

"Thirty feet," he said. "Give or take."

She frowned. "Too close." She urged Rachel slowly backwards. "I feel it."

David relinquished his sister's hand. "Okay," he told Audrey. "Take her back a little."

"I want to see it!" Rachel cried.

"Rachel, go!" David felt immediately guilty, but he'd sensed something too. The rainbow pulsed with a preternatural glow, so arresting in its coloration as to seem cartoonish, fairytale, unearthly. David fought against the tranquilizing pull. Something, or someone, was coming. Again. He glanced back at Audrey and Rachel. They had moved back farther. *Good.*

The rainbow hummed louder now, and its glow blossomed to blinding proportions. David shielded his eyes but stood his ground. The earth felt tremulous beneath him, but still he stood, and when the glare and row at last subsided, he lowered his hand and saw the rainbow was dissipating, and through the resultant gloom now materialized a figure of baffling aspect.

A Native American man sat atop a pale horse, approaching slowly out of the fading spectacle, as if from a sunset centuries past. Whether warrior or not, David could not know, but most important was the manner in which this mysterious traveler regarded him. He could hear the clop and shuffle of the horse, and occasional mutterings of its rider.

When they had neared to perhaps twenty feet, David peered back at Rachel and Audrey. "Do you see them?"

By Rachel's mesmerized expression, he knew she did.

Audrey shook her head. "No, but I can feel it. I can tell that something's there."

"Some*one*," David said, and turned back.

He could see now that the man had a bow and a quiver of arrows slung over one shoulder, and a long, tapered spear clutched in one hand. His expression, however, was more scrutinizing than hostile, as he took in this new world into which he'd emerged, and the young man with whom he'd now arrived nearly face to face.

David reached back for his mirror, the only thing constituting the mere possibility of a weapon, but then thought better of it, and returned his hands to his sides.

The man had heeled his horse mere feet in front of David, and it now stood snorting at the air and stamping one front hoof. The man atop it looked David squarely in the eyes, then motioned about with his spear.

"*Pîsim?*" he said. "*Tipiskâw pîsim? Nîpîy?*" He regarded David expectantly.

David shook his head. "I'm sorry, I don't —"

The man cut him off with a wave. He appeared exasperated, but quickly nodded, and his brow furrowed in apparent contemplation. "I can forget those times and lands to which I have traversed. I shall speak in your language."

"Thank you," David said. "How many do you speak?"

The man looked skyward, a wistful look upon his features, before meeting David's gaze once more. "As many as there are in creation."

David nodded slowly as a whirlwind of questions swirled within him. He started to speak, but stopped, uncertain what to ask or say.

"I was inquiring," said the man, gesturing again, "about your sun, your moon, your water, your land, your sky... your world."

David nodded. "What did you want to know?"

"I am the spirit incarnate of the ancient guardians," said the man. He eyed David intently. "I am divining, presently, that you are too."

David toed the ground like the stamping equine. "So I've been told."

"Then surely you must know," said the man, eyes brimming with alacrity. "Surely you may advise me if the time has come."

"I'm sorry, but what time do you mean?"

"Time that the world has gone asunder, fallen to imbalance. That the rivers and the skies have been desecrated, and that good peoples of the Earth must take a stand to set things right."

"I don't know," David said. "I'm sorry. I know we have problems, and know some things aren't good, but I don't know if it's the time you speak of."

The man studied him intently. "Very well," he said at length. "But I can feel your spirit. I sense the trajectory of your lifetimes. You sojourn toward a foretold destiny."

"Been told that too."

The man regarded him curiously. "A destiny you do not embrace?"

"All I want—" David gestured back toward his sister. "—is to find our mother."

The man's gaze traveled to Rachel and Audrey, then back to David. "The grandest destinies often culminate from the humblest beginnings." He tugged at the reins and spoke to the horse, which grunted and swept its head from side to side before turning about. Its rider shifted in the saddle and turned back a final time to David. "Should the time be at hand, you may call upon us to stand with you."

David wondered precisely how he might do so, but opted not to inquire. It would, he figured, like so many other things, reveal itself in time. He watched as man and beast grew smaller against the horizon, listening to the fading clop of hooves. When after a few minutes they had become mere specks upon the horizon, the rainbow flared again into spectacular relief. David heard Rachel exclaim behind him, and shielded his eyes as the ancient guardian and his steed disappeared into the blazing illumination. A moment later, the rainbow quivered and pulsed, and vanished entirely with a resounding pop.

When David at last turned around, Rachel and Audrey had returned beside him.

"Has he gone?" Audrey asked, softly.

"Yes," Rachel said. "And the rainbow too."

"Let's head home," David said. "I'll tell you all about it."

They headed back in the direction from which they'd come, Rachel glancing back behind them every so often. David recounted the entire episode for them, and they listened in rapt attention, but a particular consideration pressed down upon him as they went.

Why, precisely, had Audrey been unable to witness what had just happened, but Rachel had?

CHAPTER 12
Luminary Clock

SOMEONE WAS WAITING FOR THEM when they got home.

Someone stood on the street at the edge of their front lawn, regarding them with a pleasant demeanor, as though expecting them. It wasn't Marcel, or Herman, but perhaps a friend.

"Who is that?" Rachel whispered.

"I don't know," David said. "But I think he's okay." He offered her a smile, but saw in her eyes that she did not share his confidence. They stopped about ten feet from the stranger.

"Master Rose," said the man.

Master Rose. It sure sounded like something Marcel might say.

"And you are?"

"A friend of a friend," said the man, to which David smiled.

He was of medium build, brown hair, thirty-five to forty, and nothing in his demeanor suggested cause for alarm. Still, best to be sure.

"What friend?" David asked.

"Marcel, of course." The man stepped toward them and extended his hand.

Rachel slipped behind her big brother.

"Ah, dear Ms. Rachel," the man said. "I have heard so much about you too. My name is Bram." After he and

David shook hands, he stepped back and smiled. "And I am on your side."

***

DAVID STARED THROUGH THE WINDOW

of his unlit room. The moon glowed behind a drifting veil, and he could hear the wind in the treetops. Tranquil... but that was the way of things, he had learned: it was always peaceful... right up until it wasn't.

Still, the visit from Bram had renewed his confidence and his hope. Bram explained that Marcel had dispatched him to look out for David and Rachel, including keeping watch for any more wayward immortals up to no good. David, for his part, was to keep Bram posted about any key developments, whether he spotted an immortal or encountered anyone or anything strange, whatever it might be. Bram had given David a number to contact, which seemed almost incongruous in this world of magic mirrors and other strange vectors of communication, but he was grateful for another ally, regardless. His determination stemmed more than anything from the last thing Bram had told him before departing—that in the very near future, when he'd received word from Marcel to do so, he would take David to begin training in earnest.

Rachel had remained unmoved, suspicious of Bram all the while, but David could hardly blame her, after all she'd been through. He'd read her another Frost poem at bedtime: *Acquainted with the Night*. They hadn't read it before, and well after his sister had drifted off, passages lingered in his mind's eye.

I have walked out in the rain... and back in rain... I have outwalked the furthest city light... and further still at an unearthly height... one luminary clock against the sky...

He wished he could read it, that clock. All he knew was, its hands continued their advance, as did all clocks everywhere, this world or others. Whether moving him closer to or farther from the truth, he could not say. He missed Marcel. As the summer ticked away, every day felt like running in place. Marcel had implored his patience, but the waiting was torture.

Where is he?

He glanced toward his closet, the top shelf. He shouldn't do it, he knew — not after what had happened. He was nowhere close to being able to control its powers. Best to be cautious. Best to wait, to give it time.

A small voice sounded from the other side of the wall. He closed his eyes and listened. Rachel talked in her sleep sometimes. Sometimes she cried. If it continued, he would go to her. He listened. Nothing further.

He exhaled, eased from his bed, and went to the closet. He rose up on his toes and slid his hand under the pile of shirts on the top shelf. When he clutched the mirror, carrying it as one might a small bird, he returned to his bed and lay down, his back propped against the wall. Time was a luxury he did not possess. There was a girl on the other side of the wall whose heart broke anew each day.

Caution be damned.

He eyed the locket and inhaled deeply. True, he hadn't come close to mastering it, but with every experience came small nuggets of revelation. He mustn't just open it wantonly, without purpose. He must focus intently, and channel all the resolve that brimmed inside him. Marcel had gifted him the mirror, after all, as a covert means of communication, and he needed to communicate with him, to know where he was and what came next.

He closed his eyes and slowed his breath. *Show me.* He massaged the locket softly between his hands, like a meditating mystic.

In that first instant upon flipping open the lid, so fleeting as to scarcely register, he saw Marcel — was sure he did — and yet, no. The phantom image, so singular and disarming, lingered in his mind's eye. He hadn't seen Marcel — couldn't have. A winged creature had appeared, but also the face of a man, in mad pursuit. He'd been cloaked in robes that, along with his long locks, billowed behind him beneath frantic wing beats. He clutched a sword in one hand, shimmering blue, perhaps reflecting the sky of that world through which he soared — an expression of unspeakable gravity.

In another matchstick of an instant, it vanished, melting away as phantom things do, and now, in the undulant surface of the mirror, something else took shape. What appeared a great sandstorm resolved into view, and imprinted within it, darkened images of indistinct architecture — tombstones, or tablets, but the vision remained so shrouded that David could in no way be certain. All he knew was he hadn't reached Marcel, and the failure to do so afflicted him more acutely than anything he'd just glimpsed.

He watched, his focus gone, as the images churned and faded until, moments later, they'd vanished entirely, and the mirror was once again a mirror. He sighed and flipped it shut.

His gaze roamed back through his window and traced back up to the heavens. The moon glowered behind an ebbing film of clouds. David squinted, not quite able to distinguish its features. Always were things just out of sight.

He closed his eyes and clutched the locket to his chest, listening for any signs of troubled slumber. Rachel had voiced her distrust of Bram once more, at bedtime, and David again had done his best to reassure her, telling her he was a friend.

"You *have* friends," she had replied.

***

AND SO HE DID. WHEN HE awoke the next morning, he dispatched a group text asking Robert, Chester, and Amanda to meet him at sundown at the woods. He did so with a measure of guilt: although each of them had sworn on numerous occasions they were willing partners in this odyssey, the fact remained their involvement placed them in jeopardy. David wouldn't hesitate to make any sacrifice for them, but the fact he was endangering his closest friends plagued him ceaselessly.

"Sundown?" Robert's reply. "Vampires tonight?"

David grinned as he sent a shrugging emoji.

"See you there," came Amanda's response, punctuated with a red heart.

"7:41p.m.," read Chester's text. "Sundown."

David chuckled as a face palm emoji materialized from Robert.

"Thanks," David messaged. "I'm not even sure what I want to do, but that's where a lot of things started, and I want to show you some things."

A few seconds later, another text flashed in from Amanda. "Mind if I ask Audrey?"

David responded that he did not, and watched the scrolling ellipsis.

"Thanks," came the quick reply. "This might be her kind of thing."

David sent a thumbs-up.

It just might be.

CHAPTER 13
Man's Offence

ALTHOUGH THEY PROBABLY COULD have slipped from the house unnoticed, so entrenched was their father in his habit of retreating for hours on end into his study, door closed and lights dimmed, David was not about to chance bringing Rachel along. She was disappointed, but he assuaged her with a story and a snack, and the promise that his departure was focused on finding more clues.

This was true, but as he marched down the sidewalk with his friends, there was no escaping the fact that this venture was rooted almost exclusively in hope, and perhaps a healthy dose of desperation. Robert had brought Bear, who set the pace with ears and tail pointed. They walked silently, passing only a few other people along the way.

When they came parallel to the drainage tunnel, across the expanse of field from the sidewalk, David paused and turned to his friends. "This is where so much of it started — the Gentrys, Malea." His eyes met Robert's. "Getting stuck in that past life." He watched Chester's eyes narrow. "I know, guys, I know. Hard to believe, and not even sure I do, and I'm the one it's happening to. Maybe I'm just crazy. Maybe it was the concussion that day, but even that happened here." He glanced up and down the sidewalk. "No one else around, it's night, and I've got the mirror."

Bear had stopped when the group did, but now he circled and stepped within the limited orbit of his leash, sniffing at the faint breeze. His tail had fallen, but now pointed back up, and he stepped to Robert and nuzzled him and whined.

Robert nudged Chester. "Can that get across the grass?"

"Possibly," said Chester. "But not worth the risk of getting stuck." He shut the wheelchair off, locked the wheels, unsheathed his cane, and offered a wry grin. "The game is afoot."

They paused upon reaching the creek, which ran slow and quiet given the recent dry spell. Orion flickered to the southwest. The last streaks of daylight had vanished, a full and reddish moon titling low to the east as an inky band of clouds edged into a far quadrant of the sky.

"Blood moon," said Audrey.

Chester raised an eyebrow. "Are you sure? That's typically associated with a total lunar eclipse."

Audrey smiled. "Typically, but sometimes they're tied to the Harvest Moon, or the Hunter's Moon, not necessarily to an eclipse. Their reddish hue gives them the name."

"More atmosphere between us and the moon when it's first risen, low in the sky," Chester acknowledged. "The extra air bestows the reddish appearance."

Robert shook his head and chuckled. "Oy."

Audrey maintained her smile. "He's right."

"Thanks," Chester said. "Except, the Harvest and Hunter's Moon correlate on the calendar more closely to the Autumnal Equinox, if I am not mistaken."

No one present suggested that he was.

"Haven't we each seen enough," Audrey posed in a gentle voice, "to believe not everything may be as we *once* believed?"

The evening seemed to have fallen more pitch near the forest, and the moon in question lent a ghostly luster. David was about to inquire of his friends whether to venture a crossing, but paused, mouth agape, as something caught his eye. The ground beneath them, around them, was flaring violet, like it had done a few other times in the last year. He regarded his friends for their reaction, but it became quickly apparent that they did not see.

Amanda touched his arm. "What is it?"

David gestured all around them. "The flowers," he said. "You don't see them, but I do. It's happened before. First time was here, in fact — purple flowers everywhere. Amer... amerus...." He scoured his memory. "Amer-something."

"Amaranth," said Amanda and Chester in unison.

"I remember it from a poem," Amanda continued. "But no, I don't see it."

Audrey stared out into the evening, eyes roaming and wide. "I wish I could." She turned to the group. "We need to be careful. David can see things we can't, some of them dangerous. I've been there."

"Bear!" Robert threw a second hand upon the leash. "Easy."

The canine whimpered and sat, gaze fixed upon an unseen spot in the forest, tail sweeping briskly upon the ground as a low and distant rumble sounded above them.

David glanced skyward, then faced Amanda. "What poem?"

"Paradise Lost," she said, quietly. "Milton." She closed her eyes. "Immortal amaranth... a flower which once in paradise, fast by the tree of life, began to bloom...." Her eyes fluttered back open. "Trying to remember."

"But soon for man's offense," Chester chimed in, "to heaven removed, where it first grew, there grows, and flowers aloft, shading the fount of life...."

"Seriously?" Robert chided. "Didn't know you were into poetry."

Chester shrugged. "I've seen it before, so it's in my head."

Robert shrugged. "Of course, it is. Bear!" He fortified his grip once more, as the dog had leapt to his feet, growling. "Something in there."

Audrey narrowed her eyes and stared into the woods. "Someone."

David followed her gaze across the stream, past the tree line and into the obscurity of the woods. He wondered at first if the tables had turned and Audrey, familiar as she was with such matters, was seeing things that he, in fact, could not. But then he saw, shaped out of the darkness, singular and incandescent, and his mind faltered in consideration of how they could have possibly missed her. Her figure svelte and beguiling beneath what appeared an ancient robe, she knelt just beyond the tree line within a cluster of amaranth, a small bouquet gripped in one hand. She lifted it to her face and inhaled. Flaxen locks spilled out from under a gleaming wreath, and slung over her shoulder a quiver of golden arrows. Beside her, sniffing and pawing occasionally at the earth, a majestic stag.

David felt his eyes widen. *No wonder Bear was going nuts.*

"And where the river of bliss," Amanda now resumed in a whisper, "through midst of heaven rolls over elysian flowers her amber stream."

Chester's voice, likewise subdued, mingled with hers.

"With these that never fade the spirits elect, bind their resplendent locks."

"So," David said, without averting his gaze, "you see her too."

"I see her," Robert said. "She probably wonders why we're staring."

David furrowed his brow. "The arrows? The stag? Who wouldn't stare?" He felt eyes upon him, and turned to his friends.

Audrey glanced at David, then back across the stream, then back. "I see a regular woman," she said, softly. "Picking flowers." She narrowed her eyes. "Wait. I think it's actually Ms. Duffy, from the library."

"It is in fact she," said Chester. "Maybe she lives in the neighborhood. Has a dog with her."

Amanda leaned in close to David. "What do you see?"

David began to reply, but stopped cold. She was looking right at him. It was not Ms. Duffy who held his gaze. The figure had risen from her crouched position, the clutch of amaranth fallen to her feet. The stag paced slowly behind her. David watched her carefully, much as he had back in the woods at Tintagel, with the McAlister brothers. Whether she was real or imaginary or yet another figure of worlds past, he could not know. What he did know, whether his friends could see it or not, was that she'd crossed her left arm over her chest, so that her hand rested upon her right shoulder, inches from her quiver of gleaming arrows. Her right hand dangled near her right hip, poised.

"David?" Amanda eyed him intently.

He shook his head slowly and raised a finger to his lips.

The night fell quiet as the woman—an archer, clearly, of ancient lore—took a step toward the stream, toward them.

David felt his hand moving, as if it hand a mind of its own, to his pocket, to the mirror. He didn't know what it would do, what it *could* do, but it was all he had. Her eyes had been locked onto his, but now they traced his movements, observing with rapt attention the slow trajectory of his arm as he extracted the mirror from his pocket, raised it before him, and thumbed open the lid.

He'd braced for what might come, but nothing did—at least, not yet. He stared at himself in the mirror, and felt the others staring at him. His reflection began to fade, then dissolved to gray. He tensed as the nothingness deepened and swirled. He didn't know what was coming, or who, or if he might at any moment be drawn headlong once more into a world and lifetime past. The mirror thrummed in his palm.

"Step back," he urged his friends, his mouth dry.

"David," Amanda whispered near his ear. "It's Ms. Duffy. I can see her."

"No," David said. "It's not."

The individual across the stream took another step towards them—this woman, this archer, this would-be Duffy.

Bear snorted and pulled.

The stag pawed at the amaranth from behind his keeper.

David kept an eye on her left hand.

She smiled and called over to them, "Good evening, children," her voice dulcet, strong.

David wondered how it sounded to the others. He slowly lowered the mirror.

"What are you doing out at such an hour?"

"Good evening," Chester responded. "Just hanging out, taking Robert's dog for a walk." His tone suggested to David the slightest misgiving, as if trying to fathom that which he beheld.

The figure across the stream smiled and took another step forward. "Nice to see you, Chester. Nice to see each of you." Her eyes traveled back to David. "And you, Master Rose. Pray tell your blessed sister is safe at home?"

David flinched at this mention. "She is."

The archer nodded. Her arrows glinted in the moonlight. "Sweet child," she said. "She misses her mother."

David swallowed. A reasonable, even compassionate, remark, his friends must think, and perhaps it was, especially if uttered by the kindly librarian. Yet the woman entreating him from just across the stream looked poised more for battle than for books. He gripped the mirror.

"We all do," he said.

She smiled. "Your mother understood the value of a good book."

David furrowed his brow. Something began to foment in his mind, the fleeting embers of comprehension, but then things began to happen very fast. The archer extracted and loaded a fiery arrow and leveled it toward him and his friends. The mirror pulsed and heated in his hand, but as he turned to tell his friends to get down, he saw the archer had angled slightly left and sighted her weapon skyward. He followed her trajectory and his jaw fell open as his mind scrambled to register that which his eyes beheld. The southwestern stars were moving—Orion... not just flickering... *moving*... and more than a little, though a little would have been enough.

He'd taken astronomy last year, but he remembered more from a mythology unit of English class: Orion, the Huntsman. His eyes fixed first upon the belt, but then traced upward along what seemed so clearly now a torso, he couldn't fathom how he had before missed it. From there, the crooked arm and loaded arrow took shape, the defining stars illuminated vastly more so than all their brethren across the deepening sky.

"We should get back," called Chester. "That's a lot of lightning."

David thought to correct him, but clearly, they were seeing things differently. He stared, transfixed, by the incomprehensible transformation above. Orion's features were filling in — by what means David couldn't begin to fathom — but the great hunter was glaring down at them with blazing eyes, his mouth twisted into a gaping scowl, and he bellowed with such thunderous outrage that it seemed the whole universe must have trembled.

"Run, children!" The archer pulled her payload back.

Now David knew — Artemis, daughter of Zeus, sister of Apollo, goddess of the moon and of the hunt. Legend held she'd accidentally killed Orion, upon which he was immortalized as a constellation into the heavens.

"Let us help you!" Amanda called.

David glanced back at her. "No."

"She's struggling with her umbrella, David."

"Please trust me," David said, raising his voice against the decibel of the growing storm. "It's not who you think!"

They locked eyes, and after a moment, Amanda nodded and turned to their friends. "Let's go."

Chester looped an arm around Robert's shoulders, and they set off toward the sidewalk, Audrey and Amanda alongside. When they reached the sidewalk, Chester maneuvered into his wheelchair

Robert called back across the field. "David! Come on!"

"You guys go!" David shouted back, scarcely audible to himself. "I'll be right there!"

He whirled back around but began to inch backwards upon looking skyward. Orion had unfurled his first arrow, a galaxy-sized salvo which whistled toward them on a catastrophic trajectory. Artemis appeared unfazed, and loosed her own blazing volley. As David craned his neck, the fiery arrows expanded in exponential proportion in their orbit across the heavens. David shielded his eyes at the impending collision, two comets coursing headlong, and when they exploded in a deafening cannonade, the entire sky flashed white.

Now he ran, heading for the sidewalk and his friends.

"Never seen lightning like that," Audrey shouted as he reached them. "Did Ms. Duf—did she get out of there okay?"

"I think she'll be okay," David replied. The skies had opened, and daggers of heavy rain pelted them as they scrambled toward David's house. He wondered if his dad was worried. At least Rachel was safe at home. That had seemed of great importance to the goddess in the woods.

When they reached his house, his friends made a beeline across the lawn toward the shelter of the balcony.

David paused a final time at the sidewalk and turned back. The sky blazed in such a tempest that shielding his eyes from the liquid darts and squinting against the fiery pageant scarcely helped. Just before he turned away, before the intensity and implausibility of the spectacle overcame him, he registered a scene more implausible yet.

A winged figure alighted from where the mythic archer had last stood, spiraled toward the heavens and unleashed skyward a volley of flaming arrows. Her leviathan quarry, whose unearthly visage seemed now to extend the whole of the firmament, thundered in response, and discharged his own barrage of flaming projectiles — prodigious ropes of lightning that seemed in a heartbeat to close the breach between heaven and earth. The respective salvos detonated in blinding confluence.

David at last turned away, uneasy to do so, and uneasy to not, unsure the nature and outcome of that which he'd beheld, unsure if he'd even beheld it. He knew one thing, though: she'd said something — the woman, Ms. Duffy, the archer, Artemis — whoever and whatever she was. She'd said something about his mother, and about a book. Even if he'd imagined it — imagined her — something inside him had knotted in response. He'd come to heed these appeals of his own soul, even if they — *especially* if they — defied all comprehension.

His friends had made it to the refuge of the front porch, and he broke into a trot to join them. They would need to dry off, and then he'd read Rachel her story, and put her to bed. It was getting late.

CHAPTER 14
Everything in Its Time

HE AWOKE THE NEXT DAY EMBOLDENED.
'Your mother understood the value of a good book.' It had to
mean something; everything did, in this new world. The
only thing he could think of was to return to the library.
It felt too obvious, in a way, but he had nothing else to
go on.

Once more he disappointed Rachel by leaving her
behind. She enjoyed the library, and perceived in
David's demeanor that something was afoot, but if Ms.
Duffy was there, and was who she had been last night,
then all bets were off. She'd seemed — Artemis, that is —
good, but with each day David grew less confident in the
meaning of the word. She'd also seemed keenly
interested in Rachel's welfare — an outwardly good sign,
but again, who could be certain? After all, Edmund
Kane had fooled them all.

With all this in mind, David elected to go alone. His
friends had risked more than enough on his behalf, and
even though it was just the library, something felt
different. It was Saturday, a little before noon, and their
father had retreated once more into his study, so David
made Rachel lunch, set out a few of her favorite books,
and put cartoons on the television.

The blue sky was palm-printed here and there with
storybook clouds. A shrill chittering emanated from
bushes up ahead, and when a twig snapped underfoot,

the sound sent the spooked inhabitants soaring and squawking from their sanctuary. Across the street, a jogger passed from the opposite direction. David didn't recognize him, but he didn't know everyone in the neighborhood, and there was nothing unusual about the man — middle aged, brown hair, medium build. Nothing unusual about this day at all, in fact, and it was this aura of normalcy that suddenly evoked within him a different sort of dread. The world had changed — his, anyway — so that the unusual had become commonplace, with peril seemingly around every corner, and even the briefest reprieve now seemed suspect for what sinister truth it might conceal.

The sun now shone but the cemetery grounds remained slick from the previous evening's storm. Maybe he'd expected, subconsciously, to take this detour; maybe not. Sporadic visitors dotted the landscape as he wound his way toward his mother's grave.

When he reached it, he knelt and placed a hand on the tombstone. "I know you're not here, Mom, but maybe you can hear me."

A light breeze played through the treetops, sending aloft a helix of late-summer foliage. *'Then leaf subsides to leaf.'* Frost again, from one of his mother's favorites. He closed his eyes, his hand still atop the stone, and thought back to his previous few trips here: being ambushed by LaGrange; and the time before that, with the spirits and their strange preoccupation with his sister. He could see them now — beseeching, spectral faces, and gauzy forms tapering out like threads. Always were there threads, dangling just out of reach, and his inability to grasp and pull them through was excruciating.

When he was little — long before Rachel was born — his parents had taken him to a botanical garden, and he'd been mesmerized by what at the time had seemed impossibly tall sunflowers. They'd purchased seeds, prepared a spot in the front yard, and planted and watered them, and the next several mornings he'd raced outside and flattened himself to the earth and inspected the soil for the first signs of life. After a week of disappointment, he stomped back inside and told his mother he was giving up.

She'd knelt before him and taken up his hands. *'Keep faith,'* she'd said. *'Everything in its time.'*

Two mornings later, the first buds had at last breached through.

"I'm trying," he said now.

The chime of church bells brought him back, harkening the noon hour, summoning the devout to recite the Lord's Prayer. David closed his eyes and waited. *Two... three... tour....* He thought of Minister Morgan. They hadn't been back to church since the time a few months ago, when the minister had spoken of the Jewish Holy Days and an assembly of some sort, and several other things that blurred now in David's mind as the bells tolled on. *Eight... nine....* He felt bad about not having returned.

Eleven... twelve. High noon. David wondered if he should perhaps pray, but he was less certain than ever in what he believed. All he knew was that his sister believed in him, as did their mother, if she was out there. Maybe Amanda did too. He hoped so, and his heart thrummed at the thought of her. In his mind's eye, they were back in the stairwell at school, the night of the dance, just the two of them for those wondrous few minutes—just the two of them atop the world, hand in hand, even as that world closed in, time frozen just long enough to immortalize the magic of a stolen moment.

There had never been an instance — not one — when his heart hadn't gone aflutter upon seeing her, no matter what calamity might await him. He'd survived fights to the death, escaped a mythic wizard, been rescued from a past life.... He knew that was only the beginning, but none of it disarmed him compared to a single touch from Amanda, or one look into her eyes. His heart beat for her, tremulous, yet every bit as clarion as the church bells whose echoes still hung in the air.

Alas, now was not the time. His mother was out there... somewhere... and his sister faithfully awaited him at home.

He rose and brushed aside a cluster of falling leaves from his shoulder. The seasons marched on, and so too must he, not moving on, but forward — toward an answer, a clue, anything. Until then, his would be a solitary season — no choice but to weather it, come what may. He inhaled deeply, thrust his hands into his pockets, and headed for the gates.

***

NO EPIPHANY. HE'D PLUCKED A FEW

dozen books from various sections and had pored over them for hours, and while intriguing tidbits arose here and there, most were at best akin to what they'd unearthed last time — hints, suggestions, curiosities. These faint rumblings of a connection invariably faded like breath on a mirror. *Presque vu*, as Marcel had explained, but no answers. He hadn't noticed Ms. Duffy upon arrival, but on his way out he saw her at the checkout desk, assisting patrons. He got in line, and when it was his turn she smiled and gestured him forward.

"Checking out?" she inquired.

"No," David said.

"Well," she said, smiling, "may I help you find something?"

He looked down, and when he looked back up and met her eyes, he saw in them that she understood his answer.

"It is wonderful you read to your sister," she said. It occurred to David that he ought to consider this an odd statement, as he'd no idea how Ms. Duffy could possibly know he did so, but like so much else in this new world, it washed over him unremarkably.

"She likes Frost," he replied. "Mom left it for us, the book of poems."

The librarian nodded and her eyes glinted, and for a sliver of a moment, David thought he glimpsed behind them the fire with which they'd brimmed the previous evening—when she was someone, or something, else—and which had blazed from the tips of the unearthly arrows she'd discharged towards the heavens.

"She loved the book, yes," Ms. Duffy said. She glanced quickly about, then motioned David closer, leaned slightly across the counter, and in a hushed tone said, "She has always been willing to give anything for you, for each of you."

David tried to speak but his throat caught, and Ms. Duffy smiled. He knew she understood well those words which would not come.

"I know," she said. "That time is still to come. You all must—and I know you all will—keep your promises, and love one another in equal sacrifice."

"Yes."

A few people had lined up behind him in the queue. Ms. Duffy straightened up. "Very good," she said, her demeanor having returned to its previous, professional manner. "Will there be anything else?"

"No thanks," David said. He mustered a quick smile, met her eyes a final time, then turned and headed for the exit.

***

HE CHOSE A DIFFERENT POEM THAT

night: *The Last Word of a Bluebird*. It was short and sweet. Rachel smiled at its words and rhythm, and before long was drifting off.

David stayed a while at her bedside, returning to the other poem, the one Ms. Duffy had mentioned, one not befitting a bedtime story. It spoke of a holy land and holy war, and of hearts and death, and as he arrived at the final passage, he glimpsed that which their librarian had referenced, and clearly meant for him to see:

> *For a few swift gleams of the angry brand,*
> *scorning greatly not to demand,*
> *in equal sacrifice with his,*
> *the heart he bore to the Holy Land.*

Notions of Arondight sliced through his consciousness, visions of crimson and steel, and for a moment, he heard the old voices calling to him. Like a lightning strike, it was there and gone, and he turned off the lamp and sat in the quiet darkness. At length, the moonlight seeped in and chalked the room in its pale glow. He thought of sacrifice, but not his own, for this watch he kept, this post he stood, was not a burden but a bearing, to which he would always return. No, he was plagued by who else might be called upon, for already too many had been endangered on his behalf.

He started to rise from the chair but the wood creaked, and Rachel stirred, and so he eased back down and watched her toss a bit. She settled facing her window, the moonlight bathing her features like perfect porcelain. Her reflection glimmered angel-like in the windowpane, and he sat back in the chair, waiting for her breathing to settle, that if she woke and looked for him, he was sure to be there.

CHAPTER 15
Collateral Damage

THE ABSENCE OF ANY CLEAR ANSWERS, of a clear path forward, bordered on maddening. Any long stretches pent up in the house evoked pangs of futility and guilt, and so it was on that evening he went to his father's study to let him know he was heading out for a walk.

The doorframe glowed in the otherwise darkened hallway, owing to the lamplight within. David raised his hand to knock but then paused. Something felt off. He cocked his head and listened. Usually, his father was reading or working on the computer in the study, and subsequently David could hear the occasional rustling of pages or pecking of a keyboard. But now, nothing. He turned the doorknob gently and nudged the door slowly open.

He'd always been ambivalent about art classes at school, but as his eyes adjusted to the scene unfolding before him, he harkened back to a unit they'd had this past schoolyear. Chiaroscuro, it had been called — a bit tough to pronounce, and he'd never been sure he'd grasped it fully — dark and light and shadows and contrasts, but whatever the case, he thought of it now as the study came into view. The unease that arose within him owed not to what he presently observed but to that which he, upon first surveying the room, had not. His gaze had gone instantly to his father's chair, naturally, where he knew he would be sitting—where he *was* sitting, but David had somehow failed to see him, as if he'd been swallowed up—by the chair, by the study. Absorbed. The room was illuminated by the desk lamp and the drift of moonlight waxing through the curtainless window, casting the space in haphazard shadow.

"Dad?"

His father, who'd been neither reading nor typing but immersed in his chair with a catatonic stare, looked up and about upon hearing his son's voice, at last turning his head toward the doorway.

"David... hey... everything okay?"

David flinched. He knew his father meant well, but the question agitated him, nonetheless. Of course, he was not okay—none of them were—and any pretense to the contrary seemed almost a sacrilege.

"Yeah," he said.

His father studied him. "Sure?"

"Yeah. I'm going for a walk."

"Okay." As David turned to go, his father called after him. "Not chasing any conspiracy theories, I hope."

David paused, then whirled back around. "Wouldn't that at least be better than giving up?" He turned again and stomped toward the front door, hoping Rachel hadn't overheard.

He burst from the house into a warm evening, beneath a peculiar sky. It seemed somehow fractured, one half ablaze in the day's last light—pink and blue and blazing crimson—the other peaked and gray, like a sky from another day, or another world. A light breeze picked up as he strode, rattling through the tree canopies, whose leaves had already begun to turn. The summer was flying, as summers do; another season gone. His mother had loved that song, the one about the seasons, and had used to sing it to him when he was little, and years later to Rachel, spinning her gently, hand in hand.

> *The seasons they go round and round,*
> *and the painted ponies go up and down.*

As he turned the corner at the first subdivision, a dog barked from an unseen yard, echoing into the otherwise dormant night, prompting the canine to retort again in kind.

We're captive on the carousel of time. We can't return, we can only look behind from where we came.

He was tired of looking behind, no matter that the feeling of being pursued never, ever fully relented... including now. Something felt off, and that was saying something. He glanced skyward and felt his gut clench a little, as the gathering pall had commandeered a greater share of the skyline, and where the welling gray intersected the last cross-stitch of daylight, a strange indentation appeared to quiver, and then was gone. The subdivision terminated in a cul de sac, which he rounded and continued on.

And go round and round and round in the circle game.

His anger was already ebbing, succumbing to a tide of remorse for how he'd spoken to his father. He walked past Deer Creek, where he and Donovan had taken Rachel sledding just six months' prior, and past the outskirts of Moreland's Farm, where the unthinkable had — supposedly — occurred. As he cornered the next subdivision, a lone streetlight hummed and flickered on, its pale glow bleeding into the dusk and casting the empty road in anemic hue. His shadow splayed out in comical proportion, monstrous limbs striding toward him like a fiendish, alien being. A chalky halo shrouded the bulb, more ghostly than divine, and David thrust his hands in his pockets and hastened his pace.

The patter of his footsteps seemed in concert with the thrumming of his heart. It was invigorating, in a way—moving quickly, moving forward, doing anything, really, besides nothing at all—but still that air of unease attended him, inescapable no matter his pace, descending, it seemed, with nightfall. When he reached the next crossing, he finally paused. The percussion of his heart rang loudly in his ears, all the more audible without the accompaniment of his footsteps.

He caught his breath and held it a moment. *Footsteps.* He heard them now, not far at all. Not unusual, all things being equal—why would others not be about on such an evening? He exhaled, but slowed his breath, listening.

The footsteps grew louder, coming from the left.

He squinted into the darkness, but making out nothing, he pivoted and headed in the opposite direction, toward the cemetery.

Things were, after all, not equal. He would double back, that's all.

The cemetery gates crimped over him, skeletal and twined with ivy, but this home of the dead no longer unsettled him. He almost envied those within, for the peace they'd found, for the rest. Not that he had a death wish—far from it—but all peace would elude him until he'd found his mother, until he'd found the truth. Until then, not even death itself promised the slightest reprieve, for what was death and what was life, in this undiscovered world?

He turned and strode back in the direction from whence he'd come, but paused after a few steps, certain he'd heard something. Or more so felt—something within the graveyard. Too late for visitors, so groundskeepers, perhaps, or maybe some kids. As for the latter possibility, he couldn't very well pass judgment.

This felt different, though. He glanced to his left and right along the sidewalk, and seeing no one, inched closer to the ivy-wrapped gates. He angled his head and listened. For a moment, he heard only the whispering breeze and occasional chittering of birds. Then came a faint rustling of leaves. He began to straighten up, but froze upon hearing a snapping of twigs.....

...Coming from two directions, converging.

He bent back in and thumbed apart a slight breach in the ivy. His eyes at first registered nothing, so obscured were the grounds, owing to the hour and pale haze of the distant lampposts.

Whatever remained concealed from his vision nonetheless seared into his heightened consciousness. That was the thing about this world: that which you saw might well be phantom; that which remained unseen might well be as real in its shapelessness as anything. *Something* was in there; of this he had no doubt—there, and approaching.

He squinted against the gloom, and could at last distinguish two figures shaping up within the darkness. Only when they halted beneath a towering oak, near a cluster of moonlit graves, could David discern their appearance with any distinction.

When the first of them spoke, any uncertainty regarding who—or more so, what—they were quickly evaporated.

"The Assembling nears," said the slightly taller of the two, in a baritone voice.

"Yes," replied the other, raspier, gravelly. "This is why we are here. Let us not tarry with the obvious."

Both men wore trench coats, despite the season.

"Mind your words," rejoined the taller figure. "Or I shall — "

"Let us dispense with this foolishness," raspy voice interjected. "We have rendezvoused as a means to an end, that through this partnership we might divide and conquer until only we remain to seek the prize. And at that moment, rest assured we shall determine the better man."

"Aye," said baritone man. "Rest assured."

"So then," posed the other. "Our plan?"

"The Lightkeeper dwells in this world. Eliminate him, and our path to the prize grows that much simpler."

"Neither of us harkens to his incipient world," said the shorter man. "You know the rules."

"And it seems you may have forgotten," came the baritone retort. "I did not say vanquish him. Eliminate him, from this world, from this time, and then act swiftly."

"So be it. Then what next?"

A shaft of moonlight had spliced through the treetops and illuminated their faces in ghostly relief.

The tall man grinned fiendishly. "We draw him out."

"Surely," replied staccato voice, "you have discovered his residence. Why not proceed there now?"

David's heart accelerated, and he poised to break into a sprint, to beat them home, if need be.

"No," said the taller one. "His family is surely home. Such an invasion would attract unwanted attention and make a mess of things. We are to avoid collateral damage when possible."

"So be it. Then what, pray tell — and when — are we to do? I grow impatient."

"We have waited millennia," came the reply. "We may wait one day more." He narrowed his eyes and swept his gaze in a circle around the grounds.

David tensed, as it seemed his attention lingered an extra moment in his direction, but the tall man regarded his colleague once more.

"I sense a presence, and on this evening we must not tarry. Rejoin me here tomorrow at sundown. We shall devise our plan."

David stepped back from the ivy and straightened up, back stiff, mind swimming. *Others will see it*, Herman had cautioned. *And others will come.*

First LaGrange, now these latest arrivals, and certainly more to come. He yearned to contact Marcel or Herman, but without those options, perhaps the next best thing was to confide what he'd just seen to Bram, who hopefully could offer guidance, and maybe even protection.

He turned and headed briskly away, not wanting to chance an encounter with the two who would any moment now be making their way out. His head was a tempest, but one thing gnawed at him more than anything as he went: was he the presence detected by the shorter man? For no reason in particular, he reached into his pocket and withdrew the mirror, which immediately began pulsing within his grip, as a thin blue ring ignited around its periphery. The mirror called to him, whoever or whatever might in this very moment be behind it — perhaps Marcel; perhaps another; perhaps a whole new world, be it light or dark; but perhaps possessing some of the answers he so desperately sought. It had been given to him by Marcel, after all, so why hesitate?

He reached to thumb it open, but something stayed his hand. Yes, Marcel had bestowed him this gift, as he had bestowed so many—perhaps none more abiding than to trust in his own instincts. Not that they would always be right, but no matter—they would always be *his*. This time, when he'd never felt more lost, there could be no surer path. He returned the mirror to his pocket, cast a backward glance to ensure he was not being followed, then turned back around and continued home.

CHAPTER 16
Perilous World

AFTER DAVID SENT HIS TEXT ABOUT
the immortals in the cemetery, Bram had requested they
meet there the next morning. He took Rachel, since their
father was at work.

When they arrived, Bram was already there, and for
a moment his eyes seemed to narrow upon spotting
Rachel, but just as quickly his expression reset to its
customary affability.

"Good morning," he said, nodding to them both.

"Hey," David replied. He glanced at Rachel, who'd
been excited to tag along on her brother's latest
excursion, but had quickly soured upon learning with
whom they'd be rendezvousing. He'd tried again to
reassure her, explaining that he didn't get that telltale
unease around Bram, like he did with Kane and others,
so he didn't really think he could be bad.

"Anyone can be bad," she'd said.

"Thank you for meeting me," Bram said, still
smiling. "As much as you might be able to share about
the events of last evening, it shall hopefully assist me in
piecing things together, and enable me to protect you
most properly."

"Okay," David agreed, though he would have
preferred Bram not having spoken of protection.

"Excellent. If you would kindly direct us to the
location of the occurrence."

David crooked his head backwards over his right shoulder. "That way."

"Very well, then." Another smile. "I shall follow your lead."

They headed back along the sidewalk, David glancing back over his shoulder every so often. When they arrived at the approximate spot, David stopped, stepped over to the fence, and spread apart a swath of ivy until achieving a reasonable vantage.

"Here," he said.

Bram nodded, moved alongside him, and helped hold the ivy open. Rachel nuzzled closer on her brother's other side. Bram tilted his head toward the cemetery grounds. "In there?"

"Yeah. By the big oak."

Bram stared silently into the graveyard for several moments. At length, he stepped back, and David did likewise, the ivy springing back shut.

Bram turned to face him. "Tonight?"

"Yeah," David said. "Said they'd meet again at sundown."

"Thank you."

Bram's latest grin made something in his stomach knot. He looked down at Rachel, then regarded Bram. "Do you want me to meet you?"

"Heavens no," Bram quickly replied. "Though I do appreciate the courageous offer. You are not to come anywhere near this place. Marcel would insist."

"What are you going to do?"

"Nothing at all," said Bram. "Merely observe, to hopefully divine their intentions—from as safe a vantage as possible, I might add. I am no immortal, after all."

"Have you met many?" David asked.

"I have."

"Are they all like that? You know, violent? Bad?" He glanced down at Rachel, who clutched his hand tighter still, her squinting face dappled in the filtered sunlight.

"Many," said Bram, his voice even. "Maybe most. Maybe they didn't start out that way, but this world in which—forgive me—your kind live is full of temptation, and seems to compel most along that precipitous path."

"Facilis descensus Averno," David said, remembering Chester.

Bram cocked his head. "What's that?"

"Nothing."

But inside, the unease had continued to build. No, Bram wasn't immortal, but neither was Marcel, nor Herman, and both seemed impeccably—if inexplicably—versed in numerous languages and phrases and sayings, and all things old and mysterious and suggestive of this perilous world, at once ancient and new. That this small utterance from a 19th-century tale was foreign to Bram perhaps shouldn't have aroused in David the slightest misgiving, and yet, somehow, it did.

Nonetheless, on the slight chance that there was anything to his concerns, it remained imperative that Bram not suspect in him the faintest trepidation.

"Good luck tonight," David said. "I won't come near."

***

BUT HE DID. HE DIDN'T KNOW if he should feel remorseful for lying to Bram, but he didn't.

There was simply no way he could sit on the sidelines while these events transpired. There could be information about his mother, or Kane, or at the very least about the nature and next steps of this dark world. Would there be more immortals? Would they all be after David? Was Bram really on his side? Then there was that no-so-trivial matter of their direct threats to David's life. No, he would not sit home and merely await it, whatever it might be.

Their father had disappeared into his study after dinner, and when the door closed, David went to the living room where his sister was playing, and told her he was heading out for just a bit.

"You're going to the cemetery," she said — not a question.

"Yeah."

"Take me," she implored, looking up from her assemblage of stuffed animals.

"I can't." The hurt on her face cut him to the quick, but better to disappoint than endanger. "I'm sorry. Dad would be upset if I took you out in the dark."

Rachel raised her head to the window, where through the cradle of tree limbs the fast-ebbing day flared in crimson brushstrokes upon the horizon. "There's still a little light," she said.

"Not for long," he said. "I'm sorry."

She returned her attention to her animals, whom she'd arranged in a circle, as though some manner of high council. "You won't be too late?" she asked without looking up. "They won't go to bed until they get their story, you know."

David smiled. "I know. Not too late."

"You'll come back?"

"Of course, I'll come back."

She looked back up at him. "Promise?"

"Promise."

When he stepped from the house, he locked the door, checked his pocket for the mirror, and briskly set off for the cemetery. The day's last embers shimmered beneath the descending vault of night, as a glowing moon angled in the eastern sky. A handful of others were out, it being a pleasant, late-summer evening — a couple pushing a stroller; a jogger; an old man and his dog, which seemed none too pleased with his owner's leisurely pace.

After a few minutes, the outskirts of the cemetery came into view, dark and gaunt and familiar. David found it more than a bit disquieting that it had started to feel like a home away from home.

The moon and the streetlights cast the grounds in a pale glow. He slowed and contemplated the wisest approach. Bram might be observing from the spot they'd examined earlier, so best to wind his way around to another section of fence line. Even more critical, he had to avoid detection by the immortals who were set to rendezvous here at any moment.

David crept along the sidewalk, cornered onto the next straightaway, and strode swiftly until he reached a parallel location. The ivy was thankfully less copious, and he cast a glance to either side, and then behind, before stepping toward the gate.

The snap froze him in his tracks as might have a gunshot, and when he realized it had come from underfoot — from *him* — his heart revved, and he held his breath as if even the sound of it might now prove costly. When after several moments he detected neither voices nor movement, he slowly exhaled, stepped over the culprit twig, and placed both hands upon the iron slats.

He pressed his face to the gate and peered in, beholding at first only darkness, so well did the oak canopies ward the moonlight. At length, telltale features substantiated into view — the prodigious, shadowed oaks; the oblong, pale stones; as though a new world — a dead world — rising.

Only a few seconds later, two dark figures appeared and approached quickly — the immortals, like clockwork, their coattails trailing behind them as they strode. They converged once again at the great oak, the spill of moonlight casting them like ghouls against the otherwise darkened expanse. They each glanced quickly about, and David tensed with the realization that his less obscured vantage point also meant a clearer view for them. He maintained his grip, endeavored to slow his breath, and tried to remain motionless.

The shorter of the men, the less patient from the evening previous, spoke first. "And so, a day has passed. Pray tell, the time has conferred upon you some wisdom as to the measures we shall now undertake."

"Indeed," said the taller. "The Lightkeeper shall soon be within our grasp." He glanced furtively about. "I have ascertained information of the most profound import."

"About the Lightkeeper?" The taller man stepped closer to his associate.

"About the Lightkeeper, yes. Others, as well — his upholders, as well as pursuers. Those who would sacrifice all for him, and those who, like us, at this very moment seek his demise. And much, much more. Things have been set in motion beyond what we have possibly imagined."

"I can *imagine* quite a bit," said his colleague. "But compelling, nonetheless. I trust you shall understand that I should very much like to be availed of your sources."

"That," replied the taller man, "is of little consequence, compared to the gravity of this present moment. We must take heed to—"

David stared as the taller man put his finger to his lips, and both men slowly pirouetted about, sweeping their gaze over the grounds. David's heart pounded in dread that he'd been discovered. He felt his eyes widening as both immortals withdrew broadswords from their coats. Perhaps they'd yet to spot him, but clearly, they knew he was there. He gripped the iron slats, frozen in indecision—he must flee, but in the event they'd yet to catch glimpse of him, such sudden movement would surely betray his whereabouts.

As he contemplated his best course of action, a shaft of light blazed across his sightline, causing him to squint and throw his hands up over his eyes. A cacophony of voices flooded his senses—the two immortals, but others too, it seemed. Through his narrowed eyes he saw the immortals flailing against the inexplicable lightshow. The incandescence erupted from alternating vicinities of the cemetery, and as he watched the immortals stumbling about with their blades brandished, David glimpsed a handful of projectiles sailing into the expanse. Before he could register their nature, a series of skull-pounding blasts detonated from the grounds.

He clenched shut his eyes and he threw his hands to his ears, the pain crippling. In the scrambled theater of his mind's eye, he saw the two immortals propelled through the air by the force of the deafening blasts, and he cowered and cringed as the discord from within the cemetery escalated. The chaos roiled for what seemed an eternity, and when it finally abated — when the noise slowly ebbed and the searing light faded upon his eyelids — he cautiously uncovered his ears and let his aching eyes flutter open.

He saw no one in the cemetery. He glanced all around him before stepping to the fence and peering intently within, where he spied not a movement, not a sound, as if no one had been there and nothing had happened.

Other immortals? Perhaps Marcel come to save him once again? Such an attack seemed somehow unlikely from his friend. Then what, exactly? And whom? If Bram had been there, then clearly, he bore witness too, if he hadn't been himself assaulted. And who was to say David would not be next?

He unclamped his grip and backed slowly from the gates, envisioning Rachel peering out their front window, anxiously awaiting his promised return. He had to get home.

The assailant struck the instant he turned, clamping a hand over his mouth from behind, and with another hand restraining his right arm.

David flailed frantically with his left hand to reach the mirror, but it was wedged in his right back pocket, just out of reach. There was something else, though, something worse: he felt as if falling away from himself, fading quickly. As a pungent odor washed over him, he registered somewhere within his fast-dimming faculties that he'd been poisoned — chloroform, likely. He heard the clip of approaching footsteps, and felt additional hands upon him, lifting him now, for he had fallen. The night sky gazed down upon him from its fathomless depths, a great, dark sea.

"Careful with this one!" someone said.

"Get the mirror!" someone else said.

It was the last thing he could make out clearly, as the world around him disintegrated to fragments of waning sight and fractured sound. He tried to summon the will to resist, calling upon whatever reservoir of strength he prayed might yet flicker somewhere within him, but it would not come. His heart ached for what this would do to Rachel. Maybe Bram was out there somewhere, racing to his rescue. He clung to that last ember of hope, quivering in the distance, until all around him fell to black.

CHAPTER 17
Phantom Sanctuary

RACHEL CLIMBED ONTO THE COUCH in their living room, nudged apart the curtains, and peered out. Something was wrong, she just knew; David should have been home by now. He shouldn't have gone to the cemetery. Those bad men would be there, and she considered Bram among them. Maybe she should have snuck out. The ghosts at the cemetery liked her, and she could have asked for their help. She stared out at their lamplit lane, desperately hoping to glimpse her brother emerging from the shadows. He would come in and tell her what happened, and tell her it was late and she must get ready for bed. He would read her a story, and when they were sure their father was not within earshot, maybe he would tell her he'd discovered something that would bring them closer to finding Mama.

She smiled at the thought of this, and scampered closer to the windows, peering intently into the darkness. Any moment now he would appear.

Any moment.

***

DAVID FELL SLOWLY BACK INTO HIMSELF, through a lulling labyrinth of rousing consciousness. Part of him wished to stay behind, swaddled in the phantom sanctuary of that deep rest into which he'd been compelled, for he was so very tired, but as recognition awakened within him, like so many lights switched on, he knew he must push through.

He'd been out a while. He surmised this owing not merely to his lethargic state, but to the elusive fragments which had begun to suggest themselves along the periphery of his recollection. He'd been transported, obviously — more than once, and by more than one means. Pieces of it were coming back to him: being carried to a vehicle, then out like a light again; stirring upon being removed from the vehicle, only to fade once more, whether by virtue of the original chemical agent to which he'd succumbed, or additional. Next, he was certain, he was aboard a plane, and there had been multiple voices, as stood to reason, by turns menacing and frantic.

'A million for this one? What's so special about him? Hey, he's coming to....'

...Only to have been snuffed out again, but now he was awake, apparently arrived at the chosen destination, for the locomotion had at last ceased. The remnants of whatever had subdued him pooled like floating shards in his skull. He worked his tongue slowly around his lips, which felt grotesquely swollen. He didn't feel the urge to relieve himself, which surprised him, until he realized he was likely dehydrated, exacerbating his headache. His eyes were heavy, and even though he expected upon opening them to behold dungeon-like effects, whatever dim light pervaded these quarters pressed painfully upon him. He imagined at least one of his captors would be there, and he tried to focus his thoughts — he must at all costs avoid being subdued again. He would rise, retrieve the mirror, and....

The mirror. He'd forgotten.

They'd taken possession of it, and if they were who he thought they were, then by now it was in the hands

of their master, who'd clearly orchestrated David's capture —
a catastrophic turn of events. A great melancholy
overtook him: Kane had captured him, and he had no
weapon, and had never made it home. Another promise
broken, and if he would in this place, wherever it might
be, meet his end, what weighed upon him most
unbearably was not the notion of his own death, but the
heartbreak which would yet again befall his sister.

First Mom, and now me.

He felt a wetness upon his cheeks, but he gritted his
teeth and balled his fists. If this was the end, he would
not go down without a fight.

He opened his eyes.

Only a few small lamps lit the room, but, given the
prolonged darkness of his ordeal, he blinked rapidly
against the glare. Things were blurry, but he appeared
to be alone. This was good, if even a temporary reprieve.
With his head still spinning, he could use the time to
gather himself. He rubbed his neck and gazed about the
room. It was, in fact, not dungeon-like at all; it was nice,
lavish even, like a luxurious hotel. The overhead light
had been left off, as if in consideration of his comfort. He
turned his head slowly from left to right, then rose and
shuffled toward the door. When he extended his hand
to the doorknob, he paused a moment and inhaled
deeply, bracing for what — or who — might await on the
other side. He turned the knob.

Locked. *Of course, locked.*

He raised his wrist to his eyes to ascertain the time,
but they'd taken his watch — the one his mother had
given him. He felt his face contort. A moment later he,
reached for his back pocket, not for the mirror, which he
knew was gone, but for his phone, hoping. No, they'd
taken it too, of course. Maybe his father would think to

track its signal, if it were trackable. He rested his hand on the door and breathed slowly, still trying to gain his bearings. This best thing he could do was stay calm, and stay alive. He turned and surveyed the room. The bed he'd awakened upon was plush, with thick pillows, clean sheets, and a comforter. There was a large desk, atop which sat a tall mirror, two lamps, and a pitcher of ice water; a bureau; and an unlit chandelier. A handful of paintings adorned the walls: a waterfall, a countryside, a churning sea. At one corner, a bathroom, and as nature finally beckoned, David ambled to it.

When he emerged, he poured himself some water at the desk. He considered briefly that it could be poisoned, but something told him otherwise. If his captors had meant to kill him, they'd had ample opportunity. After gulping the glass of water, he breathed deeply, refilled, and drank again. He wiped a hand across his lips, pulled the chair back from the desk, and sat.

He'd needed the fluids. It was good and cold, and as he observed the ice bobbing in the settling pitcher, it occurred to him that someone had attended to his room rather recently, or else the cubes would have melted. He wished he could for a moment channel Holmes, or Dupin, or even Chester. They could riddle this out. They would consider how long the journey felt, the sounds of the engines, the twists in the road. They'd cast a glance about this very room and seize upon some seemingly trivial detail, but which upon further examination held a key to the mystery. If not one of them, perhaps someone from his past could help, another him, hopefully possessing those same keen powers of deduction that might see him through.

Yet how could he know if there'd been such a someone — such a him — much less how to call upon that wayward soul? No, it was just him—this him—on his own... again. He must take the time to assess his predicament and conjure a plan, but as always, time felt unquestionably short. He took stock of the other items on the desk—a writing pad, pen, a Bible—and scoffed. Funny, how readily the most shameless souls propped themselves upon the delusion of righteousness. He pulled the desk drawer open and found another writing pad, a few more pens, and a letter opener. He stared at this last item, with its beveled, wooden handle, protruding from which, the tapering, stainless steel blade. His fingers closed around the handle, and he gripped it as one might a knife, and held it before him. He closed his eyes and breathed deeply as things began to pulse inside him. In his mind's eye, he saw Galatine slicing through the air toward him, and his own blade, Arondight, sweeping up to meet it. His grip tightened.

From outside the room now sounded approaching footsteps, and his eyes fluttered open. He startled upon glimpsing the person staring back at him, blade in hand, eyes glinting. His grip tightened once more, but something spoke to him softly now, and he watched as the young man in the mirror slowly lowered his implement and set it upon the desk.

The footsteps paused outside his door, it seemed, and he briefly considered taking back up the blade, but he pushed back from the desk, stood, and faced the door. When he heard keys jangling, and one inserting into the lock, he grabbed the chair and lifted it before him, and once more felt things stirring within him, a vigilance emanating from a place and time long past.

He tensed as the knob turned, the key withdrew, and the door swung open towards him.

CHAPTER 18
Enchanted Inklings

THEY CAME FACE TO FACE, HE and Bram, and David was surprised to realize he wasn't surprised at all.

"My sister was right," he said.

Bram gestured at the chair still clutched in David's hands. "Why don't you put that down?"

David hesitated, then acquiesced. Not that he owed Bram the slightest reprieve. It all came back to him now, all the times he'd seen Bram prior to meeting him — jogging by, and on several other innocent occasions, hiding in plain sight, observing.

"You're a liar."

"I am compensated well for being so."

"That makes it okay?"

"Why don't you sit?" Bram gestured toward the chair. "You need your rest."

"I need to get out of here."

Bram appeared almost pained, but this washed quickly away. "I'm afraid that is out of the question. Ah! Now don't do anything foolish!"

David looked down. He'd gripped the chair again and raised it a few inches off the ground.

"You don't have the mirror, remember," said Bram.

"I don't need it."

Bram went to the foot of the bed and sat. He withdrew a small case from his shirt pocket, thumbed it

- 139 -

open, and plucked out a cigarette. He snapped the case shut, withdrew a pack of matches, plucked out and lit one, and paused the flame an inch from the cigarette. "Mind?" When David did not answer, Bram lit the smoke and extinguished the flame with a flick of his wrist.

"Where am I? What is this place?"

Bram inhaled deeply, held the cigarette away from his lips, and exhaled a ring of smoke. "I cannot disclose the former. The latter will become evident soon enough."

David gripped the chair once more, but didn't lift it. He'd tired of such remarks, of coy and suggestive words. He'd no use for them. He'd even grown impatient with Marcel a few times, but at least he trusted that Marcel had his best interest in mind, believing that some things were better learned himself, when the time came. But this wasn't Marcel. He didn't know who Bram was, and he didn't care, beyond any usefulness such information might provide in his quest to escape this place.

Bram motioned to the chair. "Again, don't waste time or energy with such posturing. You understand your predicament, and you know an attack would be counterproductive."

"What do you know about me? To say what I know."

Another billowing ring. "David Rose, recently awakened, incipient soul—" Now Bram leaned forward, eyes glinting. " —Lancelot." Another puff. "Bested your rival at Tintagel and escaped Kane. Impressive. Your hallowed weapon, however, remains in the latter's possession." He drew again at his cigarette, then rose. "Believe me yet?"

"I don't care."

"Perhaps you should."

"All I care about is getting home," David said. "I'll do whatever it takes."

Bram started to raise the cigarette, but again paused. "You've got pluck. I can see what the fuss is about, but I remind you once more, you are weaponless." He eased back the left flap of his jacket with his elbow.

David's eyes traced down to the revolver holstered in his waistband, and he said, "I have what I need, and you won't use that. You need me for something. Otherwise, you could have just shot me back home."

Bram let his jacket fall back shut, and smiled. "My compliments."

Their eyes locked briefly, and Bram slowly rose, a wry grin still etched upon his features. He stepped slowly back toward the doorway, pulled the door open, and as he stepped into the hallway said, "Keep up the fight. You're going to need it."

***

A SHORT TIME LATER, A MAN brought David dinner, asked if he needed anything, then left, locking the door again from the outside.

David poked and nibbled at his food, pacing the room like a caged cat in the intervals between. He didn't know the time, for they'd taken his phone and watch, and there was no clock in the room, and no TV — clearly by design, meant to disorient him and deny him all bearing on time and place. At length, he collapsed upon the bed, gritted his teeth, and blinked furiously. He thought of Rachel. *She* was his bearing, the thing that mattered most, and he was failing her miserably... again.

He surveyed the room, but nothing suggested his whereabouts. He was exhausted — despite his hibernation, or perhaps because of it — and his eyelids grew heavy. He felt himself drifting off, and this agitated him greatly, as though an acquiescence to his predicament. He thought it selfish, but slumber called to him, pulled at him, and he felt and saw himself being ferried out on ebbing tides. Just then, something kindled in his mind's eye, likewise entreating him, and he fought back against the weariness and forced his eyes back open.

The waterfall.

He gazed at the painting on the wall, which had not until now intrigued him the slightest. He regarded the silvery, irrepressible force coursing eternally into frothing plumes below, but now, in his mind's eye, he stood back upon the summit at Tintagel, poised over a fallen Donovan. Primal memories of lives and centuries flooded back — people, places, *hims.* And that was just it: he had at his disposal, if only he could properly channel and control it, the power and wisdom of untold lifetimes. What he wouldn't give for the mirror and his sword, but they were but tools, no matter how prolific.

He had what he needed, as he'd told Bram.

He inhaled deeply and folded his arms across his chest. The awakening at Tintagel replayed within him, vivid and acute. It was staggering, and were he not already reclined it might have brought him to his knees: the life, the death, the wonder, the loss. Darkness and light appeared in inarticulable proportions, like how you couldn't look directly at an eclipse, but must glance edgewise, that you might gain even a sense of things.

From these glimpses, these slivers, these vague but enchanted inklings, he must somehow grasp whatever strands of clarity and coherence he might. Voices were calling to him, but in tongues and from harbors he could not yet fathom, yet must. It wouldn't be easy. He recalled his elation when Marcel had appeared on the moors at Kane Manor, the one person who could always reassure and teach him, but Marcel was not here, not now, and whatever lessons he might glean, he must now extract from an obscurity as elusive as the shadows from which his mentor had emerged on that fateful evening.

So be it.

Within that cauldron churned the ingredients of boundless power and possibility.

Awareness and abilities... something, or someone, from his past that might... who might... hold the key to this latest test. It felt daunting, like trying to lasso a cloud, but this was his charge. His mother was out there, lost — same with his father, in his own way — and Rachel bore the most unfair burden of them all, relying on David with unshakable faith.

He breathed deeply again, resisted the urge to rush to the door, perhaps chair in hand, and do all in his power to barrel through. He must remain calm, and focused.

'A day at a time for now,' Marcel had told him. *'At the doorstep of eternity, that is usually somehow best.'*

He closed his eyes.

CHAPTER 19
Daylight

WHEN HE WOKE, FLEETING REMNANTS of his is slumber flared vividly in his mind, so very real, before receding away beneath tides of surging consciousness — there a moment, gone the next. *Presque vu.* Maddening, because it seemed he'd had a hold of something, but he felt a smile creeping upon his lips, for despite its elusiveness, he felt nonetheless invigorated, renewed.

He used the bathroom, and within minutes a knock came upon his door, followed by the sound of a key turning, and when the door swung open, the same man who'd brought his dinner stepped into the room with a tray of food.

"I trust this will be satisfactory," he said, setting the tray upon the desk. When he straightened up, he turned to David and gestured toward the bureau. "You should find an adequate wardrobe within. We estimated the correct size." He recrossed the room, exited, and relocked the door.

David stared a few moments before pulling back the chair and sitting down to eat. He remained unworried about the food — surely, they had not gone to such lengths, and traveled such distances, to poison him. He ate, and while images and questions and scenarios continued to teem, they felt slightly less jumbled, as if that inverted waterfall had in fact bestowed some secret wisdom, some hidden nugget left gleaming in the pan after the water and excess sediments had at last sluiced through. He could not yet define or grasp it, only discern that it was there, but that was something. No great epiphany, no definitive answer, but he was imbued with at a small glimmer of confidence and hope, as though something — or someone — had whispered to him in his dreams.

After he'd eaten, he pushed back from the desk, stood, and stretched his neck, then his arms, his back, and his legs. He lowered himself to the floor and did some pushups, then stood and turned to the mirror above the desk. He saw himself turning slowly sideways, into some manner of fighting position, and watched as his arms moved fluidly through various defensive and then striking maneuvers. It was not immediately clear to him who was leading, but he executed each motion with ease, as if he'd done so his entire life.

He squared up to his image and watched as his arms raised slowly above his head and his hands clasped together, as if around something tangible and familiar. The two figures each regarded the other stoically, before their hands came whistling down in a powerful sweep. Next came an upward slice, a step back, parry, sidestep, attack. They continued in this execution for some time, until another knock sounded, a key was inserted, and the door swung open once more.

Two unfamiliar men stepped inside, about the same age as Bram, with neatly combed dark hair, each wearing dark suits. One stood perhaps two inches taller than his colleague. They sized David up a moment.

Then the shorter of the two said, "David Rose, I hope you've had a chance to eat. Do you require anything else?"

"My watch," David said.

The men exchanged glances. "We will see about getting you one," allowed the shorter man.

"No."

They'd started to exit, but now turned back.

"*My* watch," David said.

"I will relay that request," said the shorter man. "If you wish to shower and change attire, now would be the time to do so. We shall return in thirty minutes, and escort you."

"Where?"

The taller man said, "There's someone who wishes to meet you."

***

THEY HAD DONE THEIR HOMEWORK: the clothes fit perfectly. An organized group, clearly, to have surveilled and captured him, and prepared for him in this detail. Toward what end? None spoke with a British accent, none looked familiar, and it didn't feel like Kane—perhaps a relief, but the uncertainty of who they were and what they wanted filled him, in some ways, with even greater unease.

The two men returned for him, and he followed the shorter one down a long and curving corridor, the taller one trailing. In the elegant, well-lit hallway, polished handrails wound beneath walls adorned with expensive-looking art. And 'less anyone had a mind to pilfer any of this finery, at every bend, there perched cameras and monitors. David caught glimpse of himself as they went, and didn't know who else might be watching him, only that someone surely was.

He staggered presently and lifted a hand to his eyes, for the walls had given way to floor-to-ceiling windows, and the sunlight broke over him like a wave. It had been a while since he'd seen daylight. As his eyes began to adjust, the panorama cleared into view.

"Impressive," the tall man said from close behind.

The horizon fell out before them in a boundless, watery expanse, glimmering beneath the golden hue of daybreak. David narrowed his eyes, hoping with each step and around each bend to spot land. He did not.

When a short time later the shorter man stopped at a gilded set of double-doors and removed a key from his pocket, David took one last look outside. The reality of their environment began to settle in, then sink within him. Unless he was very mistaken, he was on an island... in the middle of God knew where.

"David Rose."

The voice issued through the now open doors, reminding him of Kane in its insistence. He knew it wasn't, but whoever was now requesting him did so with an eerily similar air.

He inhaled deeply and closed his eyes. Through everything, he'd wanted to keep moving forward—toward answers, toward truth. This felt very much like falling back, but he must, at least for the moment, abide. Escape, for the time being, must give way to survival. He opened his eyes, exhaled, and entered the room.

CHAPTER 20
Price

THE LARGE, LAVISH ROOM REMINDED him of the hallways they'd traversed to arrive there. The men who'd escorted him exited and closed the doors, and David stood alone with the one who'd beckoned. The man sat behind a large, mahogany desk in a plush chair, regarding him intently, a black and white clock perched high on the wall behind him.

"Million-dollar man," the man said, and motioned to a chair. "Do sit down."

David did. The man was athletic looking, well-dressed, and younger than David had expected—perhaps about thirty—but what was age, in this upturned world?

"You are wondering where you are, and why you're here."

"I'm wondering why everyone finds it necessary to keep saying things like that," David said. "Like it's part of a game."

The man clasped his hands. "But it is, and please don't think I say that in a trivial manner—far from it. I say it with reverence, for this is the grandest of games, unlike anything the world has ever known." He leaned forward, a slight grin creeping upon his features. "But I know."

"Fine," David said. "You know. So, are you going to tell me?"

The man sat back. "I will tell you this: my name is Christian Ellerby. I am your host. You are, as you have surely deduced, quite far from home—oceans away, which you have now observed. It is not my preference to be coy, but, much as I have learned about your ki— those like you—I still cannot confirm with certainty the full range of your powers. We possess your phone, as you know, but it is possible you retain some other manner of communication. So, I'm afraid I cannot disclose our location at this time."

David inhaled deeply, working to suppress the anger simmering within him. Here, perhaps, was something he could use, something to file away for later: the apprehension this man harbored that his "guests" possessed abilities which he did not fully understand and, therefore, feared.

"So," he said, meeting Christian's gaze. "You can't tell me where I am. How about why I'm here?"

Christian regarded him a moment, yet another thing which had come to annoy David through all of this— how so many players in this "game" tended to study him, as though some inanimate object of great intrigue.

"An answer which will be revealed in due course," Christian said. "Sooner than later. I see your frustration, but once more, my explanation is grounded not in duplicity, but homage." He leaned forward once more. "Just as the immortals—just as you—had to experience your awakening—live it, breathe it, perhaps even die for it—rather than be merely told, so too is the epiphany all the more powerful when experienced here. Everything hinges on that power, David, everything I have built here, and to which I have devoted my life." He straightened back up. "I would expect you wish to understand who I am."

David did not answer.

"I will spare you the speech then, but I will say this: it would be in your interest to know me, as I am, as mentioned, your host. I am in control of all matters here, and therefore, all matters that, from this moment on, will affect you, as this has become your home."

"For now," David said.

"For as long as you live."

"So, you intend to kill me."

"Heavens, no," Christian said. "You are now my most prized possession. Whether you live or die shall be entirely up to you. You'll see. It's possible you'll live forever. You may well outlive me." His eyes glinted. "But no matter what happens, it will happen here." At this, he stood, walked around his desk, and extended his hand. "I hope to make your life as comfortable as possible. We might as well be friends."

David stood, but did not take up the hand of his unsought host. "A friend does not drug you. A friend does not kidnap the brother of a little girl whose world is already falling apart. A friend does not hold people hostage. I don't care who you are. I don't care if you own this island, the ocean, or the world. You're just one more person in my way."

The smile slowly returned to Christian's face. "I can see why the steep price," he said, slowly. "Keep hold of that edge, then. It should serve you well." He tilted his head toward the door. "Gentlemen!"

The doors swung open and the men who'd escorted David stepped inside.

David looked from them to Christian, then trudged over to the doorway. He paused when he got there, and turned back around to his host, who'd returned to his desk and was shuffling through papers.

"A million?" David said.

Christian looked up.

"You paid a million for me?"

Christian smiled. "Indeed, I did. A steep price, but I have every confidence you will justify my investment."

"Let me go," David said.

Christian regarded him, titled his head a moment, then chuckled.

"Let me go," David repeated. "Or the price will be far steeper than you can imagine."

CHAPTER 21
Enough of Hate

HE WAS NOT LET GO. HE was returned to his quarters and brought a fine lunch by the employee who'd brought his other meals, and the man told him he'd be retrieved in a few hours to tour more of the compound and attend that evening's entertainment.

It occurred to David that entertainment, like at Kane Manor, might in this place carry a far different meaning.

When several hours later a knock sounded upon his door, no subsequent sound of lock and key ensued. His visitor was affording him the courtesy of waiting for his response.

"Yeah," David called, after a moment.

When the door swung open, Bram stood in the doorway wearing a dark suit and smiling. "Ready?"

"Does it matter?"

"Ah, come now," said Bram. "I understand how you feel, but respectfully, I suggest you work to reframe your perspective. This is home now, as Christian no doubt explained. We intend to grant you every comfort possible." He stepped back through the doorway into the hall, and motioned David forward. "You might as well make the best of it." He gestured again, and David exhaled and crossed his room and stepped into the corridor.

Bram led him off in the opposite direction he'd been escorted earlier, and once more David had to shield his eyes, this time from the glare of the setting sun. He'd never seen the sun set over the ocean before, and couldn't help, despite the circumstances, be taken in. The sun calved upon the far horizon, blood-orange and purple-tinted, half-submerged, as if birthed within the glimmering waters. A prodigious finger of light extended toward them, like the fiery wake of a torpedo launched from the ends of the earth.

"Beautiful, yes?" Bram glanced back at David as they walked, like a kindly tour guide.

David did not reply. He observed several closed doors as they went, behind one of which reverberated the clamor of what sounded like an auto shop. *PRIVATE*, read the placard on the door.

A minute later, they arrived at a wide, double-door elevator, and Bram stopped and punched in several digits on the keypad. After a series of beeps and whirring, the doors drew open, revealing a small, caged enclosure. David looked on warily as Bram withdrew a small key from his pocket and inserted it into a padlock on the door. The cage door creaked as Bram pulled it back, and he signaled David forward.

David narrowed his eyes and saw a panel of buttons and controls within the cage, and now observed a series of large cables attached to the roof of the structure, an elevator of sorts, like a dumbwaiter. Nothing about this felt good, but he knew fighting would for the moment be futile. He stepped inside.

Bram followed him in and pulled the rasping door shut, and another man appeared at the elevator doors and relocked the cage. He and Bram nodded to one another, and Bram began pushing buttons as the other man withdrew.

The contraption began to quiver and hum, and David grabbed a section of caging and hung on.

Bram finished his orchestrations, glanced back at David, and faced front. "Admittedly a bit antiquated." He grabbed a section of caging as the lift jerked and began its tremulous descent. "That is by design. Where we head now, precious few ways in." He chuckled. "Or out."

"Doesn't seem very efficient," David replied, his voice spasming in rhythm with their rickety descent. "All this technology, and this is what they came up with?" He furrowed his brow. "Strange."

"Come now," said Bram, eying him almost paternally. "Why should it strike you as strange that one would go to such lengths to protect such an investment? Some things are not intended to be so readily discoverable. Surely, you've come to learn that in your world."

"It's not my world," David said. "And neither is this."

Bram sighed. "It may be hard for you to believe, but I'm rooting for you. You are... unique, and the sooner you accept things for the way they are, the greater your chance at success."

"You're right," David said. "It is very hard for me to believe. You don't usually think of kidnappers as being in your corner." He glared at Bram. "And I will never accept things the way they are. The moment I do that will be the moment I have failed."

"Defiant to the last," Bram said. "I can't help but admire that. Ah well, I was simply trying to help."

"Don't worry," David said, quietly. "You have."

He wondered what time it was back home. Maybe bedtime. Rachel would be wanting her story, or maybe a poem. Maybe their father would read her one. He hoped Dad would, but couldn't be sure. He wondered how many sleepless nights they'd endured since he'd vanished.

He sometimes skimmed the Frost book in search of poems Rachel might like. One had caught his eye of late, and though he didn't think it was quite right for her, it had stuck with him.

Some say the world will end in fire,

it began,

Some say in ice.

He braced as the elevator shuddered and lurched.

From what I've tasted of desire
I hold with those who favor fire.

He glanced at Bram, who stared straight ahead, unflinching, despite the increasing jauntiness of their drop.

But if it had to perish twice,
I think I know enough of hate
To say that for destruction ice
Is also great
And would suffice.

David's stomach catching briefly, the words still echoed in his mind. *I think I know enough of hate.* Something pulled at him from the most ancient recesses of his consciousness, and that, he'd learned, was saying something—something about the poem, something from long before. He closed his eyes and searched intently, but it lay beyond his reach, and the reach, it seemed, of every consciousness within.

The doors rattled open, and Bram stepped out and motioned David to do likewise. It felt like they'd dropped pretty far, which seemed odd, given their apparent location in the middle of the ocean.

Swallowed up, in the belly of the beast.

He followed Bram through a labyrinth of twisting hallways, passing no one, only doors and walls and paintings of strange battles, some of armies, others depicting contests between lone combatants. Some struck David as peculiar, though they were passing each so quickly he didn't have time to register any in sufficient detail. Something struck him about the weapons, though—incongruous somehow, mismatched.

At length, their path straightened, and David drew up alongside his escort, who'd paused before another locked door.

Bram punched in a code—more beeps, more whirring—but now a small, square panel drew open at face level. A pair of eyes materialized from the darkness beyond, regarding Bram at first, then David. There was no talk. The panel closed, there was a resounding pop, and the door swung inward. Bram strode forward but David hesitated, giving his eyes a moment to adjust. Bram stood just inside the doorway, awaiting him.

A dark corridor fell out before them, stone walls and floor lit only by lanterns spaced every ten feet or so, and which harkened for David those upon the drawbridge at Kane Manor. The man who'd granted their entry had receded from view, leaving only the fading clip of footsteps. Bram waited patiently as David hesitated, the similarity to Kane Manor stirring some familiar embers within him, none pleasant, yet somehow comforting. An ancient but familiar sense settled, such as had awakened within him on that fateful day beneath the eclipse, when darkness fell, but the embers of lifetimes past had sparked to life within him. This he could deal with; this he knew.

He crossed the breach, muscles tensing, eyes darting this way and that for signs of any weapon he might use. If he were to be set upon, he wanted it to be now, crazy as it seemed, that he would at least be that much closer, no matter the outcome, to some manner of resolution.

He spotted no weapons, no combatants, as Bram gestured him onward. They traversed the corridor a minute or so before the walls terminated, and the space mushroomed out into a broader expanse. He followed Bram down a set of wide, shallow steps, and saw they were not alone, as perhaps a dozen other men and women sat at various tables. David swept his gaze over each, trying to latch upon even the slightest clue or familiarity, but nothing suggested itself. He spied Christian at a center table, and saw he'd been spotted too, their host rising now to greet him.

"David Rose!" Christian extended his hand, which David shook resignedly. Christian motioned for them to sit.

Their table sat adjacent to a tall window, overlooking a stage of some sort, upon which stood a table, a few chairs, and little else. David exhaled. When he sat, his chair shifted and clanked into the window, and he glanced up sheepishly and scooted back.

"Not to worry," said Christian. "Silicon nitride, about the sturdiest transparent solid known to man. We are quite safe here."

David raised an eyebrow. "From what?"

When two servers appeared with a bounty of food and beverages, David's mouth watered. Other staff appeared and attended each table.

Christian smiled, waited until everyone had been taken care of, then turned back to David.

"They're about to begin," he said, nodding toward the window, and theater below. "And you'll see."

CHAPTER 22
A Matter of Time

THE GALLERY LIGHTS DIMMED, AND a man and woman appeared from either end of the theater below. David glanced at the other tables, where each patron dined and looked on affably.

"Isla," came from below, spoken by the man upon the stage to his counterpart.

David looked on.

"James," the woman replied.

They moved tentatively toward one another, casting uncertain glances up toward the gallery.

"What is this?" the woman asked.

The man appeared greatly distressed. "They didn't tell you." Not a question. He shook his head, and glared back up at the balcony. "I'm not surprised. Part of their game. They didn't tell me it would be you."

Isla nodded slowly. "What do they want?"

James exhaled deeply, and bent to whisper in her ear.

Her eyes widened briefly, then settled.

A moment later, they each stepped to a nearby couch, sat, and folded their arms.

"We won't do it, Christian!" James called. "You can't just kill us!"

David observed as their host lowered his glass, appearing unperturbed, and withdrew a small device from his shirt pocket. He pressed a small button, and spoke. "I have no desire to kill you. There are, however, things I can do."

David flinched at the look in his eyes, a demeanor that, for the first time, reminded him of Kane.

"Don't threaten us," Isla called. "You know what we can do."

"Oh, I do," Christian rejoined. "I most certainly do!" He returned the device to his pocket, shifted in his chair, and nodded toward the shadowed recesses of the terrace.

Toward whom, or what, David could not discern, but a moment later the stage darkened, and David felt a knot twisting inside him as he looked on.

"What is this?" James called.

The stage resolved slowly into focus, still dark, but visible, and David stared at the transforming scene. He hadn't detected any stagehands or crew of any kind, nor had there been time, but James and Isla now stood, looking bewildered, in a log cabin, by all appearances. David's mind spun, seeking to decipher it all. There were four walls, and a roof, and it was entirely enclosed, yet it remained fully visible to David, and presumably to his fellow spectators.

"James," Isla said, her voice tremulous. "What is this?"

James paced within their new space, trying the door unsuccessfully, then the lone window, also without luck. Against a near wall was propped a rifle, and James stared a moment before picking it up and turning it over in his hands. "It can't be," he muttered. "It can't be."

David eyed Christian, who leaned forward, elbows upon the table, face propped upon his open palms, like an enthralled child.

"James!" Isla had retreated to the back of the cabin. He turned and regarded her solemnly.

"Your awakening," she said. "Your first?"

"First awakenings occur in our first lifetime after death," he said. "And so on and so forth, for each lifetime after. This is something worse." He glared back up toward the gallery. "It won't work, Christian!"

"What won't?" Isla stared at him. "James?"

James moved slowly over to her, and it appeared to David that she was for the first time unnerved by his proximity.

"Incipient soul," he said. "He wants us to fight. He's baiting us, trying to provoke our instinct, our powers."

David narrowed his eyes; he could discern beads of sweat upon James' brow.

James sighed and said, "Final death comes only at the hands of one from the time of —"

"Our incipient soul," said Isla. "But I wasn't from that time, and you aren't from mine."

James nodded, but was now taking deep, deliberate breaths.

Isla exhaled as he set the rifle down and placed a hand upon the wall.

"I know," he rasped. "I know. But you know the pull, placing two immortals into the incipient time of even one...."

Isla glanced sharply up toward the gallery, but quickly returned her focus to James, who'd now doubled over, looking out the window, like a werewolf fretfully anticipating the full moon.

"Listen to me, James," she said. "Fight it. You are stronger than him... than this. We both are."

In the gallery, Christian turned and nodded once more toward the shadows.

David squinted and thought he perceived a flicker of eyeshine, and the faintest movement, a dimpling within the darkness, but then, nothing more. Something stirred distantly within him, an impression, for the time impenetrable, but there. He turned back around just as the developments below shifted again, a kaleidoscope of color and light, and when his eyes adjusted, he saw that the cabin was gone, and the immortals now teetered upon the precipice of a towering waterfall. David's eyes went to James' hands, in which the rifle from the cabin remained gripped.

"This is yours, isn't it? Isla?"

She did not at first answer. She stood, staring out over the impossible expanse, until at last, with a resigned expression, she turned to James. "Yes, my first life."

David surveyed the gallery. The guests continued to dine while watching the developments below, some conversing, but quietly, as though adhering to the etiquette of a night at the theater. David glanced back down. He was so exhausted, so consumed by his own quandary, that perhaps he was misapprehending this entire thing. Perhaps Isla and James were just actors; perhaps those weren't even their names. The transforming settings could be the work of talented engineers. Would all these people be looking on so casually, otherwise? Despite all he'd experienced, he didn't wish to believe that true. If the barbarity of this secret world to which he'd awakened were not enough, knowing others were let in on the secret was almost more than he could bear — and not other immortals, but regular people invited in. Toward what end, he was loathe to speculate. Entertainment? Profit? It struck him every bit as monstrous as anyone or anything yet.

His gaze traced back down to the rifle. Where had it come from? It hadn't been there, none of this had — not the rifle, not the cabin, not the waterfall.

Waterfall. Inside a theater.

The stage had transformed into a cabin, and the rifle appeared, in a heartbeat, a flash of light. The waterfall appeared quicker still, but there hadn't been time for stagehands to dart unnoticed onto stage and transform the setting so profoundly. It had to be technology, special effects, but... something inside him suggested otherwise. The rifle was real. He'd seen it, and saw it still. He heard it clunking against the cabin floor when James had set it down. And the waterfall... they all saw it, heard its roar. Effects, perhaps, but what of the droplets of water speckling upon the glass before him? It occurred to him that, yes, actually, it too could be an elaborate effect. Today's theme parks had stuff like that, after all. It also occurred to him that he could simply inquire.

He glanced at Christian, who had just sipped from and set back down his glass of wine. How much could he trust in the answer he might receive?

Below, the two immortals squared off on the sloping rim of the waterfall.

"Isla?" James said.

David stared as Isla withdrew a tapered dagger from the folds of her clothing.

James took a step backwards, mindful of his footing. "Where did you get that?"

"I don't know." Her voice broke. "Same place as that." She gestured at the rifle.

James glanced up at the gallery, then back at Isla. "You're stronger than this," he said, his voice tinged with solemnity. "We both are. You said it yourself."

Isla closed her eyes, then opened them, and David felt his own grow wide as he watched her angle into a combat position: sideways, her left leg forward, right leg back, bracing, her left hand in a guard position, right hand raised high and clutching the gleaming blade.

"Isla!" James held up a hand. "Wait." When she did not alter her posture, he pointed the rifle toward the waterfall, and fired.

The report reverberated throughout the gallery, and David stared as a flock of sea birds lifted from some unseen position behind the mist and fluttered away in distress.

Isla did not stand down.

"Isla," James said again, softer this time, imploring.

David inhaled deeply as James leveled the rifle directly at her.

"I'm sorry," James said.

"I know," Isla said, scarcely a whisper. "Me too."

"Stop!"

David felt the eyes of the room upon him. He realized he'd leapt from his chair, and had locked eyes with Christian, who regarded him with an expression somewhere between surprise and contempt. The latter quickly evaporated, and David derived no solace in the grin that replaced it.

"This is unprecedented," Christian said.

Two large men with firearms and radios had appeared at the edge of the gallery, but Christian motioned them away. They glanced at one another, and receded back into shadow.

"That someone objects to you making people kill each other?" David said.

Christian arose from his chair, eyes glinting. "I continue to observe why you are my greatest prize."

"Not yours," David said.

Christian seemed to consider this, then turned to face the gallery. "My deepest apologies," he announced. He snapped, and a flurry of servants materialized from the darkness, decanters and trays in hand. "Please allow your tables to be refreshed, and the proceedings will resume shortly."

David stood, unmoving, as Christian approached.

Their host took a step closer to David, leaned down and whispered, "You cannot stop me."

"I guess we're going to find out."

They locked eyes once more, and though it occurred to David he had no weapon — not a rifle, not a dagger, not a mirror — this did nothing to diminish his resolve. He didn't know what he read in Christian's eyes, and he didn't care. He would not be a part of this spectacle. They regarded each other in this manner a few moments more, like James and Isla below, who, David imagined, were now staring up at the gallery in anticipation of what would transpire next.

At length, Christian slowly nodded, and took one step back. "As I always promise," he said, eyes still on David but addressing his guests, "you will encounter mystery and surprise. This is a new one even for me." He turned now to face the gallery. "I will make it up to you, you have my word. You will get another chance to see what you came to see. For now, please enjoy your meals, as much as you want, anything."

Silence reigned at first, but then a murmuring and chatter rose as the lights went up. Servers circulated between the tables, refilling glasses and replenishing plates.

Christian turned back to David and said, "You might have cost me a lot of money, and risked my reputation. I can't have that. You cannot forestall the inevitable. It's only a matter of time."

The theater darkened, and David wondered if they were visible to James and Isla below, or if they were still even there. Perhaps they were staring up at him, this strange new captive who'd managed, if only briefly, to throw a wrench in the wheel of this terrible machinery, this grand and ancient game in which none of them had asked to be a part. The spent droplets from the now silent waterfall trickled down the glass, thin rivulets against the darkened backdrop, and once more something stoked within David, something distant, as it had when he'd glimpsed the illusory figure disappear into the shadows minutes previous — ancient tributaries, adhering to a bygone source.

"But not this time," David said.

"So it would appear."

He detected a trace of admiration.

"As for now," Christian said, "I suggest you eat something. Then, you will join me in my office."

CHAPTER 23
Prodigal Son

HE DID NOT EAT. HE KNEW they'd bring him something if requested, but he was too amped-up to think about food. They escorted him back to the elevator, back up the rickety ascent, and back to Christian's office.

Their host, clearly by means of some more expedient transport, already awaited. "You are a young man of conviction. That is good." Christian leaned forward and clasped his hands upon his desk. "But I want you to assure me you'll cause no such disturbance again. It might cost me... in many ways."

"We don't always get what we want," David said.

Christian unclasped his hands and sat back. "Indeed." He studied David a few moments, inhaled deeply, then held out his palms. "We must come to an agreement, then. I need your cooperation. I could try to oblige it, force it out of you, but that would not bode well for either of us."

David registered vaguely that it was his turn to speak, but saw no benefit in doing so. He surveyed the office: family photos, framed certificates, a variety of coffees and liquors, and on a far wall some sort of Smartboard. The trappings of a well-off businessman, but nothing here indicated any devotion to immortality, ancient feuds, or dark worlds. Yet this man had obviously discovered these worlds and staked his claim. He didn't *seem* as threatening as Kane, or Merlin, or even Donovan, but there was something unnerving about his demeanor, so confident as to be almost casual, so long as his business remained unthreatened, anyway. Business—David and all like him walked a razor's edge in this immortal contest, calamity always a breath away, but this man had leveraged all this, exploited and mined it, all for his own gain.

No, David did not feel obliged toward friendly banter.

"There must be," Christian said at length, "something that you want."

David regarded him. "I think you know."

Christian appeared exasperated. "You know I can't do that. I have never permitted anyone to leave here. It would ruin everything."

"For you."

Christian's eyes smoldered, but rather than alarm David, it heartened him. Their host had, until now, been the picture of assurance. He was frustrated now, angry. Anger, David had learned, so often bespoke fear, and both, vulnerability. He'd seen it in himself, and in others, and for the first time since being abducted to this place, he was seeing it in Christian.

"I've worked too hard to allow that." Christian leaned forward again. "There must be something else."

In his mind, David saw again the figure in the gallery who'd receded into shadow, the fiery eyes, if eyes they were—the fade to darkness. It reminded him of someone... something... but how to remember, when memories in this phantom world trailed away like rain on a window, formidable enough to sift the reservoir of one lifetime, much less many. It might be nothing, but it might not.

"Yeah," he answered at length, absently rubbing his wrist. "There is."

***

DAVID HADN'T COME HOME.

Rachel waited for what seemed forever, until her father had emerged from his study and spied her at the window. He'd begun to admonish her for being up at such an hour, but had quickly seen the anguish on his daughter's face, and rushed to her and asked what was happening. She'd explained everything, best as she could, and though she couldn't say whether he believed any of it — the immortal stuff — he'd scooped her up and taken her outside and into their car, and they'd driven to the cemetery, parked, and looked feverishly about.

They did not find him, nor encounter another living soul. Rachel was not surprised. She could feel it, the moment they'd arrived there, that her brother was gone, that something bad had happened. Her father had reassured her that it wasn't *that* late, not for a teenager in summertime, and said not to be surprised if David was home by the time they returned.

He wasn't.

She protested when her father escorted her up to bed, so that he could make some phone calls, but she heard in his voice and read in his eyes that it was pointless to argue. This upset her briefly, but then something else began to suggest itself within her, something that for the first time in a long time gave her a flicker of hope, despite how worried she was about David. She couldn't remember the last time her father had seemed so... well... alive. Even after he'd tucked her in and kissed her forehead and promised her things would be okay; even after she heard him bounding down the stairs and to his office to make phone calls; she could still hear the urgency in his voice.

She heard him calling David's friends — one by one — to see if he was there. When he wasn't, her father called the police to report David missing. She felt a tear rolling down her cheek, though she hadn't expected him to be with any of his friends. Something had happened, she just knew. She stared into the vast darkness of her unlit room; her father had forgotten to turn on her nightlight, but she wasn't upset. In her mind, she saw again the fire in his eyes, and slowly, it lit her room like a candle, and with it, her heart.

Mama was gone, and now David, but her father had at long last returned. As she dabbed her cheek with her shirtsleeve and closed her eyes, she felt a smile upon her lips, because she had remembered something else just then too. There were other friends of David that would be looking for him, friends her father hadn't called.

They were out there, and, she believed with all her heart, they knew.

**

CHRISTIAN DID NOT READILY AGREE.

He wasn't sure they'd finished examining the watch, and even then, he was reticent about returning it.

"Examining it?" David questioned. "It's a watch."

They went back and forth, but Christian at last relented and dialed another of his surrogates. Within minutes, there came a knock upon the door.

"Ambrose," called Christian. "Come in."

David did not turn around, but felt the new presence immediately. He heard the door close, and the man who'd entered sidled up alongside him.

"Meet David Rose," said Christian.

Ambrose extended a hand and David took it, unenthused. The man before him did not look as he'd anticipated, not that he'd anticipated much—just, not this. He was well-attired, with slightly graying, neatly combed hair, and wore glasses. Hard to guess his age, as something about him just looked—

"Mr. Rose," Christian said, "would like his watch."

Ambrose lowered into an adjacent chair. "And we wish to oblige him?"

"You tell me."

"I haven't found anything," Ambrose said. "Yet." He trained his gaze upon David. "But sometimes it is not the magic of the vessel alone, but the vessel in the hands of him chosen to wield it."

"Duly noted," Christian said. He turned to David. "Ambrose is our wizard," he said. "Any and all things technological or mechanical. No one better, and well-studied in the ways of *your* world."

David did not reply. It was Ambrose, he now presumed, who occupied the private office behind which he'd heard such commotion. Perhaps that explained why he'd anticipated a different appearance, dirty and disheveled, like an oil-stained mechanic scooting out from beneath a car.

"You've examined it thoroughly?" inquired Christian. "I retain unshakeable confidence in your abilities. If there were something, you'd have found it. I think we can grant this one concession."

"That world of which you speak," said Ambrose, "does not favor concession, but turns, in a heartbeat, upon advantage." He faced Christian. "I do not advise you relinquish yours."

David remained silent, taking in this exchange, which intrigued him far beyond the matter of dissenting colleagues. He wanted his watch back because it was from his mother—sacred. Clearly, though, these men, who'd constructed an empire on their expertise of such matters, suspected something greater.

"Your wisdom is appreciated, as always," Christian said. "I am demonstrating no small measure of good will for our young charge."

"Not so young," said Ambrose.

"Nevertheless."

The two men regarded each other. Ambrose finally grunted, shifted in his chair, and withdrew something from an interior pocket. He extended a closed hand to David, but then paused.

"I am keenly aware of your powers," he said, searching David's eyes. "But I dare say you are woefully oblivious to mine."

David glanced at Christian, who'd raised an eyebrow at this remark, then returned his focus to Ambrose.

"Don't be so sure," David said.

Ambrose conjured a grin, then dropped the watch into David's open palm.

"Well then," Christian said. "It appears our prodigal son possesses keen powers of observation himself. He must have seen you in the gallery."

"Indeed."

Ambrose did not turn from David, who studied him in turn, wondering—and presuming so—if Ambrose was experiencing the same epiphany. Maybe not epiphany, maybe *Presque vu*, like Marcel had taught him—tip of the tongue. He knew this man, somehow, and not just from the gallery. He felt eyes upon him as he slid the watch back upon his wrist, as though bracing for a transformation. He found himself bracing too, but

as the watch settled snug into place against his skin...
nothing. Only a quiet reassurance settled in the
nethermost reaches of his heart, like a whisper he alone
could hear.

"See now," said Christian. "Nothing to fear."

"Sometimes," said Ambrose, glancing from Christian
back to David, "that which we ought to fear most resides
not in what we've found, but what we haven't."

Christian sighed. "Truly, my old friend, my respect
for you is boundless, but prone you are to the dark side
of things. Lighten up. All I've done is extend a courtesy
to Mr. Rose here."

After a few uncomfortable silent moments, Christian
asked his wizard to escort David back to his room.

They strode silently until Ambrose paused suddenly
near an exit, and turned to David.

"Come," he said, pushing open the door. "Let us
walk."

CHAPTER 24
Servant of God

"I KNOW WHO YOU ARE," DAVID SAID.

"Of course, you do." Ambrose turned and looked far out along the muted sea.

The moon perched high and oblong above them, bifurcating the inky waters in its glimmering wake. Somewhere a seabird called, unrequited. As David's eyes traced down toward the shoreline, he noticed a long, irregular tract of timber — strange, he thought, to be rooted as it appeared, in sand and sea. As his eyes adjusted and the parcel resolved into greater clarity, he recognized it as a rather copious mangrove forest. The tangled expanse fell out in either direction as far as he could see. It vaguely reminded him of Kane Manor, of the drawbridge and moat. Although there was no comparison in terms of physical presentation, something else struck him as akin, and it occurred to him that in both instances, the bodies in question, however divergent in appearance and design, nonetheless served as formidable blockades. The island had other points and ports of access, clearly, but this was hardly one. It was impressive, though — beautiful, if somewhat eerie, especially at nighttime, spiraling endlessly away within the spectral wash of moonlight.

Ambrose stepped farther away, until obscured by shadow.

David stared as Ambrose's silhouette began to shudder, seize, and spasm. He took a step forward, instinctively wanting to assist, but then stopped. If anyone needed help in this moment, it wasn't Ambrose.

It wasn't Ambrose.

When the figure turned back about, David saw in the pale slip of moonlight that which he'd expected, not that it helped. The crimson orbs seared into him, as they had in the cave mere months ago. The suit had vanished, and in its place flowed the dark robes of the baneful wizard. The neatly coiffed hair now hung long and wild beneath a familiar hood. David's eyes widened as Merlin reached into his cloak and withdrew his wand. He cursed himself for being unprepared, for assuming the wizard wouldn't dare attack his employer's prize possession. *How could you be so stupid?*

Merlin stepped from the shadows and leveled his wand, illuminated darkly in the spill of moonlight that drifted through the foliage and shrouded them in a cauldron of shadow and light. The periphery of trees loomed skeletal and tall behind the ancient wizard, like fiendish disciples.

David felt for his sword, but he had none; nor did he possess the mirror. He glanced about, searching frantically for anything he could use. He thought to flee, but vanquished the notion; he was done running. His jaw clenched as he observed Merlin's wand beginning to kindle and spark, as it had in the cave, at Tintagel. No Malea to save him now, no Marcel; only him, however many he might be able to summon.

Come on. He closed his eyes in desperate concentration. *Come on.*

When he opened his eyes, only the two of them stood, opposed like gunslingers in imminent confrontation.

"In this most fateful of moments," the wizard sneered, "this is your best? Petrified like these trees that bear witness?"

David closed his eyes once more, and an amalgam of images danced across the reel of his mind: Lancelot, Duncan, even the warrior he'd channeled — or who had channeled him — that day with Cerratus. They churned deep within him, and he fought desperately to summon them, that they might afford him a fighting chance. Yet the more he focused, the more the images dispersed, revving up but ultimately flooding away like an engine that just wouldn't start. He opened his eyes, assumed an instinctive fighting position, and braced for the inevitable.

Merlin's wand hued blood red.

The first salvo came not of the singular, laser-beam variety David expected, and had before witnessed, but more of a rat-a-tat-tat volley — fast, but fractured just enough for him to maneuver to meet it. He swept up his left arm, crooked at the elbow, to parry the fire, and watched with rapt eyes as his fingertips welled blue and the fiery bombardment dispersed at his touch.

The great wizard paused ever so briefly, first in astonishment, then contempt, before continuing his assault.

This blast issued forth in the manner David had expected, a twisting, fiery rope, and his body swung forward to meet it, his arms now parallel to each other, palms open. He repelled the offensive as he had the first, and now braced for the next, but Merlin had paused and thrust his wand skyward. Short currents pulsed from his weapon, puncturing the darkness, and David stared incredulously, palms still outstretched, as a cleft seemed to open in the heavens.

A shower of voltage rained down, fusing with Merlin's fire in spectacular conflux. The sorcerer's wand flared white and, with a flick of his wrist, he severed the connection, and leveled his weapon at David once more. "Son of Benwick!" he bellowed. "In the incarnation of your beginning, prepare now to meet your end."

"Myrddin," David heard himself call in a voice he knew but did not recognize. "Son of the devil, servant of God, could it be my origins have escaped even you?"

For the first time, something resembling fear flashed in the wizard's eyes, but only for a heartbeat. Merlin flicked his wrist and unleashed his next onslaught.

This one surged toward David with impossible dispatch, blasting him backwards through the air. He landed and rolled back to his feet, scorched and stunned but in full-on survival mode, at the ready with whatever he had left.

Merlin swept toward him, robes trailing like some ghoulish bird of prey. When he'd come close enough that David could feel the heat of his wand, Merlin directed the weapon a final time.

David thrust out his hands—nothing else he could do—but as he observed the smoldering wand, it was the heat searing through his own fingers which now arrested his attention. He grunted—this was new, and it *hurt*—and fought to steady his hands as Merlin's next blast issued forth.

It never reached him.

David gasped as thin, blue wires pulsed from his fingertips, funneling into a vast arrowhead of luminescence that enveloped and extinguished the incoming fire.

Merlin stared in disbelief at the fading shockwaves, and immediately discharged another volley.

This time, David felt the emanation from deep within him, and braced as the firebolt coursed from his fingertips. It bored straight through the oncoming beam and into the chest of his adversary, who rocketed backwards in a brume of smoke and light. The wand flew from his hand, and David dodged an extraneous salvo as the hallowed weapon fell to the earth. He took a step forward, hesitated, then continued to where Merlin lay, the electricity still pulsing within him. The sensation unnerved him, feeling as though he might spontaneously combust.

He inhaled deeply, and let it out in small, controlled breaths. He felt things simmering down within him, but remained poised, should the great conjurer summon another attack. Who said Merlin needed a wand? The most fabled wizard in history might retain at his fingertips any number of terrible powers. David glanced at his own, still outstretched hands, which had returned at last to normal.

Merlin coughed violently and brushed smoke and bits of charred garments from his body.

David's eyes shot wide upon spying the baseball-sized crater smoldering at the center of Merlin's chest, surprised at the remorse it evoked within him. The wizard had tried to kill him, but that reality did little to stem the guilt. He wasn't in this to kill anyone; he just wanted to get home.

He tensed as Merlin propped himself up on his elbows and clutched at his chest. Perhaps another weapon lay cloaked within the still smoldering robes, but no. The wizard passed his palm slowly over the grievous wound, then again, and again. An incandescence began to form around the injury, a rosette of emerald light beneath which the laceration slowly closed and returned to color. What happened next was even stranger: Merlin extended a hand to David, imploring help.

David started to reach out, then paused, fearing this almost certainly must be a trick, designed to ensnare him or electrocute him or God only knew what. Somewhere within him, though, upon those faltering strongholds of what once was, his mother's voice called to him. *'Be kind,'* she would always tell them. She always gave to panhandlers, and one time he'd asked her if she really thought they'd use the money to help themselves.

She'd stopped and put her hands on his shoulders. *'Maybe, maybe not, but it is never wrong to show compassion.'*

'Even if you get burned,' he'd persisted, 'and then you've lost your money for nothing?'

She'd smiled, eyes glinting. *'Even then. Especially then. The moment we condition our kindness upon what we will or won't get in return... is the moment we have lost ourselves.'*

He extended his hand.

When Merlin closed his around it, David flinched in fevered anticipation of that which never came—no jolt, no voltage, no trick... for now, anyway. He widened his stance and pulled with all his strength, and when Merlin reached his feet, David stepped back warily.

"Fear not," the wizard said. "You have done well... greater than anticipated." He brushed more fragments from his cloak, then nodded toward David's hands. "That was new."

"No kidding," David said.

"You spoke to me," said Merlin.

"What?"

"Lancelot. You spoke from your incipient soul, but you said something...."

David nodded. "My origins."

"What did you mean?"

David held out his hands and Merlin flinched, ever so slightly. "I've no idea."

Merlin took a deep breath. "Well, another layer in the mystery of this grand game. A foremost one, I would say."

"What is this?" David asked. "This now. What are we doing?"

"We are speaking," Merlin said.

"Yeah, and a minute ago you were trying to kill me."

"In fact, no. Testing you. Imperative that I gauge your readiness."

"For what?"

"You know why you're here, yes? This place? Here, immortals are pitted versus one another for wager, for sport—extravagance and greed." Merlin's voice dripped with disdain. "It was prohibited, of course, by the Elders. To defile our world so wantonly... it is a sacrilege."

"Then why are you a part of it?"

The great sorcerer looked down, then to the heavens, and back to David. "We are many, but we live one life at a time, one world. We must find our way, and make our way, in each, accordingly. Why should the likes of our prosperous host enjoy all the trappings?"

"So that's it? You serve him so you can reap the benefits of those very things you just called out?"

"I do not serve him," said Merlin, tersely. "He knows not my true identity. I remain here in vigilance, that they do not, through this enterprise, disrupt the order of things." He narrowed his eyes. "That the likes of you are not prevented, ultimately, from your destiny."

"I just want to find my mom."

"One in the same," Merlin replied.

"What are you saying?"

"That you must survive, that you must prevail in this forbidden tournament."

"I won't do it," said David. "I'm not here to fight."

"You are no longer a boy!" thundered the great wizard. "We must act in our best interest, do whatever is required in fulfillment of our destiny."

"I'll do what is right."

"And you shall bear the consequences." Merlin began peering about at the ground on either side of him.

"Yes," said David. When Merlin turned around, still searching, David quickly stepped a few feet to his left.

"I could do it, you know," said Merlin. "I could kill you."

"I know," said David. "You tried to, at Tintagel."

Merlin waved his hand in dismissal. "Mere theatrics. It was not ordained that I be the one to vanquish you. Besides, *she* interfered." He scowled at the recollection of Malea.

"So, Kane is your true master?"

Merlin scoffed. "He would only wish."

"Then who?"

"You said it yourself."

"I don't know what I said. It gets weird when I'm him, when I'm... others—dreamlike."

"Son of the devil—"

"Servant of God."

"So it is said." Merlin resumed his search. At length he paused, shook his head, and whirled back to David with an outstretched hand. "You hold something of mine."

David withdrew the wand he'd pocketed when the wizard's back had been turned. "So, you can change your mind, and really kill me this time?"

"Boy," hissed Merlin, "hand it over. You couldn't begin to know how to wield its powers."

"Maybe not. Maybe I could just destroy it."

A blend of fear and anger lit across Merlin's features, realizing his destiny now resided in David's hand, which gripped the tool with which Merlin had for centuries forged his own destiny.

"What do you want?"

"An answer," said David.

Their eyes locked.

David continued. "Who do you serve?"

Merlin's eyes filled with tortured contemplation, as though his very soul listed upon the precipice of the matter.

But now, David heard his mother's words — 'keep faith' — and he extended the wand, knowing full well that his faith in this instance could cost him everything.

Merlin hesitated ever briefly, eying him, then nodded in acknowledgement and accepted the hallowed object.

David exhaled as the wizard returned the implement to the folds of his cloak.

Merlin turned slowly around, looking skyward, and said, "You inquire after that which I cannot answer."

"We always have a choice."

When Merlin turned back, he was Ambrose again, compete with impeccable suit and impeccable hair, suggesting not the slightest hint of his identity a moment previous. He nodded and said only, "Time will tell."

CHAPTER 25
A Sound of Thunder

DAVID SLEPT POORLY, HIS DREAMS fleeting and fitful and belonging to many, unsettling in ways different than usual. For so long his slumber had plagued him with the harrowing notion that someone — or something — was after him, ancient and sinister and unrelenting, but at last he'd discovered who and what that was.

Or so he'd thought; this had been different, as though the dreams themselves were haunted, pursued inescapably by some phantom huntsman of a time and world beyond all reckoning.

He'd no idea what awaited him today, but was glad to have gotten out of bed and dress. He now sat at the desk and waited. He glanced at his watch; someone would arrive soon with breakfast, most likely, and the day's itinerary. In the otherwise silent, still room, he rapped his fingers upon the desk. Waiting — for anything — had come to be an abomination.

He rose and went to the door, put his ear to it and, hearing nothing, straightened and knocked loudly upon the door, reasonably certain he'd never done so from inside a room. When after several moments no one had come, he tried the doorknob, knowing it would be futile, but it turned fully and the door yanked open. He stumbled backwards in surprise. It occurred to him this was no mistake — more likely a trap, or test, or anything other than good fortune—but it would not deter him.

He stepped from the room, glanced to either side and, seeing no one, headed off to the right.

Cameras everywhere, but so be it.

The corridor curved and he traversed it briskly, shielding his eyes when the east-facing windows fell out before him. A patchwork of violet clouds lingered beneath a dome of morning light.

Only after rounding a few more corridors did he glimpse another soul. The space opened into a generous expanse, by all appearances part cafeteria and part rec room. He stopped and took it in.

A few dozen people—a few staff and the rest... well... others, presumably like him—sat at tables, eating. Others sat in plush chairs, reading or conversing. A few played video games, and some even Ping-Pong. Some appeared to be about his age; others, in their twenties and thirties; some middle-aged; and even a handful of senior citizens.

David frowned, in consideration of how long they'd been here, but none seemed in obvious distress. Rather, they engaged in their respective activities as though at their local eatery or community center.

A few had paused in their activity, including one or two with utensils lifted to their mouths, and peered over at him. He felt like a kid hesitating in the doorway on his first day at a new school. He watched as a girl rose from one of the chairs, set down her book, and headed his way. She had dark, short-cropped hair, and hazel eyes that glinted in the sweep of morning light.

"Hi," she said upon reaching him, and extended a hand. "I'm Dani."

He took her hand. "David."

"Getting something to eat?"

"Just exploring," he said.

They went back to where she'd been sitting, and he sat in a chair adjacent hers and looked about.

Two individuals rose from a nearby table where they'd been playing chess, and approached — a slender young man with brown hair and green, narrowed eyes, and an olive-skinned girl with striking black eyes who looked no older than fourteen.

"Finally win one?" Dani inquired of the man.

He snorted. "Please."

The girl smiled. "Closer this time, though. You're getting better each day."

"Yes, Harlan, stick to it," a new voice said. "A much safer battleground for you."

Another male and female, of similar age and appearance to one another, had sidled up, the male having issued the taunting remark.

Harlan glanced over his shoulder, but did not turn around. "Mind your business, Valori."

"But you're my business," said the young man, shouldering his way past.

The woman snickered and followed her companion.

"Didn't you see?" asked Valori. "You get me tomorrow, and I'm gonna leave you lying."

"Why don't you keep on walking," David said, rising from his chair.

The pair looked him up and down, and the man said, "Another county heard from. Maybe I'll warm up with you."

David took a step forward.

"Thanks," said Harlan, stepping in. "But I've got this. You know the rules, Valori. Walk away."

"Come on," said the woman, smirking. "You'll have your way tomorrow."

The man glared at Harlan, and then David, but finally nodded. "That I will."

When they'd sauntered off, Harlan turned back to David. "Thanks, but no sense anyone else being on the wrong side of those two." He extended a hand. "Harlan Phillips."

"David Rose."

Surprise, then recognition, lit across Harlan's face. "I've heard about you."

"Nice to meet you," David said. He turned to the girl, who took his hand and smiled.

"Ruhi Khatri. It's wonderful to meet you," she said. "Even if it has to be here." She turned to Dani. "We're going for a bite. Wanna come?"

"Maybe in a little bit." Dani glanced at David.

"You sure?" asked Harlan. "We can wait."

Ruhi looked from David to Dani and smiled. "She's sure. Maybe we'll see you in a bit."

"Nice to meet you." David stood until they'd disappeared into the cafeteria, then sat back down. "Friends?"

Dani smiled. "Yeah. Important to have some, in a place like this."

"What is this place?"

"This island? Is that what you mean?" She looked pained.

"I know what the island is," David said, "and why we're here, but I mean *this* place. This room. What are we doing? Yard time at the prison?"

"No, no," Dani said. "Not quite so bad. We can come and go pretty much as we please."

"But not really."

She looked down. "Not really."

David felt instantly remorseful. She was young, like him, and while he didn't know her story, she was here, and so he knew it was, doubtless, punctuated by pain.

"What are you reading?"

She looked up, and smiled. "Bradbury. Short stories. Just finished a good one: *A Sound of Thunder.* Heard of it?"

"I think. Maybe."

She nodded. "Cool story, set in the future — time travel and all that, back to the time of dinosaurs. Kind of a look at how altering the past, even accidentally and in small ways, can dramatically alter the future. One of the characters explains how if even one mouse is killed in the past, his future mouse family won't live, and the same for animals that would have preyed on them, and stuff like that, and so on and so on, until the death of that one mouse might mean generations of people who were to come would, instead, never exist."

"Sounds cool."

Dani nodded. "Yeah. At the end, the main character looks at the bottom of his boot and sees he had stepped on a butterfly when he went off the path they were supposed to stick to, and realizes the present he has returned to has been altered in some awful ways."

"Ah, the Butterfly Effect. I've heard of that."

"Well, similar, I think, but I think that actually kind of referred to weather and things like that. Like how a butterfly flapping its wings in Mexico can trigger other random events and end up causing a hurricane in the Caribbean."

David nodded, and his gaze traveled across the large room, through the large windows and to the sea. "I think I like the story better."

"Yeah?"

"I can't let myself believe in random things," David said. "Not since... not since all this. Random events... twists of fate...." He nodded toward the book in her hand. "I'll take that. Even if bad stuff happened, at least it occurred because of what they chose."

Dani considered this as she gazed toward the window, her eyes reflecting the sunlight. "But it was accidental. He didn't step on the butterfly on purpose. He didn't plan on the chain reaction that followed."

"He left the path though, yes?" David shrugged. "That's a choice."

"That's a choice."

They fell silent. David shifted in his chair and cracked his knuckles, while Dani flipped absently through the book.

At length, she looked back up, and her gaze met his, searching. "What about all this? Us... this immortality thing... we didn't ask for this, didn't choose it."

David leaned forward in his chair. "I know. Well, maybe we did, though not us — not this us, anyway. But you're right. We didn't."

"So," Dani said. "Are they right then? Is all this predestined? Fate we can't avoid?"

"It's possible, but that doesn't mean we give up. Were still us, here and now, and even if we didn't choose this, we can still make choices, however small. If someone long ago foretold our every move, then so be it. We may never know. But hell if I'm going to sit back and wait for whatever's next." He exhaled, and sat back in the chair.

"So to speak." Dani smiled.

He regarded her quizzically a moment, then grinned. "So to speak."

She set the book on the arm of the chair and leaned forward. "You're planning something, aren't you?"

"I don't know. Maybe. I have to do something."

Her gaze traveled across the room and out the windows, to the sprawling ocean beyond. "What can you do?"

"Maybe nothing." He looked down a moment, and then back over to the cafeteria. "Your friends... what can they do? What are their abilities? What are yours?"

Dani looked solemn. "Abilities? I don't usually think of things that way."

"How do you think of them?"

"I just think in terms of who I was, who I've been, who I am now."

"Okay," David said. "I get it, but each of those people had powers, correct? Abilities. Yes?"

"I suppose so. Everybody does, but I just think of them as people living their lives."

David nodded. "Admirable, but Christian thinks of them—of us—as assets, instruments of profit. That's why he has these duels. He's making a fortune."

A faraway look glazed over Dani's features.

"Dani," David said. "What can they do, your friends? What can you do?"

"Harlan duels tomorrow," she said, quietly. "Like you heard. You'll see. It's pretty impressive, but we are worried. Valori is dangerous—him and his sister."

"That was his sister?"

"Yeah, twins—a rarity in the immortal world. They protect each other fiercely."

David looked down. "That part I understand."

"You have siblings?"

He looked back up. "A sister."

Dani smiled. "Older or younger?"

"Younger."

"Pretty protective of her?"

He swallowed. "I try."

She studied him. "At any rate, the duels are one on one. Those are the rules. So at least they can't gang up on someone."

"There are no rules," David said. "Not in this world. People like Christian think there are, but there aren't. Even if there were, most would follow only one rule: kill or be killed."

"Is that the rule you follow?"

He bit his lip, looked away, then back. "I don't know. Maybe, but not because of this game, not because of this destiny, not because of some prophecy, and definitely not because of some tournament."

"Then why?" Her voice fell quiet. "Have you killed anyone?"

"No," he said. "Well, yes, maybe. I think. Not me — not *this* me — but you know... other ones. I think I may have then."

Dani nodded, eyes glistening. "I think I have too. It's a hard thing."

"Yeah."

They were quiet a spell.

"Ruhi?" David said, at length. "What can she do?"

Dani clasped her hands together. "No one knows for sure. She is not yet awakened."

David furrowed his brow. "Really? Then why is she here? How did they even know?"

"Some immortals are so powerful that they just exude it. Abilities, as you say. Something about them just makes you know — or at least sense — how special they are. Couldn't you tell already with her?"

David nodded slowly. "Has she dueled yet? Has Christian tried to awaken her?"

"Not yet. She's not quite of age, but almost. Her birthday is in just a few weeks."

"He'll make a spectacle of it," David said. "He'll charge a fortune for a chance to see an awakening."

"We want to try to be there for her," said Dani. "When it happens, we don't want her to be alone."

"You shouldn't want it to happen at all—not here, not like this."

"Why?" Dani studied him. "You seem like you know."

"I do." He met her eyes. "What about you?"

A small grin crept across her features. "Do you really want to know?"

He followed her over to a section of window, where their reflections glinted back at them. David glanced at himself briefly, then at her, and when he saw her smiling, he looked down. She was so pretty, and so kind, and he felt guilty for feeling this way, and felt guilty for the guilt. He should not presume in the slightest that Amanda would be jealous if she knew. She was not his. Not anyone's.

"You ready?" Glass Dani looked at glass him.

"Sure." He peered through their images out to sea, wondering just what it was he should be looking for.

"Not out there," Dani whispered. "Look at me."

David felt his eyes widen as her reflection vanished in the glass, but before he could process this, a new image appeared—a woman, but older, taller, with blonde hair and a gown that seemed of some bygone era. Before he could hazard a guess about her, she disappeared, and another woman hovered in her place, this one heavier set, dark-complected and wearing gold-rimmed spectacles. She too vanished as quickly as she'd appeared, replaced by a black male, older, maybe seventy or so. No sooner did David's eyes register him than he too faded, replaced by another.

Many more appeared—male, female, younger, older, of disparate races and years—a muster-call the likes of which he'd never seen. They flashed past like one of those rapid-flipping-picture books, which you couldn't properly reckon by any one image, but rather by the evolving composite of all.

When at last it stopped, and Dani once again grinned back at him, David turned to her in appreciation. "How do you do that?"

She shrugged. "I couldn't begin to tell you. I guess that's my ability, as you might say—one of them, anyway—being able to see who I was."

"Impressive."

Dani smiled in an almost melancholy way. "It can be overwhelming, but amazing, too. To be able to find yourself like that...." She turned to him. "I can help others do it, too, if you want."

"I'd like that," he said. "I can see how it would be both: amazing to discover other lives, but overwhelming to keep it all straight, to keep track of which one you are, which one you were, and to make sure you stay who you are." He furrowed his brow and glanced her way. "Does that make sense?"

She nodded and said, "The eyes... remember that. They say the eyes are the window to your soul, which was never truer than with an immortal. They might be a different color, maybe a different shape, but that certain gleam endures from one lifetime to the next." She offered a faint smile. "The eyes always tell."

He began to reply, but stopped. He glanced at Dani and could see in her eyes that she felt it too—it had grown suddenly cold, not so much physically as... well, on the inside. A chill spiraled up his spine. From the corner of his eye, he perceived a shadow encroaching, but before he could turn to discover its origin, Dani nudged him.

"Don't," she whispered. "Just keep looking straight ahead."

He did, through the windows and to the sea, which fell out to the edge of his vision, a vast and cobalt country, undulant and glimmering beneath a fiery, rising sky.

Upon this glinting theater now trespassed a darkly attired figure, expressionless and pale, with eyes that seemed not to reflect the slightest radiance from the incandescent break of day.

David waited until he'd stalked past, and the curdling gloom within him had ebbed, before turning to his new friend.

"Gallows," Dani said, before he could inquire. "Caleb Gallows. Everyone steers clear of him. They won't even make eye contact."

David raised an eyebrow. "Why? I know any immortal can be dangerous, but what's so special about him?"

Dani frowned. "Tell me about your awakening."

"My awakening? Sure, but aren't you going to explain—"

"Just tell me. Where was it? What were the circumstances?"

"Tintagel," David said. "Cornwall, the UK. Associated with—"

"Arthur," Dani interjected with a smile. "Most of us here know, or at least discovered it, when we heard you were coming. I mean the moment itself, your awakening... what was it like?"

He turned back to the window, his gaze traveling back out to sea, as if to that hallowed time and place. "Wondrous, frightening, exhilarating, overwhelming... like darkness and light all at once, courage and fear, confidence and uncertainty, power and vulnerability. Hope." He glanced at her. "It was during the eclipse, so vivid from where we were. Darkness, but then such light...."

She touched his arm, and nodded. "That's beautiful. Mine was similar. Not the eclipse, I mean, but everything you described. Fear and darkness, yes. Uncertainty, but so much possibility and light." She turned around and gestured toward the assortment of immortals. "Same with them, every one I've ever talked to, anyway."

David nodded. "So...."

"So," Dani said, turning back to him. "Everyone but Caleb. We've heard he's a draugr, of Norse legend — a revenant, an again walker. They're reputed to live in their graves, living in mortal bodies but having returned from death, and having come from it — "

"A ghost." David narrowed his eyes.

"Perhaps. His awakening was dark, violent, blighted."

"How?"

"It wasn't like ours," Dani said, "not borne of light, or life." She looked down for a few seconds, then lifted her gaze back to his. "He was killed, murdered in cold blood. He was just a youth. That's when he awakened. That's how. In death."

"That's rough," David said. "It sounds awful, but what does all that mean? How does it make him different? Why does everyone steer clear?"

"They're afraid," Dani said, looking out the window. "No one wants to draw his name in the tournament. People think it's just a matter of time before Christian makes us...."

"Makes us what?" He swallowed hard. "Dani?"

She turned back to him with glistening eyes. "Battle to the death. It's coming. We can all feel it. Ruhi has foreseen it."

David nodded. "I wouldn't be surprised. I'll do all I can to stop it, but still, Caleb.... Why —"

"If it's a fight to the death," Dani said, grabbing his arm, "who worse to find standing opposite you in that arena than one who was born from death itself?"

CHAPTER 26
Divine Instrument

NO MATTER THAT HE'D SEEN IT countless times through the millennia, the evening moon above the clouds never failed to beguile him. He shook the moisture from his wings and gazed out across the billowing nebula, which rolled out before him like a chimerical sea. He hovered in place, waiting, until the sound of his own wingbeats was joined by those of another.

"A bit extreme, my friend?" chided his associate upon reaching him. The new arrival mopped the moisture from his brow, having likewise just breached the cloud-cover.

"They possess extraordinary technologies. We cannot be too careful. These are extreme times, brother."

"How many times have we said that?"

He gazed at the moon, at the vault of space splayed out beyond it, at the stars and moons and worlds beyond, as though he might in some way glean the answer from that incalculable expanse.

"Many," he acknowledged. "For many times it has been." He returned his attention to his friend. "Yet at no time greater than present."

"Then why tarry here, when our enemies stand ever closer to the prize?"

"Closer, but not yet there. If we assemble in defense of the site, then we've given the site away."

His friend grunted and cast his gaze far along the gauzy labyrinth. "So be it, then. Why sit back awaiting the inevitable? Why not bring the fight to them?"

"You know well why.'" He thrashed a wing in agitation. "It is not our fight to bring. We will fight if so compelled, if the order of things becomes threatened, if those to whom we are forsworn require it."

"Then what of the boy? Do we have a bearing?"

He inhaled deeply. He'd lived long enough to remember when the continent below was a hotbed of migration, long enough to remember when the continents were aligned far differently. His friend was right—countless were the times they'd confronted peril—and he'd learned eons ago to maintain a distance from his charges, a critical dispassion borne not despite compassion but because of it, so that sentiment would not cloud judgment when the fate of the many hung in the balance.

But this was a Lightkeeper, the last.

And there was something else yet, something he'd shared with no one, for not even he, who'd seen the world in its becoming, and seen it become an eternal battleground between darkness and light, could be quite certain. He'd seen generations of good souls, and Lightkeepers themselves, rise and fall, touched by the divine spark that kindled all they held sacred, that for which they fought. They had emboldened their fight, and though he'd regarded each with the greatest solemnity for their bravery and sacrifice, even then he'd understood them to be but instruments—like himself—in this epic contest for the soul of the world. He would honor, but never become attached.

And yet....

Within David Rose resided a light of its own incipience, modest but unwavering, hardly outshining that divine fire that had been conferred, nor being conflated or consumed. His lineage included some of the greatest warriors of all time, but the boy cared little for any of it. Be as he might a divine instrument in this fight for the ages, endowed with powers of countless lifetimes, but that remained of scant interest to the boy. David Rose, he'd come to understand, did not regard himself — would not — as any such instrument. Rather, David would, in time, wield these abilities as instruments in the fight that mattered most to him: protecting his sister, finding his mother, and reuniting his family. He'd seen the fire in the boy's eyes when it came to the girl, and it was unlike any he'd glimpsed in the mortal world. A kid looking out for his sister — not something instructed, bestowed, or ordained, but simply something within — and from this devotion emanated an unequivocal incandescence.

It was this light, modest but inextinguishable, that had so disarmed him in this commission. "I have an idea," he told his friend, at last. "Malea searches as we speak." He withdrew an object from the folds of his vestment. "He is, as you know, without the mirror."

"All the more reason to find him quickly. Find him, and free him, and let us get on with this."

"Wherever he is, they cannot vanquish him. And whatever his ordeal, his powers and conviction will grow. The naiad will find him, and when the time is right, so will we."

"Fine. What of the woman?"

"She lives. Kane knows full well the prophecy."

"Where does he keep her?"

"We are searching."

A blade of lightning sawed along the far ridges of the thunderhead. Then another. The cloud flared briefly in a kaleidoscope of color, like a lava lamp such as had become fashionable for the humans of today, followed by a peal of thunder.

"We have lost the woman," his companion said. "We have lost the boy. Kane nears the prize, and yet we wait?"

"We must keep faith," he said, quietly.

A strident crowing rose from below, growing louder until a formation of large fowl crested the cloud-cover and soared off, honking, above the flickering overlay below. Dark bodies, pale beaks and underbellies, gracefully negotiated these rarefied heights with slow, powerful wingbeats.

"Rüppell's griffon vultures," he said. "They flew in far greater numbers not a thousand years ago. Endangered now."

His friend appeared unmoved. "Might I remind you," he said, setting his own wings to motion and angling slightly away. "So are we."

He watched him go, soaring off with greater dispatch than had the griffons into the approaching storm. Only when he'd disappeared did he accelerate his own wingbeats, angle slightly downward, and dive back down through the fomenting vortex below.

CHAPTER 27
Provenance

HE READ IT INSTANTLY IN THE man's eyes.

This man maintained a countenance utterly distinct from those who'd entered over the interminable days and evenings previous to report his quest unrequited. This man was one of his top lieutenants, but that did nothing to disguise the abject fawning of his demeanor. He'd long-since wearied of such genuflection, but it seemed unavoidable these days—fearful and self-serving sycophants. Few remained who truly appreciated the provenance of their duty.

"We have found it, my liege." The lieutenant's eyes were rapt with anticipation. He removed his hat, mopped his brow, and shifted where he stood.

Kane removed a cigar, one of his finest, from the pocket of his flawlessly creased shirt. He studied the man—shifting and obsequious—then struck a wooden match and held the cigar at a forty-five-degree angle a few inches from the flame, rotating it methodically between his thumb and index finger. He extinguished the match with a snap of his wrist, and checked the integrity of the light.

"Thank you," Kane said.

The man appeared instantly crestfallen. He regarded Kane, fidgeted with his cap, and shifted some more, like someone expecting a tip. "Yes sir," he said at last, and executed a slight bow.

Kane narrowed his eyes. "Our work has only just begun. Finding it was merely the first step. We must extract it, possess it, and convey it to our destination. Then, and only then, shall we achieve victory."

The man settled into some manner of resignation. "Yes, my lord, but at last, it is ours."

Kane exhaled a tight plume of smoke, and examined the light once more. "Not quite yet. They are watching us."

The lieutenant's face lit hopefully. "We can handle them, master. Our forces can repel them presently, and it shall be ours in no time. Just give the word and—"

"Not them." Kane rose from behind his desk.

The man flinched and took a step backwards.

"You've done well, Lieutenant, but do not try my patience. Triple the contingent at the site, and await my orders. Leave me now."

When the man had gone, Kane stood looking at the space he'd just occupied, as though to be certain the man would not reappear. A ligature of smoke wafted across the room, gray and amber in the lamplight. He'd thought he might feel more emboldened by the news, and reckoned his temperance a result of the very perspective he'd just articulated to his lieutenant, but there was something else.

Him. The boy. Lightkeeper.

Their last encounter lingered in his mind, something beyond the obvious failure to dispatch him. He'd glimpsed in the boy's eyes an incontrovertible resolve, felt it in his grip—along with all the fear and uncertainty, even in spite of it—and understood in that moment the path to their respective destinies must again one day converge. Something in the lad's assurance had unnerved him, angered him, and he bristled now to think he'd let it. For the balance of his lifetime, he'd known that grand moment awaited, when he must lead his forces and face down their enemies. If that meant vanquishing the Lightkeeper, extinguishing all manner of insurgent immortals and the hope they kindled, he relished the opportunity. Yet the one who'd stood face to face with him at Kane Manor and returned his grip was not the Lightkeeper—not in that moment, anyway. Not the Lightkeeper and not Lancelot, nor any of the figures who'd risen through the centuries to arrive at that fateful day. They were there, unmistakably, and would in time make the boy formidable, but on that day, they'd scarcely scratched the surface. When David had met his eyes, he'd done so only with his own—just him, a boy... David Rose.

Something which should have been a trifle, an afterthought, a favorable observation: it clearly had meant the boy was not ready. He'd been unpracticed and uncertain in the channeling of past lives, and of the powers that attended them. Yes, Lancelot had risen that day beneath the eclipse, but that could be chalked up to the inevitable surge of the awakening, and perhaps even to an assist from the girl. Otherwise, things might well have been different. Yet something in all this had gotten to him, something in the boy's irreverence—his will.

Kane drew upon the cigar, held it a moment, exhaled. His time would come. For now, let the boy navigate the tribulations with his captors. Kane could have stopped them, that evening of the boy's capture. As sophisticated as Ellerby's operation was, he'd no idea what he was up against. He thought he did, but he didn't. Kane's associates had relayed to him that the boy's abduction was imminent, and he'd ordered them to hold back. He could focus more attentively on the prize with the Lightkeeper sidelined. Plus, others had been there that night, just as he'd cautioned.

Let Ellerby have him for a while. Let him bring pain to the boy.

Truth was, Ellerby's enterprise was sheer sacrilege, an abomination, and would be dealt with in time. For now, it would serve a purpose.

Kane crossed the room and stepped from his quarters into the warm and starlit night. He drew on the cigar, and it flared orange in the blackness, a dragon's eye. A latticework of stars flickered in the otherwise sightless depths of space. He spied the Big Dipper, and his gaze traced along its handle, through Polaris and down to the M-shaped constellation he knew to be Cassiopeia. There resided the telltale torso of Pegasus, of ancient lore. He smiled at the mortal way of things, ascribing mythical status to that which their minds could not fathom, and their hearts too daunted to try. What they didn't know, couldn't hurt them, or so they thought. Ignorance was bliss, a luxury he could not afford.

He drew on the cigar, held it, exhaled, and watched the smoke curl like an emancipated genie into the darkness of night. He inhaled deeply, taking in the singular bouquet of the desert—the sand and the dryness, the subtle herbal hints. He noted the smell of rain, though there was no rain, for always did it lurk in the inherent architecture of such environments, the divergent twin, as always there was, and always would there be.

He breathed it all in, and now he smiled, alone in the darkness, at the intoxication of it all. He smiled at that which lay fallow in the unseen distance, in the unearthed bowels of this forsaken place, and at that which lay beneath. He could smell it, feel it, even hear the faint whispers rousing from their ancient slumber. It would all be his, soon enough.

CHAPTER 28
We Are You

A MAN BROUGHT DAVID BREAKFAST that morning, set it on the desk, and informed him that guests were free that morning to roam the grounds, inside or out, for recreational time, provided they did not trespass into any prohibited areas, as the plethora of warning signs throughout the compound so distinguished.

David picked at his food, yawning and rubbing his eyes, exhausted in every possible way. Thoughts of family and friends drifted through his consciousness. He missed them terribly, and hope became more fleeting with each passing day. For all his surges of bravado, for all the whispers of forgone lives, there were increasing moments like this, when it was just him, powerless and alone, without any practical notion of how to escape this predicament. He could see Rachel, peering through tear-streaked eyes out their living room window for the big brother who'd broken his promise. He saw their father, receding further into the chair in his study, eyes vacant, merely another fixture in that dark and dreary space. He saw Robert and Chester, his steadfast friends, but even they seemed increasingly like fading memories.

And Amanda... he saw her too, as he always did, kind and thoughtful and more beautiful than all the poets of the world could ever summon the words to describe. Whatever grace remained in the world, whatever light, she was these things incarnate, setting his heart to flutter with butterfly wings. As he sat there now in the pale lamplight—no measure of bravado, no ancient powers—not one piece of this grand, immortal game held a matchstick to the revelation of her touch.

His head drooped, and he welled with shame at his despondence, for in his mind's eye he could see his mother, and knew she was still out there somewhere, counting on him, believing in him. He must fight on. It was no epiphany, no sudden surge of confidence, just a quiet reminder of that covenant that coursed within him, and from which he would not turn. He lifted his head, and took a last bite of his breakfast. Maybe he would go outside today, perhaps to the beach. Maybe the fresh air and sea would help clear his head. He pushed back from his chair and stood, but when he turned for the door, something lured his attention from the corner of his eye, something in the mirror.

Just the reflection of his own movement, doubtless, but when he glanced at the glass, he froze at the fading image of what he swore he'd seen: a pale, gaunt, darkly attired figure, regarding him with sunken and condemning eyes, as though to mark him. He was there, and then gone.

David shook his head, and turned back for the door.

When he went outside—glad to be able to do so, despite the ubiquitous presence of cameras and guards—he was especially pleased to spot Dani, Ruhi, and Harlan strolling about the grounds. They'd noticed him as well, paused their gate, and waved him over. Together they headed for a row of beautiful, if unusual, trees, as the ascending sun had already made for a sweltering morning.

"Flamboyant trees," Ruhi said.

They sat down beneath one as their friend went on to explain the name derived from its crest of blood-orange flowers. The sun rose over the sea, and the morning light, similarly colored, spliced exquisitely through the tree limbs. When the wind blew, the seed pods rattled beneath the leaves like maracas.

David reckoned he might appreciate the beauty of it all under any other circumstance but this, were they on this island of their own choosing, and could leave when desired. Their reality pressed in upon him like the rising tide, from all around, and despite being surrounded by new friends, he'd never felt more like an island himself. The sunlight glinted off the tree limbs and painted the leaves golden, and it made him think of that Frost poem, which made him think of Rachel, for it had always been her favorite: *Nature's first green is gold.*

He wondered how she was. He'd tried not to dwell on those thoughts... about Rachel, and their father, about Robert, Chester, and Amanda. It would distract him from the task at hand, from this new normal, which itself was so daunting that at times he simply was too exhausted to think of anything else.

Then leaf subsides to leaf.

But he must think of them. Now, more than ever, he must think of them — his family and his friends — for they were his touchstones, and this gulf imposed between them must not numb him to that truth. It must, in fact, embolden him. He must think of them; he must live for them; and remember that when the last leaf fell, it was only another season come to pass, another just behind it, and all of them would be together again one day to welcome it.

They sat for a while, getting to know each other, and David sensed their keen curiosity about his story — again, word of him had gotten around, so very peculiar to him though that was — but also their desire to not pressure him. When at length his friends said they were going back inside to get something to eat, David said he'd rejoin them in a bit, but that first he wanted to take a walk.

Men with guns guarded the beach, though the notion of someone making a swim for it was beyond preposterous. The guards — four, each wearing dark suits and dark sunglasses — followed him at a respectable distance as he walked along the shore. A gentle tide rolled in. If one didn't know better, it might appear an idyllic morning, an ocean sunrise on a dream vacation — except, of course, for the guns. David had noticed more and more of them — armed guards — as the days passed. He understood well the gravity of this: Christian was dead serious about preventing escape, or trouble of any kind.

David paused and lifted a hand to shield his eyes as he looked out upon the sea. The sun peaked from an architecture of coral clouds, like a new world rising. He lowered his gaze to avert the glare, and was startled to observe the tide receding rapidly back out to sea, farther than it should be. A large swath of seabed emerged into view, and he knew what this usually meant, but when he glanced back over to the guards, they seemed somehow not to be seeing it.

Besides, nothing anymore was what it usually meant, and so he stood in place and waited, come what may.

The tide had rolled back as far as he could see, and a labyrinth of storm clouds had rolled in. Presently, he detected something shifting within the haze. He squinted and stared as whatever it was gradually resolved into some semblance of definition. He cast another glance at the guards. Nothing.

Out to sea, the shapes at last clarified, and he could make out a stampede of white horses thundering toward shore, triangular in formation, like birds, and riderless, save the lead animal, upon which sat a gleaming, unequivocal figure. The still rising sun gilded his armor, and David knew who it was, or was supposed to be. When the herd reached shore, the rider held up a hand, and the horses slowed and stood snorting and stepping impatiently about.

"You're not here," David called. He didn't know if the guards had heard him, and he didn't much care.

"If *you* are," said Lancelot, raising the visor of his helmet, "then so too am I."

When the knight's hand fell away from his face, David flinched upon observing not Lancelot's visage, but his own.

"You're just in my head, right?"

"We are," replied his armored counterpart, "and we are not." David's eyes narrowed as spectral figures substantiated briefly into view upon each animal, before fading away like lightning. "We are not here, but have been here all along—before you, even. We are you, and you are us."

"What do you want?"

At this, Lancelot, his horse, and the horse nearest him shimmered and faded, and in their place appeared two different figures. It was him—David—and Marcel, back on the moors at Kane Manor.

"Your mother," Marcel said, just as he had on that evening. "The ancients foretold of the Time of Sacrifice.... There is something they seek...."

David on the beach stared as the scene shimmered and transformed once more, and now stood Amanda and Chester, back along the creek that evening just a few weeks back.

"Immortal amarant," said Amanda, "a flower which once in paradise, fast by the tree of life, began to bloom...."

"But soon for man's offence," Chester chimed in, just as he had, "to heaven removed, where it first grew, there grows, and flowers aloft, shading the fount of life...."

The images shimmered again, and David watched and waited for whatever—or whoever—was next. Whether memory, hallucination, or trick of the mind, he imagined he should be extracting from all of it some grand epiphany, but none had come. He looked on as the figures faded out, supplanted this time by none other than Minister Morgan at his pulpit.

"God," intoned the kindly cleric, just as he had those months back, "determines who is to be written into the Book of Life and who is not. The ancient view embraces this quite literally, believing that such tablets exist. God opens these books each year and marks folks for the Book of Life or Book of Death...."

The minister began to fade, and David wondered how long this would endure—maybe until he got the message. He glanced over at the guards, who appeared impassive and bored. When he looked back out to sea, his heart went to his throat. The horses had faded, so too all other figures, save one.

She stood shrouded in a halo of mist and morning light before their mother's grave, on a brisk fall day, her eyes locked with his own. "Promise," Rachel said, then, and now.

"I do," he said.

Rachel smiled and her eyes lit with all the grace of the world, and then she and all before him shimmered and hued briefly blue, as Arondight had, before fading from sight. The sea came rolling back, and the sky settled back into its previous repose, the sun just a bit higher upon its trajectory.

David turned to go, but something along the edge of his vision wrested his attention back out to sea. He thought, at first, it must be a dolphin, but no. Two small but unmistakable fins, above a taut and dark blue torso, breached the waves. He squinted into the glare, and though he couldn't be certain, he could have sworn he spied a pair of eyes staring back, emerald like the sea they mirrored, then gone.

CHAPTER 29
How Loud Their Wings

THE MAN BELIEVED IN GOD, AND as such believed in good. It followed that if there was good, it must stand against evil, and so he believed in evil too. Still, nothing he witnessed on that day reconciled with anything he'd ever known. It had all happened so very fast, yet would remain seared into his consciousness, into his mind's eye, into his every dream or nightmare, for the remainder of his days.

The arrival of the two men had been unusual enough: one, their employer, appeared out of nowhere; and a somewhat older man, equally unannounced, materialized outside the dig site in clear opposition to the other. They conversed with a peculiar calm, which belied the consequence that freighted their every word. yet it was what happened next that imprinted itself into the very fabric of the man's soul, an abiding burden.

His children would learned quickly never to inquire or speak of it, and their children too, when the time came. It would be evident enough in his eyes, in the solemnity of his expression, and in the way his breath at times would trail away, mournful-sounding, vagabond, like the foghorn of a vessel forever adrift.

He saw it whether he wished to or not, and he almost never wished to, save for those interminable dead of night hours that would at times beset him, when he'd turn from his wife so that, should she wake, she'd still think him sleeping. In truth, he stared rapt and unblinking into the void, beseeching answers which would not come.

Their spades had been replaced by firearms, his and his fellow laborers', though they'd not been told what they were safeguarding, only that it was of the gravest import. They could feel it in their blood and bones, the gravity of the thing, almost literally, such did it pull at them — something older than they, older than all men, older than the sands beneath their feet. At times, it felt not of this world, but in places inside them that ran deeper than blood and bones, in remote, inarticulable regions of cellular knowing, each of them understood.

Whatever this thing was, for which they'd toiled and searched under ceaseless duress and threats and an unsparing sun, until their bodies broke and bled, and which now, upon at last unearthing it, they defended with their very lives — it wasn't whether it was of this world, but whether this world was of it.

"You must stand down," their employer, the somewhat younger appearing of the two, had said. "You surely know you cannot prevail. Besides — " Here the man smirked, and his voice dripped with vitriol. " — I have found it, not you. My prize to keep."

"I was not looking," said the older man. "Nor should have you. Nor anyone."

"Can you be so callow," replied the first, his voice tinged with melancholy. "After all these years? At any rate — " He gestured now at the armed laborers. " — my find is protected, as you can very well see."

The older man appeared undaunted. "You would commit such sacrilege, as to bring hostilities to such a place?"

"How long have you known me?"

At that moment, a fluttering sounded, and a great shadow crosscut the infernal desert glare. Presently, another man appeared alongside the older man. The overseer appeared briefly nonplussed, before regaining his previous air.

"She has brought news of her search," the new arrival informed his colleague.

The older man nodded and, without diverting his gaze from his adversary, said, "Take leave now, and bring the news to the family. Then shall we prepare our travels."

His associate narrowed his eyes and glanced at their antagonist, and the armed laborers. "I suggest you might need me to linger a short while more."

"Each second is precious," the older man said. "I require no support. Take your leave, as I have directed."

His associate frowned, but then nodded solemnly and, after a final glance at their rival, turned to depart. His countenance seemed to shimmer and become undulant as he strode, though the desert was renowned for playing tricks on the eyes, and on the mind. The man grew smaller against the glare and sands, until he was but shadow, and then, gone.

"This place must not be defiled," the older man called. "And these innocents not subjected to that which you would here provoke."

"Then we are agreed," their employer called back. "You shall stand down. Men!"

The laborers leveled their weapons, though by their expressions, the man reckoned each of them to be as conflicted as was he. He could not explain this turmoil: they had received orders from their employer, and besides, this interloper was unknown to them, and poised to plunder that which was not his, just as their employer had said.

And yet....

"Search your hearts," the older man called, addressing the laborers now in their native tongue. "Your souls. You are men of honor and faith. You do not wish to be party to this sacrilege, much less shed blood on holy ground." He returned his attention to their employer.

"After all this time," he called, "no matter our quarrels, I have considered you more principled than this. I beseech you one last time, abandon this ill-contrived pursuit, and take leave. If you shall not, then at the very least, affirm my faith in you, that you will spare these innocents and leave the matter between the two of us to decide."

"Quarrels?" Their employer's tone dripped with incredulity. "Is that what you think this is?" They glared at one another across the sweltering divide between them, neither speaking, a strange armistice, which the man knew would prove all fleeting—like the eerie, silent skies before a storm. "But if you are willing to be discovered," their master called out at last, "then so be it!" He gestured to the laborers. "Stand down, but at the ready!"

The laborers looked on wide-eyed as their employer advanced.

"Take leave!" the older man called out to them, standing his ground. "Take leave and take shelter. For the sake of your own welfare, turn your gaze away!"

"You shall do no such thing!" retorted their employer, who'd neared within ten meters of his foe. "You are in my employ, and shall obey me accordingly!"

The laborers regarded one another uncertainly. Some began a slow retreat, while others remained in place, shifting where they stood. The man remained in the ranks of the latter—out of duty, perhaps, and perhaps honor, though in that moment and all to follow, he was never again certain as to which allegiance that word was pledged.

When the strange figures at last converged, each weaponless as far as the man could see, there erupted upon that parched theater an inferno that rendered the desert glare pale by comparison. He'd turned to flee — futile, given the force with which he was a moment later blasted through the air — but not before beholding two images he considered then, and would always consider, impossible.

Two beings flared briefly into meticulous relief, not against the backdrop of the flames, but within them: a demon, clawed and horned and malignant, taking up arms against a winged figure of indescribable beauty.

There and gone, like fading ink.

***

RACHEL COULDN'T REMEMBER THE LAST time her father had turned on the overhead light in his study. Ever since Mama had gone, he sat only by lamplight, or sometimes in darkness. Since David had gone missing, though, the light of his own eyes, dimmed and hopeless for so very long, had flickered back to life.

On this evening, her father had summoned David's closest friends — Robert, Chester, and Amanda. When they'd arrived, he escorted them back to his study, fully lit and chairs set out, and when they'd sat, he turned to Rachel and gently ushered her from the room.

"TV is on for you, sweetie," he told her. "Please go to the living room. I won't be too long."

She folded her arms and gave him that look that usually caused him — and used to cause Mama, and most any grownups — to relent. She saw in her father's eyes that it would not be so this time, and so she made another face and shuffled off. When she'd turned the corner, she stopped and listened. For a moment, only silence greeted her, but then she heard the door close and, after waiting a few seconds, she slipped off her shoes and tiptoed back to the study.

The doorknob was at eye-level but the hallway light made it hard to see, so she stood on her toes and flicked it off, then returned to the doorknob and squinted through the keyhole. Her father sat behind his desk, with David's friends seated and facing him, Chester and Robert on either end, Amanda in the middle. Rachel wondered if David missed Amanda. He probably did. She wondered if he missed *her*, too. She very much missed him.

"Thank you for coming," her father said. He leaned forward over his desk, hands clasped, and regarded each of them. "I've lost my wife. I'll not lose my boy."

"What did the police say?" asked Chester.

"They don't have answers. They've examined the cemetery, and retraced what would have most likely have been his route home. They've talked to you guys, and to me. He didn't seem in a bad state — well, any more so than all he's gone through in the last year — didn't seem to me or anyone else that he was on the brink of running away or...." Her father's voice trailed off for a spell. "Or harming himself."

"He wouldn't do that," Robert said.

"I don't think so, either," said Rachel's dad.

"So, they had no ideas?" Amanda asked.

"I'm afraid not. They'll keep looking, but I don't expect them to find him."

Rachel heard herself gasp, and threw a hand to her mouth and kept still as she could, but no one else seemed to have heard.

"I had to try them," her father continued, "but I have finally started to accept that whatever has been going on in the last year — maybe for much longer — cannot be explained by typical means. I can't go so far as to say I believe in everything David had been telling me, but at some point, when the typical explanations continue to fail, one must consider scenarios he never before believed possible."

"When you have eliminated the impossible," said Chester, "whatever remains — however improbable — "

"Must be the truth." Her father smiled. "I was a Holmes fan too."

Chester said, "Truth be told — "

"Yeah, yeah," groaned Robert. "You prefer Dew Pen."

"Dupin."

"A fan of his too," her father said. "And I fear that what we may have here is a Purloined Letter, a clue, or at least facts, and circumstances, that have been hiding in plain sight."

Rachel stepped from the door and rubbed her neck. She was a bit hungry, and there was ice cream in the freezer. She thought very hard about getting some, but decided to return to the keyhole.

"I very much understand," said Chester. "I do not — cannot — endorse much of what others have insisted to be true in all this. And yet, conventional explanations, as you've noted, have failed. Also, I've seen things that, as I sit here, I still cannot adequately explain."

"Same here," said Amanda, urgency in her voice. "I struggle to believe it too, but I believe in your son, Mr. Rose. I very much believe in him."

Rachel watched her father turn his head briefly away, drag a shirtsleeve across his eyes, and the turn back. "Thank you, Amanda. It's high time I demonstrate that same faith."

"So now what?" Robert leaned forward in his chair. "What do we do?"

Her father's eyes narrowed. "I think we must indeed channel Holmes, or Dupin, whatever your preference. We must think analytically. No matter what was happening — and it could have been anything — is it possible, after telling his sister he'd be back, David would have left of his own free will, without saying a word to anyone? Without being in touch since?"

"Anything is possible," said Chester. "Perhaps that was the only way to keep you guys safe. You and Rachel. Even us."

"No, he wouldn't," said Amanda, and all eyes fell upon her. "He would not break his promise to Rachel, not if he could help it."

Rachel smiled from her spot at the keyhole, but then felt it melting away. If David wouldn't have broken his promise, then....

"Then he couldn't help it," said her father. "Then he was taken against his will."

The room fell quiet, and Rachel's breathing sounded suddenly and frightfully loud to her. She held her breath for a few seconds.

Robert at last broke the silence. "Kane?"

"Maybe," said Amanda. "But something tells me no. Marcel had told David that was unlikely."

"But not impossible," Chester said.

"What about that other immortal?" suggested Robert. "That guy from the cemetery? What about him or others who might have come?"

"Okay," said Rachel's father. "Maybe Kane, maybe not. Maybe these others you speak of, whom I've no idea about. And this talk of immortality...."

"Remember," Amanda said sweetly, "when you have eliminated the impossible...."

"Okay," said Rachel's father. "Okay, you're right. Unfortunately, that makes the path forward even more uncertain. Where do we even begin to look? And how? Is there anyone else who knows about this stuff that could help? Anyone... well... on our side?"

Rachel stepped back from the doorknob and cocked her head. She'd heard something, maybe the TV, but it seemed to have come from the front door, or just outside—a *whooshing*. Mama had taken them to a bird sanctuary one time, and she remembered the red-tailed hawks and how big and pretty they were, and how loud their wings sounded. She crept to the front door, pressed her ear to it, and listened.

"I still say," said a familiar voice, "we must pursue Kane. He should never have been allowed to possess it."

"I have told you," replied another voice, one that made a smile spread over Rachel's face. "There was no choice. After our standoff, Kane ordered the innocents to engage me. They would have all been lost."

"A tiny price."

"The moment we believe that, then we are lost as well."

Even though her father had told her never to do it, she reached up and unlocked the door and pulled it open. The two individuals she knew were there stood looking down at her in surprise. She smiled up at them, and they smiled back. She let them in, and headed for the study.

Her father was already standing in the hallway, David's friends behind him. All of them just stared.

She glanced up at their new visitors, then back at her father. "It's okay, Daddy. They're on our side."

CHAPTER 30
Restraint

DAVID RECEIVED BREAKFAST THE NEXT morning in his room, was told to dress comfortably, and then was escorted back down to the bowels of the compound. His guides led him to an enclosed viewing area, where upon entering he saw Dani, Harlan, Ruhi, and roughly a dozen others, including James and Isla, and the Valori twins, both wearing red track suits and stretching.

As soon as David stepped inside, his escorts, saying nothing, pulled the steel door shut. It locked with a resounding snap.

Dani and Ruhi waved him over to where they leaned against a handrail, beneath the floor-to-ceiling plexiglass, or whatever Christian had said it was constructed of.

"Good morning," said Dani. "Harlan is about to go in. Have you seen any of this yet?"

David nodded, and pointed through the glass, up to the guest gallery from which he'd observed on his first evening here.

"Ah," said Dani. "He really does covet you."

"But here he is now," said the male Valori, who'd slunk up behind them. "Same as us."

"You should just worry about your match, Lars," Dani said.

Lars glanced to the far side of the enclosure, where Harlan sat alone on a bench, smoking a cigarette. "I'm not too worried," he snorted, and went back over to his sister.

"*He* doesn't look too worried, either," David said, crooking his head toward Harlan.

"No," said Ruhi, "he's not."

David raised an eyebrow and was about to say something, but just then an interior door swung open and a short, bespectacled woman in a white lab coat peered out at them. "Phillips!" she called. "Valori! You're up."

The twins bumped fists, and Lars headed for the open door. When he reached David, he angled his shoulder slightly into his, jostling him, and cast a smirking glance back as he cornered out of sight.

"Okay, Phillips," called the woman in the doorway. "Put that out and come on."

Harlan exhaled a perfect set of smoke rings, which a moment later vanished entirely, along with the cigarette itself. Dani gave him a quick pat on the shoulder, and he bent to hug Ruhi before heading for the door. He winked at David as he passed.

"Be careful," David said.

They all turned and faced the window, and looked out as the two contestants were escorted onto what looked like a coliseum battlefield. David had witnessed the evolving expanse that first night, and wondered if this was the real shape of the place, or perhaps more sleight of hand from Merlin, or whatever technology and effects Christian had come to possess. In any case, the two men had been directed to opposing places on the field, perhaps fifty paces apart.

David narrowed his eyes as a female figure appeared in the glass and approached, then quickly realized it was the Valori sister, come up behind them, arms folded across her chest.

"You should have said a better goodbye," she told them.

None of them turned around.

"Maybe you should have, Ella," said Dani.

"Foolish girl," Ella replied, and she started to reach for Dani, but Ruhi turned quickly about and smiled up at her, and Ella froze mid-reach.

"Why don't you watch here, Ella?" Ruhi said, indicating the open rail beside her.

Ella grunted, but Ruhi kept her gaze, and David watched with fascination as something in Ella's icy stare softened — barely, almost imperceptibly, but there. Ella swallowed and stepped over beside Ruhi and grabbed the rail.

Out on the battleground, Lars stood glaring at his opponent, who in turn glanced this way and that at his surroundings, probably looking for something to use, though from his vantage, David could not detect many options. A faint buzzing sounded, then a dull *whoosh*, like when the principal turned on the intercom for morning announcements at school.

A moment later, Christian's voice issued forth. "Welcome, ladies and gentlemen, combatants and guests to Valori versus Phillips. May the contest begin!"

There was a *click*, and David stared as Lars burst into a headlong sprint toward Harlan. He imagined himself in Harlan's shoes, and his body pulsed with latent notions of what he would do. *'Evade,'* whispered ancient voices. *'Parry.'*

Harlan did neither. He waited until Lars was nearly upon him — David cringing at what appeared the imminent impact — before breaking into a sprint of his own.

Lars broke stride ever so slightly, thrown a bit by this development, before resuming his pursuit.

A murmuring arose within the enclosure as the action before them unfolded. The combatants more resembled track stars, as Harlan had taken to the periphery of the field, flying about it with lanky but effective strides. Lars' face twisted in contempt as he stampeded after his quarry. Harlan would begin to slow, and just as Lars was nearly upon him, and the murmuring would rise, he would accelerate again, just out of reach. This continued for several laps.

David glanced at Ella, who looked on in frustration and disbelief.

"Your friend is a coward," she said to them, after yet another pass.

"There are no style points," Dani said.

David glanced up at the viewing gallery. He could not see him, but imagined Christian to be turning some shade of embarrassed red. This was not the sort of action his guests had paid so handsomely to see.

On the field, Lars appeared to become slightly winded, despite the impressive physical conditioning he and his sister both seemed to harbor. His power, it appeared, was of a more juggernaut variety, straight on and explosive, as his adversary seemed all too aware. Lars was tiring, but on their next pass, the terrain beneath the combatants began to billow and transform. The earth in many places crumbled and caved, until the field was riddled with craters of varying sizes. They all looked on as Harlan long-jumped over one sizable hole, Lars following suit, but at the next depression, Harlan stopped suddenly, arms flailing, the hole clearly too much to attempt. Before he could determine a satisfactory detour, Lars slammed into him full force from behind, with such momentum that Harlan's head snapped back and forward and back again. A gasp rose up in the enclosure as Harlan went careening through the air, eclipsing the chasm and landing face first several yards away.

David turned and observed the horror upon Dani's and Ruhi's faces, and the creeping grin upon Ella's. He didn't know if Christian was keeping tabs on their waiting pen, but he gestured angrily toward the cameras.

"That was cowardly," he said.

Ella smirked. "There are no style points."

Down below, Lars set upon Harlan, pouncing onto his back and raining sledgehammer blows upon his head and back with clenched fists.

David grimaced, spun from the rail, and went to the interior door, which of course was locked. He tried the steel door through which they'd entered, but with the same result. He glared back up at one of the cameras and raised an index finger. "I warned you," he said.

"Harlan!"

David whirled back at the agonized tone of Dani's cry.

Lars' assault continued unabated.

"Why's he not fighting back?" Dani pleaded.

David returned to the spot he'd vacated beside her, leaned forward to grip the rail, and beheld the unfolding barbarity. Up in his gallery, David knew, Christian and his guests looked on with intrigue, enjoying their decadent fare. He narrowed his eyes and took in the continuing assault.

"I think he is," he said at last.

Harlan had crossed his arms over the back of his head, like they'd taught the kids to do in a tornado drill at David's school. Though his arms and back were bearing a terrible brunt, the blows at last had begun to slow. At length, Harlan rolled over, kicked his opponent in the face, and rose, teetering, to his feet. His shirt was torn, his face bloodied and bruised, his right eye swollen half shut; clearly, some of the blows had been glancing, and found their way through Harlan's defenses.

Lars — likewise bloodied — staggered to his feet and raised his trembling arms.

Harlan motioned him forward, and when Lars obliged, Harlan sidestepped and stuck out a foot, over which Lars promptly tripped, pitching forward onto the ground. Harlan wobbled over to him, looking down, then raised his head toward the gallery.

After the familiar buzz and low *whoosh*, Christian's voice again issued forth. "It is not yet decided." His words echoed through the otherwise hushed arena.

David wondered what Christian expected Harlan to do — expected any of them to do, under such circumstances. His thoughts traveled back to his awakening at Tintagel, when he'd managed to get the better of Donovan — Gawain — and held the tip of his vaunted blade at the throat of his one-time brother.

Upon the battlefield, Harlan seemed — to David's relief — inclined toward the same restraint. He looked down at Lars, then back up at the gallery, and shook his head.

"Very well." Hardly acceptance in Christian's voice.

A door at the far end of the arena lifted open, and two men wheeled out a cart of various weaponry — no firearms, but that seemed to be the only thing missing. It contained swords, crossbows, javelins, throwing stars and more. The men retreated through the door.

Lars gathered himself to his feet, emboldened, it seemed, by this turn of events.

Harlan's eyes grew wide, and he cast a glance back toward the waiting pen.

"Game on," Lars hissed. He hobbled to the cart and placed his hands on either end of it, sizing up the bounty. At length, he lifted one of the crossbows, compact and preloaded, and turned back to his adversary. "I suggest you choose something. I won't wait long."

"Pick a weapon," Dani pleaded. "Pick a weapon."

Harlan did not pick a weapon. He slowly backpedaled away from where Lars stood, watching for holes as he stepped.

Ruhi leaned forward, appearing anguished, her forehead pressed against the glass. *Pick a weapon,* David saw her mouth say silently. Her eyes grew wide, and a vein pulsed on the side of her neck.

A distinct crackling arose within the enclosure, and David glanced briefly toward the battlefield, assuming it to have come from there, but it had not.

The glass around Ruhi's forehead had begun to fissure, a spiderweb of fractures emanating out like ripples in a pond. A few of the other immortals had noticed, and now took a few steps back, staring.

Dani placed a hand upon Ruhi's shoulder. "Ruhi," she said, gently. "Ruhi, stop."

The girl's eyes fluttered rapidly, the fissuring ceased, and Ruhi stepped from the rail and regarded Dani imploringly. Dani put her arm around her, and together they looked back out upon the field.

Lars' head was titled quizzically as he regarded his opponent, who stood twenty feet off, hand painting the air as might a mime on a spring day at the park.

Harlan rotated both hands rapidly before him, and soon David understood why. Their theater had begun again to transform — by Harlan's hand, apparently — but not all of it. The outer circles of the arena darkened, but otherwise remained as previous, a cratered field imprinted along its periphery by the countless footprints of the two men who now stood opposed in a rectangular slip of light at the center of the expanse. Within this space had appeared what could best be described as a living room, replete with a desk, couch, and chairs. Upon the couch sat an attractive woman, wearing a look of severity.

Lars stood before her, crossbow leveled. "What is this?" He cast a quick glance to the upper gallery.

"Is that any way to greet your mother?" The woman on the couch folded her arms.

Lars cocked his head, then lowered his weapon.

"That's better," said the woman upon the couch.

"Mom?"

David glanced to his left.

Ella's eyes were narrowed, her eyebrows raised, as she pressed her face to the window.

David returned his attention to the arena, and spied Harlan standing in the shadows, just outside the square of light. His lips seemed to be moving, and David squinted in an effort to read him. He couldn't quite make things out, but as the woman on the couch spoke again, he realized Harlan's lips were moving in unison with her words. *...been taking care of your sis –*

" – ter? Well, have you?"

Lars glanced up at the gallery, then back at the figure on the couch. "Yes, Mother, you know I have."

"Don't lie –"

--to me. You know I can tell when you're lying. Now put down that weapon. Other than his lips, Harlan stood perfectly motionless.

Ella balled her fist and banged hard on the glass. "No! Lars, no! Don't listen!"

"He can't hear you," Ruhi said, politely.

Ella shot her a glare.

Inside the arena, Lars heeded the woman on the couch, and David looked on, mesmerized, as the crossbow fell to the ground.

"That's better," said the woman. "Now tell me why you have forsaken sweet Ella."

"I've not forsaken her, Mother, I've not. It's just...."

The woman on the couch regarded him expectantly.

"It's just that I *always* have to look out for her," Lars said, looking down. "My whole life, from day one, it's never been just about me."

"In this life," said the woman, "it never is. You would do well to accept that."

Lars looked back up, plaintively. "Just once," he said. "That's all I ask. Just once. Let me fly on my own."

"Even if your ambition comes at the expense of the one you are forsworn to safekeep?"

"I would never endanger her."

"But you have, Son. You have. You have set off on your own, so many times and in so many ways, leaving her behind. You are twins, each the other's covenant—double the power, if that bond held fast, but also double the vulnerability. You have endangered her. It pains me to say it."

Lars glanced up, and David turned and saw Ella looking down. When he looked back out to the arena, Harlan had stepped from the shadows, retrieved the fallen crossbow, and retreated a few steps.

Light returned to the whole of the arena, and the trappings of the living room slowly vanished—the chairs, the desk, the couch, the woman upon it. Lars briefly held his arms out as her image faded.

David felt a twinge of compassion, but marveled at what Harlan had done. He'd not before witnessed this sort of power, except perhaps from Merlin.

"Enough!" Harlan gestured up toward the gallery.

Lars seemed to be coming out of it, but appeared now to be lacking his previous fight.

Harlan had the crossbow.

An uneasy silence ensued, and then the arena lit brighter still, the far door lifted, and the same men who'd brought the weapons emerged once again. One escorted a dejected Lars off the field, while the other retrieved the crossbow from Harlan, who hesitated a moment before handing it over. Then the two of them headed off and disappeared through the same door.

At that same moment, the interior door opened in the waiting pen, and the same woman in the white coat leaned in, scoured her clipboard, and called out two names.

David didn't recognize them, and felt a bit guilty at his relief—no one, of course, ought to be compelled into such hostilities. None of this should be happening.

He watched the new pair escorted out onto the field, and imagined Christian and his guests watching intently from their perch above. He inhaled deeply, looking forward to the moment he would help bring it all to an end.

CHAPTER 31
The Thinnest Line

"I'M COMING WITH YOU."

Rachel beamed, partly at the news that David had been located, and partly at the look in her father's eyes, which were awash with resolve. He appeared in this moment a far different man than he had for so many solitary nights in his study — far more alive.

They'd gone to the living room, where everyone could sit, and presently Marcel leaned forward from his spot on the couch and said, "Admirable, sir, but you are needed here." He nodded toward Rachel. "You are needed by her. They will not so readily give up the fight. There are countless others captive there, and though I hope to avoid it, our arrival may well instigate extreme hostilities."

"All the more reason I should go. I am his father. It should be me."

"Sir." Marcel's eyes brimmed with unease, the only such instance Rachel could remember. "This is an extraordinary development, dangerous beyond all reckoning, with countless immortals, whose allegiance and disposition we've no way to predict, and an enterprise protected by scores of mercenaries. It shall be all we can do to find and extricate your son. Our mission becomes far more arduous if we must — with all respect — be at the same time safeguarding you."

Her father shook his head, clearly frustrated, but for the moment argued no further.

"Besides," said Herman, adjacent Marcel, "who will look after her? We shall be oceans away."

"We can look after her," Amanda said from her chair, and all eyes fell upon her. "She can stay with me. We'll keep her safe, all of us." She regarded her friends. "Right?"

Robert regarded the visitors on the couch. "Right."

Chester cleared his throat. "Right."

Rachel smiled.

Her father turned to her. "What about you, angel? Are you okay with that? Just until I'm back?"

She looked from Chester to Robert to Amanda, who smiled at her with kindness in her eyes, and turned back to her father. "Yes, if it means you'll bring David back."

Her father returned his attention to their guests. "You see? She'll be looked after. I won't get in your way, I swear." He leaned forward. "I'm his father."

Marcel and Herman glanced at one another, and at length, the former released a heavy sigh. "Very well, I'll be in a spate of trouble from this."

"With whom?" Chester asked.

Marcel didn't answer. He signaled his companion, and they rose and headed for the front door, everyone else following.

"Wait," said Rachel's father. "How do we get there, wherever it is? Where is it? When do we leave?"

Marcel turned back. "Soon, but not just yet. I'm afraid we've other business to attend to first, to aid us in our mission." He opened the door.

"Like what?" Robert inquired.

"Something we must retrieve," said Herman.

"Something," said Marcel, "and someone." He locked eyes with Rachel's father. "Pack light, try to rest, and be ready. When the time comes, we shall depart at a moment's notice. To each of you—" He regarded Amanda, Robert and Chester. "—understand fully the commission to which you have here agreed. You are entrusted with the most precious cargo. I do not anticipate any attempts against her, but it is hardly beyond the range of possibility. You are but children yourselves, but you must forswear to protect her by all means necessary." He paused, and cast his gaze over each of them a final time. "Is that understood?"

When they'd assented, Marcel crouched before Rachel and placed a hand on her shoulder. "Sweet child, your strength throughout all of this has been remarkable. I fear I must implore you to keep it up. Stay strong." He nodded back over his shoulder. "And look out for them too, if you don't mind."

"I don't mind," she said.

Marcel smiled, looked into her eyes a moment longer, then stood and glanced at Rachel's father. "A moment's notice...." He nodded to Herman and stepped through the doorway.

They kept the door open, watching the two men stride off into the evening, across the street, and past the flickering lamppost, until they grew small and disappeared into the darkness.

***

THE TOURNAMENT CONTINUED.

David observed closely, every contest, mostly in dread of a catastrophic result but also scouting for tendencies in the other immortals, should he be pitted against them. He hoped not to be picked—not out of fear, which he surely felt, but in apprehension of how far they'd be expected to go. Would he be able to pull away his blade, as he had at Tintagel—not that he had a blade... not his, anyway.

He paid particular attention to how each contest concluded, when Christian would call an end to things. Slowly, but unquestionably, he perceived that Dani had been correct: things were becoming increasingly violent, going a bit further each time, injuries being incurred, building toward an inevitable—and unconscionable—end.

On this particular evening, when Dani's name was called, David's head snapped up in anticipation of the name that would follow. It was one he hadn't before heard, but when its claimant rose from a bench at the far end of the holding pen, David's heart began to pound and his blood ran cold. When he registered the immortal beside whom Dani's rival had been seated, he instantly knew, and his blood ran colder still.

"End it quickly, Mason," said the still seated one in a raspy, unmistakable voice.

The immortals from the cemetery.

They'd not escaped the grounds that night, but had, like David, been seized. The gravity of this enterprise sank within him like an anchor, and the prospects of unmooring from this unreckoned place and finding his way home felt suddenly and terribly dim. Yet he must focus on the present, for his friend would in moments be squaring off against this dangerous adversary, and Christian had been permitting—if not directing—the contests to career further and further into more treacherous territory.

He turned to Dani, who'd risen from her seat beside him, head lowered as Ruhi whispered into her right ear.

When they'd finished, David touched Dani's arm and said, "Careful, I've seen this guy before. I think he's dangerous."

Dani managed a smile. "Thanks, they all are."

David and Ruhi stood, leaned against the railing, and watched intently as their friend and her opponent were escorted onto the field.

"You know him," Ruhi said.

David glanced at her. "Not exactly, but yes, I've seen him. Never seen him fight, but I have the feeling he's powerful. Old."

"I can feel it too," said Ruhi.

David thought to ask her how she could sense that, when she'd yet to awaken, but he thought better of it and refocused his attention on the battlefield. The chosen immortals opposed one another from perhaps twenty feet apart. David discerned no weapons at their disposal, but soon the landscape began to transform, the arena darkened, and the unfolding event became as night. A gray and turreted castle loomed over the combatants, shrouded — impossibly — in gleaming moonlight. David tensed as the newly conjured setting evoked something deep within. It wasn't Kane Manor, nor anywhere he recognized, but still... it had set something roiling inside him. He flinched as someone touched his forearm, and looked down to see Ruhi regarding him with a worrisome expression.

"I'm okay," he said. "It's just...."

"I know."

They turned back to the new world shaped-up before them, where Mason seemed to be basking in the metamorphosis. His features smoldered in the moonlight, craven and eager, and when he spied the cache of assorted weaponry freshly scattered on the reshaped earth, he grinned ghoulishly, and bent to retrieve his selection. When he arose, the spear gripped in his hand glinted in the preternatural glow.

"His awakening," a voice said from David's other side.

David glanced to where the other immortal from the cemetery, the taller one, had sidled up. If he knew who David was, he wasn't showing it.

He glanced at David and Ruhi and said, "She doesn't have a chance."

David turned to Ruhi, prepared to reassure her, but was surprised to observe her composed, even confident, demeanor. He turned back to the unfolding battle.

"I suggest, dear lady," Mason called across the field, "you pick a weapon. No mercy or reprieve will you receive from me!"

David couldn't help but agree with his admonition. *Come on, Dani, pick a weapon.*

Dani made no indication of the slightest intent to do so. She stood her ground, arms folded, wearing a similar expression as Ruhi.

"Your opponent speaks wisely," came an announcement by Christian over the PA system. "I will not pause the contest should you refuse to compete."

David glared up at the viewing gallery, where Christian and his guests no doubt reclined behind the safety of the special glass, dining in extravagance as they beheld their entertainment. What kind of people were these? For all his apprehension of the new and dark world into which he had at Tintagel awakened, he was beginning to wonder if there was more to fear from that which he'd known all along.

"Very well, then," Christian intoned, before the system clicked off.

Dani remained poised as before.

Mason grinned again, snarled, and charged.

David pressed his hands against the cold glass, heart pounding.

The immortal made it about halfway across the expanse between them before stopping in his tracks.

From his peripheral vision, David perceived that several others had moved up to the glass to get a better look. His own attention had been focused upon Mason, but now he glanced over to Dani, only to find that she wasn't there. Not exactly. Not the Dani who seconds before had been poised in strangely confident posture, as her armed adversary approached, and not just one. A quick headcount revealed no fewer than six Danis, some of whom David recognized from their first encounter, when she'd revealed her ability to David in the glass — four women and two men, of different ages, races, and sizes.

The six slowly fanned out into a semi-circle, still weaponless, it appeared, but each bearing defensive postures.

Mason rotated slowly to size up each incarnation as he rubbed the stubble of his chin. He then leveled the spear at the most centered figure, an older male, where Dani had previously stood.

"You!" he called, and charged again.

David pressed his face to the glass as the other five Danis converged upon the advancing hostile. He flinched as a scream reverberated throughout the arena — Dani's scream — and stared as Mason appeared suddenly airborne and sprawling through the air. David frantically wiped away the fog that had formed from his fretful breathing.

Dani's immortals had swarmed upon their fallen foe — all but one: he who'd been Mason's target.

David narrowed his eyes and beheld the ailing figure clutching at his left shoulder, which was blossoming deeply crimson. "Dani."

He glanced to his right to see Ruhi standing, face pressed to the glass, a single tear ebbing down her cheek. He turned back to the arena. One of Dani's charges — a young female — had retrieved Mason's spear and leveled it inches from his throat. David saw himself back at Tintagel, holding Arondight in similar proximity to Donovan. He stared again as each of Dani's standing five rubbed briefly at their left shoulders, as though soothing a minor injury.

The fallen incarnation was not so fortunate. He lay gasping upon the earth, the fog of his breath issuing into the spectral night. His hands, compressed over his grievous wound, had darkened with blood, and now his body began to spasm and transform, and moments later Dani herself reappeared, sporting the same injury.

David slammed his fist against the unsparing glass. "Help her!" He whirled around and faced one of the ceiling cameras. "Help her now!"

"There will be a victor," came Christian's voice through the speakers. "Then anyone requiring assistance shall be so availed."

David whirled back toward the arena. "Finish him!" he cried, hoping desperately that Dani would hear him and instruct her surrogates accordingly.

"She will not do that," Ruhi whispered.

"She'd rather die?"

"To abandon who you are," said Ruhi, her voice tinged with a melancholy that seemed to bore its way to his very soul, "is in its own way, a death."

David slammed his fist against the glass once more... and again.

The ancillary door swung open and the woman with the clipboard regarded him from the doorway with a scowl. "You will cease this behavior at once."

David felt his face contort. *This behavior?* He pounded again upon the glass, harder this time. And again. He heard the door shut and knew the woman was approaching.

"Move," he whispered, and after glancing quickly up at him, Ruhi stepped back from the glass. When the woman reached for David's arm, he slid to his left, whirled about, and seized her left arm in turn. The clipboard went flying and clattered to the ground, and the woman gasped as David subdued her in an armbar and pressed her writhing torso against the glass.

"David!" Ruhi was staring at him in disbelief.

The other immortals, including the taller one from the graveyard, looked on in equal incredulity. He took a halting step forward, but David bent the writhing woman's neck forward with one arm until she grimaced.

"Don't!" he warned the tall man, and anyone else inclined to intervene.

"You'll pay for this!" the woman spat.

"Christian!" He knew they were being monitored through the various cameras.

Even the combatants in the arena had turned their attention to this unprecedented turn of events. Dani's envoys, those conjured visages of lifetimes past, had cocked their heads and peered toward the holding pen, and Dani herself, clutching at her still hemorrhaging wound, lifted her head and was peering toward them.

"End this!" David called. "Or—"

"David...." Ruhi again, a whisper this time. Their eyes met. "Do not abandon who you are."

He started to reply, but stopped, devoid of explanation. A heavy disquietude fomented within him, a discordant medley seeking an articulation that would not come. So many voices.... that they might at last coalesce into some semblance of solidarity, like Dani's emissaries, and other immortals who'd mastered that power of communion that continued to elude him. Perhaps Ruhi was correct, and what he'd done — what he was doing this very moment — was a betrayal of who he was, and of all that those who cared about him believed him to be. Yes, she was surely right, but as he glared back into the arena, he knew only that Dani was bleeding out, and so damn all the voices, and whatever judgment might befall him, because, whoever he was, he would not stand by and watch his friend fall.

When the arena lights came on and medical attendants rushed across the field to the combatants, David exhaled deeply and released his shaken captive, who was assisted away by additional medics. When he saw the tears of shock and pain streaming down her cheeks, his insides knotted, and he felt his own eyes glistening. He turned to Ruhi, but words failed him once more.

Another figure appeared in the doorway and summoned him with a crook of his index finger.

Ambrose.

He reckoned Ambrose would escort him to Christian, to answer for what he'd done, and then off to whatever punishment awaited.

The concealed wizard spoke not a word as they ascended from the bowels of the compound aboard the clattering lift, and when the doors at last rattled open and they stepped forth, he motioned David to follow him outside. They walked silently beneath a three quarters moon, which provided the lone illumination in a deep and darkening sky, until Ambrose veered onto a narrow cutaway to their right. Manicured bushes lined the brief segue, which soon fell out into an elegant courtyard adorned with lush gardens, stone benches, and decorative fountains that rippled like the footsteps of children in the otherwise muted night. Several cameras inclined down from their perches.

Ambrose paced to the center of the expanse and gazed skyward. "So many moons I have seen," he muttered, as if to himself.

"I have to answer for what I did," David said. "What's it going to be?"

"What would you say?" Ambrose replied, without turning around. "What punishment befits the crime?"

"Just tell me," David said. "Just do it, whatever it is. I know what I did was wrong—wasn't who I am."

"Wasn't it?"

David squinted as the figure before him began to blur and convulse, and when it turned around, David saw that it was Merlin, his eyes glinting in the cadaverous wash of moonlight.

"The distinction between right and wrong, between good and bad," said the wizard, "can be a very thin line—the thinnest line."

David gestured up toward one of the cameras. "Won't they see us?"

The sorcerer chortled. "I have lived a long time, and am not, shall we say, without my enchantments."

David nodded. "Of course. So, what now? Doesn't Christian want me punished?"

Merlin smirked. "Surely, he does, though not on the grounds you might assume. He cannot have disruption, chaos, so what you did was of course unacceptable, and you would be wise to avoid a repeat, but you remain his prized possession, and he still harbors every intention of exploiting you to the fullest."

"So, he wants me to fight, to duel?"

"Yes, and that day is coming soon, doubtless, when he has conjured the proper challenge and recruited the highest bidders."

"He's taking things farther and farther," David said.

"Yes."

"How far will he go?"

"There is," said Merlin evenly, "but one end to which such paths lead."

"Then I must stop him."

"A noble aspiration, but for all your powers, remember you are weaponless, and up against adversaries who are not. You have no sword, no mirror."

"You could change that," David said. "You could return the mirror to me. They speak of honor, in this world, don't they? Of code... right and wrong? The mirror was given to me. It is not Christian's to keep, or yours."

"You have lived generations," Merlin said, "but are nevertheless in the infancy of understanding that. In time, should you survive it, you shall learn."

"Learn what?"

"Honor, code, truth, right and wrong: their meaning bends to the will of those with the power to shape them to their own purpose."

For a moment, they stood silent, poised in the cast of moonlight, accompanied by only the rippling of the fountains and the whisper of the unseen tide, bending to no purpose but its own.

David sighed. "Even my little sister knows that can't be true. Those things, no one person can decide."

"Except you?"

"I never said that." He paused. "Have you opened it?"

This inquiry seemed to catch the wizard somewhat off guard. "I have not."

"That surprises me," David said. "Hasn't Christian asked you to?"

Merlin smiled. "You know he has."

"Then why?"

"Why would you suppose? Honor? Code?"

David squinted through the darkness at the glinting eyes of the timeless figure across the courtyard, trying to read the unreadable.

"Fear," he said at last.

Merlin flinched as through struck. "You will return now to your quarters." He whirled about and stalked off into the darkness.

CHAPTER 32
The Draugr

DAVID AWOKE TO A CHILL IN the room. When he'd rubbed the sleep from his eyes, he spotted the note about three feet from his door, curled at the edges and penned in black ink. He thought perhaps he'd heard it being slid beneath his door like a whisper, delivered from without by an icy hand.

He swung his legs off the bed, stood a moment, yawning, then padded over and retrieved the paper.

> *Ek dare þú.*
> *Caleb G~*

He'd no idea the tongue, but was reasonably certain what it meant, owing to its author. That was the thing about this world: it intoned a language wholly its own, regardless of words or the inclination of its audience to receive it, cutting across lands and lifetimes, a great and whistling blade, rendering likewise its ultimate implications in blood. That language now coursed through his veins, pulsing with a chorus of voices—he knew not how many, only that blood was what bound them. His ability to decipher them might well be the one thing to ensure his would not be the last.

At any rate, he'd been challenged by none other than Caleb Gallows, the Draugr—he who came from death. No mystery, then, the chill that curdled within him like sudden winter, but within this gloom kindled an ember of resolve. This date with Gallows could mean the worst for him, except that one thing remained even worse than death: sitting around awaiting it. In this world of immortality, time was running out, an hourglass conducted by every hand, it seemed, but his own. This duel might just be one way to change that.

When he left his room, he found the first employee he could and asked the man to take him to see the woman he'd injured in the gallery. The staff person regarded him quizzically at first, then stepped away and spoke furtively into his radio. After a moment, he stepped back over to David and escorted him to the woman's office in a far corridor of the compound.

She tensed upon seeing him, and seemed surprised — even briefly moved — by his contrition, but quickly regained a dispassionate air.

"Apology accepted," she said. "See to it you behave in no such manner again."

He ate breakfast with Ruhi, then accompanied her to the infirmary. Harlan had only recently been released back to his quarters, still recovering from his injuries. The infirmary more resembled a prison; when David and Ruhi entered, an armed guard stepped before them and inquired as to their business. Upon their reply, he murmured into his radio, and the door to an adjoining room opened.

A friendly-looking woman stepped through and motioned them forward. "She's doing better," she said.

David thought he recognized her as an immortal he'd seen around the compound.

"Dr. Ainsely... yes, I'm a captive too," she said, apparently noticing his perplexion. "I talked them into letting me check on patients." She glanced about, then leaned toward them. "I don't exactly have great faith in their commitment of care." She straightened back up, smiled, and exited the room.

They spied Dani immediately, in a bed at the end of the next room, being attended to by a nurse, and she smiled and sat up upon seeing them.

Another guard stood inside the door.

"Just a short visit," said the nurse, briefly checking Dani's wound before exiting.

David pulled two chairs bedside, and he and Ruhi sat. They asked how she was feeling and talked about her duel and the incident in the gallery, and when David mentioned the note he'd received from Gallows that morning, Dani's face became awash in concern.

"It's okay," he said, before she could put voice to her obvious distress. "I can handle him."

"It's not you," Dani said, her voice lowered. "And it's not even him — Gallows." She peered over the guard, and lowered her voice further yet. "It's Christian. You are his great possession — his prize. He wouldn't be letting you duel — not yet — unless people had paid top dollar to see it, and unless he's planning to give them quite the show. Unless he's willing to let things go as far as they might go. Until...."

"She's right," Ruhi said, glancing between the two of them. "I can feel it. I have seen it in his eyes. He is willing to let this one be to the death."

"I know. It's all been headed to this." David inhaled deeply, then slowly let it out. "But I can handle it, and if I can't... well, he's not from my timeline, or whatever the rules are. He can't kill me, not for good, anyway." He smiled weakly.

Ruhi looked down.

Dani touched David's arm. "Please don't say that."

"Hey! Why so down?" He regarded his two friends, knowing quite well the answer. "It might not come to that. Let's cheer up. Let's just focus on you getting better, okay?"

"Okay," the guard called from across the room. "Time's up."

David shot a glance at him, but then stood, as did Ruhi. They both leaned down and gave Dani a gentle hug.

"We'll be back," David said.

"You better."

They had neared the door when Dani called after them.

"Do be careful... with Gallows. No one here has ever fought him before. No one knows what they can do. There are only the legends."

"Thanks," David said. "I will be."

They turned back around and exited past the guard and out of the room. Dani's warning hung over him as they headed back toward their quarters, but so too did another consideration: No one here had fought *him* either.

***

HE'D SPENT MORE TIME IN GRAVEYARDS

lately than he could have ever imagined, but nonetheless did not expect, upon entering the arena, to be stepping forth into another.

Whether more special effects, or force of will by Gallows himself, he could not know, but now the contest had truly begun — no introductions, no choosing of weapons. It was dark — a conjured evening palely lit by conjured moonlight — and though he could not spy his opponent, he felt to his bones that he was there. He couldn't make out the upper gallery, but knew Christian and his guests were up there, behind their impervious enclosure, indulging in the fine trappings and decadent fare, awaiting the show.

No time for outrage. He'd no sword, no mirror, no weapon or means of defense to speak of, and somewhere in the creeping darkness lurked an adversary whose motives and methods remained as elusive as the shadows that attended him. He considered only survival of the moment, that he just might make it to the next.

If these were effects, they were good ones. The tombstones were real, solid and cold to the touch, inscribed in a hand he didn't recognize. They weren't speaking to him — the graves, or their inhabitants — as they had that day in the cemetery with Marcel, but that only meant he occupied a time and place with which he was unfamiliar. All of it felt unfamiliar, not the least of which this notion of Draugrs, of which Dani had spoken. Not borne of light, she had said. He was killed, murdered in cold blood.

This world was dark and cold and unequivocal, as if it could not have been anything other, and had never been. The terrain was hardly uniform or pristine. Portions sloped up or down, and some stones looked well kept, others less so. Some distance away, a spade leaned against what appeared a freshly excavated mound of dirt. A conjured memory might have been too flawless in its presentation. No, he was there — here — wherever and whenever here was. He felt a chill bump ascending his spine, and knew the moment was close at hand.

Good. He wished Gallows would call him out, challenge him, berate him, whatever might be his preference, but he'd never heard the man utter a word. Not ever. So be it. He'd come to understand that where words failed, time and mortality intoned as a language all their own.

He thought to call out to Gallows, but just as quickly dismissed the notion. His opponent was hardly apt to reply in kind. No, they would wage this contest in the still of silence. A gray and palpable fog had descended, draping over the moonlit stones. He peered into the depthless void before him, but the dark and fog had reduced the landscape into scant more than a shapeless impression. He set forward deliberately, one hand outstretched to ward off an attack or accidental collision with a stone or tree or whatever else. He stumbled more than once as he proceeded, owing to the mottled terrain, and was forced to lower his eyes to watch his footing. This, he knew, was ill-advised, and tendered his already slim chances of spying an attack virtually nil.

He stopped walking, cast a glance about, and lowered himself slowly to the ground. "Sorry," he said softly, to whosever's stone he'd propped his back against.

He wondered if Caleb were armed, had been given weapons, unfair an advantage as that would be. *'Foul is fair and fair is foul.'* He remembered the utterance vividly, on that warm evening not so long ago, watching Amanda perform on stage. Nothing was as it seemed. Nothing had been for quite some time, and he harbored no illusion that Christian might be burdened in the slightest by considerations of fair play.

A deep inhale, a slow release, and the fog of his breath drifted into the darkness like a wayward spirit. Better to stay put than continue lumbering about, making himself easy prey. Let Gallows find him, but then what? Again, weaponless... or was he? He closed his eyes, endeavoring to perceive, somewhere in the muster of lifetimes past, some attribute that might serve him in this moment. He saw himself on that great hill back at Tintagel, the mighty Arondight humming in his grip, instructing him.

Come on, he thought, and felt his heart rate kicking back up. The chill in the arena deepened, with Gallows doubtless soon to be upon him. *Tell me.*

No answer came, save for silence, that frequent bedfellow of the dark. No hallowed weapon had come within his grasp. They were watching him — his friends, Christian and his gawking guests, other immortals — and perhaps watching Gallows too, wherever he lurked. Perhaps they were like fans at a horror film, calling out desperately to the witless protagonist upon the screen. *'Behind you! He's behind you!'* His heart accelerated and, as if in accompaniment, his eyes flew open. He scrambled to his feet and whirled about, prepared to encounter Gallows, but gazed only upon the procession of stones trailing into obscurity. He peered into the darkness, that he might distinguish a shape, a shadow, a clue. Birds trilled somewhere in the invisible distance, and now sounded the forlorn howl of what David could only assume was a wolf, here in the arena. Of course, it wasn't the arena at this moment in time — not for him. God only knew, and perhaps Gallows, what moment in time it was.

No sign of the Draugr. No movement at all. *No matter.*

David set forth once more across the rutted terrain, in this world that couldn't be, yet inescapably was. The gravestones hove into view as he went, spectral and jagged, glinting in the moonlight like monstrous fangs. Rows of stones fell out to either side as he progressed, and he crooked his neck left and right with every step, in hopes of spying his adversary before an ambush, yet still no sign. He vaguely wondered if in any past lives he harbored the power of great deduction, or keen premonition, that he might sleuth Gallows out, roust him from his refuge, and compel this confrontation to its final end.

When he neared the row with the open grave, he paused, for an even greater chill had descended, the same he'd felt upon first glimpsing Gallows that day with Dani. He felt his heart accelerating and was sure he could hear it, frightfully loud upon this theatre of the dead. He glanced to either side, then whirled about in apprehension of finding Gallows right there upon him, but once again, only darkness. Ever and always, darkness. Everyone did all in their power to avoid Gallows, the Draugr, this strange and mysterious soul who evoked fear in mortals and immortals alike, but David wanted nothing more in that moment than to encounter him.

When he turned back around, Gallows appeared, as if in answer, rising from the unearthed grave—not clambering out and standing, but rising, rigid and upright, hands clasped across his chest, as though a ghostly puppet. He was attired in what appeared old-century funeral wear—black trousers and vest, a white, buttoned shirt—and bore a pallor of pale death, but what apprehended David's attention was the reddish blot that spread like a flowering rose across Gallows' chest.

David ducked instinctively and glanced quickly about, but then remembered Dani's account of his opponent's cryptic awakening. *Born of Death.* He spun back to Gallows, who now loomed, suspended, a few feet above the open grave, regarding David with a malevolence death itself had yet to fathom.

This is new: a levitating adversary.

David assumed a defensive posture, but this, surely, was rooted in the muscle memory of more traditional battles, like fencing or hand-to-hand combat, but not this, whatever *this* was. Would Gallows fly at him like a deranged missile? Fire upon him with some yet revealed weapon? He braced for whatever onslaught might be forthcoming, but when several moments later it had not, he couldn't help but yearn for it, desperately, that he would at last discern and decipher it, and muster all that he might in response. *Evade,* he'd learned in lifetimes past, *parry.*

Still nothing. Still Gallows hovered over him in the moonlit gloom, glowering down at him like a hellbent wraith.

The silence weighed upon David like an anchor. The trifling. He glared back up at his looming adversary. "Let's get on with it!"

"You are not in control here," Gallows retorted, the first time David had heard him speak, his voice old-world and strange, deep yet shrill, as cold and piercing as the chill that conducted it. His face twisted in contempt. *"Lightkeeper."*

Their eyes met, and David flinched, surprising himself. "Neither of us is in control," he replied. "Or haven't you figured that out?"

Gallows narrowed his gaze, unsettling David further still. *'Everyone steers clear of him,'* Dani had told him. *'They won't even make eye contact.'*

"Tonight, I am," Gallows said, maintaining his glare.

David wanted to look away, felt a profound imperative to do so, but resisted. Not that a stare-down would decide this matter, but somehow it seemed important he not succumb. He looked on as Gallows slowly drifted back to earth, settling mere feet from David, bloodstained and pale and regarding him fiendishly.

"The great David Rose. All that matters is your quest, your timeline. Well...." He took a long stride toward David, bringing them face to face. "Not to me."

David grimaced, owing not only the disquieting glare, but so too now an overpowering reek, but not body odor, at least not the normal kind. Gallows smelled of blood and bones and dust. He smelled of death.

"I don't claim to be any more important than anyone else," David said. "We're both just pawns in this game. But if you're too stupid to see that, then you give me no choice."

Gallows sneered and his eyes narrowed, searching David's own, searing into them, beyond them, as if into his very soul, as though scouring the manifest of every embodiment he'd ever been.

The stench and chill overwhelmed David, and he was certain Gallows could feel the trepidation of his pounding heart.

"Arrogance." Gallows sniffed. "But also fear. It's a wonder you've survived this long."

He suddenly took a step back and to the side, and David moved with him, poised for any sudden attack. Gallows kept moving, circling him slowly, and David matched the pirouette in turn. Their shadows undulated as they moved, like ghoulish marionettes in a fateful danse macabre.

"I fear your luck is at an end," said Gallows. "No more lifetimes for you."

"I never thought there would be," David said, continuing the strange rotation. "But I will do what I must in this one."

Gallows laughed—a grotesque, incongruous report—and at last came to a stop. They had in essence reversed positions, David now standing near the grave from which Gallows had minutes earlier risen.

"Search your heart," Gallows told him, maintaining his infernal glare. "You are at last doubting whether that is any longer true."

My heart? What could Gallows know of it?

Yet, something was amiss; he could feel it, feel the icy grip upon it, and he knew it to be Gallows', a cold and skeletal hand protruded somehow from that abominable stare, those sunken, lifeless eyes. That heart, which moments previous had been spurred to full gallop from adrenaline and fear, now seemed to be slowing, languishing, helplessly succumbing to the cloak of gloom that Gallows had wrought. His opponent took a strident step forward, and David felt himself taking a corresponding step back.

No! He tried to will himself forward, towards his adversary, but his legs felt as slowed and heavy as his heart, and he could only look on as Gallows moved closer still.

He hoped very much that his life wouldn't flash before his eyes—as an immortal, a luxury he couldn't afford. He hoped for an epiphany, some bolt of lightning power or perception that would jolt him from this spell. A bolt of lightning itself would be just fine, but... nothing. Only darkness presented itself, illuminated solely by that ghastly, pale countenance of his adversary, Gallows, the Draugr, who had inched ever closer, a living death.

"I cannot kill you," Gallows hissed. "Not for good, anyway, but I can consign you. I can defeat you here and now, and in so doing, sentence you to that same purgatory that has been my life." He took a swift and sudden step forward, closing the final space between them.

David felt himself retreating, once more against his beseeching will, and saw his arms flailing to either side. When he thudded against the dirt floor, the breath rushed out of him, and he fought desperately to recapture it as the dark figure stood over the grave, looking down at him like night itself.

"And now, David Rose, we switch places, you and I. You shall rise, as I did, but so too, rise in death." Gallows reached for something.

David felt his eyes grow rapt upon observing the unmistakable silhouette of the spade he'd seen propped against the mound of dirt. *Come on. Where's Lancelot? Or Duncan? Any of them? Any of me?*

He tried again to call them, but none would answer, and he welled with shame that their storied legacy seemed poised to meet such an unbecoming end. He thought of his friends—here on the island, and those back home—and of his family. The inspiration they evoked had yet to fail him, yet still his body lay listless, the life and will ebbing from him. He had failed them all.

When the first heap of shoveled earth came cascading down, he closed his eyes and mouth and winced as the dirt pelted him, and spit away those bits that had still managed to breach his lips, and turned his head and brought his arms up over his face before the next salvo could do likewise. A third layer came, then a fourth. He vaguely wondered if Christian might at last declare a victor and call an end to this, but understood immediately the folly of such thinking. Mercy and reason were hardly the currency of this realm. Besides, Christian was probably furious at him — the great David

Rose, his prized possession, going down without a fight. Another layer. Another. This was happening.

Rachel, forgive me.

His breathing, which had scarcely come back to him, once again grew labored, and distant. The world was falling away from him, or he from it—a netherworld of boundless shadow—except....

In his mind's eye, he stood back upon the hill at Tintagel, beneath the eclipse, as the legendary diamond ring effect transpired, at first but the faintest of glimmers, but slowly spreading. Where there had been darkness, light. His arms and angled posture had prevented his face from becoming submerged—so far, anyway—and when he forced his eyes ever so slightly open, he squinted in amazement at the illumination he beheld.

My watch.

The watch from his mother, which did not possess a light, nonetheless gleamed now like a beacon in the blackness of this would-be tomb. He could still hear Gallows holding court above, as he continued to rain more dirt upon David, but even Gallows, even what was happening, became for the moment, secondary. The watch, this last, best connection to his mother, not only glowed impossibly, but upon its face now materialized another unmistakable one.

'If you need me, truly need me, I'll know.'

He felt his mouth spreading into a helpless grin, and happily spat away the invading soil.

"David," Marcel said, his voice wonderfully, if inexplicably, clarion. "I am heartened to at last make contact. Pray tell, I haven't caught you at a bad time?"

CHAPTER 33
Rising Up

'*SOMETIMES, IT IS NOT THE MAGIC* of the
*vessel alone, but the vessel in the hands of him chosen to wield
it.*' Such had been Merlin's words to his unwitting liege.
The watch was not a light, not a phone, and not a magic
mirror. It was nothing David had ever thought to wield,
and yet, each day, each moment in this new world, was
an unlearning, a humbling, a looking askance at all that
had been, a looking anew at all that couldn't be, but
somehow was.

Marcel had spoken quickly, given the urgency of
David's message, and the obvious predicament in
which he'd found David. He instructed David as to
what he must do, both at present and in the days to
follow.

A reservoir of adrenaline simmered within David
in consideration of the news, but first things first. He
maneuvered to his back, braced his arms against either
side of the dirt walls, and propped himself up. Layers of
earth cascaded from his chest, and when the next
shovelful came, he shook his head fiercely, pushed off
from the walls, and rose. The grave was deep, perhaps
with great exertion scalable, but he knew Gallows
would turn the spade upon him the moment he might
breach the surface. No, he required something else. He
thought about what Marcel had said, and Merlin, and
raised his arm before him so that the watch was sighted

upward, and closed his eyes as another heap of soil rained down.

Rise.

And he did. He watched in amazement as a golden shaft of light blazed forth from his watch, piercing the darkness, and then looked down and stared in disbelief as his feet left the ground. He harbored no illusion that he could fly, but his heart soared in wonder. He knew it was but the power of the moment—call it magic, maybe—but it infused him with the same exhilaration he'd felt upon first wielding Arondight, and when he'd first beheld the otherworldly incandescence of the mirror. The beam from his watch propelled him, pressing back upon him like a counterweight until he breached the surface.

Gallows did not, in fact, attack him, but stumbled back wildly. The first flickering of fear colored his eyes as he beheld his adversary rising up from that abode he himself had occupied minutes previous.

As soon as David cleared the grave, his feet again gained purchase upon the ground, and the illumination from his watch faded as quickly as it had come. No matter. He'd had no intention of turning it upon Gallows, who had relinquished the spade and stood, transfixed, looking a great deal less ominous. This fight was over, and that was precisely the point of it; that was David's stand. He wasn't here to fight; he was here to survive, and to leave, and to help the others leave too.

He peered into the darkness at where he reasoned the spectator gallery to be. This time, he did not call out, for he knew Christian could see him, had seen him, could see what he could do. And while he likely was brimming with anticipation of even greater duels now, he hopefully read in David' s eyes the futility of pursuing this one further.

When the lights came up, and a handful of attendants marched onto the field to check on both combatants, David exhaled in relief. He needed to rest, and then, to act. The enormity of what Marcel had shared with him was dawning more fully upon him. There was a reckoning at hand, and like so many other things in this world, it presented the countervailing bedfellows of hope—of the grandest nature—and danger—of the gravest sort. This time, far more lives than his own hung in the balance, and rested in his hands.

This included Ruhi, their pre-immortal friend, whose suspected powers were anticipated and coveted so intently by Christian.

***

RUHI'S BIRTHDAY WAS TWO DAYS

away, and they told David the next morning that, as expected, her "gift" from their gracious host was an invitation to her first duel.

David was unfamiliar with her opponent, but it hardly mattered. "We cannot let her fight," he told his friends as they ate breakfast.

Dani had watched David's duel on the TV monitor, and had been released from the infirmary just that morning. She still looked banged up.

Harlan did too, even though he'd been released several days previous. He sported a pair of sunglasses to hide his lingering black eyes. "No," he said. "We can't."

"To awaken in violence...." Dani shook her head.

"That's how it happened with me," David said, softly. "Maybe with a lot of us."

"But it doesn't have to happen to her," Dani said. "She is too innocent, too good."

Harlan took a swig of juice and nodded. "And too powerful. No way to know what could happen."

"There is a way," Dani corrected. "And Christian wants to find out. He's charging a pretty penny for it, no doubt."

David shifted in his chair and surveyed the area. "Where is she?"

"In her room," Dani said, her voice low and tinged with melancholy. "She wasn't hungry."

"Can't much blame her," Harlan said. He pounded his fist on the table, rattling their trays. "That son of a bitch.... Some birthday present! A gift to himself."

David nodded. "But one he won't get to open." His friends regarded him intently, and he leaned forward and lowered his voice. "You haven't asked me how I escaped that grave last night."

"We saw it," Harlan replied. He nodded at David's wrist. "Your watch... it was like a rocket ship. How, I haven't a clue, but I learned long ago to stop questioning things."

David smiled. "Never stop questioning things. There was something more it did, before the part you saw, while I was still down there." He eyed the watch wistfully.

Dani put a hand on his arm. "What did it do?"

"It called me," David said, shrugging. "I don't know how, but it did, like the mirror had done before, and it was Marcel."

Harlan removed his sunglasses and regarded David with narrowed eyes. "Your friend?"

David smiled. "Yeah, my friend."

Dani said, "What did he say?"

David swiveled once again and swept his gaze around the rec hall. He waited for a few immortals to pass by with their trays, then turned back to the table.

"He said Ruhi won't have to fight, because there's a different fight coming."

His friends leaned forward, their eyes rapt.

"Well, he didn't mention Ruhi," David said. "He doesn't know her, but what he told me amounts to that. Let's finish up and go see her. She won't fight on her birthday, because we're going to get out of here before then."

***

RUHI HAD BEEN SURPRISED AND grateful at the news, but extremely worried. "Christian won't let us go without a fight," she said. "He'll stop at nothing if he sees us rising up against him. I believe you, David, that your friends are as remarkable and as powerful as you say, but there are only a few of them. Christian has dozens, just based on what we've seen, likely as many more as he might need to summon."

"But that's the thing," David said. "As many as he might need to summon. We won't plan to wait around and find out. How many are here at any one time? Where does he summon more from? How do they get here?"

"By ship," Dani said. "Not sure from where, but we've seen it before, shifts of workers arriving, supplies. Sometimes one of those small planes comes, the kind that can land in the water. Christian no doubt controls these waters, and maybe the airspace too."

David considered that for a moment. "Okay, it won't be easy, but it's a chance, and even a small chance is better than none. Besides, they're mortal — all of them, as far as we know. We have an advantage, no matter how many of them there are."

Dani said, "But you're assuming all of the immortals will side with us. What if they don't?"

David raised an eyebrow. "They're all captives. You really think any of them would forego a chance at freedom, and side with the one who robbed them of it?"

Dani shook her head and sighed. "I think each of us has learned to never assume. What about the Valoris? What about Gallows?"

"I know," he said. "I know. They're bad, but still, wouldn't they swallow their pride and join us if it meant getting out of here and having the freedom to go be evil to their heart's content?"

"Sometimes," said Ruhi, her eyes alight with the wisdom of lives yet lived, "an evil heart is content to forsake freedom, at the chance to deny another theirs. We must not be surprised at with whom they might ally."

They fell silent for a while, steeped in the gravity of that to come.

At length, Harlan nodded again at David's wrist and said, "We're forgetting one other thing: Ambrose. He had your watch. He had to know its powers, even if you didn't. Why would he allow you to have it back? Maybe he's on our side. It could make every difference."

"Yeah," David ceded. "It could, but I just don't know. He warned Christian against giving it back to me, and he attacked me, but I saw something in his eyes... heard something in his voice."

Dani said, "What did you hear?"

"I wish I knew." David let out an exasperated breath. "I still don't always know what the voices in my own head are telling me."

Harlan huffed. "Well, it might be worth finding out."

"Sure," said David. "I'll just tell him we're planning to escape tomorrow, and if he'd like to help us, great, but if not, to please not say anything." He nudged Harlan's shoulder. "Just playing. Gotta still be able to laugh a little, huh?"

"Forgive me," said Ruhi. "I commend the spirit in which it is tendered, but this is no laughing matter."

David let go of his smile. "No, it's not. We need to know where people stand, and we need to find out as quickly and carefully as possible." He turned back to Harlan. "I think you're going to be the key."

CHAPTER 34
One Small Candle

A GROUP MESSAGE OF ANY SORT was, of course, out of the question, even if they'd had the means to accomplish it; so too the notion of alerting the other immortals one by one—simply not enough time. But when Harlan had defeated Lars Valori, an ember had lit in David's mind. He didn't know what exactly, and he didn't know when, only that Harlan's unique power of illusion would be called upon in some manner, when the time came.

The time was now.

They would gather and address the other immortals at dinner that evening, hoping as many as possible would indeed be present. Dani's caution regarding the loyalties of each immortal was not lost upon David: they would not summon Gallows, the Valoris, or the two who'd been abducted that night from the graveyard, or a handful of others, but that wasn't the half of it. The entire matter would require no small degree of subterfuge, and a Herculean effort on Harlan's part.

When they arrived for dinner, David and his friends got their food and proceeded to a table at a far end of the dining hall. Some other immortals were already seated at various tables; others were still arriving. When a few minutes later it appeared those who were going to be there, were there, David turned to

Harlan, who was wearing the same torn shirt from his duel, which he'd called his "Badge of Honor."

"Ready?"

Harlan nodded, clasped his hands together as though in some manner of communion, and swept his gaze over the entirety of the hall. After a few moments, he unclasped his hands and spread them slowly apart in front of him, as though parting an invisible curtain.

David rose quietly from his chair and headed over to the nearest table. "Hey," he said, as the five occupants looked up. "Sorry to bother you guys, but I need to share some important news. I'm asking everyone to gather at our table for a few minutes." He nodded over his shoulder.

"What news?" inquired one, a female with short, dark hair.

"I need to tell everyone at once," David explained. "No time for anything else."

A young man at the table scoffed and crooked his head toward the pair of guards across the hall. "They'll know something's up."

David said. "No, they won't, not if we're quick enough."

Perhaps ten minutes later, he had navigated to every table, save for those occupied by dubious immortals, and though there were some close calls, as each cohort indicated varying degrees of skepticism, they now gathered around David's table, where Ruhi and Dani had in the meantime pulled a few spare tables and chairs alongside. More than a few of them, David included, cast an occasional, nervous glance toward the guards and uninvited immortals, but thus far, Harlan's enchantment seemed to have gone undetected. David couldn't help but marvel at the scene: Harlan had conjured a flawless replica of the dining hall from just prior to David getting up to solicit the others — immortals at various tables eating; others heading to or from the food line. What had been, as far as the eye could see, still was; and beneath this summoned veil, what was, had never been.

"We have a chance to get out of here," David told the assembled group. "Tomorrow. I am sorry for such little notice, and it won't be easy. It'll be a fight. And it'll depend on each and every one of us." He paused, letting it all sink in.

He glanced at Harlan, who continued to paint the air. A vein in his neck throbbed, and beads of sweat tinted his forehead, as if holding the entirety of the hall in his hands.

David turned back to the group, having no time to spare. He told them what Marcel had told him: that there would be a rescue attempt, that it would only be Marcel and a few allies, and that help would be needed, lest they be hopelessly outnumbered.

The immortals listened, and for the most part did not interject, honoring David's request — in consideration of time and Harlan's obvious strain — to let him say his piece, before asking questions. When he'd finished, he glanced once more at Harlan's panorama, and then Harlan himself.

"How much longer?" he asked.

"Five minutes," Harlan rasped, without breaking his gaze from his handiwork. "Maybe."

David turned back to the group. "So, who's in?"

The immortals cast glances at one another, murmuring, and a few hands slowly rose.

"Come on," said a man about halfway down the row of tables. He cast a glance to the immortals to either side of him. "We're just going to take his word for all this? How do we know any of it is true, that he even had such a conversation—through his watch, no less? And even if he did, did he hear correctly? You know?"

The group fell silent As David checked on Harlan, who was blinking furiously as sweat streamed into his eyes.

Ruhi took a napkin and gently mopped his brow.

"Thanks," Harlan said.

"No time to argue," David told the group. "I have nothing to gain by making this up. What I said happened, happened." He gestured at Harlan, Dani and Ruhi. "We're getting out of here. At least we're going to try. Each of you has the chance to do the same."

"Okay," said a woman a few seats to David's right. "Even if we believe you, that this man, this friend of yours, told you this, we don't know him at all. We don't know what he is or isn't capable of. Christian has countless guards, and guns."

"Not countless," Ruhi said. "About twenty-five, or thirty, at any given time."

"How do you know?" David tapped his temple. "Do you feel how many? Get a sense of these things?"

Ruhi giggled. "Actually, yes, but also, I count. When you're somewhere a long time, you take in your environment, notice things, learn." She shrugged. "Even if it's just to pass the time."

"Fine," said the woman who'd voiced her concern. "Thirty. Thirty with guns. God knows what else. Even if we believe you, even if we go along—we could lose our lives in the process."

The immortals each looked up at David, who, without hesitation, said, "Yes, you could. I would not do you the dishonor of denying that."

"Okay," replied the woman. "Then why chance it? Yes, we're captives here, but we're alive, at least."

"For now," Dani said.

David glanced again at Harlan, as more murmurs spread throughout the group.

"Maybe a minute," Harlan gasped.

David turned back to the group. "We're out of time. I've told you all I can. The more who join us, the better our chances, but the choice lies with each of you. You must decide what you think is right. All I ask is that you not give us away."

Isla, whom they had observed with James that first night in the arena, said, "How will we know it's happening?"

"I don't know," David said quietly. "I am sorry. I wish I had a way to safely signal each of you, but I don't." He felt a hand on his arm, and glanced down at Ruhi.

"I do," she said.

***

OVER HER PROTESTATIONS, AS SHE did not wish to distract from their preparations, they celebrated Ruhi that evening. Her birthday — and, as far as Christian was concerned, her duel, and awakening — would come in two days, but the rescue attempt would be tomorrow. Although they each voiced their intention to celebrate together on her actual day, each understood that which need not be spoken: tomorrow was not guaranteed, nor the following day, nor any subsequent.

Dani had prevailed upon one of the kindly culinary staff to bake a small cake, and they took it outside with some small plates and plastic utensils, and set it atop the balustrade that lined that section of the compound.

Night had fallen, the sea moving tremulously not far off — black, rolling hills beneath a placid moon. A flamboyant tree rattled and swayed just off the veranda.

"They only gave me one candle," Dani said, apologetically.

Ruhi touched her arm. "You didn't have to do any of this."

Dani's eyes welled and glinted in the moonlight. She threw her arms around Ruhi and embraced her. "You are the brightest light I've ever known. One small candle is the least we could do." She stepped back and wiped a hand across her eyes. "Of course, they wouldn't give me any matches."

"Don't want us playing with fire," said Harlan. "Hmphh."

"I'm sorry," Dani told Ruhi.

"Please don't be," Ruhi said, smiling. "I am grateful to each of you."

Dani broke into a broad smile. "Well, we can still sing to you, even if it's a bit early."

"Wait a minute," Harlan interjected. "David, can't you conjure a light? You certainly did last night."

David glanced at his watch and said, "I don't know how that happened, and I don't know how to make it happen again. I could blow us all up."

Harlan shrugged. "Maybe Ambrose did something to it."

"I would put nothing past him," said a voice belonging to none of them. Ambrose stepped from the shadows, and approached.

David stood between him and his friends. "How long were you standing there?"

"You should know as well as anyone the futility of judging time, especially in a place like this." Ambrose nodded to each of David's friends, then raised an eyebrow upon spying the cake, in the center of which perched the unlit candle. "As for tinkering with your timepiece, I did nothing of the sort."

"Fine," David said. "Now, if you don't mind—"

"Why would I mind?" Ambrose said. "I was just coming to return another of your possessions, should that be satisfactory to you." He slipped a hand into his shirt pocket. "Nor have I meddled with this one." He withdrew the item, and extended it to David.

David gazed at it. "Why are you doing this? Does this mean—"

"Once again, preoccupied with those things unknown. What is time, in our world? What does 'why' mean? Platitudes proffered for which there can be no answer, roads taken which have no end." He leaned close to David's ear and dropped his voice to a whisper. "My reasons are my own."

At this, he whirled about and strode off in the direction from whence he'd come. When he suddenly raised a hand and snapped his fingers, David flinched in instinctive anticipation of a hex, but when he turned around to check on his friends, he saw they were fine, but that the solitary candle on the cake had now lit.

"Well," said Harlan, "that was interesting." He nodded toward the new object in David's hand. "What the heck is that?"

David rotated the mirror slowly between his fingers. "It's a long story."

"Hey, you didn't tell him about tomorrow."

David peered into the shadowed recesses into which Ambrose had disappeared. "He knows."

"Anyway," said Dani. "You should make a wish, Ruhi."

They all looked at their young friend, who was gazing up through the lightly swaying branches at the latticework of stars materializing against the darkening sky.

Harlan followed her gaze. "Anything interesting?"

Ruhi smiled. "Aquila," she said.

Harlan appeared bemused. "Tequila?"

Ruhi giggled. "Aquila. Constellation on the celestial equator. Latin for eagle. Can you see the wings?"

They all craned their necks, and peered.

Ruhi explained, "Aquila represents the bird that carried the thunderbolts of Zeus."

"In mythology," Harlan said.

Ruhi shrugged. "So it is said, but who can say for sure? Who's to say we're not creating our own, here and now."

"I think I see it," Dani said, squinting toward the heavens. "The wings. There's a lot up there."

"There is indeed," said Ruhi. "See the brightest one? That's Altair. It's one vertex of The Summer Triangle."

"The Summer Triangle?" David chuckled. "Sounds like a bad romantic comedy." He glanced quickly at Dani, then back skyward.

Ruhi smiled. "It's an astronomical asterism in the northern celestial hemisphere. The defining vertices of the triangle are Altair, Deneb, and Vega, each the brightest star of its constellation."

"Somebody likes astronomy," Harlan said.

"I like eagles," Ruhi said. "My earliest memories are of my grandmother telling me stories before bedtime. She would sit cross-legged on the floor in our main room, near the fire, and hold me in her lap and tell me stories until I slept. It felt like the safest place in the world. My favorite story was about a great eagle that would come to the villages in time of dire need. It came when there was a battle, or a flood, or any time the village, or even a single one of its members, needed help."

Ruhi glanced at her friends before lifting her gaze once more. "And when my grandmother died, I went outside and waited and waited for the great eagle to come and escort her body, and to make everything better, and even after dark I refused to come in until finally my father came out and held me and explained that the eagle would indeed be coming, but in spirit, to escort my grandmother's soul."

She lowered her head to her chest, then once more regarded them. "Ever since then, whenever I miss her, or am frightened, I think of her on eagle's wings, gently soaring into the sunset, and the peaceful world beyond." She smiled, and her eyes wore a faraway look. "People have always found comfort in their own ways."

Dani smiled and put an arm around her shoulder. "Come on, the candle's lit. Let's sing."

And so they did. They sang to Ruhi, who stood beaming shyly in the moonlight, their voices trailing away on unknown winds, against which the small candle bowed but did not extinguish. It flickered and danced against the backdrop of the dark and rolling sea, so very small in comparison, but if regarded just right, as bright and brilliant as anything any of them had ever seen.

CHAPTER 35
One If by Land

THE QUESTION OF MERLIN'S ALLEGIANCE weighed heavily upon David's mind. Harlan had been right: it could make every difference. And what about the other immortals, the ones they'd confided in that evening? On whose side would they come down, when the time came? He also worried greatly about how he would know that the game was afoot, to quote Holmes. There hadn't exactly been an abundance of time when Marcel had "called." He only knew they were coming — Marcel and perhaps a few others — and there was bound to be a battle.

David hadn't the slightest clue by what means they were coming — by plane or by ship — or if perhaps they had somehow already infiltrated the island and were preparing to storm the compound. It reminded him of the Longfellow poem back in grade school: One if by land, and two if by sea. Would there be a signal? Would he know it if he saw it? These considerations and countless others conspired with the sheer anticipation of the moment to render it a fretful, restless night.

He wasn't certain he'd slept — more of a fitful stupor — but when the hands of his watch showed 6:00, he slipped from bed already dressed. He'd clutched the mirror to his chest throughout the night, ever so tempted to flip it open and try to reach Marcel, but had resisted. *Too dangerous.* Same with his watch, not that he'd the faintest idea how to make that happen. Nonetheless, he at last possessed both items, and this provided him no small measure of comfort. If only he had his sword....

They'd agreed to meet at 6:30 in case things began sooner than later. They got breakfast, knowing they needed strength, but none ate much given the state of their nerves. A smattering of other immortals had entered the hall, getting breakfast, moving languidly in the warm swath of morning light. A few took notice of David and his friends and looked their way an extra few seconds, as though expecting some signal, but, receiving none, they continued about their business. Even the kitchen staff and the guards seemed mellowed and nonchalant, yawning and sipping coffee. Just another day on the island. Sounded nice, when you thought of it that way.

David shook his head.

"What?" Harlan set down his mug and regarded him.

"Nothing," David said. "It's just so weird, the staff shuffling around like everything's normal. They have no idea what's coming."

"I hope not," Harlan replied. "As far as they're concerned, everything is normal."

"Shame on them," said Dani, quietly, looking up from her untouched food, "for ever accepting any of this as normal."

"Okay, okay," Harlan acknowledged. "I agree. I'm just saying...."

David checked his watch. "What time is the first duel today?"

"9:00," answered Dani.

David nodded and took a deep breath. "I hope it starts before then. It'll be really tough if we're all down there."

"Can't you try the mirror," Harlan asked. "To try to reach him?"

"I'm supposed to be careful with it, and I don't really know what it can do."

"But you know it can do that," Harlan said. "Right? I mean, it's worked before."

"Marcel said I would know. I've seen it do other things, some amazing, some I couldn't even begin to describe, and it's done some things to me I can't risk happening again."

Harlan shrugged, nodded, and stabbed at his food.

Dani turned to Ruhi and said, "You doing okay? Are you sure you're up to this?"

Ruhi smiled weakly and nodded.

Dani put an arm around her.

They sat a while longer, swaddled in the amber glaze of sunlight and the comfort of words which needed not be spoken.

A couple minutes later, Ambrose appeared at the far end of the room, paused at the entrance, so that part of him was illuminated by the sunlit room while the rest remained obscured in shadow, and summoned one of the guards with a crook of his finger.

"Wonder what he wants," said Harlan.

They didn't have to wait long. The summoned guard cast a glance around the hall and, upon spotting their table, was now heading their way.

David eyed his approach before casting a wary eye back toward Ambrose. Several other immortals had paused to watch the guard. By the time he'd reached their table, David was standing to receive him.

"Mr. Ellerby requires your presence," said the guard.

David raised an eyebrow at first, then remembered. It had been a while since he'd heard Christian's last name. "Now?"

"Now."

David nodded, and turned back a final time to his friends. He placed a hand on Ruhi's shoulder, and they briefly locked eyes. He then nodded at each of them, turned back around, and headed off with the guard toward Ambrose.

***

AMBROSE EXCORTED HIM SILENTLY

on the long, winding walk to Christian's office, the corridor flaring brightly each time the wall gave way to windows. David held a hand to his eyes and peered out in each instance, more hoping than expecting to catch a glimpse of an arriving ship, as if one could just glide on in undetected, or undeterred. Yet something was afoot; he could feel it. Why else would Christian have summoned him? There were few coincidences in this world.

He spotted no ship, however, and no sign, just the fire of daybreak upon the gilded waters, so blinding in its brilliance as to offer not the slightest illumination. So it was that when at last they reached the stately doors of Christian's office, Ambrose—Merlin—paused and addressed him.

"Every soul has his prize, and his price," he said. "I have lived a long time, and little remains of more intrigue than that which each of us discovers we hold most dear."

When the doors swung open into Christian's office, David knew, instantly. He saw him, knew him, even though his back was turned and his modest frame was scarcely visible behind the lavish chair in which he sat.

Bram, the one who'd abducted him, sat nearby, and they both faced Christian, who sat, smiling and imperious, behind his desk. The black and white clock ticked high on the wall behind him.

"David Rose," Christian entreated. "Do come in." He gestured to an empty seat in between the seated men, and David approached it.

Ambrose strode past the desk and sidled up against the wall behind Christian, looking over his shoulder, expressionless.

"You have met Bram," Christian said, in an amicable tone, "and I do believe you are familiar with our visitor."

When Marcel turned to greet him, David forgot all sense of cover, should any have been required, and embraced him so forcefully that Marcel grunted in surprise, but then reciprocated. David stepped back and straightened up, and when Marcel motioned with his eyes to the empty chair, he nodded and sat.

"Your kind," said Christian, "continue to amaze me." He nodded toward Marcel, while keeping his eyes fixed on David's. "Never before has one discovered our enterprise." He now trained his gaze upon Marcel. "Much less managed to breach it."

If this were to solicit an explanation from Marcel, none appeared forthcoming.

"Well," said Christian, leaning forward with clasped hands. "Our guest here has tendered a most interesting offer, a deal." He nodded at David. "It must be nice, having such a friend. Believe me, it is quite rare."

David glanced at Marcel before returning his attention to Christian. "What deal?"

Marcel turned to face him. "He'll let you go."

David felt his eyes go wide.

"In return," Marcel continued, "I will leave his—" He paused and cleared his throat. "—enterprise... unrevealed and undisturbed."

It was Christian's turn to clear his throat. "And?"

Marcel glared at Christian, and turned back to David. "And, you are to fight one more duel. Tonight."

"Not just any duel," Christian noted. "You will match against one of your dear friends, if we have observed correctly. Dani, I believe?" He looked to Bram for affirmation.

David felt his fists balling as if they had a mind of their own. "You aren't even sure of her name? You're just pairing us because we're friends? That brings you enjoyment?"

"Oh, the friendship is simply happenstance," Christian replied. "Though it does make for a more compelling story, and that always pleases my guests. But that is secondary. The revelation, the *pièce de résistance*, is something our wizard here has unearthed in his endless study of your ways." He leaned forward, eyes glinting.

David cast a glance at Ambrose, who stood, still impassive, behind his boss.

"You and your little friend," Christian said, "your opponent this evening, share the same timeline, as it were—same original lifetime. Incipient souls, I think you call it?"

David slumped back in his chair and shook his head. "I won't hurt her, and I don't think she'll hurt me."

"You'll do more than that," Christian said. "This is a first, at my tournaments, and I have charged a premium. From what I understand, two immortals from the same lifetimes, thrust onto the battlefield, will be unable to resist the call to arms, the call to combat."

David glared at Christian for a few maddening seconds, then turned to Marcel. "That is your deal?"

Marcel nodded once. "It is."

David regarded him intently, this man he'd yearned for so very long to finally see, the man who would rescue him and the others. He searched Marcel for a sign, studied his face and read his eyes for the faintest glimmer, the quickest wink, something to assure him that this was all part of the plan, intended to misdirect and appease Christian, so that the true rescue could unfold. But he observed in Marcel only the most resolute affirmation of that which he'd spoken, and he felt in his heart the first-ever pangs of disappointment in his sacred friend.

How could he agree to such terms?

And there was a matter of even greater consequence. He turned back to Christian and looked him squarely in the eyes. "I'll duel, but then you let us go." He felt all eyes on him.

Christian furrowed his brow. "Indeed, that is as I have described. You and your friend here will then be free to go, should you survive the duel."

David shook his head. "No, not just us. *Us!* Every immortal. Everyone you abducted. Everyone whose lives you stole."

The room grew heavy with the ensuing silence as David kept his gaze fixed upon Christian's. Behind Christian, the clock ticked away the seconds. It seemed the only sound in the world.

At length, Marcel cleared his throat again and addressed their host. "I wonder if you might grant us just a few minutes alone."

CHAPTER 36
Where Souls Were Kindred

THEY WERE ATTENDED BY ARMED guards, as expected, but Christian had at least permitted them to walk outside, along the beach. Once at the water, David was embarrassed to feel his heart accelerating, in hopes once more of spotting a ship, a submersible, some magical vessel onto which they would somehow make their implausible escape.

No, Christian understood there was no risk of this, and ever the businessman, the dealmaker, if granting this small request increased the chances of his deal being realized, he was happy to oblige. That he had assented to free David, however, that he had in such short order come to view forfeiting his prized catch as somehow a good deal, was nothing short of astonishing.

Marcel had convinced him, clearly, that it was in his best interest to do so.

"I won't hurt her," David said.

He glanced back at the guards, who were keeping pace while allowing them a little space — fifteen feet or so. Between the distance and steady thrum of the surf, David doubted they'd be overheard.

Saltwater perfumed the air, along with the scent of flowers from the nearby gardens. A smattering of gulls cawed and dove in the distance. David peered eastward, where the sun calved upon the far horizon, half submerged, gleaming spokes lifting from the golden orb like fiery digits. A medley of cotton-candy clouds hung languidly about.

Marcel replied without breaking stride. "You may try to avoid doing so, but when incipient souls are thrust together, sometimes there is no choice."

"You always have a choice," David said. "Haven't you taught me that?"

"It would appear," said Marcel, sounding momentarily distant, "I do not have all the answers for which you so kindly give me credit. You heard Christian: this is the first time he has matched incipient souls. His guests have paid him well. He will require a decisive victor."

"Then I'll let her win, even if she hurts me a little."

"You are incipient souls!"

David flinched at the sharpness in his friend's voice.

"There is no *little*. If you let her win, she may well kill you, and there would be no coming back."

"And no coming back for her. I won't do it."

They walked silently a while, until at length, Marcel replied. "Your sense of honor and principle never fails to inspire me, a ceaseless reminder of why you are who you are."

"But?"

"But there have been developments, wheels in motion, the ramifications of which cannot be overstated. Which, it pains me to say, renders your position, however admirable, trivial by comparison."

"Trivial? These people have been abducted. Some will die. None will see their families ever again, or their friends. That's trivial?"

"It brings me no pleasure to say it, but relative to all that hangs in the balance, yes, it is. All that matters is freeing you, and at the soonest possible hour."

"Then why have me duel? Why not now?"

"Sometimes we bargain," Marcel said. "To do otherwise would have meant a fight, and that could take longer, and risk more, than the slight acquiescence I agreed to."

"Slight acquiescence? Don't you care about these people? Their lives will be lost. What about Ruhi? She isn't even awakened yet. Do you know what he has planned for her?"

Marcel stopped and turned to face him. He held a hand up toward the guards, who thankfully paused their gait, and waited.

"Of course, I care," Marcel said. "But I haven't the luxury to succumb to it, or all could be lost, including incalculably more lives than theirs." He gripped David by both shoulders, so tightly it surprised him. "It is because we care that we must steel ourselves. It is because we feel that we must learn not to feel too much. Not yet."

David squinted. "It's that serious, these developments?"

Marcel straightened up, looked skyward, and nodded. "Having lived as long as I have, I am disinclined toward hyperbole. And still, I tell you now, these developments are as grave as mankind has ever faced."

"My mother," David said. "If I go now, will I see her?"

"I cannot promise it, but this is our best—and perhaps only—chance."

It was David's turn to glance toward to the heavens. Here at long last was his best chance to fulfill his promise to Rachel, to do all in his power to find their mom, but she had retained faith too, their mother—in him. *'The moment we cease to do right,'* she'd told him, *'is the moment we have lost ourselves.'*

"I'm sorry," he said, "but I won't hurt her, and I won't leave the others behind."

Their eyes locked, wordlessly conveying all that, in that moment, was required. No greater articulation existed, where souls were kindred, than those things unsaid. They looked out to the shimmering, placid waters, as if to an unseen storm they knew to be gathering.

"This will delay things," Marcel said. "It'll be a fight."

David turned back. "It was always going to be."

It might have been the reflection of sea and sun, but David thought he caught that familiar twinkle in Marcel's eyes. Marcel nodded toward David's feet, and David glanced down to observe a ring of violet flowers encircling him.

Amaranth. The nearest gardens lay a hundred feet inland. "There isn't much time."

"Where immortality is concerned," said Marcel, "there never is."

***

IT FELT TO DAVID LESS A plan than a gambit, a Hail Mary pass like quarterbacks would throw in desperate hope that someone, somehow, would pull off a miracle. What he and Marcel had agreed to, in those last fleeting moments before the guards insisted they return, might require just that. One in a million was better than zero, but should that miracle elude them, they might never escape this place, or even survive.

Marcel watched from the spectator gallery that evening, along with Christian's VIP guests. The other immortals were not in the bullpen, as usually required for their possible inclusion in a random draw, for tonight was anything but random, a marquee contest between incipient souls, one being him — the talk of the immortals, David Rose, Christian's prized possession. It was good the others were not there, if their plan were to stand any chance. It would, however, render matters that much tougher there below.

For now, he must focus on Dani. She stood perhaps fifty feet across the arena from him, but he could read upon her face the same foreboding that gnawed presently at him. She surely wondered if their plan stood a chance, whether either of them would get to find out. They'd been given swords — had been forced to take them — and they each gripped their unsolicited blades with one hand at the handle, letting the tapered end rest upon the earth.... For now.

"Welcome, honored guests, on this unprecedented occasion!" Christian's proclamation through the sound system wrested away their attention. "You shall journey back in time to bear witness to a phenomenon at once sobering and exhilarating: a battle between not just two immortals, but incipient souls. There are no greater stakes. An immortal may only be truly vanquished by another whose soul was born of the same lifetime. Our intrepid warriors — dear friends, as it so happens — stand upon our battlefield, awaiting the call to arms. Good luck to you both. And to our dear guests... enjoy!"

David simmered, but forced the anger back down for now, determined that Christian would get what he had coming. He knew he shouldn't feel that way, but he did. That would have to wait, as now he must focus.

The lights in the spectator gallery dimmed, the dome of the arena darkened and disappeared, and the ground beneath them began to undulate and transform.

His arms flared out to either side to maintain balance, the sword heavy as he did so, and he could see Dani likewise attempting to maintain herself.

It felt different from his duel with Gallows. This felt more like that day in the woods, propped against the oak tree, when the world had fallen away and others risen, including the one in which he'd landed, like Dorothy upon Oz, and where he might otherwise still be marooned, had it not been for Robert. He saw his best friend now in his mind's eye, and his heart filled with a terrible melancholy, but the image quickly faded. People, recollections, and feelings welled within him and galloped past, falling from memory like the collapsing world around them, there a moment then gone, phantoms, as though belonging to a consciousness no longer his own.

When the sky finally ceased rushing past, and the ground beneath them steadied, he was unsurprised to observe that which had shaped up before them, where the arena mere moments ago had been. It wasn't Tintagel or Camelot looming over them, but a castle, nonetheless — perhaps Dani's.

Except... it was no longer Dani who stood across the landscape from him. Or perhaps it was — just a very different Dani than he'd known, different from the one who'd stood across the arena from him not two minutes previous. She was now a he, bedecked in full armor, though helmetless, a full beard and unruly shock of hair tufting in the evening breeze. An unfamiliar visage, but familiar indeed was the surge of hostility now coursing through David's veins. By virtue of this rival tribesman, or the immortal pull, he could not say, but he felt old instinct rousing, and slowly retrieved his sword from the scabbard in which he now found it ensconced.

He too had transformed, without intention—so many times had he tried, but failed—back to his incipient soul: Lancelot. He lifted his weapon into the moonlit night, brimming with power and purpose and fear—the latter owing to the diminishing recollection of who he'd just been, and the fading restraint that seemed to have attended it. He was Lancelot, knight and warrior, and he was home. Whoever else he was, and all other matters, would simply have to wait until he'd discharged his present duty: vanquishing this wayward enemy who now approached.

His adversary's blade gleamed in the evening luster, at the ready, and he didn't have to regard his own weapon to know it was not Arondight. No matter. Like the finest soldiers, he maintained many swords at his disposal. Still, something gnawed at him from within regarding his most hallowed blade—a consideration for another time, as the enemy was nearly upon him, the moment nigh. He thought to inquire of his rival's name, but reproached himself silently for such a notion. This was a duel, a battle of will and skill, power and prowess, a contest likely to prove, for at least one of them, their last.

No, let's not be tendering introductions.

Yet still, that gnawing *something* remained, and this agitated him in no small measure. He was Lancelot, guided unflinchingly by honor, strength, and a determination more unrelenting and unequivocal than in all the kingdom, or beyond.

That determination, he prayed, would foment up and through him in that very moment, as his opponent set upon him, their swords clattering together like a bladesmith's forge. A volley of sparks showered from the point of impact, fading like embers, only to be replaced by the ensuing salvo, and again, and again.

He is skilled, thought Lancelot. *This much is clear.*

Years of unrivaled dominance had burdened him at times with overconfidence, but this early barrage had arrested his attention. Yet it was hardly the only thing that had. The strange foreboding, which whispered to him like a voice from some lifetime past, returned. Yet he had no lifetime past. He was Lancelot, the first and only, and must without distraction attend to the mortal contest in which he now engaged.

And yet....

He parried the next blow, rained upon him with precision and ferocity, and in one motion countered with a powerful strike of his own.

His opponent grunted, but immediately rejoined the fray with renewed vigor.

Lancelot responded in kind, understanding swordfights were not intended to be marathon affairs. Fatigue would soon set in for both, rendering it anybody's contest. Lancelot thus parried the next salvo, pushed his adversary back with the hilt of his blade, and charged, sword brandished, two-handed, above his head. When he brought it down, he felt instantly that his opponent was at last weakening—the opening he needed, the turning point that every swordsman in the land prayed would arise in his favor. He swung his weapon skyward once more, and without pause swept it down upon the defensively postured blade of the weakening knight. He repeated this until his adversary had fallen to his knees, and could no longer lift his weapon.

Lancelot stood over his vanquished foe, panting in exertion, and said, "Raise your head, sir. You have battled valiantly." He always had insisted upon meeting an opponent's gaze, even the most reviled enemy, before dispatching him. To do otherwise was cowardly. When the fallen knight did as exhorted, their eyes locked, and Lancelot flinched at what he saw — at whom. He could not yet place it, but now came once more those whispers from beyond.

Look, they called. *The eyes always tell.*

The eyes of his adversary now suggested that which the elusive whispers could not. Through their own articulation, they conveyed him back to that time and place and purpose upon which mere minutes ago he'd stood. *They'd* stood... him and Dani. He David, and she Dani. Dani. The fallen man before him. David, the youth inside this borrowed frame. Never had he experienced anything like this: he was Lancelot du Lac, one of the greatest knights of the Round Table, and yet, he wasn't. Perhaps, more aptly stated, he was, but not *just* Lancelot. Ghostly tales of possession had haunted the land from time immemorial, none of which he'd subscribed to, and no aspect of which evoked in him the slightest fear. He was Lancelot.

And yet....

This extraordinary development felt less an occupancy than a union. He was Lancelot, and he was David, from divergent lifetimes, yet all at once. Here and now.

I am you now?

Yes, and you were me. Forgive this brief intrusion sir. Until we meet again.

He gripped his sword with one hand, and grabbed the shoulder of his adversary with the other. "Make tight the grip upon your blade," he said. "Now hang on."

He watched as the ancient sky descended, as stars and worlds tumbled past, as light and darkness flared and swam, until all converged in a kaleidoscope of time and place beyond all telling. He clenched his eyes so tightly shut that they hurt, and hoped his friend was doing likewise. The ground beneath them shifted, far more unsettling than had it merely shaken. It was no earthquake, and no storm; it was a world falling, transforming beneath their feet, until he could gain no purchase and pedaled there upon the nothingness, two wayward, wingless travelers upon the thoroughfare of the heavens, that only it would see them home.

He tightened his grip upon Dani's shoulder. *Almost there,* he told himself. Perhaps wishing would make it so.

Not home, exactly, but *back* — to where they'd stood not long ago, upon the fashioned battlefield of this forsaken place, unwilling participants in this forbidden tournament. He took a calming breath, for their plan — fleeting though their time to devise one had been — appeared, at least for the moment, to have held. For when he opened his aching eyes, and the world stopped spinning and at last resolved into view, he saw they had indeed returned to the arena. It was just him, David, and her, Dani, as she had been before their soul-crossed journey through millennia past. Hardly lost upon him was how narrowly they'd dodged disaster, how rapidly they'd immersed into their incipient selves, how close to striking a fatal blow he'd come. They'd been pretty confident in their ability to remain themselves, but how quickly a gaping hole had been blasted through that veneer.

Thank goodness for the eyes... and Dani's wisdom.

Still, Christian would demand a decisive victory, given the stakes, and for the satisfaction of his high-priced guests. David wasn't certain what the spectators had been able to see when he and Dani had been transformed, but now was the time to play their hand, and pray it worked well enough — and long enough — to give them a fighting chance.

He released his grip from Dani's shoulder. "Okay," he whispered, and took a step backwards.

His friend crumpled to the ground. Her arm fell back, her weapon clattering against the earth of the arena floor and skittering from her grip. Her other arm and hand came to rest upon her chest, as they'd discussed.

David stepped to her, leveled the edge of his blade a few inches from her throat, then slowly raised his head toward the spectator gallery, behind which Christian and his dignitaries doubtlessly stared, attention rapt. He lifted his weapon away from Dani, turned to face the gallery full on, and rested his blade upon the earth before him, hands clasped over the scabbard. He stared up at the darkened gallery, and reckoned their host was staring right back.

In the purview of his mind's eye, their gazes now fixed upon the other's, and David slowly and unequivocally shook his head.

CHAPTER 37
The Desperation of a Moment

IT SEEMED A PECULIAR TIME TO think about Newton, but then again, not really. The last time had been in the school office months ago, when Cerratus had attempted through hypnosis to induce David's awakening. The Third Law of Motion: *For every action there is an equal and opposite reaction.* It had helped him stave off the counselor's dastardly attempts that day, in the simmering impatience it had stoked, at ceaselessly playing the pawn in this unwanted game. He hadn't known a thing about physics, and still didn't, but he had learned that there were times he could — and must — be the one to play his hand. He must be the one to dictate the moves upon the chess board, even should it — and in this case, he was banking on the likelihood it would — result in an equal and opposite reaction. Or worse.

Sure enough, the crackling of the PA system prefaced the announcement.

"You are immortals," intoned Christian's voice, absent its usual cordiality. "You are incipient souls. The duel will have its victor. One lives, one dies."

David flinched, though he'd come to understand this day would come. It stirred within him an unbridled sense of revolt, not at what might happen to him and Dani, for their plan was well in motion, but rather, to the others, should it fail.

And so, it mustn't.

He maintained his grip upon his weapon, his gaze upon the gallery, and again shook his head. Silence pervaded the arena, the sort you could almost see for its quivering anticipation.

"Ready?" David whispered.

"Ready," Dani whispered back.

"Shouldn't be long."

It wasn't. The iron doors at the far end of the arena hummed and rattled open, and four guards emerged and strode toward them.

"Four of them," David said. "Tasers, I think. Holstered, for the moment."

The PA system crackled, and Christian bellowed, "It would be unfortunate to be coerced into resumption. The choice is yours."

"She's hurt," David called when the guards had moved within earshot. "At least get her medical attention first. Otherwise, it'll be liking shooting fish in a barrel."

"Then count yourself lucky," one of the guards scoffed.

Another stepped past him and peered down at Dani, whose breath now rattled out in halting, rasping intervals. "What are her injuries?" she asked.

"Not sure," David said, "but I pierced through her armor. We had armor when we... back in—"

"Yes," the woman said tersely, crouching down to get a better look. "We saw."

David nodded toward where Dani's hand rested upon her chest, as if staunching a wound, and said, "It may have gone through a lung." He watched as the guard's eyes narrowed, and tightened the grip upon his sword. "Thank you."

The guard glanced up with rebuke in her eyes and said, "Don't. I am just ascertaining if you are being forthright, or—"

"Or full of shit," said one of the other guards.

All in one motion, Dani retrieved her sword, sat up, and crooked her other arm around the throat of the crouching guard.

The other three rushed forward, but David beat them there and held his blade aloft. "Don't," he warned, as one of them went for his taser. He heard rasping behind him, and the scrabbling of feet upon the earth. "Got her?" he called back.

"Got her," Dani said.

"Come on," spat one of the guards, his hand twitching upon his holster. "He can't stop all of us."

"True," David said, "but which one of you wants to be first?"

The men kept their hands upon their holsters, but for the moment made no effort to unsheathe their weapons. As they eyed one another uncertainly, the arena fell quiet once more—a standstill.

The PA crackled. "Don't be foolish!" Christian cried. "Release her at once, or I will send more guards!"

Please.

"Very well, then!"

Dani and her captive stood, Dani's arm still crooked around the woman's neck, her sword still poised.

"Let's go." David took a step backwards, brandishing his sword at the seething guards before him. "Don't move!"

He glanced quickly back again, to ensure Dani and the woman had begun their retreat to the back of the arena. No exits there; the way off the field, and to the elevator, was at the opposite end.

Good. He remembered the first time Bram had escorted him down the small and clattering lift. *Where we head now, precious few ways in.* David smiled. *Or out.*

When they reached the far end, Dani leaned against the curved wall for support, maintaining her grip around the guard's neck. David stopped a few feet in front of them, fixing his eyes on the three guards, and the iron doors through which they'd come. He didn't have to wait long.

Another contingent of guards marched imperiously through the opening, this time with guns, and they were not holstered. They strode briskly to where their three associates stood, and David held his sword aloft as he watched them confer. Slowly, the new arrivals fanned out left and right, until they'd formed a semi-circle.

David counted quickly: a dozen new arrivals, making sixteen total, counting the hostage. He swallowed, as each guard leveled their weapons.

"David...."

"It's okay," he called back to Dani. "They won't shoot."

"What?" rasped their captive. "Of course, they will. You think Christian prizes life more than fortune? Than power?"

"Not our lives," David replied. "But yours."

She laughed, a choking, incongruous sound. "Then you truly are a fool!"

"David...."

"It's okay, Dani," he said again, but his heart welled with remorse.

Too many times he'd placed an innocent in harm's way, all to serve his grand purpose. Even Marcel had seemed to think their sacrifice might be necessary, and justified, but David couldn't think like that. He wouldn't... even if deep inside, within the darkest corners of his wayward soul, he knew it to be true.

He turned to face Dani. "I know he'll stop at nothing, but they won't shoot yet. She's right." He nodded at the captive guard. "He'll do anything to protect his power, and his investments, but remember, we're part of that investment. He'll do all he can to negotiate the best possible outcome, before going that far. And we haven't yet played our hand." He looked into her eyes. "Will you trust me?"

Dani nodded, and David felt his blood coursing with the solemnity of her affirmation. He nodded in return, set his jaw, whirled back around, and once more raised his sword.

"Give it up!" called a tall guard at the center of their formation. "You are surrounded."

"I've faced worse," David replied.

The guard shook his head, withdrew a radio from his pocket, and spoke briefly into it.

David stared past him to the iron doors — waiting, hoping. He endured that briefest yet most interminable of intervals, when everything hangs in the balance, and time is but a prayer; when in the desperation of a moment, all the world resolves into meticulous resolution.

Any second now.

When they barreled through, David's heart soared. There were eight of them, which meant twenty-four total, here below in the arena. Ruhi has sworn that there were thirty, max, on any given day within the compound. That meant a half-dozen or so remained above.

When the reinforcements reached the formation of their peers, the guard who'd called out began his advance, flanked by two additional men on either side, and the new arrivals fell into line in their wake.

"Now, David!" The fear was palpable in Dani's voice.

He kept the sword leveled with one hand, and moved the other to his back pocket.

The guards were perhaps fifty feet away, and closing fast.

"Not yet," David said.

Forty feet. Thirty.

"David!"

Twenty.

"Now!" he cried.

The now-freed guard raced past him. "He's got something!" she called to her colleagues.

And so he did. He flipped the mirror open as Dani moved shoulder to shoulder with him.

The guards halted ten feet shy of them, and leveled their weapons.

"Drop the swords," the leader ordered, and then, with furrowed brow, "and the mirror."

"He's right," David whispered.

"What?"

"We leave our swords. Too dangerous to have them sucked in with us."

"We may need them!" Dani pleaded.

"Not worth the risk. Do it."

Their blades clanked to the arena floor.

"Good," the guard called. "Now the mirror."

By then, it was too late, even had David been inclined to oblige. A gleaming vortex spiraled out of the face of the mirror, of a hue and composition he could not possibly determine. He turned to Dani, and their eyes met a final time.

"Together!" he cried, and they bowed their heads toward the rising funnel, stepped forward, and he clenched his jaw and closed his eyes as he felt himself being drawn in.

He thought of Rachel, that should these be his final thoughts, the last would be of her. That should they not make it out, she would find comfort, find peace — somehow, some way. In that strange theater of his mind's eye, he saw her, smiling at him from within a sanctuary of resplendent light, somehow more luminous than even that of the gleaming tunnel into which he and Dani now spun. He smiled, exhaled deeply, and surrendered.

CHAPTER 38
A Rising Tide

THEY LANDED—AT LEAST IT FELT to him like landing—face-first upon the sand, exhausted and disheveled, like shipwrecked survivors after struggling to shore. He'd clearly overshot, but was beyond grateful that they'd made it through, alive and, he cautiously surmised, in one piece. The world continued spinning, though less dramatically than it had upon their journey.

Through blurry eyes he spied the mirror a few feet off, having caromed from his hand upon impact. He crawled to retrieve it and snapped the lid shut. As his vision cleared, he saw they'd emerged on the side of the island with the prodigious expanse of mangroves, obscuring their view of the compound.

He slid over to Dani and placed a hand on her shoulder. "You okay?"

She lifted her head slowly, brushed sand from her face and hair, and nodded. "I think so. You?"

"I think so."

"Well," she said, raising to her knees. "That was... different." She looked at him. "How did you do that?"

"I really don't know." He turned the mirror in his hands. "I just focused the best I could, and remembered what Marcel told me: 'Envision what you want, and why you want it.'"

He wobbled to his feet, slid the mirror into his pocket, and held out his arm for Dani to brace upon as she staggered up. He turned his head in either direction.

"Probably easier to walk around," he said.

Dani looked out to sea, where the sun sank upon the far horizon, yielding beneath a dome of dark blue dusk. "I don't see a ship." She turned back. "Is there a ship? Wouldn't Christian intercept it?"

"I don't know," David said. "But I doubt it would be here on this side."

"So, you're not sure how we're supposed to get out of here? Get off the island?"

"Sorry." He looked past the mangroves toward the compound. "Marcel may still be in there. He can tell us."

"Do you trust him?"

"I do."

"Okay."

In her voice, David registered an unequivocal leap of faith.

"Let's do it," she said.

David nodded, managed a smile, and together they set forth around the stretch of mangroves.

"Whatever we find in there," David said, "it might be happening fast. It might be bad. We'll have to be ready to act, and maybe to do things we've never done, and never wanted to do."

"Understood," Dani said without breaking stride. "Envision what you want—"

"And why you want it."

It was Dani's turn to smile.

A quarter moon had settled into a far quadrant of eastern sky, lending to their path a candlelight glow that, under any other circumstance, would have rendered it an idyllic seaside stroll. The mangroves stretched out a considerable distance along the shore, and the two quickened their pace. When at last they had circumvented them, headed toward the compound, and reached the nearest doors, they paused and turned to one another.

"Whatever happens," David said, "thank you. You've been —"

Dani cut him off by wrapping him in a tight embrace, and said, "Thank you."

They straightened up, and David grasped the long, curving handle of the perimeter door at which they'd arrived. Their eyes met, Dani nodded, and David pulled.

It was, of course, locked.

David groaned.

Dani laughed and put a hand on his elbow when he glanced her way. "I'm sorry, it's just kinda funny. We just escaped about thirty guards by traveling through a mirror, but here we are thwarted by a locked door."

David smiled, surveyed their surroundings, and moved to retrieve a nearby stone. "Step back," he told Dani, and they both did.

He cocked his arm, but paused. Something didn't seem quite right — not always easy to distinguish, in this world upended. He narrowed his eyes and listened. Any second now, he reckoned, the sounds of bedlam would arise — immortals everywhere, and Christian's guards. The fight might be well underway. Yet no such sounds were forthcoming — no sounds at all, in fact.

"David." Dani had cupped her hands around her eyes, and was staring through the locked glass doors. "Look."

He didn't quite know what he expected to see when he moved to the door, cupped his hands over his eyes, and peered in, but... not this. When his eyes adjusted and the space inside resolved into view, he observed only Harlan, in his badge-of-honor torn shirt, cross-legged on the ground and painting the air with his open palms, as David had seen him do on two occasions previous. He was conjuring.

Across the hall, angled down toward where Harlan sat, perched one of the countless pairs of camera and screens. David stared wide-eyed at what they revealed, or, more to the point, what they didn't—namely, Harlan himself. The monitor, set though they were in real time, depicted an empty corridor, save for the occasional immortal or staff passing by, none of whom, David could plainly observe, was in actuality anywhere to be found.

He turned to Dani.

"I see it," she said.

"That must mean—"

Before he could finish, a face suddenly materialized on the other side of the glass, startling him. But then he smiled.

Ruhi flinched, clearly surprised as well, but when she registered who it was, she broke into an ear-to-ear grin. She pushed open the door and stepped outside, but before they could even greet her, another immortal appeared behind her and came through, and another, and another after that.

David could hear the swooshing footfalls of several others in tow, but no voices. They'd known to keep quiet, which was good. The escape was on.

"Ruhi," David said, as their friend stepped to the side to allow the procession to file past. "How did you—"

"Shh." Dani pressed a finger to her lips as the line of immortals continued through. She gestured toward Ruhi, and tapped her own forehead.

David nodded. He'd been concerned all along how'd they'd be able to communicate, when the time came, but now he had his answer. Ruhi had said she'd be able to do it, and she had. He regarded her briefly in amazement.

She's not even awakened yet.

He turned back to the doors, and in between the passing immortals saw Harlan in the same spot upon the floor, continuing his vigil. David glanced up at the monitor: still projecting Harlan's creations. The plan was working... for now.

Christian — and anyone else watching — had seen what had transpired, had watched as David and Dani had disappeared into the vortex. Of course, they didn't know where the two had come out, that they were still there, upon the property. Harlan's artistry had prevented the cameras from picking it up — again, for the time being, meaning for as long as Harlan could hold out and remain undiscovered. It wouldn't be long now, either way. Christian and his soldiers — and the immortals siding with them — would be onto them soon enough. Their ruse to lure as many guards as possible into the arena had paid off, but only for the moment. They'd be slowed by the limited means of access into and out of the arena, but would be in pursuit soon enough — armed and primed to do whatever necessary to prevent escape.

They must get off the island now, and David's heart revved with not only the urgency of the moment, but uncertainty of the next phase of their plan. Was this the right exit? Was there a ship, and if so, where? And where in the world was Marcel?

"Hey!"

David's attention snapped back towards the corridor, from which the accusing voice had issued, and where Harlan still sat, composing, his face strained in exertion. One of Christian's men had yelled. This was no surprise, as not every agent had been dispatched down to the arena, and it had been only a matter of time before someone on ground level had made the rounds. David watched as the man's face transformed in realization, as he glanced from Harlan to the monitor, and then outside.

"Code Red!" he shouted back over his shoulder, down the corridor. He then fumbled for his radio.

David flew to him and grabbed his hand, and as they struggled, David saw that the commotion had broken Harlan's focus, and that the monitor had reverted back to reality. It was all now plain to see, for whoever might be watching, but David had more immediate concerns. Forget the radio—the monitors had given them away—the revolver for which the man now grasped posed the gravest danger.

Harlan blinked away the cobwebs, and upon registering the transpiring struggle, scrambled to his feet and rushed to David's aid.

The guard was strong, and it was all they could do to prevent him from getting to his gun. Harlan and the guard came face to face, and the latter snapped his head forward into Harlan's nose. Harlan yelped and stumbled backwards.

Though David's instinct was to assist his friend, he saw the guard had seized the opportunity to withdraw his weapon. Without thinking, he swiftly chopped at his wrist, as though executing a sweep of his broadsword, and the gun went clattering to the ground.

Harlan, eyes fluttering, darted to it, scooped it up, and leveled it at the seething guard.

"You'll pay for that," the guard spat, rubbing his wrist. "Both of you."

"We've been paying," Harlan said.

David motioned to the guard. "On the ground now, face down. Hands on your head."

The guard scowled but, after a moment, complied.

Dani stepped through the doors and into the corridor, and briefly paused to take in the scene. "That's everyone," she said. "Everyone who's coming, anyway. Thirty-three, Ruhi says. Are you okay?"

Harlan wiped his shirtsleeve across his bloodied nose and said, "Fine."

Dani's eyes traced up to the monitors. She turned to David. "They're seeing this. What next?"

The answer came before he could provide one, which, given his uncertainty, was just as well — not the answer he wanted, but the expected one, at any rate. Around the corner now appeared Christian, flanked by a guard on either side.

Only two, at least. No Marcel.

David's heart hammered. Marcel had either slipped away, and was at that moment orchestrating the next steps of their escape, or.... *No.* He pushed the thought from his mind.

"Impressive!" Christian called. His men had drawn their guns, and when they neared to within fifteen feet, Christian held up a hand, and the three of them paused.

Harlan directed his own weapon in their direction.

"To have drawn my contingent to the arena," Christian continued, "and whatever magic that was to get you here." He paused and narrowed his eyes at Harlan. "Easy there! No need to take this any further. Your first time with a revolver?" He indicated the guards on either side of him, each of whom had their weapon sighted, motionless, upon Harlan.

"You can get up now," Christian called to the still-prone guard. "And you—" He regarded Harlan and shrugged. "—let's do the smart thing, and set your weapon—*my* weapon—upon the ground. We'll put this all behind us and go back to the way things were. Call your friends back in here. Where possibly can they think they're going?"

David glanced at his friends before turning back to Christian. "There's no going back."

The amicable demeanor Christian had maintained despite the standoff melted away. His eyes narrowed and set. "Understand this, you have lived many lifetimes. The implications of that, of immortality, are beyond anything I could possibly know—the indescribable summits, the unspeakable valleys, the pain, the joy, the love, the hate, the life, the death, the loss. I am awed by the perspective all of it—all those lifetimes—has surely conferred, truly. But you see, I have but this lifetime. Only this. And so, I possess neither the time nor perspective, however grand it might be, to be patient when all I have worked for my entire life—my one and only life—is suddenly imperiled. This will not stand."

"Then we will fall," David said. "But this is the stand we take." His heart pounded at the imminence of whatever would happen next. He was frightened, naturally—guns were drawn, and Christian had just laid things bare—but exhilarated nonetheless, that finally, they'd reached a tipping point. Finally, the moment of truth had arrived.

"Are you willing to die?" asked Christian.

"I've done it before," said David. "Are you willing to kill?"

"I think you know."

"Perhaps, but you know the cost. We're not zombies. We won't come back to life. That's not how it works. You kill us, and your precious operation is over. Your tournament dies. You'll be all out of players."

"I can get more."

David nodded. "Maybe, but the price you pay may be greater still. There are things you don't know, people you don't know."

"Yes," said Christian. "I've met your friend."

"Not Marcel. Others, and not all want to save me. Some want me dead, but by their hand, not yours."

"I think you're bluffing," Christian said. "At any rate, I don't want you dead. I'd prefer you very much alive. All of you. We'll try to see to that, though it will depend on you."

Out of the corner of his eye, David saw the gun trembling in Harlan's grip.

"My patience grows thin." Christian gestured outside, where the gathered immortals stood, awaiting instruction. "Would you lead them over the proverbial cliff, or in this case, to the bottom of the sea? There is no escape."

"We're not done yet," David said. Inside, he was not so sure — no Marcel, no ship.

"Your friend?" Christian scoffed. "An impressive gentleman, I grant you, but a bit long in the tooth, I'd say."

"Longer than you know," interrupted a new and welcome voice.

David's heart soared at the sight of Marcel standing in the doorway, attired in a long cloak.

"Slipped away for a wardrobe change?" Christian appeared bemused. "I fear it won't help you."

"That's not what you should fear." Marcel's eyes narrowed As he approached and placed a hand upon Harlan's shoulder. "Stand down, friend. Go now... each of you. Lead the others to the shore."

Christian snorted and glared at David. "My guards are coming any minute now. If by some miracle you even make it to the water, what then? The only ships in these parts belong to me. I would reconsider his advice, were I you."

David glanced at Marcel, then back at their host. "You're not."

He nodded at Harlan and Dani, and together they backed out of the corridor as Marcel stepped aside. Only when they were outside did Harlan lower his weapon.

David gazed out at the restless immortals, standing in limbo between the compound and the sea, and turned back to Marcel. "Which way? Around the mangroves?"

"Through," he said.

David furrowed his brow. "That'll slow us down."

"Yes," Marcel acknowledged. "And them as well."

"Enough," Christian interjected. "You're terribly outnumbered, and hopelessly out-armed."

"You are, of course, quite right," Marcel replied. "But you are an intelligent man, to have amassed and orchestrated all this. Clearly, you have gained at least some insight into our world."

"And?"

"And so, surely, you know something of its nature, its power, its inability to be measured in any conventional sense." Marcel gestured out to sea, where the last flares of daylight shimmered and broke upon the water. "Its origins lay well beyond our vision, its strength building not one by one, like so many stones assembled, but exponentially, like the tide we now behold — a gathering storm."

He turned back to Christian. "It is as if to tell the ocean it's outnumbered, because it is but one — to stand before it with your soldiers and their guns... like so many stones assembled. Then watch as they sink — inevitably — beneath that rising tide."

"Ever the orator," Christian said, withdrawing his own revolver now. "But I tire of the speeches. I'll offer one last chance: stand down, or it is you who falls today."

From within the compound came the clamor of voices and racing footsteps.

"As I said, you are outnumbered." Christian sighted his weapon upon Marcel. "Do the wise thing, and live to fight another day."

"Your faith in my wisdom appears misplaced." Marcel reached into his cloak and withdrew a long and gleaming sword.

David stared, transfixed, not merely at the sight of Marcel brandishing a weapon, but at the sight of the weapon itself. Even Arondight seemed somehow ordinary by comparison.

"David," Marcel said. "Go."

CHAPTER 39
A Moment Immortalized

IN A WORLD WHERE THE UNIMAGINABLE had become commonplace, and hardly anything any longer came as a surprise, the sight of Marcel poised there like some centurion, sword gleaming in the tallow embers of the day's last light, froze David in his tracks. He knew time was of the essence, yet he could not break from this spellbinding turn of events. For so very long had answers eluded him, but here, now, silhouetted in the doorway of the compound, seemed to stand an unequivocal resolution to a question he'd never asked.

He knew he must snap out of it, must turn and run and along with the others take flight through the labyrinth of mangroves, beyond which, if Marcel had by some miracle arranged it, would await their means of escape, and freedom. Yet something held him in place, pressing in on him, rooting him like the mangroves to the soil — one last glimpse at the indelible image before him, for in this eternal world, a moment immortalized and imprinted into the consciousness like an inscription upon stone. His heart pounded in exhilaration as well as fear: not a sword in this world could parry the salvo that might at any moment now be discharged upon his friend; yet there Marcel stood, resolute in his posture, seemingly convinced that his, in fact, would do just that.

"David," Dani said gently but insistently. "Come on."

He turned and faced the congregated immortals, who anxiously regarded him for instruction, just as he had regarded Marcel.

"Go!" he called, breaking into a trot toward them. He motioned toward the mangroves, which coiled in the background like some fiendish creature of the deep.

The last brushstrokes of sunset faded upon the horizon, a brilliant watercolor washing slowly away. A vault of darkness rose over the sea, against which flickered a latticework of stars, fixed and cold and unequivocal, presiding in their order above a world which knew anything but. The mangroves imprinted against the fallen night as though ink-stenciled. The fight was coming, David knew; that it would transpire in darkness seemed somehow fitting. A certain clarity belonged to nightfall: once your eyes adjusted, what was there, was there—unobscured by shadow, unblinded by light.

His fellow immortals seemed less certain. Some had begun to do as instructed, but many others lingered, taking a step or two, then pausing and looking back.

"Go!" David cried again.

Some still hesitated, but when they observed the majority complying, they whirled about and followed suit. The thrum of the surf increased with every step, but accompanying it now came the clamor of Christian's arriving forces.

David desperately wished to stop and take another glance backwards, or even to return to Marcel's side, but he resisted the call and kept on sprinting. As soon as he breached the tree line, it was as if they'd entered another world, a nighttime world, and he reckoned it would so appear even had it been the heart of day. The crucible of trunks and limbs spiraled overhead into a dense foliage, through which scant illumination managed to seep through. The water lapped at their ankles immediately, deeper as they went, and they splashed their way through methodically, as the poor visibility and jutting limbs presented a formidable obstacle course.

Why would Marcel have chosen this shoreline to send a rescue, if a rescue in fact awaited? And even if it has to be this, it would have been so much simpler to circumvent this monstrous impediment, even though it would be taking the long way around.

Still, his faith in his mentor remained unshakeable: Christian's forces were coming — he could hear their voices growing louder — and the group of immortals would be fish in a barrel were they set upon in the open. Through the mangroves — not *despite* the obstacle it posed, but *because* of it — they stood their best and perhaps only chance. Yet something else dawned upon him as he forded his way through the murky waters and snarled limbs, which jutted like timbered warriors lost to time. Not only did he harbor abiding faith in Marcel; so too did Marcel harbor the very same in him. This realization kindled in him not only great pride, but what with each day he was coming to better understand as a requisite responsibility. Marcel would do his best — was at this very moment doing so — to hold off Christian's forces, but it was up to David to lead the others through this daunting entanglement, and then hopefully to freedom on the other side — whatever happened, whatever it took.

It would take quite a bit, for the voices grew both louder and closer, and the group's progress had slowed to a crawl. He saw some bodies, and his heart jumped very briefly, but he quickly realized those folks had tripped, and each in turn scrambled back to their feet and forged ahead.

David remembered an old saying from a legendary basketball coach: *'Be quick, but don't hurry.'*

"Careful!" he called ahead. "One tree at a time. One branch. Watch your step and pull yourself forward. We'll get there!" *I hope.*

He wished desperately to cast a glance behind but for now resisted. They were coming, of this there was no doubt, but it struck him that the number of voices sounded somehow fewer than had seemed the case back at the compound. Perhaps Marcel had stopped a few — whatever that had entailed — or perhaps some had simply routed in either direction around the mangroves, to ensure the fleeing immortals would be surrounded, with no escape. Perhaps Marcel lay stricken where he'd moments ago so valiantly stood.

David clenched his jaw. He should go back, despite what Marcel had said. This man had been his saving grace through all of this, in more ways than he could possibly count. He was his mentor, his teacher, his protector. He was his friend.

He grabbed the nearest, jutting branch, and whirled around.

Something whistled past his face, and again. He heard a groan, whirled back around, and then he understood. *Tasers.* He rushed to where an immortal lay writhing on the ground. They were in ankle-deep water, and the targeted immortal had fallen face first, convulsing, face submerged. David grasped the long, metal string, plucked the still pulsing dart from the immortal, and flung it aside. He lifted the fallen young man, turned him, and cradled him as he turned back to face their attackers. He tried to slow his mind within the tumult of adrenaline and fear that pervaded him.

They have tasers. This is bad. But for now, they aren't using their guns. This is good... if we can still somehow escape.

He knew that if it came down to only two choices — kill them, or risk escape and exposure of his enterprise — Christian would under no circumstances chance the latter.

He peered through the twilight for a quick headcount: eight guards that he could make out. There could be more, but he must contend for now with what he knew. They had fanned out in groups of two, three of which slogged around and onward, tasers aimed, firing intermittently. More groaning arose, and the sound of bodies in the water.

David balled his fists as one of the duos was nearly upon him, taser still leveled.

"Give it up, Rose!" another called. "We have you dead to rights."

David looked down at his stricken comrade, who inhaled deeply and grimaced, and said, "What's your name?"

"Bates," he said.

"I'm David. Can you sit?"

"I think so."

David grabbed him under his armpits and pulled him to the nearest tree trunk, against which he helped prop him as comfortably as possible. Their eyes locked momentarily, Bates nodded, and David stood and turned back to face their attackers. The other three duos had forged ahead, but the men whom he now confronted were poised not ten feet away, tasers leveled, and even in the dusky gloom, David could make out their holstered firearms. His heart pounded as he grabbed one of the jutting, robust branches to steady himself. He thought to reach for the mirror, but couldn't be confident in what it would or wouldn't do in this moment, and any such gesture would surely provoke the guards. In his mind's eye, he saw Marcel materializing to save him, as he'd done multiple times before, but he quickly jettisoned this childish notion. This was one of those moments — the darkest hour, do or die — and he must answer the call, right here, right now. There was only him.

Or was there?

It had been the longest time since he'd felt it, and never when he'd tried, but here it came, and none too soon, effervescing from the most subterranean regions of his soul. His veins pulsed and his muscles twitched, accompanied by an incipient whisper, a calling, a strength. The branch strained and began to crack beneath his grip. He was uncertain what the guards read now in his own eyes, but in theirs, he now registered a sliver of something besides the obvious hostility. For the first time, he saw fear.

Good.

For the moment, however, it seemed only to exacerbate the danger, as their fingers twitched nervously upon the triggers.

"Come with us, Rose. You can make this easy."

The branch creaked.

He smiled. "So can you."

One of the guards spat. "Have it your way, kid." They stomped forward, weapons sighted.

Suddenly, David stood back at Tintagel, in the shadows of the great eclipse — memory rising, Lancelot rising — and he was there and he was here, all at once and all as one. The branch snapped beneath his grip and he swung it as he might have Arondight, slicing into the forearms of the nearest guard, who cursed as his taser went flying. The other fumbled at his trigger, and David swung the branch upwards, adjusting his grip as he did so, and with two hands thrust the limb with all his might into the face of the bewildered man. The guard yelped, blood spurting, and David flinched as the taser discharged, followed by a plunk as it dropped into the water.

The bloodied guard stumbled backwards, tripped upon some knotted roots, and fell. By this time, the first guard had his wits back about him and was reaching for his gun.

Before he could withdraw it, Bates grabbed him in a bearhug from behind, restraining him.

David wrested the gun from the struggling man's holster, sloshed a few steps backwards, aimed it at him, and said, "Stop fighting."

The guard's face twisted in contempt, but when he at last acquiesced, David waded over to the fallen guard, who lay prone in the water, glassy-eyed and semi-conscious. He withdrew the man's gun, tucked it in his own waistband, then gripped him beneath his armpits. With a grunt, he hoisted the man into a sitting position and propped him against one of the sturdy trunks.

"What are you doing?" Bates asked.

"He's out of it," David said. "He was going to go under. He would have drowned."

"He was trying to kill us," Bates said. "If he gets another chance, he'll try again."

"I know."

"So?"

"So, we're not like them."

Bates narrowed his eyes. "So, what now?"

"Let him go," David said.

Bates grunted but did as instructed, then waded over to stand beside him.

David leveled the gun at the guard, then gestured with it at the man he'd assisted. "Take him," he said.

The guard glared at them momentarily while rubbing his wrist, then turned and bent to assist his muttering colleague.

David extended both firearms to Bates and said, "Only if you have to."

Bates took one, then hesitated. "What about you?"

"I can't," David said.

Bates shrugged and accepted the second weapon.

As the uninjured guard scooped up his colleague beneath the arms and began their arduous retreat, there arose a chorus of more splashing and strident voices — more guards, and at least the three other pairs remained out there, the ones who'd forged past them in pursuit of the others.

David and Bates eyed one another. The final embers of day flickered like fireflies. Only pale drifts of filtered moonlight to guide their way. They turned back seaward, where their fellow immortals had proceeded per David's instruction, and where they had been pursued.

Over the surf came the frenzied sound of the continued chase — splashing feet, anguished cries, each one of which pierced David as though he himself had been struck. They stepped urgently, holding their hands out before them so as to avoid running face-first into a tapered branch, but the night had fallen so dark as to render visibility virtually nil.

Figuring he had no choice, David reached to his back pocket and withdrew the mirror. "Stand clear," he told Bates.

He took a deep breath, flipped the mirror open, and waited.

Nothing.

He exhaled. *Come on, light. Light.*

He felt it first, a surge of energy fomenting within the handle, then saw it coursing forth in a brilliant trajectory of radiance. He started to smile, but just as quickly grimaced, as the scene before them materialized in terrible relief. The illuminated expanse fell out before them like a graveyard, bodies slumped against tree trunks, or half-submerged in the inky waters.

"Holy shit," said Bates. "What do we do?"

The splashing, and the voices, impossible now to pinpoint, grew louder by the second.

"We help them." David waded over to the nearest of the fallen. "No one left behind."

"They'll catch us."

"Yes." David exhaled in relief upon observing the rising and falling chest of the immortal he'd bent to, a middle-aged woman. He tore the pulsing prongs from her back and discarded them. "And then we'll fight."

Bates nodded, regarding the two firearms in his possession.

The pandemonium around them escalated to fever pitch: the staccato bursts of shouting, the pop and hum of tasers fired, the anguished cries, the splashing, and the stomping chase.

Beyond the spectral glow of the mirror, only darkness lay beyond. David snapped the lid shut and returned the mirror to his pocket, so he could use both hands to assist the stricken immortal.

And then he stopped.

Bates cocked his head. "Do you hear that?"

He didn't. He didn't hear a thing. All had fallen still around them, silent—no sloshing, no cries, no trilling of the birds above the surf, or even the surf itself—as though stayed by a great and unseen hand. It was as if the world held its collective breath upon the precipice of a moment.

Now, from the fathomless depths flickered the faintest hints of illumination, merely a suggestion at first, an outline, but there all the same. It soon expanded, like the reawakening of a cold and distant star, and then the voices came—different from those before, only a few, but clarion, familiar. They came on like a wave, and now all else returned too—the crashing surf, the frenzied splashing, the frantic cries. Only now the cries were imbued with something different, something more.

When the first shimmers of indelible blue materialized in the closing distance, David's heart welled with unflinching resolve. He helped the recovering immortal to her feet. "Can you walk?"

She inhaled deeply, tremulously, then slowly let it out and said,

"I think so."

David gestured to another struggling immortal to their right. "Help her," he told Bates.

When they'd assisted the fallen within eyesight—four of them—they regarded one another in the moonlight. Behind them, the pursuing guards had nearly arrived, by the sound of things. Up ahead, still beyond their vision, the battle had been joined. David met the gaze of each, then slowly nodded, and together they turned and continued onward, toward the shore, and toward the fight.

The game was afoot.

CHAPTER 40
Revelation

THEY FOUND TWO MORE IMMORTALS almost immediately—a male and female—and aided both before forging onward together. By then, the pursuing guards had reached them and were firing tasers, and the immortals took cover behind the tree trunks. The sound of discharging tasers mixed with the occasional crackling and voices of the guards' radios.

"Here!" Bates extended one of the guns to the nearest immortal. "What's your name? I don't need two!"

The immortal shook her head. "Jackie!" she cried above the bedlam. "And no thanks. I don't need any!" She flattened herself against the tree.

David blinked and rubbed his eyes, as her outline became blurry and unsubstantial. A dart whistled past his head, and he jerked backwards, and when he glanced back at where the woman had stood, she had vanished entirely.

"I'll take one!" said another of the other immortals they'd rescued, crouched behind a nearby trunk with hand extended.

Bates let one salvo whistle past, then another, and handed over one of the firearms.

"Thanks!" the recipient said. "I'm Stefan!"

"Bates!"

"Only if you must!" David called to them. "We are not killers."

Bates spun to face him. "With all due respect, that's not for you to decide!"

David nodded, as Bates was correct. There was always a choice, and during those times when it seemed there wasn't, those choices mattered most. He could not impose his choice upon another. At this moment, he could hardly slight any of them for employing whatever means necessary to survive, or avoid capture, the latter of which meant not only reprisal but a lifetime of captivity.

"They're behind the trees!"

The guards had inched closer, not ten feet away, and now fanned out around them, sloshing through the water, encircling them.

"Guns!" The nearest guard had spotted Bates and the other armed immortal, and quickly holstered his taser and withdrew his semi-automatic.

Each of the other three did likewise.

"Drop your weapons!" ordered the nearest. "Or we will fire!"

David's heart pounded and his mind raced. He'd hoped to avoid this scenario. He slowly inched his hand toward his back pocket, thinking he could conjure something from the mirror — anything — but any sudden movement might —

"Aghh!"

They froze as the nearest guard pitched face-first into the water, his firearm flying from his grip and vanishing with a kerplunk. He floundered violently about, as though trying to swim for it, and it became quickly apparent he was struggling against more than the elements, and David stared in amazement as the immortal who'd vanished moments ago materialized as though from thin air upon the guard's back.

"Hey!" Another guard splashed forward to join the fray.

David moved quickly to intercept him, grabbed him in an armbar and twisted with all his might, until the guard cursed and his gun plopped into the roiling waters.

When another of the guards rushed forth, Bates jumped onto his back and clubbed him on the back of the head with the butt end of the revolver. The guard exclaimed and continued to fight, but when Bates clubbed him again, the man pitched forward into the water. Bates paused a moment, panting, before turning the unconscious guard to his back and hoisting him upon a nearby tangle of roots.

The guard David had intercepted was strong and fighting back. So too the immortal Jackie had felled, by the looks of it. Meanwhile, Stefan and the remaining guard faced one another in stand-off, each leveling their weapon point blank. The other immortals of their group had backpedaled away, frightened and unarmed, and David saw they had an opening.

"Go!" he called to them. "Run! Stefan, Bates, give them cover!"

The guard squaring off with Stefan momentarily leveled his weapon in their direction, but now Bates took a step toward him and pointed his gun at the guard, who, outnumbered, grimaced and slowly lowered his weapon.

"Go!" David shouted once more.

The immortals looked on hesitatingly from their shadowed positions, then whirled about and disappeared in the other direction, toward shore.

David and Jackie disengaged from their opponents and waded toward Stefan and Bates, and the four stood shoulder to shoulder.

The guards with whom they'd struggled did likewise with their armed colleague.

Suddenly, a loud crackling issued forth, and David flinched, thinking it at first another taser discharge, but then one of the guards reached for his radio.

"Leave it," David said.

"We don't take orders from you," the guard said, but when Bates aimed his weapon at him, the guard let his hand fall to his side.

"What is the status?" Christian's voice rang out. "Leader One, talk to me."

More crackling, followed by a heavy silence, and then....

"Situation critical." More crackling, with shouts and splashing in the background. "Something is happening."

"*What is happening?*" Christian's voice carried a tenor David had not yet heard, but knew he one day might. This day.

More crackling. More chaos.

"Escape!" came the disjointed reply. "Permission for lethal force!"

Silence. Then crackling.

"Permission granted. Not a soul must escape. But do *all* in your power to bring them back alive."

More crackling, and the radios went silent.

In the ensuing, terrible, brief interval, their standoff continued, and David waited with a pit in his stomach for the inevitable. When a few moments later a shot rang out, he closed his eyes, but just as quickly forced them back open.

"You see?" said the guard he'd tackled. "We tried to warn you."

Another gunshot sounded, followed by cries in the darkness, and other sounds David could not distinguish.

From beyond the guards, from the direction of the compound, more voices rang out.

"More are coming," the guard said. "Put down the guns. This doesn't have to end badly for you!"

Bates and Stefan did not budge.

David narrowed his eyes and listened. Yes, others were nearing from the direction of the compound — Christian's reinforcements, doubtless — but so too were the voices and sounds of struggle getting closer from the opposite direction. He glanced behind him, in the direction of the shore, and stared as flashes of light erupted, followed immediately by earsplitting percussions. Then he saw it again, the trace of vivid blue, there, then fading, but growing closer by the second.

He squinted through the gloom at Bates and Stefan, who kept their weapons leveled, but their arms were beginning to slump, hands beginning to quiver. No wonder, given the stress and exhaustion. It wasn't easy to hold your arms aloft for an extended period under any circumstances, much less these.

The guard with the gun had maintained his posture as well, seemingly more comfortable, which stood to reason.

The sounds grew louder all around, closing in — opposing waves, with them at the confluence. He and Jackie exchanged glances, and Bates and Stefan looked briefly back.

More shouting. More shots. More cries.

"Steady," David said. The agonized uncertainty of who'd been shot, of who'd be next, weighted his heart, but he must not let it paralyze him. He withdrew the mirror and prepared to flip it open.

The new arrivals converged in unison from both directions and stormed onto the scene, water flying in their wake, weapons drawn, their appearance so perfectly timed that David thought it must have been coordinated. Then his eyes adjusted, and he saw who it was, and the distinction between their weapons, and revelation came like a second awakening. Though he knew they remained in the fight of their lives, for the first time, he knew unequivocally that this was one they would win.

"Master Rose," said Herman, wading alongside David. He, like Marcel, wore a long cloak and, also like Marcel, brandished an immaculate sword that gleamed remarkably in the pale slip of moonlight.

Herman was the same, diminutive size as David remembered, but beholding him now, in this fateful impasse, he didn't exactly seem bigger, but rather, possessing of such a capacity to influence this moment that it rendered size or stature—anybody's—of little consequence. He who now stood beside Herman arrested David's attention greater still, and explained in a heartbeat the traces of blue he'd glimpsed.

"Hey," Donovan said, grinning broadly.

"Hey," David said back, and felt himself breaking into a wide grin, belying the ominous circumstances of their reunion, just as though they were back in his backyard, building the treehouse and horsing around.

"I think this belongs to you." Herman took a respectful step back as Donovan turned Arondight horizontal to the ground and presented it with two hands to its rightful owner.

When David's hands closed around the familiar handle, his body pulsed with invigoration, as the hallowed blade hued a celestial blue. The tip appeared stained crimson, and he narrowed his eyes at this but did not, for the moment, inquire. He felt all eyes upon him, even the newly arrived guards, and knew without looking that they'd drawn and sighted their guns upon him. For the moment, they were of no consequence. He gave himself over to the rush of power and of purpose, to the reunification of man and weapon, of man and himself.

He raised his head and regarded the brother he was sure he'd lost. "Thank you."

Donovan nodded, reached into a long scabbard clipped to his waist, and withdraw his own vaunted blade, Galatine. Together, the three of them — Donovan, Herman, and David — angled into defensive postures, swords aloft and glinting.

Christian's reinforcements had provided guns to the guards who'd been disarmed, and each of them — eight in total — sighted their weapons upon the incongruous trio.

"You have all performed valiantly!" Herman called to the other immortals. "Pray tell, take your leave. Head for shore, but remain at the ready, as you may encounter further hostility along the way."

"No offense," called Bates, glancing at Herman while keeping his weapon trained upon the guards, "but don't you at least want the guns?"

"Thank you, no," Herman replied. "Retain them in your possession, and use them only if you must."

"They're going to shoot," insisted Stefan, "the moment we are gone."

"Yes," replied Herman, as calmly as one discussing the weather. "I very much expect they shall."

David squinted through the haze of darkness and glinting moonlight in an effort to read the faces of their adversaries, wondering why they hadn't begun firing. The swords were impressive — otherworldly — and

Stefan and Bates still pointed their guns, but... swords were still swords, and eights guns were well more than two. Furthermore, Christian had granted permission for lethal force to prevent the escape of the immortals, if all else had failed.

That's it. Has to be. One last attempt to talk sense into us and return us – and as many immortals as possible – to their boss alive. Otherwise, his vile operation would, though preserved, be decimated.

"Then do the smart thing," called one of Christian's new arrivals, his weapon leveled at Herman. "Drop the weapons, the swords." Now he pointed the gun at Stefan and Bates. "The guns." And finally, David. "The mirror."

"Back slowly away," Herman directed the immortals.

After glancing briefly at one another, they each complied, including Stefan and Bates, who kept their guns leveled all the while.

When they'd disappeared into the recesses of the mangroves, Herman returned his attention to the guards and said, "You have your orders, and I have mine. I cannot fault you for that which you could not possibly know, but I would gently suggest you.... What is the phrase? Live to fight another day."

The guard who'd ordered them to disarm sneered. "So said the man with a sword, to the man with a gun. I don't know who you are, old man, and I don't much care. You want to commit suicide, that's your prerogative, but you really want to take two kids with you?"

"You don't know who we are," said Donovan. "We're— "

"Who we are is of no consequence," Herman interjected. "All that matters is we have arrived here at this impasse, and time is frightfully short. One of us must stand down now, and I assure you, good sir, it shall not be us."

The guard shook his head. "Is that right, boys? We have the numbers. We have the guns. Does he speak for you?"

"He speaks for all of us," came a new voice.

David's eyes shot wide and he cast his gaze about the darkness until he found her—found them.

Dani stood about ten feet to his left, aiming a revolver at the guards. Fanning out around her in a wide circumference were no fewer than eight other armed figures, some male, some female—difficult to discern in the shadows, but there.

Other immortals, David thought at first, but almost immediately realized better. *Not other immortals, but rather, variations of the same.* He reckoned he was the only one, besides Dani, who knew, and it was imperative that remain the case.

The guards appeared flustered, leveling their weapons from one Dani to the next.

"Easy," said the one who'd been engaging them.

David glanced edgewise at Herman, who had not wavered in his posture, sword still gleaming and aloft, eyes steely and set. David looked past him to Donovan, who likewise maintained his position, but whose eyes were wide and rapt in anticipation of the moment.

"We have the numbers," said Dani, the real Dani. "We have the guns."

The guards glared, their guns still leveled.

"Set down your weapons," said Herman. "All of them. Cast them aside, and retreat."

"We can take them!" blurted one of the guards. "Look at them. They've probably never fired a gun! And them—" He gestured with his revolver at the trio with the swords. "We'll put them down in a heartbeat."

Their leader stared at Herman, who stared back, sword still poised. It hadn't wavered an inch.

Night had come full on, but so too now the light of Arondight, for the moment dispelling the darkness and casting each of the players upon this stage in vivid relief. David searched the eyes of their adversaries, saw their eyes searching back.

The lead guard locked eyes with Herman. "Toss your weapons," he instructed his charges. "And stand down." His gaze remained fixed on Herman's. "They won't get far, and they'll be greeted before they even make it through." He slowly lowered his gun and turned to regard his team. "Now do as I have ordered."

The guards complied, though the immortals couldn't be sure they'd discarded every weapon. The guards then retreated.

When they'd gone far enough as to have disappeared from sight, David and his friends turned and headed back in the other direction, toward the beach. Donovan stared in wonder as all of the gun-wielding immortals but the true Dani faded as they went.

If Herman had noticed, he was certainly unfazed.

"Thanks," David told Dani as they forged on. "How bad is it?"

"Pretty bad," she admitted. "But it could have been worse." She nodded toward Donovan and Herman. "They stopped most of the shots. I don't know how, but they did."

"Most?"

"Too much chatter," Herman said. "Keep your focus. We must press on."

"How," David inquired quietly of Donovan as they walked, "did you do that?"

Donovan glanced at his sword, which he'd been using to cut through prodigious tangles of branches that hung from the canopy of mangroves like stalactites. "I don't even know. I think these have more power than we realized."

David nodded, and carefully circumvented a clump of roots. Arondight continued to shimmer blue as they sojourned, lighting his way — their way.

"Do not overestimate it," cautioned Herman. "No matter its power, no sword, no wand, and no weapon are a worthy substitute for vigilance and fortitude."

Donovan glanced over at David as if to say, *'yeah, but vigilance and fortitude don't stop bullets.'* Thankfully, he kept his musings to himself.

They pressed on.

There were more bodies — alive, thankfully. Most had been tased, and they stopped and aided each of them, until they could rise and walk. Together, they all ventured forth.

At one point, David veered to avoid a clump of roots, but then looked again and saw it wasn't roots but another body, a guard this time, and he knew instantly that the man was dead. The color had drained from his face and from his skin wherever it was visible. David looked at the man's hands, saw one was missing, and understood right then the crimson stain upon his sword. The dead man wore an expression of pronounced wonder, his eyes rapt and unseeing, and it occurred to David that you never noticed the glint in someone's eyes... until you didn't.

If the others had seen the dead man, they didn't say, and David bowed his head a moment before turning and catching up with the group.

They were getting closer, the surf plainly audible in rhythmic intervals, like short bursts of wind, and the moonlight more appreciably pervaded the thinning expanse through which they trekked. The blue glow of Arondight dimmed as David at last caught glimpse of the shore—coinciding, perhaps, with his relief and slightly lessened sense of danger. There was still so much he didn't understand.

When they at last emerged from the tree line, some of them stumbling, some limping, each addled with that wearying blend of adrenaline and exhaustion, they peered about in every direction, like rescued miners exposed to daylight for the first time in days. Of course, there was no daylight, but the effect felt briefly similar, so shrouded had been the belly of the mangroves.

When David stepped farther toward shore and then turned to face the mangroves, he was stunned to catch glimpse of the upper reaches of the compound, not terribly far off. They hadn't traveled very far at all, despite the toll. He only hoped that the toll exacted upon Christian's forces had been at least as debilitating.

For the moment, it appeared it had, as he neither saw nor heard any sign of guards. The rest of the immortals awaited them, and some cheered as they emerged from the tree line, relieved and elated that they were not more guards. It was hard to make out their faces, and David scanned quickly for Ruhi and Harlan. It was hard to say whether all who'd set off through the mangroves—upon his instruction—now stood before them near the shore.

David peered out at the darkened sea. No ship. His heart sank again, but as he started to turn back around, something flickered along the periphery of his vision, and he paused and glanced back. In the distance, a smattering of lights appeared, disjointed at first, but quickly their relationship suggested itself in David's mind, like when you followed a trajectory of random stars until suddenly, wondrously, a magnificent constellation materialized before your eyes. His mind now registered the unseen mosaic of the distant lights — a ship, most certainly, far offshore, of course, lest it run aground in the shallows. He thought to inquire if it was there to rescue them, but knew, of course, it was. His heart soared and he turned back around to search the faces of his friends, to see if they'd seen it, but what he saw — other than in Herman — was alarm, and then he saw why.

Behind him, out at sea, he heard the rush of smaller boats approaching — their transports, maybe, to the larger ship — but it seemed they were too late.

The jeeps roared to a stop on either side of them, four in total, kicking up mud and sand and water, and a handful of armed guards quickly jumped forth from each.

David narrowed his eyes upon spotting Christian amongst their ranks.

David turned to Herman, whose demeanor remained one of unflinching resolve. After a glance to either side, Herman took a step back, so as to have the best possible vantage toward both flanks, and once more, raised his sword aloft.

CHAPTER 41
Thirty-Three

DAVID SAW THEM NOW IN HIS mind's eye, the other bodies, mostly guards but not all, and his stomach turned and he counted them and there were five, and counting the guard they'd passed in the mangroves, that made six — six lives lost, at least — because he'd insisted upon this great escape.

He thought of Ruhi, and what she'd said about remaining true to who you were. His mother wouldn't have wanted him to leave anyone behind.

Mom. She was out there, somewhere, captive just as he had been, and this reality assuaged his guilt at least a little. Marcel had said there'd been developments, big ones, and that they likely involved her.

He narrowed his eyes and peered at each of the bodies, not wanting, but needing, to see their faces, remember them — even the guards, whose involvement in all this was inexcusable. Yes, even them, for they were people, someone's child, parent, sibling, spouse. He would remember them for the rest of his days, but as he thought of his mother, out there somewhere, her time running frightfully short, this was a penance he simply must bear.

The time was now, the moment here. Arondight began to thrum and shimmer its telltale blue. Like Herman and Donovan beside him, he raised his sword.

Christian strolled over to them, still flanked by guards on either side, their guns drawn and pointed.

When they neared to within ten feet, Christian stopped, surveyed the scene, and shook his head forlornly.

"It didn't have to be this way," he said.

"And it wouldn't have been, had you not pursued this enterprise."

David whirled around at the voice of Marcel, as if having appeared out of nowhere. The approaching boats had yet to arrive — David could hear them clipping along through the waves — and he hadn't observed Marcel emerging from the mangroves, or from either periphery. Thus, he did not begrudge the perplexity on the faces of Christian and the guards. Nonetheless, he felt his heart elate in anticipation and relief.

"You've killed on this day, sir," said Christian. "You and your associates. You must bear the consequences for that."

"Go ahead," said Donovan. "You'll end up in jail too."

David, heart pounding in anticipation of the inevitable, said, "I don't think those are the consequences he means."

"Our young prodigy speaks wisely," Christian said. He withdrew a small revolver from his waistband, checked it, cocked it, and leveled it at Marcel. "Thrown down your weapons, all of you."

David tensed, but then squinted through the darkness as Christian suddenly clutched at his temple and doubled over, as though struck.

"Sir? Sir!" The guard to Christian's left bent to assist him, but then grimaced, dropped his weapon, and likewise pressed his hands to his head.

David stared as another guard, and another, and soon each of them, writhed in distress.

Then he saw.

The other immortals had massed along the shoreline, some glancing feverishly to sea before returning their attention to the showdown unfolding before them. He saw Harlan, Dani, Isla, James. Others, he recognized, some, he didn't, but there, so unassuming that he had to look twice and squint to be certain, stood Ruhi, head bowed, an index finger pressed to either side of her temple. Her lips seemed to be moving, scarcely perceptible but moving, the duress of their adversaries in apparent lockstep with her silent incantations — Ruhi, not yet awakened but clearly possessing of powers beyond which any of them had reckoned.

When the next guard who doubled over discharged his weapon, whether intentionally or otherwise, those guards who had managed to keep hold of their firearms took that as their cue, and began firing.

Once again, in the ensuing rush of madness, the world resolved into excruciating clarity: Donovan and Herman flourished their swords and advanced, and David did likewise; Marcel came alongside them but, for the moment, weaponless. David braced for the impact of those bullets which would surely find their way through. His ears pricked as a great tumult arose from the throng of immortals behind him, a medley of responses that seemed to include indeterminate parts fight and flight. He perceived, along the periphery of his vision, some of the immortals rushing to join the fray, so many, in fact, he knew Dani and Harlan must be employing their powers of illusion. Inasmuch as this would reduce the live targets, he knew they must act swiftly in the narrow window of opportunity this would afford.

The shots continued to ring out, and from the sound and ensuing reactions, he could tell Bates and Stefan, and perhaps a few others, were firing back.

Then came the cries, heartrending, ringing out after each report from the sporadically erupting firearms. A few guards crumpled, writhing, but he could tell most of the fallen were behind him, among the ranks of the immortals. They had to end this quickly.

They were almost to the first line of guards, some of whom remained postured in distress, while others, though afflicted, still pointed their guns. Some had retreated to the tree line, apparently convinced they were taking more fire than could possibly be the case. David caught glimpse of Dani, standing and summoning her duplicates, and saw Harlan beside her, conjuring his own creation. Their courage stirred David, but his heart revved in fear for them, given their sitting duck status right there in the open. Even if Harlan had misdirected their vision, shots were still ringing out at random, and David knew it was only a matter of time before some landed.

Almost to the first line of guards, something flashed beside him. He glanced and saw that Marcel was no longer there. He thought to chance a quick glance behind, to see if Marcel had retreated or been struck, but now his attention was wrested by a similar flash just up ahead, as if something had been there for a heartbeat, left now to his mind's eye to decipher just what it had been.

And what it had done.

The two guards alongside whom the apparition had so briefly materialized stood dumbfounded, looking at turns at their hands and at the sand beneath them, and for their weapons that were no longer there.

Ruhi's hex had apparently waned as more shots came, more cries, more flashes, more guards left staring. It occurred to David that some of this might be the work of Dani or Harlan, or other immortals — perhaps even Merlin, though he dare not take for granted the allegiance of the ancient wizard. Perhaps the brew of exhaustion and adrenaline consuming him was playing tricks on his mind.

The shots dwindled, and now in the brief interludes of stillness arose the thrum of watercraft. David hazarded a look back and, sure enough, a cadre of smaller vessels had idled up to shore.

"Fall back."

David whirled back around to see Marcel beside them once more.

"Back to shore," Marcel said. "We will gather the fallen. Form a perimeter so the boats may be boarded."

David did as instructed, exhausted but emboldened. Once again, Marcel had saved him. The fight wasn't over yet, their escape hardly assured, but they'd been seconds away from combat with Christian's guards, his heart pounding, less in fear of what might befall him than dreading what he himself might do. The ghostly face of the corpse in the mangroves drifted across the theater of his conscience.

They slowly backpedaled to the shoreline, the sound of arriving boats revving behind them.

"The wounded first!" someone cried. "Then all others. Nobody left behind!"

"Thirty-three," came Dani's familiar voice. "There should be thirty-three. Where is Ruhi?" This last utterance was freighted with panic.

Before David could turn around, his attention was drawn once more to the tree line, where, through the gloom of moonlight shadow, now emerged five dark figures. Their features remained for the moment indistinguishable, but he knew... from their shapes, their strides, and from their absence until this moment. More than anything, he knew from the way this world, and these moments, seemed inevitably to unfold. When they'd come near enough, and their faces resolved at last into view, it was mere corroboration.

The group included the Valori twins, the men from the graveyard, and lastly, somewhat beside them but walking, as ever, his own path, Caleb Gallows, the draugr. All but Gallows brandished swords.

Christian had sidled up alongside them, speaking in short bursts into his radio, then pocketing it and regarding the would-be defectors once again. Many of the guards, even having been relieved of their weapons, had recovered their faculties and fallen in behind their boss.

"I don't usually give so many chances," Christian said. "But I shall offer you this last."

David glanced to his right, where Marcel, Herman, and Donovan stood poised. He couldn't help but notice the glint of Donovan's eyes, as if he were anxious for a fight.

"You answer to a calling well beyond the bantering of this small mortal," Marcel said, looking at each of the five new arrivals in turn. "Spare yourselves the dishonor of remaining under his sway."

Christian's face twisted in contempt.

"We made a deal for ourselves," spat the shorter of the immortals from the cemetery. "A good one." He gestured with his sword. "But we won't spare you."

"Continue boarding!" Marcel called out to those behind him.

David shot a quick glance to the boats. The immortals waded through the shallows and were assisted into each craft by shadowed figures. Some immortals were carrying others.

Christian turned to his band of five. "You know what to do."

David was unsurprised to see Christian motion his guards to fall back—another duel to entertain him. What was surprising was just how shameless the immortals who presently stood across from him could be, to fail to grasp how exploited they continued to be. Or how they simply didn't care. Maybe that was just it. This world—the immortal world—teemed with wonder, and many beautiful things, but so too was it blighted with darkness, almost as if the worst of humanity—hatred, feuds, vengeance, greed—compounded itself one century, one lifetime, after the next.

As usual, he had no time to ponder it, as their opponents set quickly upon them, four against three. Gallows remained for the moment a spectator, rooted where he stood, a shadow within the shadows. Lars Valori had rushed David, and they squared off now, the clanging of their swords joining the sounds of the bedlam behind them. Ella Valori, as well as Mason, the tall man from the cemetery, charged Herman, while Donovan and the other immortal from the cemetery engaged.

David needed to focus, as Lars was powerful and quick. David parried and countered his strikes with every ounce of strength he could muster. Whether he was Lancelot in this most fateful of moments, or just David, he did not know, and in his heart of hearts, he knew it did not matter. His heart was Lancelot's, and Lancelot's his, and so too for every him he'd ever been, or might again, one day, yet be.

A loud whistling passed frightfully close and, realizing it had not been from Lars but rather the blade of one of the nearby combatants, he edged a few feet away, casting another quick glance at Gallows as he did so. The draugr met his eye, as if to say, *'we're next.'*

David refocused his attention upon Valori, who relentlessly maintained his attack. David continued to parry the heavy blows, reminding himself that immortals, for all their powers, were not superhuman. Sooner or later, Lars would tire. He remembered watching a boxing match once with his father, and being surprised when he cast doubt on the prospects of the aggressor. "He's gonna punch himself out," he'd said, and sure enough, the blows had slowed, the arms had grown heavy and dropped, and the other fighter, who'd been bobbing and weaving and blocking, soon took advantage.

He chanced a quick glance edgewise. Donovan, perhaps channeling Gawain, had forged a decided advantage and seemed to be wearing down his adversary.

Marcel called out, "Time grows short!"

David's eyes grew wide as he watched Herman flourish his sword in lightning-quick strokes, and both of his opponents fall stricken to the sand. They did not appear to be fatally wounded, but sufficiently incapacitated that their blades dropped to the ground, and they made no effort to retrieve them.

Lars set upon David once more, and once more, he parried, and jabbed, this strike finding its way through. Lars grunted in anger and pain and struck again, but this time the assault was palpably weaker—he was punching himself out. Another cry issued forth, and David permitted himself a sideways glance.

Donovan had felled the graveyard immortal, who sat gasping upon his hands and knees, one hand still clutching his sword, the other, his side, where a crimson wound had begun to foment. Donovan stood over him, Galatine poised for a deciding blow.

"No," Marcel said.

Donovan paused a moment, then lowered his weapon and stepped slowly back.

David could feel their eyes upon him — Marcel, Herman, Donovan... and Christian too, and the guards. So too the immortals behind him, those yet to board the watercrafts and head for the ship. And Gallows, whose gaze burned into him like destiny unfulfilled. No one interfered, as it should be — just him and Valori, to the finish.

Lars unclasped his bloody hand from his side, raised his sword high, and with a terrible cry lunged forward a final time.

David sidestepped, parried the strike easily, and swept his blade into Valori's torso, opposite side from the first incursion. His actions had been seamless, automatic, and yet somehow, he'd managed to think there shouldn't be any major arteries there. No, his opponent would not have granted him any similar consideration, but no matter. He remembered Ruhi's sage wisdom, and his mother's too, all the times she'd reminded them that doing right ought never be predicated upon the odds of reciprocity.

Lars exclaimed again, cursed at David, and dropped to his knees. His sword remained gripped in his bloody palms, but he would not raise it again.

"Now then," called Marcel. "The last vessel awaits."

David began to turn but something froze him, held him back. Someone. He angled toward Gallows, and met his cryptic stare.

"You guys board," he called back behind him. "I'll be right there."

"Master Rose," Marcel called. "We must tarry no further."

No, we mustn't. But he could not turn away. Gallows nodded at David's sword and smirked, and after a brief moment, David released his grip and let Arondight fall to the ground.

"David!" Donovan yelled. "Are you crazy?"

Yes. Perhaps I am. But who, anymore, can say?

Gallows' features twisted into something approximating a grin. It was warm out, humid—they were seaside, after all—but David felt the familiar chill riding up his spine, as he had during their first encounter. He balled his fists, but it felt slow, labored, more strenuous than it should have. His body slowed down, his breathing. Donovan had been right—he shouldn't have relinquished his weapon, as the draugr had clearly not relinquished his.

The grin of his adversary shaped into grotesque proportion as he observed David's duress and slowly approached.

David's arms felt lethargic, heavy, like the fighter who'd punched himself out. He wondered what Gallows would do to him. Strike him? Pierce him through with some hidden blade? Drain the life from him through this cursed spell?

He vaguely registered a cry from behind him, from the waters, and the ensuing, frantic splashing. He didn't turn but rather stared in wonder into the eyes of his would-be executioner, which grew wide with bewilderment, and then, unmistakably, fear.

The new arrival tackled Gallows with such force that the draugr emitted a louder sound than David had ever heard from him, echoing forth as the wind was blasted from his body. Both he and his attacker flew like a missile several yards past. The two figures tumbled and rolled and crashed, and the stranger started raining blows upon the draugr before either had even come to a stop.

But... not a stranger.

David felt his own grin—boyish and large and silly looking, doubtless—cresting over his features, and the cold and lethargy melting quickly away. Well before the man stopped punching, Gallows no longer offering the slightest resistance, and before Marcel called out the man's name, David knew, and his heart soared higher than at any previous moment since all this had started.

"Well done, Mr. Rose," called Marcel from the shallows. "And now, if you don't mind terribly, I must insist we at long last take our leave."

CHAPTER 42
On Eagle's Wings

THE AIR IS WARM, BUT THE sea colder than he expected. He is overwhelmed with exhilaration and fatigue, and his father helps him to the watercraft. The sea thrums with the sound of the tide and revving motors. Forgetting something? He looks, and Donovan is smiling, extending Arondight to him once more. He accepts it, smiles, and shakes his head. What would Marcel have said? But his father is here, and it's all he can think of. That, and a million and one questions. But they must wait.

"Incoming!"

David twisted in his seat toward the sound of roaring engines, twin beams, boring through the darkness, framing in their wake the outlines of the vessels on which they perched. No surprise, as Christian was always going to fight until the bitter end.

David turned back around to their own boat's operator, who had voiced the warning. "Do we have guns?" he cried.

Their pilot either couldn't hear him, or chose not to respond. "Hang on!" he called back to his passengers, and gunned the engine.

David rocked back against his seat, his body momentarily airborne, but his father secured him with a tight arm around his shoulder. David smiled his thanks, then twisted back around and squinted at the blinding confluence of the approaching lights, and their own.

It didn't appear their craft had weapons, but he harbored little doubt the closing vessels did.

As if in confirmation, a burst of assault-rifle fire rang out.

"Everybody down!" Marcel called.

Everyone but Marcel and their pilot flattened themselves as best as possible within the cramped quarters of the boat. David remained facing the stern, his eyes scarcely above the rim of the craft, squinting to see beneath the protective arm of his father and the dancing lights upon the otherwise darkened sea. Amidst it all, he was surprised to glimpse what appeared to be a dolphin jumping past, in the roiling breach between the vessels. Then another volley of gunfire erupted, and he flinched as several rounds pinged sharply against the exterior of their craft.

"Hang on!" cried their pilot again, steering into evasive maneuvers.

The lights swam crazily, and David felt his father's grip tighten.

"The lights," Marcel called, calmly.

The pilot looked at Marcel, then nodded and switched off the stern lights. The sea immediately grew more distinguishable from their now shadowed vantage.

A moment later, the dolphin resurfaced in a perfect arc, shimmering in the moonlight, a solitary creature. David recalled that most traveled in pods, but when this one breached a third time, he understood. When one of Christian's men shouted, "What the hell is that!" David knew that despite their exposure to the immortal world, they would not possibly believe the answer.

They were to about to find out, anyway.

The space between their boat and the others began to foment and swirl, and the pursuing vessels swerved in a desperate attempt to circumvent the inexplicable cauldron unfurling before them. The tempest moved with them, though, cutting them off.

As he squinted against the sudden maelstrom, David felt as though back in the cave at Tintagel — Merlin's cave. When Malea had thwarted the great wizard with a similar demonstration, and likewise now, when he locked his gaze upon the epicenter of the squall, he perceived the same lightning-fast locomotion of the elusive naiad.

He glanced up and saw his father craning to see, while still pressing upon his son to stay low. Their eyes met. "Lots to tell you!" David exclaimed.

When he turned back, he saw they'd put more distance between themselves and their pursuers. A great wave rose in the churning chasm, and David stared as it coiled and bent and spiraled into a tall and whirling waterspout. The pursuing crafts veered even farther about, one in either direction, but the vortex expanded with them, like some sentient storm, and the last David spied of them, they had circled about, idling, no longer in pursuit.

"Stay low," Marcel called. "They may still fire."

When they arrived at the larger ship, they were helped aboard with the utmost urgency by some of the other immortals, and a handful of individuals David had never seen. Interspersed at a handful of positions stood some of these strangers, keeping watch. If they were armed, they kept the weapons hidden from view. He heard a rapid fluttering, like a bedsheet in the wind, and craned his neck. He was surprised to behold another unrecognized individual poised high up in the crow's nest of the ship. He furrowed his brow, reasonably certain the berth had been unoccupied when he'd first climbed aboard, but then again, he hadn't really fixated upon it, and in all the commotion, surely he'd missed the ascending figure.

He was hard to miss now. His hair was long, so too his beard, billowing in the wind along with his long, gray robes, yet his demeanor remained fixed, unflappable, staring out to sea in silent vigil, as though a statue attired and adorned and placed there for effect. He looked less old than ancient, even for this world, or any David had ever seen.

As ever, he'd no time for such contemplations. As the sounds of Christian's boats diminished in the distance, and as everyone settled in on board, the sights and sounds of the grim ordeal they had at last managed to escape settled in as well. Several immortals lay stricken upon the deck and were being attended to, and a few others were carried to cabins below, presumably for rest and aid.

"David." His father gripped him by either shoulder, so tightly that he almost lost grip of his sword. "Are you okay?"

"I'm okay."

"Get to a safe place," his father said. "I need to try and go help."

Please, David thought, as he watched his father head off toward an ailing immortal, *let them live.* A terrible thought arose within him—a rationale—and though he fought to quickly suppress it, there was no denying what it had been. *But if any do die,* he'd thought, ashamed to admit it, *at least they will live again.*

Not in this lifetime, though—not for their families, friends, and loved ones. He dare not entertain such a justification—none of them dare—for to his way of thinking, such a notion embodied the very worst of this eternal struggle into which he'd been thrust. It trivialized lives, like pages being turned in a book, when in truth each page, each soul upon them, mattered more than anyone else had any right to say. If any would on this day perish, their eventual rebirth would be of little solace to their loved ones, even if such an eventuality were by those loved ones to be believed. The loss would be just as crushing and indelible, just as devastating. It would alter the course of many lives... forever... all because of his conviction that it had been up to him to lead the rest to freedom — all because of this grand and glorious game.

"Please," he called to Marcel, who was at that moment walking briskly past. "I need to help."

Marcel paused and turned to face him. "We are attending to those in need, but I commend you for your willingness." He glanced up toward the crow's nest, and then back at David. "We are not out of harm's way just yet. You must remain at the ready, should the battle be rejoined."

David tightened his grip on Arondight. "I'll be ready."

Marcel nodded solemnly, and ventured off.

"David!" a familiar voice called.

He peered about, through shadow and light and the bustling of anxious figures.

"David... this way!"

Harlan was wearing an undershirt, and David wondered briefly where his other shirt had gone, but in the grand scheme of things it seemed to matter little. He smiled to see him, but it faded as quickly as it had formed, as David registered the severity upon the face of his friend.

"What is it?" David asked upon reaching him. *Don't you mean who?*

"Hurry!"

Harlan turned and walked so briskly toward a far end of the deck that David had to jog to keep up, steadying Arondight carefully as he went. Although not a stormy night, the wind upon the open sea lashed at them, and through tearing eyes, and past the interspersing crowd, he spotted the crouching figures toward whom Harlan now hurried.

Please, he repeated, from the deepest recesses of his heart. *Let them live.*

He glanced briefly skyward, and spied once more the cloaked figure in the crow's nest, standing expressionless above these frantic moments of life and death. David couldn't help but wonder just how many he'd seen. A pageant of stars had arrayed in the unbounded night sky, flickering from their far-flung stations as though to guide them.

When he collided with Harlan, his eyes traced back down and his heart dropped at what he beheld. Ruhi lay prone on the deck, two figures kneeling on either side, feverishly attending her. David recognized one of them as an immortal, Dr. Ainsley from the infirmary. The other, a male, he did not know. Dani sat cross-legged, cradling Ruhi's head, stroking her hair gently and talking to her. The man bent over Ruhi, applying pressure to her torso with a bundle of white towels, which quickly darkened. Dr. Ainsley cut a long strip from a shirt—Harlan's, David observed—and fashioned a tourniquet.

"Please," Dr. Ainsley said, glancing up at David. "Kneel on her other side."

David quickly did as told, setting his sword down. As soon as his knees touched the deck, Dr. Ainsley gently tucked a hand under Ruhi's back, and nodded toward David to do likewise.

"Carefully," she said. She threaded the strip under Ruhi's back as the assisting man removed the towels.

David reached under his friend, aghast at the thought of hurting her, but she only made a slight wheezing. He felt for the strip of cloth, grabbed it, and pulled it through. He extended it over Ruhi to the doctor, who pulled it to the end gripped in her other hand, and tightened it over the grievous wound.

Ruhi looked up into Dani's eyes, her breathing shallow and her lips turning blue.

"Pressure is dropping," Dr. Ainsley said, and her eyes met those of the unknown man. "She needs surgery."

"Then let's do it," David said. "Can we do that here, on the ship? It must have equipment."

Dr. Ainsley wore a pained expression as she softly replied, "Not that kind. She needs to get off this ship. She needs to be airlifted to a hospital, and fast."

"Then do it," David cried. He looked at the doctor, and then up at Marcel, who had just made his way over. "We have to call."

Marcel looked past David to Ruhi, and his eyes filled with a great melancholy. "I am afraid there is no time."

"Forget our mission!" David cried, leaping to his feet. "Forget Kane. Forget me! She is all the matters right now."

"That's not what he meant," said Dr. Ainsley, looking from Marcel to David.

David looked into Marcel's eyes, and saw that the doctor was right, that Marcel was indeed speaking of Ruhi's time, and doing so from the vantage of one who had seen more of it than any of them gathered presently in this vigil, than all others on this ship combined.

David looked at Harlan, whose face quivered in desperation. His hands twitched in futile yearning to do something, anything, to help, but not even his greatest conjuring could forestall this. He regarded David, and together they knelt beside Dani, one on either side.

Harlan wiped a hand across his eyes and smiled at Ruhi. "I'm here." He took up one of her hands.

David clasped the other. It felt so small, and cold. "We all are."

Ruhi smiled, and slowly turned her head to look at each of them. She looked like she wished to speak, but no longer had the strength. Each breath came shallower than the one preceding it, and further between.

"Look," Dani told her, still caressing her hair. "At the sky, Ruhi. The constellations. Aquila. Can you see the wings?"

Ruhi looked past her friend, skyward, her eyes reflecting the starlight.

"Fly, Ruhi, my sweet friend," Dani said. "On eagle's wings, into your grandmother's arms." A tear fell from her cheek onto Ruhi's forehead, and she bent down and kissed the spot. When she sat back up, Ruhi's breaths had stopped, and her eyes were fixed upon a far and distant spot in the heavens.

David blinked fiercely and clenched his jaw.

Harlan closed his eyes and lowered his head.

The man who had been assisting slowly stood, took a step backward, and respectfully bowed his head.

Dr. Ainsley looked at each of them. "I am so sorry," she said. "May we take solace that one day she will—"

She stopped abruptly and looked up at Marcel, who had put a hand on her shoulder and slowly shaken his head. Dr. Ainsley regarded him uncertainly a moment, then nodded, rose, and stood next to Marcel and the other man. They stood silently, heads lowered.

Dani, Harlan, and David remained at their friend's side. The sights and sounds and even the buffeting winds all seemed to fade away, until it was just them, four friends. How long they remained there, David could not tell. He knew only that Dani cradled Ruhi's head in her lap for quite some time, and he and Harlan held her hands, and that after at last relinquishing it, he would feel it there for a very long time to come.

CHAPTER 43
One More Day

ONE OTHER HAD DIED, AN IMMORTAL named Sam. He'd had his awakening, unlike Ruhi, but this did little to diminish the solemnity in Marcel's voice upon relaying the news. Several more were injured, some seriously, but were expected to make it. They sat, exhausted, in chairs in a lounge — David, Harlan, Dani, and Donovan — as Marcel updated them to the best of his ability.

Herman stood nearby, listening, while David's father was still off helping attend to the wounded.

David and his friends had been given blankets and bottles of water and power bars, to combat their dehydration and fatigue.

The bodies of Sam and Ruhi must of course be returned to their families. David vaguely wondered what explanations would be given — about their passing, about all of this — but knew in his heart that Marcel would do the right and honest thing, and do all in his power to bring comfort to their loved ones. There were details and logistics — lots of them — but they floated in and out of David's consciousness as Marcel spoke: where they would go first, based upon the medical treatment needed most urgently; and where to next, based upon getting folks home. Someone inquired about the not insignificant matter of them having commandeered a ship that was not theirs, but as for this matter, Marcel appeared entirely unperturbed.

"One more day," David said, to no one in particular. "Christian was going to make her awaken. I should have let him."

Dani leaned forward in her chair and placed a hand on his.

He looked at Marcel and said, "I will carry this with me forever."

Marcel nodded solemnly. "Yes, and a great many other things, this as consequential as any other. You will carry it, and so too the burden of neither permitting it to distract you from the work ahead, nor permitting that work to anesthetize you against that grief you bear."

David nodded, grateful Marcel had not attempted to assuage him. Marcel spoke a while longer, but soon David felt himself drifting off. He thought at some point later he heard, or perhaps he had been dreaming, Marcel and Herman speaking in hushed tones.

"For as long as I have known you," he thought Herman said, "you have spoken only truth."

"You are questioning," he thought Marcel replied, "whether I have here done otherwise?"

"How many millenia, how many lifetimes ago, did we learn the importance of doing the very thing you advised him he must not?"

There was silence, and then the Marcel still there in the lounge, or in David's head, replied, "How many millennia, how many lifetimes ago, did we so too learn that our learning never ends? He is the Light Keeper for a reason. The longer we live, is it not more incumbent upon us to keep hold of just what it is we all live for?"

***

MARCEL JOINED THEM EARLY THAT

evening at David's house, some three or four days after setting sail—time, to David, once more a blur. They all gathered, David's family and his friends, as Marcel shared all he could about the road ahead. It involved that which Kane had discovered and taken, and yes, Marcel told them, it almost certainly involved their mom. It would be a difficult journey, he cautioned, and it would be a fight. When Donovan noted pridefully that they'd won the last one, Marcel regarded him in such a manner that all present immediately understood: that contest had paled in comparison to that which awaited.

David's friends wanted to come, but knew that they could not. Their parents had been shielded as much as possible from this world, and no way would they let their children head off on such a perilous expedition. There was no way David would think to ask them.

Rachel would be coming, though this had been a matter of considerable deliberation. There was no minimizing the danger involved, and this at first inclined their father to leave her once more behind. But when he asked Marcel if there was a chance at finding his wife, his children's mother, and Marcel affirmed the possibility, he began to reconsider. When Marcel pulled him aside—so that Rachel could not overhear, but David did—and quietly conveyed the possibility he hoped desperately would not come to fruition but could, that this might portend the last chance for them to see her, he was decided.

Much to her satisfaction, Rachel would be joining them.

Their father pressed Marcel for elaboration of this latest caveat, clearly devastated at the thought, and Marcel assured him he didn't know much for certain, but would as soon as possible disclose all that he possibly could.

"There's something more, isn't there?" David asked Marcel, when they had a brief moment alone. "About Rachel. Herman told you what happened at the cemetery?"

"He did," Marcel replied, with the gravest of expressions. "And yes, there is quite possibly something more."

As ominous scenarios began to flood over him, David said, "But does that mean it's better if she does come, or that she doesn't?"

"I am so very sorry, Master Rose," Marcel said. "But I truly do not know."

***

THEY WALKED TO THE CREEK BY the woods, the last place they'd all been together before this night. Summer was nearly over, the sun fading quicker by the day, and its final streaks on this evening did not disappoint, providing a lavender dome, gilded here and there with streaks of gold.

They remained mostly quiet, there beneath the violet pageant, basking in fellowship and the unfailing articulation of that which need not be said. Sure, they'd shared and answered what they could — David and Donovan — to the best of their ability, and to the extent their exhaustion would permit. They'd shared and answered, and then the others had shared too, about all they'd been up to there at home, and David soaked it all in, deriving comfort from it all. But what mattered most, they each knew well, resided not in all that had happened, but in what was yet to come.

When the veil of night at last descended and a crescent moon titled in a far corner of the sky, they decided it was time to depart.

"More peaceful than the last time here," Chester noted.

"Yeah," said David. "For now."

"So, when are you leaving?" Robert asked, as he assisted Chester across the field. "It was all a blur back there, with Marcel."

"Day after tomorrow," David said. "Need a day to get ready, and hopefully rest, but time is short, he said."

"Isn't it always?" Robert replied, shaking his head. "So, you're here one more day."

"One more day."

They walked silently a while, until Donovan sidled up beside David and nudged his shoulder. "Merlin," he said.

David furrowed his brow. "What about him?"

"Did you see him? At the fight? When everything was going down?"

David thought for a few seconds. "No."

"Me neither. I wonder if he's still there, or more importantly, whose side he's on."

"He didn't help us," David said.

"But he didn't try to stop us, either."

At length, David fell back in the procession, until he was side by side with Amanda.

She smiled, as though having waited for him to do so.

"Thank you," he told her, looking her square in the eyes. Those beautiful eyes glittered now in the moonlight, and had from the first entranced him with a radiance all their own. "Thank you for keeping Rachel. Thank you for my sister."

She took up his hand. "It was my honor." As they neared David's house, Amanda nodded up ahead, toward Donovan. "So, what has that been like? Having him back?"

"He was amazing, I have to admit, to do all he did to help us, especially knowing how hard it must be because of what happened with his mom. I don't think we would have made it without him."

"That's great," Amanda said, but her face crinkled.

David stopped and turned to her. "But...."

"I don't mean to be cynical, but I just wonder... I mean... he did try to kill you."

"I know, but it wasn't him. Well, it was but it wasn't." David sighed. "I guess we're all still trying to figure out who we are."

Amanda nodded, and they resumed walking, still hand in hand. It occurred to David that such an inquiry might be well be applicable to the two of them, but he thought better than to pose the question, and walked on, grateful beyond all telling for each moment, and each step—however fleeting—that remained.

***

IT WAS BEDTIME, WHICH MEANT A

story or a poem. David had smiled when Amanda had returned the Frost collection to him, glad Rachel had brought it along for her stay. He wondered what she'd choose tonight.

Their father got her ready and tucked her in, and when he returned downstairs to let David know she was ready for her story, Marcel smiled and placed a gentle hand upon David's wrist as he rose to head upstairs

"She enjoys a good book?"

David regarded him a moment, then nodded. "Like our mother."

"Yes," Marcel said, eyes glinting. "Like your mother." He relinquished his grip. "Go to her. And then, pray tell, rest, for the next chapter in our story entails no less than the most important book the world has ever known."

***

RACHEL DIDN'T WANT A BOOK ON

this evening—no book, no poem. The only story she wanted was what had happened to David during his time away, but she soon grew impatient even with this, and turned her focus to their imminent quest.

"When do we leave?" she asked, so small there beneath her blanket, eyes wide in the wash of moonlight spilling through her window. She often chose not to draw the curtains, preferring to drift off to the sight of the stars and moon, and awaken to the morning light.

"Day after tomorrow," David said.

"Why not tomorrow? Why not now?"

"We need to pack," he told her. "And we need to rest." That Marcel and Herman and their associates likely needed to finalize their planning, was a point with which she need not be troubled.

"I don't need to rest," Rachel insisted, starting to sit up. "I can go now."

David smiled, and gently coaxed her back down. "Soon. Before you know it."

"Don't you want to find Mama?"

"More than anything."

"Then—"

He raised a finger to his lips and brushed aside a strand of hair that had fallen over her eyes. "You heard Marcel. It's not going to be easy. You need your rest. We all do. Mama will need us at our strongest, okay?"

Rachel started to reply, then stopped, nodded, and turned to face the window.

"Look at all those stars," he told her, softly. "Imagine they'll light our way. Trace with your eyes from each one to the next, like connecting the dots, and soon enough, you'll be there."

He stayed beside her until her breathing slowed and her eyes fluttered shut, and even then, stayed a while longer. A good thing, too, as moments before he was about to tiptoe out, her eyes eased back open.

She turned to him and asked again, "When do we leave?"

"Day after tomorrow," he said.

"So, we're here one more day?"

"One more day."

THE END

Acknowledgements

My deepest gratitude to my family and friends for their unyielding support, to my beta readers, and to my publisher, Evolved Publishing. It truly takes a village, folks.

About the Author

From childhood I kindled three dreams: to one day become a father, a writer, and a baseball player.

Two of three ain't bad. (I shall neither confirm nor deny holding out deluded hope for the third.) Most of what I write is fiction, but not all. I write the occasional article and guest post, and conduct some interviews. I'm an English major, have a masters in social work, and have been a nonprofit leader for many years. I am crazy for sports and animals, am helplessly in love with the written word, and am eternally grateful for my family, who make me luckier than I could ever deserve.

For more, please visit Daryl Rothman online at:
Website: www.DarylRothman.com
Goodreads: Daryl Rothman
Twitter: @DRothmanWrites
Facebook: @AuthorDarylRothman

What's Next?

Watch for the third book in this "David Rose" series to release in late 2025.

David Rose and the Days of Awe

Marcel has returned from a mysterious excursion with possible news of David Rose's mother, in addition to a revelation which threatens to upend the course of human history.

Not even a year from discovering his immortality and the sinister world into which he has awakened, David has survived a swordfight, eluded a dark wizard, and pulled off a harrowing escape after being abducted to a hidden compound and forced to compete in a forbidden tournament of immortals.

What matters to him above all else is protecting his little sister, rescuing their mother, and reuniting their family once and for all. But now, their enemies have obtained a weapon of ancient and unspeakable power.

Once again, David's in a race against time in this world that time forgot. He must find his mother before it's too late—not just to save her, but also himself and, just maybe, the entire world.

More from Evolved Publishing

We offer great books across multiple genres, featuring high-quality editing (which we believe is second-to-none) and fantastic covers.

As a hybrid small press, your support as loyal readers is so important to us, and we have strived, with tireless dedication and sheer determination, to deliver on the promise of our motto:
QUALITY IS PRIORITY #1!

Please check out all of our great books, which you can find at this link:
www.EvolvedPub.com/Catalog/

Thank you!